Praise for

OFF THE WILD COAST OF BRITTANY

"Blackwell moves smoothly between the two time periods. . . . The author's fans will be pleased." —*Publishers Weekly*

Praise for

THE VINEYARDS OF CHAMPAGNE

"A beautifully captivating story of wartime tenacity and tenderness that celebrates the sweetest bonds of human relationships and the courage to love again after loss. So exquisitely rich in detail you'll feel bubbles on your tongue."

—Susan Meissner, bestselling author of *The Last Year of the War*

"The allure of the decades-old mystery of missing letters juxtaposed against the history of the caves of Champagne makes for a satisfying page-turner." —*Publishers Weekly*

"Blackwell's exquisite talent at interweaving the past with the present is on full display in her latest . . . telling the universal story of grief, loss, and human resilience." —*Booklist*

Praise for

THE LOST CAROUSEL OF PROVENCE

"Blackwell uses an outsider's passion to shine a light into the dark past of a broken family and how a sweet wooden rabbit can bring them together again." —The Associated Press

"Plan your trip to Provence now. In this meticulously researched novel, Juliet Blackwell deftly navigates three time periods, taking us from contemporary California to both the Belle Époque and Nazi-occupied France as she spins a story as charming as an antique carousel." —Sally Koslow, author of *Another Side of Paradise*

"An untrusting American orphan meets a dysfunctional French family—and each turns out to possess wisdom that helps the other to heal from old, old wounds. With crystalline imagery, vivid characters, and lively prose, Juliet Blackwell redefines what family means in a way that will touch readers long after they've read the last page. As Cady points her camera at one antique carousel after another, this novel should come with a warning: Will cause enormous desire to travel to France." —Stephen P. Kiernan, author of *The Baker's Secret*

"Narrating from several perspectives, Blackwell weaves together a tale of love lost, repressed passion, and finding a sense of belonging that should utterly charm and delight readers new to her and current fans alike." —*Booklist*

Praise for

LETTERS FROM PARIS

"Blackwell seamlessly incorporates details about art, cast making, and the City of Light . . . [and] especially stuns in the aftermath of the main story by unleashing a twist that is both a complete surprise and a point that expertly ties everything together."

—*Publishers Weekly*

"Bestselling author Blackwell brings us another captivating tale from the City of Light. . . . This romantic and picturesque novel shows us that even the most broken people can find what makes them whole again."

—*Booklist*

"Blackwell paints a picture of Paris that is both artistically romantic and realistically harsh . . . a compelling story of Paris, art, and love throughout history."

—*Kirkus Reviews*

"Blackwell has woven a great tale of mystery, artistry, history, and a little romance. With plenty of backstory and tidbits about Parisian life in the nineteenth century, there's something for everyone in this recommended read."

—*Library Journal*

Praise for

THE PARIS KEY

"A charming protagonist and a deep well of family secrets, all gorgeously set in the City of Light."

—Michelle Gable, international bestselling author of *I'll See You in Paris*

"[A] witty, warm, winsome novel . . . [Blackwell's] generation-spanning tale combines intrigue and passion with a flawless ear for language and a gift for sensory detail."

—Sophie Littlefield, bestselling author of *The Guilty One*

ALSO BY JULIET BLACKWELL

THE PARIS SHOWROOM

Juliet Blackwell

BERKLEY
NEW YORK

BERKLEY
An imprint of Penguin Random House LLC
penguinrandomhouse.com

Copyright © 2022 by Julie Goodson-Lawes
Readers Guide copyright © 2022 by Julie Goodson-Lawes
Excerpt from *Off the Wild Coast of Brittany* copyright © 2021 by Julie Goodson-Lawes

Library of Congress Cataloging-in-Publication Data

Names: Blackwell, Juliet, author.
Title: The Paris showroom / Juliet Blackwell.
Description: First edition. | New York : Berkley, 2022. | Includes bibliographical references.
Identifiers: LCCN 2021044398 (print) | LCCN 2021044399 (ebook) |
ISBN 9780593097878 (trade paperback) | ISBN 9780593097885 (ebook)
Subjects: LCSH: World War, 1939-1945--Underground movements--France--Fiction. |
LCGFT: Historical fiction. | Novels.
Classification: LCC PS3602.L32578 P39 2022 (print) |
LCC PS3602.L32578 (ebook) | DDC 813/.6--dc23
LC record available at https://lccn.loc.gov/2021044398
LC ebook record available at https://lccn.loc.gov/2021044399

First Edition: April 2022

Printed in the United States of America
1st Printing

Book design by Alison Cnockaert

To Bob Lawes
Proud veteran, loyal friend, extraordinary father
Thank you

what didn't you do to bury me
but you forgot I was a seed

—DINOS CHRISTIANOPOULOS,
THE BODY AND THE WORMWOOD

THE
PARIS
SHOWROOM

1

Capucine

Winter 1944
RUE DU FAUBOURG SAINT-MARTIN,
TENTH ARRONDISSEMENT, PARIS

*I*N MY GRANDMOTHER'S generation, twirling a fan in one's left hand meant: *We are watched.*

As far as I knew, our captors did not understand the arcane language of fans. Still, when Isedore, the young woman who slept on the cot next to mine, picked up a fan and toyed with it, I glanced over at the guards just in case. The two men seemed absorbed in their game of cards, which they played upon a marble-topped and gilded Louis XIV side table, so I returned my attention to my project, keeping my movements small.

I doubted I would be noticed, shielded as I was by a blanket hung for privacy and by a well-placed trunk. The guards seldom paid us much mind. Most of the captives were Jews married to Aryans, or the wives of prisoners of war, though a handful were "antisocials," like me. By and large, we did as we were told. The alternative was deportation.

There were far worse places to be held prisoner by the Nazis.

I pressed another pleat into the sheet of heavy drawing paper that I had slipped into my work smock yesterday as I sorted through a shipment of goods from an artist's ransacked atelier. The artist signed his pieces "Michel Gainsbourg"; apparently his name was Jewish enough to prompt his arrest but not sufficiently well-known that the Nazi elite vied to possess his artwork. Some of Gainsbourg's dreamy watercolors and elegant sketches might be displayed on the showroom floor below, while the rest would be loaded onto trains bound for Germany. There, they might grace the residences of the loyal *Herrenvolk* who had lost their homes in the Allied bombings, or adorn the walls of those who simply wanted something new and pretty to spruce things up. It was an enduring mystery to me how the Nazis could so revile the Jews yet covet their art, their furniture, their clothing. Even their ordinary kitchen utensils.

But then, not much that happened in the Lévitan department store made sense.

Truckload after never-ending truckload, the looted household goods arrived nestled in straw-filled wooden crates, as though packed by loving hands. We prisoners sorted and cleaned and repaired the items, some of which would be displayed in the downstairs showrooms, as though there was nothing at all unusual about where they had come from. As though the store's rightful owner, Monsieur Lévitan, had not been forced to flee to the south of France, just steps ahead of the secret police.

Once we had arranged the stolen items in tasteful displays on the department store counters, Nazi officials and their wives—or, more often, their French mistresses—would wander the aisles like plump, greedy children let loose in a candy store. Their avaricious eyes gleamed as they snatched up family heirlooms as well as every-day items: valuable cloisonné vases and old desk lamps, centuries-old grandfather clocks and ancient pianos, fine bone china and well-used cast-iron skillets.

The Nazis called their project *Möbel Aktion,* or Operation Fur-niture. It was a special branch of the *Organisation Todt,* an organiza-tion of forced-labor camps that supported the war efforts of the Third Reich. The goal of Operation Furniture was simple: to strip the Jews' homes and businesses of all they possessed so that the Nazis and their followers might live more comfortably.

And so that the Jews would have nothing to return to—if they returned at all.

Stiff with cold, my fingers moved slowly. Muscle memory soon found the right place to force the fold so that the fan would snap open properly, and as my hands settled into the familiar rhythm, my mind was free to wander. Madame Schreyer's fever had spiked last night, and the other prisoners in her pod were attempting to hide her illness from the guards, lest she be deported to wherever it was they sent us when we were no longer useful: back to Drancy, on the outskirts of Paris, or more likely to camps in Germany and, beyond, in Poland. Madame Schreyer was pale and wan, her coffee brown eyes appeared sunken, and her hands trembled. For now, at least, only her fellow prisoners knew just how weak she had become. Af-ter all, none of us was looking our best.

Folding a fan is akin to the Japanese art of *orikami,* creating something magical, even miraculous, from an ordinary sheet of pa-per. The delicate watercolor sketch of a shepherdess with her flock meant the finished fan would be not only useful but also lovely, just as a proper fan should be. Back in our shop—in my father's shop, La Maison Benoît—we created works of art from silk and peacock feathers, with carved ivory stays gilded in gold. Before the war, our fans had been in demand by the finest fashion houses. Before the war, I spent my nights in the jazz clubs of Montmartre, reveling in the knowledge that we were the lucky ones. We had survived the War of 1914 and freed ourselves from the suffocating weight of tradition, and were creating a new society filled with art and music and openness. Before the war, Charles and I had exulted in wine and song and each other, secure in the belief that the worst days were behind us and that beauty and joy lay ahead.

Charles. I felt the familiar pang deep in my belly but continued with the methodical pleating of the paper, doing my best to ignore the ache.

"Are you all right, Capu?" Isedore was fine boned and olive skinned, with huge near-black eyes that seemed unable to keep from betraying every emotion that passed through her heart. *"Ça va?"*

"Oui, ça va." I was fine, I said, though we both knew it was a lie. None of us was fine, could possibly be fine, given our circumstances.

Isedore was not much younger than my daughter, Mathilde, who was just turning twenty-one. Two years older than I had been when I gave birth to her.

Just before my arrest, I had made Mathilde a special birthday gift: a fan with carved ivory monture, inlaid with tortoiseshell and mother-of-pearl chinoiserie ornament, silk painted with the scene of a ballerina dancing on a seashore, and topped with a line of brilliantly hued ostrich and peacock feathers. It was an outrageous work of art, the likes of which were rarely seen anymore and for which, I was sure, my daughter had absolutely no use.

But it was all I could do.

I had poured my maternal love, inadequate though it was, into that fan, and had tucked it into one of La Maison Benoît's signature leather-covered boxes along with a key to the "language of fans." As a small child, Mathilde had excelled at the subtle unspoken language, flitting around the shop and gesturing with the grace of a five-year-old coquette in the making.

My father and I used to laugh so hard we cried.

Did she remember? Or did Mathilde now simply say what was on her mind, giving voice to the thoughts so many of us found distressing to utter? It was hard to imagine; my daughter had been a secretive child, quiet, polite, and obedient—so unlike me. Such traits had helped Mathilde to fit in with her father's conservative parents, and over the years they had blossomed under her mami and papi's stewardship.

Our estrangement had saved her. Her grandparents were good, stolid French Catholics who would keep her safe. If the price of that safety was Mathilde's disdain for me, I was more than happy to pay it.

I was startled from my thoughts by the sound of a shout, as the younger guard crowed over a winning hand while the other guard complained loudly and riffled through the cards, implying something shady had occurred. I took advantage of their distraction to get to my feet and edge over toward one of the huge arched attic windows.

We had been ordered to stay away from the windows, and the guards had piled crates in front of them to block our access. But by subtly angling the crates a bit this way and that a little at a time, we prisoners had created an inconspicuous path through the obstacles so that occasionally one of us dared to peek outside, hoping to spy an Aryan wife or mother, in-laws or perhaps a brave neighbor or two loitering on the sidewalk below. The other day a young man named Jérôme had managed to drop a note to his girlfriend without being spotted, but most often the prize was a mere glimpse of a loved one, a furtive wave of a hand. The locking of eyes. The crucial, precious recognition that one had not been forgotten.

I peered through the smudged glass to the street below, though I knew it was fruitless. Mathilde would not come looking for me. She had no reason to seek out the mother who had abandoned her.

But . . . if she *had* been there and had tilted her face to gaze up at the department store's attic windows, and if she remembered the language of fans that we had once shared, I knew what I would have done.

I would have drawn the fan across my eyes: *I am sorry.*

2

Mathilde

*T*HE THREE YOUNG women made a pretty picture on the busy terrace of the Café de la Paix. Bridgette was blond and blue-eyed, Simone was sleek and dark featured, and in the gentle sun, Mathilde's hair shone a honey-tinted strawberry. They wore their thick coats against the chill of late winter: Mathilde's red wool, Simone's royal blue, and Bridgette's patchwork of cleverly repurposed gray serge.

As their aproned waiter set three demitasses of "coffee"—in reality, a roasted-barley-and-chicory concoction—on the tiny wrought iron café table, Simone regarded a tall, strapping soldier from under her soot-darkened lashes. When he returned her stare, she looked away but graced him with a flirtatious smile.

"*Arrête*, Simone," Bridgette hissed in a fierce whisper. "Stop that."

Simone shot Bridgette a withering look and sat back in the metal chair with an exasperated flounce. "I don't mean to be harsh,

Bridg, but you haven't been any fun since this stupid war began. Don't I deserve a little pleasure after spending a month in the muddy countryside with my *grandpère* and *grandmère*, Monsieur et Madame Ennuyeux?"

"Simone, you mustn't refer to your grandparents that way," said Mathilde. "It's disrespectful."

"I'm just being honest, Mathilde," Simone said with a shrug. "They are *so* boring. I cannot imagine how you put up with your grandparents, day in, day out. Mine think they're living in the last century."

"There's nothing wrong with being traditional," said Mathilde.

"Maybe for you," Simone said. "Me, I prefer to live a little while I am young. We'll marry and have babies and become fat and boring housewives soon enough."

"You might," Bridgette said, and sipped her ersatz coffee. "But not I."

"*Bof!* We shall see. Do you know, there is not a single healthy young man in the entire French countryside? Those that haven't been sent to work with the *Service du Travail Obligatoire* are all ugly, or toothless, or missing an arm or a leg. Not like these fellows . . ."

Simone smiled at another uniformed officer, but, vexingly, his pale eyes were fixed on Bridgette.

The Germans always go for the blondes, Mathilde imagined her friend saying. Simone often cursed her dark mane, claiming that if she had access to hair dye, she would fix that soon enough. The last time Mathilde had been at her childhood friend's house, Simone confessed she would give anything to be like the beautiful Annabella, the platinum blond French movie star whom they had worshipped before Annabella abandoned France for Hollywood.

"They're *Germans*, Simone," said Bridgette, keeping her voice low. "German soldiers. I know you never paid attention in history class, but remember the last war?"

"This is different," said Simone.

"In what way?"

Simone waved her hand dismissively. "That one was about an archduke or something, right? I mean, it was just ridiculous. This time we're not fighting. We're . . . finding a way to live together. And besides," she added as another officer brushed past their table. "They're so *handsome*."

"You are not the only one with family in the countryside, Simone," said Bridgette, her lips tight with anger. "I visit my family in Claye-Souilly often, and the men there are very handsome."

"Not these days, they're not. Even those who still have all their teeth and limbs are so grim, so gray," said Simone with a sigh. "And not many have enough francs to pay for this coffee, much less buy me a nice meal."

"Because of the Germans, which was my original point," said Bridgette.

"*Please*, let's not ruin my birthday coffee with such talk," said Mathilde, adding a bit of saccharin to her cup since there was no sugar or cream to be had. "It's been so long since the three of us have been together. Can't we just enjoy one another?"

Mathilde loved seeing her old school friends, but lately their get-togethers tended to devolve into spats like this one. It wasn't a dispute over politics exactly since none of them truly understood what was happening in their country or in the world, much less what their future might hold. The *Pariser Zeitung* was the only newspaper still permitted to publish, and it extolled the virtues of collaboration, its articles devoted to praising how well the German and French cultures complemented each other. Editorials paid tribute to Parisian restaurants, museums, and nightlife.

Still, Mathilde was dismayed to see familiar Jewish businesses defaced with slurs, ransacked, and abandoned—a fine jewelry store in the Marais, her favorite chocolatier near the Place des Vosges—and lately there were whispers of mass arrests and the deportation of French citizens as well as immigrants, though no one seemed to know where they were sent or why. Not far from her house in Neuilly-sur-Seine, a group of young Jewish children was being cared for by nuns after their parents had been hauled away to an unknown fate. How could that be justified?

Her paternal grandparents—Mami Yvette and Papi Auguste—counseled Mathilde to cooperate with the Vichy authorities. Even Father Guillaume, their parish priest, lectured his parishioners to accommodate the occupiers. *"Rendez à César ce qui appartient à César, et à Dieu ce qui appartient à Dieu,"* he had read from the pulpit during the Sunday Mass two days after the German troops swept into Paris. Render unto Caesar what is Caesar's and unto God what is God's.

Under Papi Auguste's direction, the Renault automobile factory where he was a vice president had retooled to produce engine parts for the fearsome *Luftwaffe.* Just last night, Papi had announced with satisfaction, over a dinner of black-market grouse prepared in a delicate cream sauce, that business had never been so good.

As she listened now to her friends argue, Mathilde could see both sides: There was no denying that the German soldiers had an attractive, healthy way about them that their own people seemed to have lost, the famously brash Parisian confidence having leached away under the humiliation of the Occupation. But Simone's father was a well-paid bureaucrat who worked for the Vichy government, while Bridgette's family was so poor that she often dressed in her old school uniform or in outfits fashioned from the various scraps of material that littered the floor of the family's tailor shop. Bridgette's father had lost a leg defending Reims in the War of 1914, and Bridgette had confided to Mathilde that lately he was compelled to produce bespoke suits at the whims of the Nazi elite, even if it meant that he and his wife went for days without sleep and were paid only a fraction of what the suits were worth.

Mathilde did not know what to think. As usual.

There was a lull in the conversation. Around them, the café's terrace was abuzz with conversation: customers hailing waiters, schoolgirls flirting with soldiers, and a long queue of Parisians in front of a nearby boulangerie patiently waiting their turn to purchase the day's baguette. Except for the fact that so many of the men wore German uniforms, and the people in line possessed haggard faces and clutched ration coupons, the scene was reminiscent of life in Paris before the war.

Mathilde suddenly found it unbearable that they should all be pretending that nothing had changed. But what was truly bothering her wasn't the war per se, but the contents of the long box she carried in her bag.

"What's wrong, Mathilde?" Bridgette's astute blue eyes studied Mathilde's face. "Have you heard from your mother?"

Mathilde shook her head. Unable to find the right words, she pulled the box from her bag, letting the embossed gilt stenciling on the smooth leather box speak for her: La Maison Benoît.

"A fan?" asked Bridgette.

"My mother made it for me. I guess she didn't have a chance to send it before she . . ." Mathilde hesitated, then took another sip of her espresso and set it back down before finding the courage to finish the sentence. "Before she was arrested. She and my grandfather both."

Bridgette's hand froze in midair as she lifted her cup, and Simone's eyes widened and her mouth gaped open. A long moment of silence passed.

"*What?* When?" asked Bridgette.

"I'm not sure," said Mathilde, fighting back tears. "Maybe a month or so ago. It was only last night that we received the news from her apartment's concierge, Madame Laurent."

"Arrested? But—I don't understand." Simone leaned in, for once taking care that others seated at the crowded café did not overhear. "Why was your mother arrested? You're not a Jew. Or . . . are you?"

"No, of course not. It was because of the newsletter. Her father's newsletter."

Mathilde hesitated to call her mother's father, Bruno, her grandfather even though she had lived in his home when she was little and could still recall the sound of his easy laugh, how he used to throw her into the air and tickle her. But to Mathilde, her true *grandpère* was Papi Auguste, a man whose name suited him completely: Dignified and thoroughly French, he dressed in a three-piece suit, complete with a pocket watch and monocle, even on his days off work.

"He's a . . . you know . . . Bruno's a communist."

"*Shhhh,*" Bridgette said, glancing around. "You mustn't say things like that anymore."

"But that makes no sense," Simone whispered. "Why would your mother be arrested for her father's beliefs?"

"Guilt by association—haven't you heard?" murmured Bridgette. "It doesn't take much these days."

"We're not really sure," said Mathilde. "It's not like anyone tells you why. The only reason we learned of it was because Madame Laurent wrote a letter telling us they had been arrested, but it was delayed in the mail. She also sent me this fan."

After the package arrived, Mathilde had left the fancy leather box on the marble-topped demilune table in the foyer for a full two days, unopened, until Mami Yvette reminded her that a proper young lady did not ignore her mother, even if she did not respect her mother's choices. Mathilde had lifted the lid slowly, with trepidation. Nestled within the box was the most beautiful fan she had ever seen: ornate carved ivory stays studded with mother-of-pearl and tortoiseshell, tips gilded in gold. When splayed opened, the fan revealed a pleated painting of a ballerina dancing upon the ocean shore. The scene was topped with iridescent peacock feathers and fluffy ostrich plumes. Fully extended, the fan spanned nearly two feet.

"Madame Laurent wrote that my mother made the fan for my birthday," Mathilde uttered, her voice strange to her own ears, as hollow as her heart.

"May I?" said Simone, reaching for it.

Mathilde nodded.

Simone opened the fan in front of her face, revealing only her eyes above the feathered top. She batted her eyelashes, then laughed as she lowered the fan. "I mean, it's awfully old-fashioned—who uses fans anymore? But still, it's very pretty. Maybe you could hang it on the wall."

She handed the fan to Bridgette, who stroked the feathers as she studied the painting and the carved stays.

"Your mother was always so . . . ," Bridgette said in a wistful voice.

"Glamorous," Simone said with a sigh.

When Mathilde was very young, her mother would sweep into her "bedroom"—a palette made of blankets and pillows on the bottom shelf of a large armoire—to kiss her good night before going out for the evening. Capucine literally sparkled as the light reflected off the rhinestones and bugle beads of her fringed flapper dresses. Her dark hair was coiffed in a chic bob, a fan always dangled from her wrist, and she smelled of clove cigarettes, powder, and the subtlest hint of perspiration mixed with her signature scent: the perfume called Habanita de Molinard.

But that had been before Mathilde went to live with Mami Yvette and Papi Auguste Duplantier in their big square house in Neuilly-sur-Seine, an affluent suburb to the west of Paris proper. There, she slept in a canopied princess bed in a room with tall casement windows and French doors that opened onto a delicate Juliet balcony. There, she had a huge dollhouse to play with in the redecorated bedroom of her father, Roger Duplantier, who had died when she was still an infant. He had been an only child, so Mami Yvette liked to say that Mathilde was the daughter she had never had, and because of that, she would always be grateful for Capucine, even though Capucine was a lost soul, mingling as she did with artists and foreigners, with jazz musicians and vulgar Americans.

The Duplantier family honored the Pope and did as Father Guillaume told them they must. They had never approved of Capucine, much less Capucine's father, Bruno the godless communist, still less the fact, discussed only in whispers, that Capucine had been with child before she and Roger hurriedly exchanged marriage vows.

Mathilde used to stand on that delicate Juliet balcony, peer down the tree-lined, cobblestoned rue Pierret and wonder when her mother would return to take her back to La Maison Benoît.

For a while, Capucine had come to visit regularly, showering Mathilde with kisses and smiles and bearing gifts of brightly colored Bakelite bangles and freshly baked madeleines. Mami Yvette served tea in the parlor and watched with stiff-necked disapproval as mother and daughter chatted on the uncomfortable horsehair sofa. Mathilde would cry when her mother left, begging her to take her with her, but Capucine would shake her head and go, leaving Mathilde to fall in a heap in Mami Yvette's arms, Mami stroking her hair and telling her, "Maybe next time." Until, eventually, there was no next time and Capucine did not return.

As Mathilde grew and matured, the pain of her mother's abandonment calcified into bitter shards. Yes, she was healthy and warm, loved and well nourished. Yes, she went to an exclusive private school for girls and dressed in pretty and fashionable clothes. Yes, she attended Mass every Sunday, took Communion, and went to confession more than she probably needed to, considering her largely blameless life, and thus was in no danger of the fiery torments to which Father Guillaume insisted her mother would be condemned in punishment for her wicked ways. Mathilde tried to put her mother behind her. *"Le passé est passé,"* Papi Auguste was fond of saying. What's past is past, and her mother belonged to the past.

But part of Mathilde never stopped missing her little nest in the big armoire, the memory of her joyful, irrepressible mother sweeping in and scooping her up in the middle of the night, feathers wafting about them as they danced around the workroom. To this day, a part of Mathilde remained on that balcony, yearning for the mother who hadn't come back.

And now?

My mother is a prisoner of the Nazis. Mathilde repeated the words in her mind as if to bring herself to believe them. Papi Auguste had always muttered that Capucine was immoral, degenerate, and dangerous, and would come to no good end, but still, Mathilde could not believe she had been arrested.

"Where are they being held?" asked Bridgette, her soft voice even kinder than usual.

To Mathilde's surprise, she found her friend's sympathy grating.

"Yes! You should go see them," said Simone. "Maybe there's a way to help. Your *grandpère* is an important man at the Renault factory—surely he could do something."

"Or you could use your own money," Bridgette suggested. "Maybe hire a lawyer or bribe someone or . . . something. Aren't you meant to inherit soon?"

Mathilde nodded. "It's supposed to be my dowry, though."

Simone scoffed. "Your 'dowry'? What is this, 1910?"

"But even . . . even if I could help, or talk my papi into helping, we don't know where they *are*."

After reading the letter from Madame Laurent, Papi Auguste had gotten to his feet at the head of the dining room table, raised his glass of wine in a toast, and declared, "The Lord works in mysterious ways." Mami Yvette cast her husband a disapproving look and gave Mathilde a hug, but Mathilde knew her grandmother agreed with him.

Letting the tears fall, Mathilde shook her head and repeated in a whisper: "We don't even know where they are."

3

Capucine

*P*APER HAS A memory.

Once a fold is created, the paper is forever changed and can never again be truly flattened. Even if dampened and ironed, it will never regain its original shape, because the integrity of the fibers has been broken. A fold is a fracture.

A fold leaves a scar.

"It's so pretty," Isedore proclaimed, watching over my shoulder as I drew a little border of daisies and daffodils along the edge with a colored pencil.

Officially we weren't supposed to keep any of the items that came in, but the guards rarely begrudged our petty theft of candle stubs, broken figurines, or similar items destined for the bonfire. Most were also amenable to bribery, so I traded a fan to one of the guards in exchange for a box of half-dried paints and stubby pencils seized from Monsieur Gainsbourg's studio.

"I'll finish it off with some lace I saved from a torn wedding dress," I said. "Bruno always said a fan must be beautiful as well as functional."

Isedore cocked her head, her long mahogany hair falling over one shoulder. "Why do you call him Bruno, Capu? He is your father, no?"

"He is," I said with a smile. "But a very unusual one. Very . . . forward-thinking."

"Is he still at Drancy?" Isedore asked, her voice an irritatingly gentle whisper.

The question stabbed at my heart, dousing me with doubt and fear. I didn't know where he was. That was one of the hardest things to deal with since this war began: Between the propaganda and lies, the innuendo and threats, the Nazis ensured none of us knew anything. Not for certain.

The last time I had seen Bruno, his dark eyes, which had always flashed with passion—for his art, for his daughter, for his longing to change the world for the better—had been shadowed with sorrow and disillusionment. He was stricken, his countenance wan and gray from hunger and defeat. And guilt.

"Denounce me, Capu," Bruno whispered as we stood in line at Drancy, the former French military barracks now used as a prison camp for the Third Reich.

Murmurs ran up and down the long queue, rumors swirling, as we newly arrested struggled to comprehend what had happened, what *would* happen, to us. Why had we been detained, yanked from our homes, and forced to stand in line for hours without food or water or access to a bathroom? We had been given five minutes to pack a precious few of our worldly belongings into a single suitcase: I had brought two framed photos, one of Mathilde and another of me and Charles; a pencil and notebook; and, ludicrously, a handful of our cherished exotic feathers. In my panic, I had not thought to bring anything practical except a single change of clothing. No toothbrush, not even a comb.

"I will *not* denounce my own father," I snapped, anxiety lending my voice a harsh edge. "Don't be ridiculous."

"You must, *ma fille*," Bruno insisted, his own voice shaky but determined. "It is the only way to save yourself. And it is my fault you are here. It is all my fault."

"They're just going to force us to work, Bruno. Maybe it won't be so bad. We know how to work."

He shook his gray head. "How can you deny what has been happening these past few years, Capu? Have you not seen what the Nazis have done to Paris? They are a different kind of enemy."

Even now. Even after being arrested, standing in line at Drancy, I could hardly comprehend what was happening to our country. I spoke enough German to understand the guards who amused themselves by taunting the prisoners, most of whom were Jewish, with vague threats veiled in vicious smiles: *Look! We will light special candles for Hanukkah.* The menace behind their words sent a chill down my spine.

Another murmur coursed through the line like a wave: The officials were looking for people skilled in furniture repair, clock making, and interior design to work in Paris. I pounced on it like a lifeline.

"Listen, Bruno," I whispered. "Did you hear that?"

"Do not be gullible, Capu," he said. "The Nazis need weapons, not furniture. Why would they ask for any such thing?"

"I have no idea. But I say we volunteer."

"We're not experts in furniture, much less interior design."

"They don't know that," I said. "We've made decorative fans for wall hangings, and anyway, we understand the world of fashion and design. I met Émile-Jacques Ruhlmann more than once. We can make a good case for ourselves."

My father fixed me with a gaze that was both fierce and unbearably sad. "I will not lift my pinkie finger to help a fascist. You listen to me, Capu: I will never debase myself to work for the Nazis."

"If it means I can stay in Paris," I said, "I'll do what they say."

"Then you will be a pawn in their game, *ma fille.*"

"Maybe. But I'll be a pawn in Paris, Papa. Who knows where we'll end up otherwise?"

"Paris is not what it used to be, Capu. Paris has broken my heart, and she will break yours. And there is no need for you to kneel at their feet and beg to serve as their decorator. Here is what you must do: Denounce me and my beliefs, claim to be a good Catholic like your in-laws, and I'm sure . . . I'm sure they must let you go."

He said this last with a firm nod of conviction as if trying to convince himself.

But, of course, I refused to denounce my father. And in any case, as far as I could tell, personal denunciations or declarations of Catholic faith or claims of innocence failed to secure anyone's release, at least for those of us without a connection to someone in power.

At long last, a group of thirty prisoners was shoved into the office of the *Kanzlei*, where we were ordered to complete a number of forms detailing our pedigree. This was more for the Jewish prisoners than for my father and me; the officers hoped to ferret out immigrants and to determine who might be only partly Jewish or had Aryan spouses and in-laws.

Bruno's pedigree was thoroughly French, and my mother had been born in Paris to a family of Italian merchants. Good Catholics all. Our crime was political, not ethnic or religious. I rarely used my married name, Duplantier, but I wrote it down on my form. My husband's parents had tormented me enough through the years that I felt no compunction using their name now if it would help.

The interviewer sitting behind a raised desk was a large, square-faced man with a jagged scar along one cheek. One by one we were called up to speak with him. When it was my turn, I smiled, gazing up through my lashes.

"I have connections to the finest Parisian couture houses, monsieur," I said. "I formerly worked for the designer Louise Boulanger at her atelier on rue Royale."

That was a gross exaggeration. I had done some featherwork for Louise Boulanger in the late 1920s, and in return she had given me a simple shift of apricot satin with a dyed ombré skirt of ostrich plumes. I would never forget the feel of that feathered skirt as I danced in Charles's arms, swaying to the jazz. The plush softness of the plumes brushing my stockinged legs. The mingled scents of tobacco and perfume. The heat, the music, the beat that seemed to go beyond the here and now to call up a kind of ethereal strumming, a song of nature and beauty and truth and grace that lifted and healed us after the brokenness of the Great War . . .

The man behind the desk snorted and looked at me askance. "You're in fashion design?"

"Yes, indeed," I said, cringing at the pleading note in my voice. I was still clad in the plain work apron and headscarf I had been wearing when we were arrested. "You must forgive my appearance; I was in the workroom when . . . summoned. I'm also very skilled with furniture and in interior design. In fact, Émile-Jacques Ruhlmann was a very good friend of mine, right up until his untimely death, may he rest in peace."

"Who's that?"

"A famous French furniture maker and interior designer. The father of the Art Deco style? My point is, I could be of service."

"Uh-huh," he grunted. He read through the papers, making a note in the margins.

I couldn't keep my eyes from that scar: Pink and shiny, it winked at me when he talked. I wondered whether it was a relic of the Great War, a souvenir from a French soldier. The last war had fostered such acrid resentment between our two countries; the German people had been humiliated by their loss and ruined by the terms of the armistice, and we French had been maddened by the years of brutal hunger, shortages, and pervasive fear—not to mention the millions of death notices from the war department delivered into the trembling hands of mothers and fathers who understood, before opening the envelopes, that their worlds had blown up just as surely as their children had.

"You're not a Jew," he said. "And your in-laws are Aryan. But you were declared antisocial. Why?"

"My father—" I cut myself short, appalled at what I was about to say. "I mean, I was accused of being a communist, or antisocial, but I assure you—"

"*Genug jetzt!*" He cut me off, made another note on the papers, stamped them, and beckoned to the next person in line: Bruno.

I stepped over to the next desk, where an unsmiling young woman handed me a small square of green paper, assigned me to block thirteen, and ordered me to join the line on the other side of the room.

I watched, mouth dry and heart pounding, as Bruno raised his stubbled chin and refused to so much as speak a word or fill out a form. I was not surprised; diplomacy had never been Bruno's strong suit. He and Monsieur Accambray, the fruit monger across the street from La Maison Benoît, had maintained a petty feud so long running, I doubted either man could remember how it had begun. In some ways Bruno's quick temper and his refusal to suffer fools were two of the characteristics that endeared him to our elite customers.

The interviewer glared at my father, made a note on his blank forms, and stamped them with a *thunk* that reverberated like a gunshot. A different clerk handed my father a purple slip of paper and gave him a none-too-gentle shove toward a much bigger line of people, all of whom held purple tickets.

Another man spoke briefly to the interviewer, then was sent to take his place next to me. He was tall and thin but strong-looking, with the dark, heavy-lidded eyes of a tortured poet. While most of us were whimpering, shaking, or shuffling in our distress, he conveyed an air of quiet calm.

"*Bonjour*, madame," he murmured as casually as though we were waiting in line at the bank.

"*Bonjour*, monsieur," I responded in pure reflex. I noticed his square of paper was red. "What do the colors signify?"

"Red is for Jewish spouses of Aryans," he said in a low, deep voice. "Green, like yours, means you are awaiting clarification of your papers. The Germans love their categories, and we defy an easy label. They don't quite know what to do with us."

My father stood in his line across the hall, unspeaking, not meeting my eyes, clutching his purple ticket.

"And what does purple mean?" I asked.

"To be deported."

I took in a long, shaky breath, fighting nausea.

"That category is very clear, I regret to say." The young man's dark eyes searched my face. "Do you have someone in that group?"

Unable to find my voice, I nodded.

"I am very sorry," he said, placing a gentle hand on my upper arm. A wave of reassuring warmth reached through the thin fabric of my sleeve.

My voice shook as I finally found the words: "It's— He's my father. Where will they be deported *to*?"

The man shook his head. None of us knew any more now than we had when our neighbors and local shopkeepers began to disappear, leaving behind everything they owned.

Our group was ordered to move. As we shuffled out of the *Kanzlei* and toward our assigned quarters, I looked over my shoulder to catch a final glimpse of my father. Bruno's wan face suddenly lit up with a big smile, and he gave me a jaunty wink. Like he used to before the war.

That was the last time I saw my father. *Papa.*

Three days later I was ordered onto a covered lorry that slowly lurched its way to Paris, where it pulled up to the rear loading dock of the Lévitan department store on rue du Faubourg Saint-Martin, in the tenth arrondissement. About thirty of us huddled on the dock, shivering in the late-winter air, while our things were searched, rough hands riffling through hastily packed valises and pillowcases and tossing anything considered valuable or *verboten*— forbidden—onto one of two piles: the first, items to be kept by the Germans; the second, items to be destroyed.

A French police officer searched through my bag. He looked very young, his chubby cheeks roughened with pockmarks. He seemed perplexed by the feathers but let them be. But he froze when he discovered the framed photo of Charles and me together in an embrace, Charles grinning down at me, me smiling up at him. In love.

The guard met my eyes as he set the photo, facedown, on the pile destined for the bonfire.

My mouth opened to protest, but before I could say anything he said in a low voice: "I am doing you a favor. They must not see this."

"What do you mean?" I whispered.

He leaned toward me and replied, "You will be deported, no questions asked."

"I . . . Thank you," I said. *Charles.* My Charles. I imagined his precious face, and our love, consumed by the flames.

The young officer nodded briefly and moved on to the next prisoner, the next valise.

Eventually we were herded up a wide stairwell to the main floor of the department store, where a vast assortment of sofas and chairs, housewares and china, was on display. The sound of our boots on the stone floor seemed to echo throughout the showroom as we were escorted into one corner.

"Pay attention, everyone," said a German guard in heavily accented French. She was stout, of medium height, her face wide and bland, her light brown eyes cold and unyielding. "I am Pettit, and you will do as I say, here or anywhere, now and always. Remain silent and give your attention to Herr Direktor Kohn."

A large bald man in his forties stepped forward. Herr Direktor Kohn walked with a noticeable limp, and when he spoke, his voice was surprisingly high and raspy, as if he had stolen it from someone else. We had to listen closely to understand him.

"It is a great privilege to be chosen for the satellite camp known as Lager Ost. You will be sorted into pods of ten prisoners and assigned a number to which you will respond without fail. The rules are simple: Remain quiet, do what the guards tell you, and work hard. I have no tolerance for malingerers. Anyone found shirking their duties will have their food taken away, their work hours extended, and their things confiscated—or they will be immediately deported, at my discretion. Perhaps because you are in Paris you will be tempted to try to get in touch with friends or people in the neighborhood. This you will not do. Anyone attempting to make contact with the good citizens of Paris—the free citizens of Paris—will immediately be sent to Drancy, and from there perhaps to Bergen-Belsen or to Auschwitz. Anyone attempting to escape will be shot on sight, and their entire pod immediately deported. I suggest you think of your compatriots before abandoning them to such a fate."

And with that, Herr Direktor Kohn turned on his heel and strode down a nondescript hall whose signage indicated it led to the former offices of the department store management.

"Excuse me, Madame Pettit." A young woman, whom I later learned was Isedore, raised her hand as though she were in school. "Herr Direktor Kohn mentioned Auschwitz. Where is that?"

Pettit gave her a sickly smile. "It is at the end of the railroad tracks. The very end. Now put this on." She handed her a numbered armband, demanded her name and date of birth, and made a note in a large ledger.

I was issued an armband with the number 123 and assigned to a pod of ten women that was led up a broad stairwell to the fourth-floor attic. This was where I, and my equally bewildered compatriots, had lived ever since, spending our days unloading, sorting, cleaning, and repairing items pillaged from Jewish homes and businesses.

"My parents have already been killed," Isedore said softly now, bringing me back to the present. "My parents and my little brothers. All of them. I'm sure of it."

My hands, busy with the fan, stilled, and I focused on the young woman's near-black eyes.

"You can't think like that, Isedore," I said, shaking my head. "Now that the Allied forces are fighting to free us, I am sure things will change. The Germans will be defeated, everyone will come back, and your family will be reunited. And Paris will be Paris once again. You'll see."

"Do you really think so?"

"I do," I said with a nod, trying to convince myself. I wondered whether Mathilde had been notified of my arrest, and whether she might assume I had been killed. Would she care . . . ?

Surely, she would. Despite everything.

Some of the wealthier inmates were able to bribe the guards to post letters to family members. I had no money, but perhaps I could piece together a fan nice enough to entice a guard to do the same for me. But what would I say? And more important . . . would it endanger Mathilde if anyone found out we were communicating?

"Mordecai says the Nazis intend to kill every Israelite in Europe," Isedore continued. "He says those who are deported will never return, are probably already dead."

I glanced at the master jeweler with the decided paunch and long gray beard. Mordecai Krivine was perched on the edge of his cot, deep in discussion with a younger man sitting cross-legged on the floor. Mordecai was quick with advice, but also with a laugh, and he maintained the Jewish traditions—and his sense of humor— as best he could under the circumstances. There was no rabbi in Lévitan, so Mordecai had stepped into the role of spiritual guide for many of the prisoners, most of whom were Jews deemed "undeportable" by virtue of their mixed blood or mixed marriages, or who fell into one of the other categories that meant their disappearance would likely provoke a public outcry. The only non-Jews in Lévitan were the spouses of French soldiers being held as prisoners of war and those labeled "antisocial," like me and Madame Savanier, a *gitane.*

As the tall man in line at the *Kanzlei* had pointed out, our occupiers loved categories.

Isedore was unmarried and both her parents were Jewish, but she had saved herself by claiming a mastery in clockworks, having worked in her father's shop since she was a child, much as I had worked beside my father. On the shelf above her bed, she kept a beautiful rococo clock—its face cracked and its mechanism broken beyond repair—to remind her of better times. The Germans had stolen thousands of valuable timepieces and needed experienced hands to clean and restore the antiques and to ensure the mechanisms kept accurate time.

Our occupiers also valued timeliness.

"Isedore, I really don't think—"

"*Number 123!*" barked one of the guards.

I jumped, appalled to hear my number called out on a Sunday, the one day of the week we were not required to work. My heart pounded and my mouth went dry.

"Yes?" I shoved the now-completed fan under my blanket and stood.

"Capucine Benoît Duplantier?" Pettit knew my name perfectly well but preferred to reduce me to my number: 123.

Most of the guards, like the young man who had searched my bag upon my arrival, were French police working for the puppet Vichy government. But Pettit was German and seemed to harbor a deep resentment of humanity in general. She spoke fluent French but preferred to go on tirades in her native tongue, most of which we felt fortunate not to understand.

"Follow me. Herr Direktor wants to see you," she said.

"Why?" I asked, trying not to betray my nervousness.

"Wear your smock," she snapped.

Shortly after our arrival in Lévitan, two inmates had been tasked with creating the smocks from bolts of cheap black material seized from a fabric store. Usually, we wore whatever clothes we had brought with us, however threadbare, but when we were summoned before the Nazi officials, we were expected to be presentable and interchangeable, clad in our matching outfits. Mine had a red triangle sewn on the front, indicating that I was a political enemy of the Third Reich. The Jews wore yellow stars, and Madame Savanier had been issued a black triangle with a "Z," for *Zigeuner*, which meant "Gypsy." To the Nazis, being a Rom was a crime.

I locked eyes with Isedore as I took my work smock down from my shelf and slipped it on over my dress.

Isedore glanced at the spot where I had hidden Madame Schreyer's fan and whispered, "I'll get it to her."

I nodded my thanks. Our pod had long since made a pact: If any of us was taken away, our possessions were to be shared with the others before the guards had a chance to confiscate them for themselves or toss them atop the bonfire.

"Hurry up," snapped Pettit.

"You look quite fetching today," I said as I joined her. "New hairdo?"

"Just move."

Pettit led me to the stairs; the elevator was reserved for freight. Wordlessly, we descended three stories to the main level. When I coughed in my nervousness, the sound ricocheted throughout the wide stairwell.

Pushing through the doors that led to the main showroom, I

wondered what the store had been like before the war. I imagined the aisles full of customers perusing the displays, hardworking families dreaming of new bedroom sets and master suites, dining room tables and chifforobes and china cabinets. Smiling shopgirls standing at the ready to assist.

Now, though the vast space was still full of furniture and other goods, it had the feeling of an abandoned building. We prisoners were allowed in the main showroom only when we were setting items out on display for inspection or serving the Nazi "customers."

As we approached the director's office, a group of ten men shuffled out. Their faces had the resigned, closed expression common to those of us in captivity. Pettit yanked me to the side to let them pass.

A few days ago, a prisoner had tried to escape by hiding in an empty crate in the back of a moving truck. He had been summarily shot on the loading dock, and the next day his entire pod had been deported. These men, I assumed, were their replacements.

I recognized one man: the tall, handsome fellow I had spoken to at the *Kanzlei*, who held a red ticket because his wife was Aryan. He met my gaze and nodded almost imperceptibly.

"Boyfriend?" Pettit snickered as the group passed by.

"Only in his dreams," I said, trying to keep my tone light.

We had not been expressly forbidden from forming friendships or even pursuing love affairs, but I did not want to take any chances. Besides, while many of the guards were civil enough, and willing to look the other way while we pilfered books or wallpaper paste or other minor objects, I did not trust Pettit. For some reason she appeared to tolerate me more than she did the others, but I sensed in her a simmering well of anger. She could be easygoing one moment and in the next strike a prisoner viciously with the butt of her gun for some perceived infraction. Bruno used to lecture me on the writings of Sigmund Freud, so I was familiar with his psychological theories and wondered about Pettit's background, what might have happened to her as a child. How it was that, of all the paths she might have followed, she wound up working as a Nazi prison guard in Paris.

"*Mach schnell.*" Pettit gestured with her head toward the non-descript hallway. "Hurry up."

Discolored squares on the wall indicated where artwork had been taken down, leaving bald patches that had been partly covered over by Nazi propaganda posters. In one, birds with human features carried banners that read "The English, our good friends" and "*Vive de Gaulle,*" above the slogan, "The tall tales always come from the same nest." It seemed an unnecessarily convoluted way of calling the British liars. When my step slowed as I read the slogan, Pettit shoved me roughly between the shoulder blades.

"Move!"

Down the hallway was the store director's office. It was stuffy inside and overly warm, creating an overlay of sweat upon my cold fear. The scent of smoke from the bonfire that nearly always burned outside made me doubly nervous. It reminded me of the guards at Drancy mocking the prisoners with their talk of lighting candles for Hanukkah.

In this world of secrets, the camp gossip grapevine thrived. I had learned that Herr Direktor Kohn had been injured early in the war and thus was assigned to the comfortable job of director of Lévitan, one of Drancy's three satellite work camps in Paris. But rather than embrace the luxurious Parisian post, Kohn seemed embarrassed by it and by his injuries, and his shame spooled out the way it often did for cruel men: in taking delight in humiliating and hurting others.

The only time Kohn was accommodating was when his immediate superior, Baron Von Braun, the Oberführer of all the internment camps in Paris, came to inspect the goods—and the prisoners—at Lévitan. During these visits, Kohn smiled obsequiously, the air palpable with dread that Von Braun might find something amiss. We prisoners snapped to, not for Kohn's sake, but for our own. Von Braun had once pulled an inmate out from behind a counter and ordered her deported for having given him a "strange look."

Now Kohn was seated behind the massive desk from which, I assumed, Monsieur Lévitan had once run his store. With his narrowed blue eyes the commandant looked me up and down. He spoke decent French, and I knew a little basic German from school, but Pettit stood to one side at attention, ready to translate.

"You are Capucine Benoît Duplantier of La Maison Benoît?" he asked in his wispy voice.

"Yes, sir."

"What did you do there?"

"I was a fan maker with my father. We had connections to some of the finest couture—"

He cut me off. "Do you know a Mademoiselle Abrielle Garnier?"

My instinct was to remain mute. Never loquacious to begin with, Parisians had become even more tight-lipped during the Occupation. Words mattered; words could kill. I had been arrested because of my father's alleged crime of "ideological degeneracy," and admitting even a casual connection to someone the Nazis were suspicious of could lead to condemnation. On the other hand, since Kohn had asked me about Abrielle, he must already have had reason to think we were acquainted.

"Well?" he demanded.

"*Oui*, monsieur," I said.

Yes, I knew her. Abrielle Garnier had big green-gold eyes and bouncy yellow hair, was petite and doll-like, and spoke in a breathy little-girl voice. I had known Abrielle in those heady days when I frequented the cafés and jazz clubs of Montmartre and was in demand as a model for the likes of Matisse, Picasso, and Léger. I had known Abrielle Garnier when I danced, wearing the apricot gown with ostrich feathers designed by Louise Boulanger, in the arms of the man I loved

I felt a surge of pure rage.

Unless I was mistaken, Abrielle Garnier was the one who had betrayed my father and me to the Gestapo.

4

Mathilde

AFTER EXCHANGING GOOD-BYES at the café, the young women grabbed their bikes and went their separate ways, promising to meet again soon.

Mathilde had told her friends she was off to buy a new pair of stockings, which was a lie she would have to confess to Father Guillaume on Sunday. She had no need of new stockings, not that it would matter if she did. Ever since the Germans had taken over, many stores had closed, those that were still open had half-empty shelves, and nothing could be purchased without a precious ration ticket. A robust black market quickly sprang up to fill the void, and even Papi Auguste participated, proud of his ability to provide well for his lovely wife and precious granddaughter.

But she felt too restless to go straight home. Pausing on a street corner in front of a small carousel, Mathilde leaned her bike against a tree and took a seat on a bench to watch the noisy, colorful contraption spin round and round. Most Parisian children had long since been sent out of the city to live with family in the relative safety of the countryside, so the carousel held half a dozen young women who cooed and flirted with the men watching them, most of whom wore uniforms of the *Wehrmacht*, or German army. One of the soldiers began to toss chestnuts and candy at the women as they passed by, and the women hooted and laughed, reaching out for the goodies.

Mathilde had read that the Nazis were so pleased with Parisian culture that they were determined to keep the city unspoiled, a playground for the *Herrenvolk*, their loyal followers. Even common soldiers were given leave in the *Ville Lumière*, the City of Light. The Germans had a slogan for it: *Jeder einmal in Paris*. Everyone, once, in Paris.

Her grandparents counseled her that war was difficult, that they must count their blessings, and that their patience would be rewarded when the world returned to normal.

But the laughter of the women on the carousel and the leering expressions of the men in uniform grated. Just three doors down the street, the display windows of a neighborhood hardware store had been shattered and a crude Star of David painted on the door in red paint that dripped like blood. Paris had been altered, twisted, contorted into an amusement for the Nazis and the *Wehrmacht*.

My mother is a prisoner.

Mathilde retrieved the letter from her bag, smoothed it out, and reread the four succinct sentences she had long since memorized:

> *I am so very sorry to inform you that your mother and*
> *grandfather have been arrested, and your grandfather's*
> *store ransacked. I did what I could to intervene, but to*

no avail. All the soldiers would tell me was that the pair
were being taken to Drancy, and the S.S. officer in
charge spat when he pronounced them communists,
undesirables. I am heartbroken.

The letter was dated more than a month ago and was signed
Madame Antoinette Laurent, the concierge of the building that
housed her grandfather's shop.

Mathilde had been thirteen years old the last time she had dared
visit La Maison Benoît. She had lied to her grandparents, claiming
she was meeting a friend after school to stroll through the Jardin
du Luxembourg. She remembered edging slowly, warily, down the
cobblestoned street. As if the wagons full of flowers and trinkets or
the unfamiliar people milling about the neighborhood might infect
her. The fruit monger across the street seemed to glare at her.
Shops lined both sides of rue Saint-Sauveur, a solid block of store-
fronts broken only by the occasional wooden or iron door leading
to an interior courtyard ringed by apartments. It was a cityscape
utterly unlike what she was used to in Neuilly-sur-Seine with its
large, quiet detached homes.

It was hard for Mathilde to believe that she had spent the first
five years of her life here, on this narrow street that now felt so
foreign, so strange, and smelled vaguely of rotten fruit, which reminded her of a long-ago trip she had taken with Mami and Papi to
visit the Duomo in Florence.

La Maison Benoît's lemon yellow façade was graced with the
sinuous lines of the Art Nouveau school of design. The style appealed to her, though Mami Yvette and Papi Auguste did not approve of Art Nouveau, much less the more recent Art Deco style.
Their old stone home was reassuringly stolid and square, the inte-

rior paneled with the heavy dark woods of the Victorian era. Old-fashioned swaths of carved garlands and cupids frolicked about, crowning the mantelpieces and her own princess bed.

Mathilde remembered how she had approached La Maison Benoît's multipaned bay window and peeked in, not even sure what she was hoping to see. She spied Bruno, bent over a large ledger on the counter, apparently alone. To her surprise, the fan shop was neat as a pin. Bruno was an avowed communist, and somehow Mathilde had assumed his political beliefs would have translated into a chaotic lifestyle and lackadaisical housekeeping. Instead, pretty glass apothecary jars were filled with shells and beads and feathers, and the shop's signature gold-embossed leather boxes were stacked high on the shelves that lined the shop's rear wall, below which were rows of neatly labeled and wide but shallow drawers.

And there were fans everywhere, pinned to the walls and perched atop shelves: some made of fluffy plumes while others were demure, some monochrome while others were wildly colorful, even iridescent. Many of the fans had no feathers at all but were made of folded paper or silk, featuring delicately painted cartouches of dancers or birds or bucolic bliss.

Mathilde had lingered on the sidewalk, trying to work up the courage to fling open the door, stride inside, and address her grandfather as she had rehearsed in her imagination. She was poised to enact her plan when two well-dressed women approached the shop. Wearing chic feathered chapeaux and carrying matching reticules, they were conversing animatedly, gesturing with their hands and laughing.

In what felt like a mockery of her daydream, one of the women opened the front door with a flourish and the pair marched in.

Mathilde remembered the sound of the shop's bell ringing out,

Bruno closing the ledger and coming around the gleaming counter to greet the women, trading kisses and hailing them as old friends.

And then Bruno glanced over to the window, and their eyes met through the glass.

Her breath caught in her throat. He tilted his head in question. She quailed and ran away.

"Mathilde? *C'est toi?*" Bruno called after her from the shop door. "Is that you, Mathilde? *Ma petite fille?* Come back!"

She did not stop. She did not look back.

Mathilde had rushed straight to the confessional at the Cathédrale Notre-Dame, where the priest admonished her for disobeying her grandparents and gave her a penance. She prayed on her rosary, kneeling on the hard stone floor for nearly an hour, relishing the pain, knowing she deserved it.

But when she reached home, her guilt returned. Mami Yvette took one look at her and asked what was wrong. Mathilde might have worked up the courage to tell her grandmother the truth, except that she didn't understand herself why seeing the beautiful La Maison Benoît, with its chic clients and splendid fans and feathers and shells, her grandfather Bruno looking happy and relaxed, had upset her so. She could not find the words.

And now, eight years later, watching the carousel make its incessant circles, Mathilde pondered: Dared she venture to rue Saint-Sauveur, see if she could find a clue as to her mother's whereabouts?

Her grandparents would not approve. And given the way things were, it might be dangerous even to admit a connection to someone who had been arrested.

Still . . . Mathilde couldn't bear the thought of going back to Neuilly-sur-Seine, not in her current mood.

It didn't take long to get there on her bike. Mathilde turned onto rue Saint-Sauveur, then got off and walked the bicycle the rest of the way. As she had the last time, she felt wary, as though the shop might reach out to her, enfold her in its orbit until she could not—or would not *want* to—break away, as her mother had always done with the artists and musicians she had befriended.

As she drew closer, Mathilde noticed details she hadn't before: a crack in a windowpane, chips in the weathered paint on the door. But then, as Mami Yvette said, the city was not at its best these days: Everywhere there were blackened façades, rusted gates, peeling paint. The war had not been good to France, and her looks had suffered. Even the famously fashionable Parisians could not perm their hair or find new clothes or cosmetics.

Mathilde leaned her bike against the stone wall and approached La Maison Benoît's display window.

Cupping her gloved hands around her eyes to block out the sunlight, she peered inside to find the store was in shambles: boxes overturned, their contents spilling out, fans splayed on the floor, feathers strewn everywhere. Incongruously, she was reminded of a time, years ago, when Bridgette had spent the night and they had had a pillow fight, the downy white feathers escaping the ticking and filling the air like snowflakes, floating down onto her princess bed.

"They are closed," came a woman's voice from behind her.

Mathilde spun around to see an elderly woman: plump and kindly looking, despite her frown, and at least four inches shorter than Mathilde, with her long gray hair gathered up in an old-fashioned bun.

Madame Antoinette Laurent. The concierge.

Mathilde had fleeting little-girl memories of Madame Laurent: the softness of her lap, the scent of vanilla that surrounded her, the taste of her homemade madeleines. But madame was much smaller than Mathilde remembered.

"Madame Laurent, it's me. Mathilde."

The woman squinted at her for a moment and then grinned: "*Mathilde?* Oh, but of course you are! I should have recognized you, my dear. You look so much like your mother."

"Truly?" Mathilde asked, her hand touching the strawberry blond braid on her shoulder. Mami Yvette had always praised Mathilde's fair hair, which she had inherited from her father, though she had her mother's dark eyes.

The old woman chuckled. "Your coloring is different, but I speak of your face. In any case, call me Antoinette. We have no need for 'madame' between us. Don't you remember that I used to baby-sit you?"

They stood staring at each other for a moment. Mathilde felt her mouth gape the way it sometimes did when she was at a loss for words. It was a habit Mami Yvette had tried to train out of her.

"I am so sorry, child," said Antoinette, the smile falling from her face. "So very sorry about your dear mother and your grandfather. Tell me, have you received any word?"

Mathilde shook her head.

"I don't know what to make of it, of any of it," said the old woman. Her rheumy eyes fixed on the storefront. "I would never have imagined such a thing was possible in *la belle France*. Bruno and Capucine both! Such good souls."

The chaos of the street behind them reflected Mathilde's thoughts: jostled and jangly. Three adolescent boys ran by, laughing and try-ing to tag one another with what appeared to be a dead bird. A sad-looking flower vendor called out, her weary voice anemic, try-ing to entice customers by claiming her violets were on sale. Two women argued over a small basket of apples, waving their ration coupons at the grumpy fruit monger.

"You knew my mother well?" Mathilde asked as though the question had just occurred to her. She remembered Antoinette from her childhood, but somehow, in her mind, Bruno and Capucine existed in their own universe, independent of all else. She had learned a term in Latin class that seemed to apply: *sui generis.*

"Well, I should think so!" Antoinette replied. "Your grandfather had this shop, and lived in the apartment behind it, even before I became the concierge, so many years ago now. Do come in out of all this noise, *ma fille.* Come in for a cup of tea, and we will talk."

Mathilde did not want to talk. Not about her mother, or her grandfather, or what had happened to the fan shop. Not about the war, or what life had been like before the war, and especially not about how much she took after her mother. She wanted to flee from this old woman and this cacophonous street, maybe escape into the sweet darkness of a movie theater, where she wouldn't have to talk to anyone. Perhaps she could find a film playing that wasn't too long, and she could still make it back to Neuilly-sur-Seine in time for dinner. Maybe . . .

Mathilde opened her mouth to bid madame adieu, but instead said, "Thank you, yes. I would love a cup of tea."

ANTOINETTE LED THE way through a door in the huge wooden gate that separated the building's interior courtyard from the street and provided privacy for the residents of the apartments that encircled the cobblestoned courtyard. In the old days, before the war, window boxes had been filled with trailing flowers, their charming red and pink blooms cascading down in glorious contrast with the gray stone walls. Nowadays those lucky enough to find seeds planted their window boxes with winter vegetables: kale and squash, a few hearty herbs to enliven bland meals. Most of the planters, though, were full of brown weeds or nothing at all.

For the past twenty-some years, Antoinette Laurent had seen to the needs of the building and its residents. She kept the courtyard tidy and swept the sidewalk out front, distributed the mail, took messages for the residents, arranged for repairs, and collected the rents for the landlord, a wealthy retired businessman who had long since decamped to the Loire Valley, where he lived in an eighteenth-century manor house acquired for a song from an impoverished aristocratic family.

The position suited Antoinette. Her duties kept her busy and provided numerous opportunities to offer motherly advice to troubled tenants and to cluck over the children to whom she snuck sweets and cookies. And yet she had her solitude, time to herself in the flat that was included as part of her pension. The accommodations were not large, just a small bedroom and bath, the tiniest of galley kitchens with a window that opened onto the courtyard, and a sitting room that overlooked the street and the main door so she could keep an eye on who came and went.

She had no need for more. Here she fostered her memories, tended the diminutive shrine where she lit candles when she could not force herself to attend Mass. These days, the religious rite was inevitably led by a priest so old, he stumbled through the Latin liturgy or by a cleric so young, he could not possibly know anything about real life, about hardship and sacrifice.

Antoinette had no quarrel with the Church, but she would leave God the Father and the Holy Ghost to others; Mary, the mother of Christ, was the one who had truly suffered. First as a naïve teenager carrying a child she had not expected to, and then as an anguished mother cradling the body of her brutalized son.

Mary was the one who understood suffering.

And speaking of naïve teenagers . . . Antoinette escorted Mathilde into her apartment, watching as the girl turned her head this way and that, her gaze locking on the colorful shrine in an otherwise unadorned corner. But then, Antoinette realized that Mathilde was no longer a teenager, for Capucine had made the fan for Mathilde's twenty-first birthday. She looked, and acted, younger than her age. But perhaps Antoinette's own age was playing a trick on her: Mathilde would always live in Antoinette's imagination as a little girl sobbing from a nightmare in the days when troubles could be assuaged with cocoa and cookies.

"I'm so glad to see you again, after all these years," said Antoinette as she went into the kitchenette to put the water on for tea. "*S'il te plaît*, take your coat off, have a seat at the table, or feel free to look around, as you wish. Oh, and the cat's name is Croissant," she added with a chuckle as a pale ginger tabby jumped up on the windowsill and let out a demanding *meow*.

Mathilde hung her red coat and bag on the peg by the door, then went to pet the cat, scratching it under its chin as it arched and leaned into her with a raspy purr.

"Do you mind if I wash my hands?" Mathilde asked, after. "I'm actually allergic to cats, not supposed to touch them, but I can't resist."

"Oh, I remember, now that you mention it. How is your asthma?"

"I do believe I've grown out of it," Mathilde said as she washed her hands at the kitchen sink. "Mami Yvette treated me with a special tincture from the thorn apple plant."

"I'm glad she's taken such good care of you."

Mathilde dried her hands on a gingham kitchen towel, then meandered around the apartment. Clasping her hands behind her back, as though afraid of spoiling something, she leaned forward to examine four framed photos arranged in a half circle on a bright orange cloth on a table in one corner of the room. The shrine was decorated with colorful paper flowers, dried herbs, several extravagant feathers in a painted ceramic vase, seashells, and handwritten notes and cards. A silver cross hung on one wall and a small painted figurine of the Virgin Mary stood on the table alongside the photographs.

"Who are they?" Mathilde asked, gesturing with her head to the photos.

"The baby is my sweet Charlotte," said Antoinette, coming to join Mathilde and picking up the framed photo. She gazed at it a moment, kissed the glass, then gently set it back down. "She was my first, but she only lived a few days."

In fact, the photo had been taken after baby Charlotte died, because there had not been time to take one while she lived. Antoinette had held her tiny daughter's lifeless body in her arms, and she remembered thinking when the photographer ordered her not to move, for fear of ruining the exposure, that it would be the easiest thing in this world to remain as still as her Charlotte, for she had no wish even to breathe.

"And the boy is my sweet Jean-Louis. He was taken by the influenza at the age of ten." Again, Antoinette went through the ritual, placing a kiss on the glass before setting it down. "And here is my youngest, my sweet Richard."

Every time she picked up the framed photograph of the handsome young soldier, Antoinette could hear in her mind and her heart his exuberant off-key singing, remember the way he used to tease her while she stood at the stove, cajoling her into baking his favorite chocolate soufflé. She could see the tilt of his jaunty smile as he boarded the train and hear his last words to her: *"Don't worry, Ma. I'm bulletproof!"*

Bulletproof, perhaps, but not gasproof. "He was killed in the Great War, in an attack on the river Marne."

"You lost *all* your children?" asked Mathilde, her eyes wide.

Tears glinted in Antoinette's eyes, but she nodded and smiled gently.

"And your husband?" Mathilde asked.

"Gaston, my husband, passed not long after Richard."

Also on the altar sat a photo of Gaston and Antoinette, taken when they were young and hopeful. When her dear Gaston was still alive, when he still smiled, still played the violin as he had when he first serenaded Antoinette and convinced her to marry him.

Gaston had been her rock, holding her and supporting her, keeping her tethered to this world when they lost Charlotte and then Jean-Louis. But the death of their last child, their only child to live to adulthood, their hale and hearty miracle boy, Richard, had devastated him. Gaston never again picked up his beloved violin, and Antoinette had not been able to revive his interest in music or even coax him to join her on her evening constitutionals about the neighborhood. After receiving that dreaded, dreadful notice from the war office, Gaston faded away, bit by bit, disappearing before her very eyes as he succumbed to a broken heart. Three months after Richard's death, Gaston began his own journey to reunite with his children in the world beyond. In the heaven that had been promised to them.

Or so Antoinette tried to tell herself. When she lost her husband in addition to all her children, her heart had toughened and become calloused, a devastating wound covered in a ropy scar. She had been a good Catholic her entire life, going to Mass on Sundays and sometimes Wednesday evenings as well. She had sent her children to the nuns to learn the catechism, and taught them to respect God and their neighbors, to do unto others as they would have others do unto them. Where others occasionally criticized the priests, Antoinette had held her tongue out of respect.

The loss of her family changed her. She turned away from the Church, though not from her faith, and began to worship at her own altar. And now that God was allowing neighbors and friends to be taken away in the backs of covered lorries to who knew what fate . . . Antoinette did not know what to believe anymore. She would never have thought it possible in her beloved Paris.

But if there was one thing she had learned with age, it was that with every passing day, she was less sure of what she knew.

"Let's sit and have our tea," said Antoinette, gesturing for Mathilde to join her by the window at a small table upon which she had laid out a steaming pot and two eggshell-thin teacups, one decorated with the painting of a peach, the other with a pear.

Mathilde took a seat and gazed out the pristine windowpane at the street: the fruit shop across the street; the small flower stand; a paperboy hawking the latest edition of the *Pariser Zeitung*, the German-controlled newspaper that urged Parisians to be patient, assured them that all would be well, that the war would soon be over.

"I've been expecting you," said Antoinette, patting Mathilde's hand. "I felt sure you couldn't stay away. But I mailed the package ages ago."

"We only just received it," Mathilde said.

Antoinette's hands stilled as she poured tea into their cups. "Was it censored?"

"How do you mean?"

"Don't you know? Like so many other things these days, the post has become not only unreliable but surveilled." Antoinette glanced at the unopened letter on her mantelpiece, partially hidden by a vase from her departed mother. It was addressed to Madame Capucine Benoît, and it came from America, from a Mr. Charles Moore. It was a miracle it had made it past the censors. "Well, no matter. When the soldiers came for your mother and grandfather, I gave them quite an earful, let me tell you. If the Germans or the Vichy want to send this old woman away, I've given them plenty of reason already."

Mathilde remained silent.

"I suppose I should have delivered it in person," Antoinette continued. "But the truth is, I don't get around as well as I used to, and the streetcars are as unreliable as the mail these days."

"Do you know where my mother and Bruno were taken?"

Antoinette shook her head.

"Could we have . . . " Mathilde began, then paused to formulate the words. "I mean, do you think we could have done something, had we known about it sooner? My papi Auguste knows people, I think. Maybe he could make inquiries . . . ?"

"It couldn't hurt to ask, but I doubt your grandfather Duplantier would be willing to help. Don't you?"

Mathilde cast her eyes down and sipped her tea. Her pinkie finger crooked up elegantly as she grasped the handle of the delicate teacup.

She is in every way a proper young lady. Quiet, polite, modest. Her grandparents must be very proud of their creation.

"My grandparents always said that Capucine—that my mother is a . . . bad influence," said Mathilde.

Antoinette smiled. "Oh, I imagine they said much more than that."

"I'm sure I don't know what you mean," said Mathilde.

"I've known many men like your grandfather Duplantier, and I am willing to bet he called your mother *une putain*," said Antoinette. "But the truth is, Mathilde, that is a word most often used by men to describe women who dare to defy them. Your mother was beaten down by this war, and this Occupation, like all of us. But she has always been very brave. One of the bravest people I've ever known."

UNE PUTAIN. A whore. An ugly word made even uglier coming from the mouth of an aged and allegedly wise woman. *Grandpère* Auguste had never used that word in Mathilde's presence, she was sure, for she would have remembered if he had. Still . . . many times Mathilde had snuck out of bed at night and sat at the top of the stairs, listening to her grandparents conversing in the parlor. Mami Yvette's soft voice was but a murmur, but Papi Auguste's deep voice carried as he spat out his contempt for Capucine, the wild woman who had bewitched his son.

And brave? Antoinette's words hovered in the air as Mathilde accepted their truth. Her mother *was* courageous. Glamorous, as Bridgette had said, and striking to be sure, but more than that: Capucine was brash and bold, the kind of woman who dared to make her own way in this world. Defiant. Brave.

The realization quite literally took Mathilde's breath away. It was as disconcerting as learning the earth had reversed its spin so that the sun now rose in the west. No, she thought, it was as if the sun had been rising in the west all along, and she had somehow failed to notice.

Unable to meet the implied criticism in Antoinette's soft hazel gaze, Mathilde concentrated on her tea. It smelled oddly herbal and tasted bitter, not at all like her mami Yvette's fine black tea from Ceylon. It was probably an improvised concoction of dried leaves and grasses; according to Mami Yvette, who never failed to remind Mathilde how fortunate they were, thanks to Papi Auguste, real tea was hard to come by for most Parisians. For ordinary Parisians.

"You have no idea how life was for women before," said Antoinette, returning to the kitchen to lay a slice of bread and a dollop of jam on a china plate. "The painful corsets! The heavy skirts! We could scarcely move in the clothes we had to wear, dragging our hems in the muddy streets. And we couldn't even imagine cutting our hair. The first time I saw Capucine with her hair bobbed, I nearly fell out of my chair."

"I've never been very interested in fashion," Mathilde said with a shrug.

Some of her girlfriends, Simone especially, had envied Bruno's connections to the couture houses of Paris, but that sort of thing had never mattered much to Mathilde. It did make her wonder, though. How did an avowed communist like Bruno justify making his living by selling exorbitantly priced fans to the wealthy elite?

Papi Auguste had declared Bruno "a rank hypocrite," and Mami Yvette had concurred.

"It wasn't just a matter of fashion," said Antoinette as she came back to the table and set a small bit of dried fish in front of the cat purring on the windowsill. "It kept women in line, unable to move freely, to be seen as true helpmates, much less men's equals. It was as if we were . . . Well, it's hard to describe, but have you seen those cardboard cutouts of movie stars in front of movie theaters?"

Mathilde nodded and gave a shy smile. "I love the movies."

"So do I!" said Antoinette as though pleased to find they had something in common. "So many of us, men and women both, were like those cutouts: attractive but one-dimensional. But not your mother. Your mother is fully three-dimensional and always has been. Yes, she stayed out late at night and slept late in the morning, and perhaps spent too much time in the jazz clubs she loved so much. And I know your grandparents disapproved of her *copain*, of her beau. I really didn't understand it myself until I joined them one night at the club."

Antoinette leaned forward, her voice becoming more intense. "They were not merely playing music and dancing, Mathilde. They were lifting their eyes, seeking something deeper, more important. They were creating a new world of possibility, of openness, of expression. Have you never wondered what it would be like to embrace the life you desire despite societal expectations? To have the freedom to love whomever you want, no matter their religion or background?"

Mathilde was so busy trying to digest the meaning behind the old woman's words that she was unprepared to be asked a question. She felt flustered, as though she had been called up to the front of the class while she had been doodling.

So Mathilde channeled Mami Yvette, saying primly: "I'm sure I have no idea what you're talking about."

Antoinette's fixed gaze made her squirm. For some reason, Mathilde thought of those Jewish children in Neuilly, their big sad eyes in the window. Why had their parents been taken away, and where had they gone? Everyone referred to them as orphans—did that mean their parents were never coming back?

Mathilde felt suddenly suffocated in this tiny apartment, full of the faces of the dead. They seemed to peer at her from their frames, sizing her up and finding her wanting. *I shouldn't have come here, much less agreed to talk to this virtual stranger about my mother, of all people.* Mami and Papi always warned her about those with dangerous views who would seduce her as surely as the serpent in the Garden of Eden had seduced Eve.

Mathilde had agreed to come in for a cup of tea only because she had remembered the old woman from her childhood: the way she always carried the scent of vanilla, the way she used to bake Mathilde's favorite cookies and cradle the girl in her soft lap.

A child's memories. Mami Yvette often chided her for this: Mathilde was no longer a child, and she must put away childish things. It said so in the Bible: *Lorsque j'étais enfant, je parlais comme un enfant, je pensais comme un enfant, je raisonnais comme un enfant; lorsque je suis devenu homme, j'ai fait disparaître ce qui était de l'enfant.*

"Well," Mathilde said, rising so quickly the table rattled, leaving half a cup of tea and the untouched plate of bread and jam. "I thank you for your hospitality, madame, but I really must go now."

She grabbed her bag and coat and headed for the door before Antoinette had a chance to speak. The old woman pushed herself up from the table and trailed Mathilde out the door and into the courtyard.

"Mathilde, wait. *Attends.* Before you go, wouldn't you like to see the shop?" Antoinette said to her back. A key ring rattled as she held it up. "I have the key."

Mathilde turned back, stoked by a surge of anger. "Why would I?"

"Because it was once your home. And whatever is there is yours. It is your inheritance."

Mathilde's lips parted in surprise. Her grandparents often spoke of leaving their estate to Mathilde—or, more precisely, to Mathilde's future husband and their children. But Mathilde had never thought of La Maison Benoît that way.

"What would I do with a bunch of dirty old feathers?" Mathilde scoffed, this time channeling Papi Auguste, the words ringing hollow in her own ears as she fled through the door in the wooden gate, averting her eyes from the lemon yellow façade of Bruno's shop as she grabbed her bicycle from where it stood propped against the stone wall.

The bike's tires hissed on the damp cobblestones as she pedaled as fast as she could, putting distance between herself and rue Saint-Sauveur, Madame Antoinette Laurent, and La Maison Benoît.

Between herself and her immoral inheritance.

5

Capucine

TWO WEEKS AGO, Abrielle Garnier walked into the main showroom of the Lévitan, but not as a prisoner. As a customer.

When visitors were expected, a group of us women was put to work on the showroom floor. On that day, I had been assigned to housewares and had gathered the finest items that had come in that week: cut crystal water glasses, etched Baccarat bowls, Waterford champagne glasses—both flutes and coupes—silver tea sets, carafes, wine decanters. Each piece had to be pristine and sparkling so as not to suggest any trace of its former owner.

Working in housewares was one of the least coveted jobs for us prisoners. The items often arrived caked in food and stained with drink, as if snatched from the tables of those dragged away in the middle of a meal, and our hands became chafed and raw from scrubbing the items with harsh detergent in cold water. But that wasn't the worst part. There was a pathos to it: the dirty dishes a memento of the last moment their rightful owners might have been happy, their families gathered together in their home, breaking bread—or whatever passed for bread these days.

The only job more heartbreaking was sorting through children's things. Once-cherished wooden toys, tiny hand-knitted sweaters, even nappies and safety pins. We schooled ourselves not to speculate on the fate of the children, but even the most hardened among us occasionally broke down when folding a tiny embroidered pillowcase, imagining the downy head that once lay upon it.

We were rarely told who would be coming to the store, so we took no chances and prepared as though it were Baron Von Braun himself, whom we privately referred to as "the Toad" because of his squat figure and bulging eyes. Von Braun stopped in frequently, ostensibly to assess the goods and to inspect the prisoners but also to show off for visiting dignitaries. He loved to brag about the "little skirts and trousers for little German children" being sewn by the prisoners and bound for the Fatherland. In reality, the talented Lévitan seamstresses spent most of their time crafting bespoke suits for the Nazi elite and dresses for their Parisian mistresses. Still, a set of the diminutive skirts and trousers were kept on display, and Von Braun never failed to point them out.

Clad in my headscarf and black smock, I had scrubbed and dusted and arranged the housewares section, making sure each item was displayed to its best effect, until I had nothing to do except wait at my station behind the counter, eyes downcast. The anticipation filled me with anxiety, a yearning for the relative safety of the group huddled together in the attic, or those out by the loading docks sorting through the crates of looted goods. At least there a person stood a chance of fitting in, of skating by in a crowd of faces.

Standing here in the main showroom, I felt too open, too exposed.

As I straightened my shoulders and concentrated on breathing, I had a sudden vivid memory of Bruno taking me to the Galeries Lafayette, the famous department store in the ninth arrondissement, near the Paris Opera House. It was 1919, just after the end of the Great War. The celebrated pilot Jules Védrines had performed the amazing feat of landing his airplane on the store's massive rooftop. Bruno's eyes were shiny with little-boy excitement as he explained that Védrines's aircraft was a Caudron G.3, a single-engine biplane. *I have always dreamed of riding in an airplane one day*, Bruno confessed, nudging her with his elbow. *What do you say, Capu? Up into the clouds, and beyond!*

Over the years I had returned to the Galeries Lafayette with school friends to watch a fashion show or to *ooh* and *aah* over merchandise we could not possibly afford. Just visiting the stunning building—with its Art Nouveau dome, elegant balconies overlooking the main showroom, and panoramic view of Paris from the top floors—was a treat unto itself.

Lévitan's architecture was nice, its main floor also graced with arches and a second-floor balcony overlooking the showroom, but it was not nearly so grand. Before the war, Lévitan's stated purpose had been to serve the working classes, not the bourgeoisie.

And now I stood as a prisoner behind a store counter, in a cruel mockery of those carefree days spent wandering the aisles of the Galeries Lafayette.

There was a commotion near the management offices, and a group of German officers appeared. Most were dressed in ornate uniforms graced with eagles, with fine overcoats on their shoulders, and exhibiting expressions of haughty disdain, and were trailed by a clutch of sycophants. High-ranking Nazis and their attachés, I presumed. Herr Direktor Kohn scurried after them, all but bowing and scraping in his eagerness to please.

I leaned over to make a final adjustment to the Baccarat crystal goblets, so that they might better catch the light, and froze. I recognized that high little-girl voice even before I saw her hanging on the arm of a Nazi commander, preening and flirting: Abrielle Garnier.

Our eyes met. We stared at each other for a long moment and she widened her green-gold eyes, apparently as stunned to see me as I was to see her.

On second thought, it made perfect sense that Abrielle would have attached herself to the enemy—and an officer, no less.

Abrielle smiled up at her companion, patting his arm and batting her eyes coquettishly. Tall and bearlike, he appeared to be in his late forties, with pale blue eyes, high cheekbones, and a thick neck. I imagined he had a devoted *frau* and several little *kinder* waiting for him back home in the Fatherland, but it seemed almost de rigueur for ambitious German officers stationed in Paris to sport French mistresses on their arms.

"Couldn't we look over there, *Bärchen*?" Abrielle said, pointing to the opposite side of the shop floor and leading him away from my counter.

"Anything you want, *Maus*," he responded in a jovial voice. "You only turn twenty-nine once!"

I happened to know that Abrielle was only a few years my junior, which meant she was in her mid to late thirties. But her petite stature and girlish mannerisms had always made her seem much younger, a fiction no doubt bolstered by the pampered life she was clearly enjoying. Pretty little Abrielle was a stark contrast to ex-hausted me, what with my ungroomed hair tied up in a scarf, my face bare of makeup, my hands chapped from washing dishes. Back in the day, in Montmartre, we had been rivals, but now? We might have been a bubbly daughter and her careworn mother.

"So, tell me, what would you like for your birthday?" The officer, fatherly and indulgent, gazed fondly at Abrielle.

"It certainly won't be found in dishwares, *mein Herr*," she said with a tinkling laugh. "Where are the furniture and the fine art? The apartment is so dull and boring! I heard from one of the girls that Bassano has nicer things. Or maybe Austerlitz?"

"Yes, we'll visit the other locales and see what they might have for the apartment," said the officer. "But while we're here, I want to get something special just for you. What do you say? Shall we take a peek at the jewelry?"

"Oh, yes, please!" Abrielle said, fluttering her mascaraed eye-lashes.

I remained silent and stoic, my eyes lowered as the couple walked away. We had not exchanged a single word.

I had never cared for Abrielle Garnier. Other than vying for modeling jobs in Montmartre, we hadn't had any real quarrels, but she grated on me. But now, watching her flirt with her Nazi officer, I tasted the bile of loathing for the woman who had betrayed my father and me and further separated me from my daughter.

I vowed that if I had a chance, I would get my revenge. Somehow.

"WHY DO YOU ask me about Abrielle Garnier?" I asked Herr Direktor Kohn, trying not to fidget as I stood in front of Monsieur Lévitan's former desk in the director's office.

"I ask the questions here," Kohn snapped, and shuffled some papers.

I stared at the floor. Bruno always counseled me to treat the occupiers as if they were wild animals: unpredictable, easy to set off, often lethal. *Move slowly,* he said. *Don't look them in the eye. Be still, be silent, act small. Try to pass unnoticed.*

After a pause, Kohn said, "She requested you."

"Requested me to do what?" I bit my tongue as soon as I said it. He had just ordered me not to ask questions. But this time, Kohn answered.

"I have no inkling as to what might be in a woman's mind. But she is a special friend of Herr Pflüger, and so if Mademoiselle Garnier wants your assistance, you will provide it."

"Yes, of course, I will, Herr Direktor. It will be my pleasure," I said, hoping my obsequious manner would please him.

He nodded and continued, more patiently: "I believe she needs your help to decorate her apartment."

"I don't understand."

He frowned. "You are trained in interior design, are you not?"

"Certainly, Herr Direktor. I worked with Émile-Jacques Ruhlmann when he still had his workshop on the rue de Lisbonne."

I had never worked for Ruhlmann. But I had once gone to a party at his workshop, and though he was much older than I, we had run in similar circles in the late twenties and might well have mingled at one of Gertrude Stein's soirées or shared a drunken evening at Bricktop's nightclub. But if this situation didn't call for exaggeration, I didn't know what did.

"He a Jew?" Kohn asked.

"I . . ." So much for name-dropping. "I really don't know. He's a well-known designer and decorated a pavilion at the Paris World's

Fair in ... 1925 ..." I trailed off, realizing the director had no interest in what I was saying.

Kohn grunted. "I suppose that sort of thing matters to some. What matters to me is this: Herr Pflüger is an officer of the Third Reich, and we must make him happy. You will therefore assist Mademoiselle Garnier and do as she asks."

"*Ja, Herr Direktor.*"

"But let me make this clear: If you try to escape, if you attempt to contact anyone on the street, if you misbehave in any way, if you embarrass me or displease Herr Pflüger, you will be shot and your entire pod sent to Auschwitz. There are plenty more where you all came from."

"I understand. *Ich verstehe.*"

"Review the inventory for artwork and fine furniture so you will know what to suggest. Be ready to go."

"Will I be coming back?"

He waved his hand and Pettit gestured toward the door. As I walked down the nondescript hallway, my skin grew clammy as the cloying warmth of the director's office was replaced by the showroom's frigid chill.

"You're a design expert, huh?" Pettit said with a snort as we climbed back to the attic, our footsteps echoing in the stairwell.

"Of course I am. Don't I always comment on your outfits?" I asked. "Speaking of which, I love that color on you."

She looked down at her chest, then frowned. "It's a uniform."

"But you fill it out so well."

In Montmartre in the late twenties, I had been something of a fashion icon in my glittering dresses of beads and sequins, accessorized with my outrageous fans. But then the Depression hit, Hitler rose to power, the jazz clubs began to close, and my beloved

Charles left. And then came the pervasive dread and scarcity of the Occupation, and what had remained of my brash, bold ways seemed to have been muted, eroded away as surely as a torrent of water stripped a hillside of its vegetation.

Or maybe it was simply that I was nearing my fortieth birthday. Middle-aged, I suppose.

Charles used to tease me, saying that he couldn't wait to see his Fan Girl with gray hair and wrinkles. He had assumed we would remain together forever, braving this world side by side, arm in arm. But more than a year ago, I asked him to stop writing me and to move on with his life, as I would move on with mine. A thousand times since, I had wondered whether he had, in fact, done so. Whether he had found another woman to cherish and to hold, to share his music and his smile and his love.

Pettit shoved me, wrenching my thoughts out of the past and back to the prickly present. *What was Abrielle thinking?* Why would she have requested me personally? Why take the chance of admitting she knew me? Was she playing a dangerous game, or was she simply as vacuous as I remembered, unable to grasp the precarious reality of her situation—and mine?

In the last war, the War of 1914, the Germans had been our enemy, plain and simple. This time, they filled our cafés and nightclubs as customers, and even stopped by La Maison Benoît to purchase items for loved ones back home—demanding them at deeply discounted prices, of course. And then they had come back and arrested us.

The Nazis were inscrutable, capricious, unpredictable. It made me breathless, trying to figure out how to react, what I was supposed to do and say, feeling as if I were acting in a play for which I had no script.

Still . . . as we climbed the three flights of stairs to the fourth-floor attic, excitement mounted at the thought of getting out of this building after so many weeks of staring at the same walls, seeing the same faces, breathing the same stale air. I longed to be on the streets of Paris, to feel the sun on my face, to fill my lungs with fresh breezes.

I wasn't sure how long I had been in Lévitan, but it felt like years.

I tried to stuff it down, to stifle the excitement, to remind myself that anticipation was dangerous, hope was hurtful. I forced my thoughts away, shoving my emotions into a make-believe fan box the way I had done since the day my mother left when I was five.

MY ROBIN'S-EGG BLUE dress was my favorite. When I rocked back and forth, my skirts would swing like a bell.

"Pay attention, Capu," said my father. *Faites attention.*

Bruno hoisted me up onto the worktable, and I continued to swing my legs, enjoying the gentle swish of my blue skirts on my legs, watching my shiny black patent leather shoes as they caught the light from the front window. My mother and father stood side by side and asked if I wanted to go to Italy with my mother, Suzette, or stay in the little fan shop in Paris with my father. I liked our home and the fans, so I chose to stay.

That was the last time I saw my mother. Clad in a green velvet coat, Suzette was sobbing as she scurried out of La Maison Benoît, the little shop bell ringing as if sounding an alarm.

"Don't cry, Capu. It's you and me now," said Papa. "You and me against the world."

In her haste, my mother had forgotten her prized fan, nestled in its custom satin-lined leather box with the name of the shop embossed in gold. Through the years, the box remained just where she had left it, on the wooden chair with the woven rush seat next to the door. Bruno and I never spoke of it, much less of Suzette, and though Bruno was known for his scathing criticisms of unreasonable clients and obnoxious neighbors, he never uttered a single word against the woman who had left her husband and daughter.

Neither of us was willing to touch the fan, so it remained there, on the wooden chair by the door, as if Suzette might at any moment return for it.

Over the years, whenever I encountered something difficult or incomprehensible, shameful, or painful, I imagined stuffing those sensations into a similar fan box located deep within my chest. I would shove whatever was bothering me inside and close the lid, my very own Pandora's box of suppressed emotions. Into the box went the bewilderment of my mother's departure, my accidental pregnancy, the disdain of my in-laws, and the sudden death of my young husband, Roger.

And then my abandonment of my own daughter, Mathilde, the departure of Charles, the loss of Bruno . . . and somehow along the way, the loss of myself.

Put it in the box, Capucine. Close the lid. Leave it there.

6

$\mathcal{A}$NTOINETTE WATCHED THE girl flee. There was no other way to describe it: Mathilde was running away, as from the scene of a crime.

Antoinette had not known Mathilde's father well. Roger Duplantier was handsome, and he had seemed nice enough, though Antoinette failed to discern anything special about him. Certainly nothing to deserve a fascinating young woman such as Capucine Benoît. But then, when he and Capucine started seeing each other they had been children themselves, really, younger than Mathilde was now. Nor had Bruno been impressed. He would have preferred that Capucine choose a man who shared his radical political ideas. But Roger proved to be a rebel in his own quiet way, loving Capucine and insisting upon marrying her when he found out she was with child, standing by her in the face of his parents' disapproval.

Auguste Duplantier had done his best to co-opt his son into the bourgeois life, to employ Roger alongside him in the Renault factory, away from the temptations of the artistic life. Perhaps he would have succeeded if his son had lived longer. Certainly, Auguste and Yvette Duplantier seemed to have converted Mathilde into a life of social conformity.

Was Mathilde truly a demure bourgeois woman who would do what was expected and marry a man of whom her grandparents approved, live the sheltered life of a well-bred young wife?

No, Antoinette thought. *Surely not.* The girl had Capucine's blood running through her veins. She just needed time to find her place, her balance. Antoinette might not know much, but she knew this: People had phenomenal depths, and rarely were those depths discovered, much less plumbed, until they were tested.

The German Occupation was a test as serious as they came.

MATHILDE WENT STRAIGHT to Cathédrale Notre-Dame, as though acknowledging her sins right away might keep them from sticking through the magical intervention of the confessional. Also, she preferred to confess to a priest she did not know. The nuns had taught that the privacy of the confessional was sacrosanct, but even so Mathilde did not trust *Père* Guillaume not to share her secrets with her grandparents, for Papi Auguste was a pillar of their parish and a generous donor to the Church.

But perhaps harboring such doubts about her parish priest and her grandfather was yet another sin for which she should atone. She made a mental note to mention that in the confessional as well.

Mathilde liked Notre-Dame. The damp smell of the ancient stone, the medieval harshness of the chilly, humid walls alongside the ethereal beauty of the huge stained glass rosettes, the way the colored light illuminated the cathedral as if the beams were dancing for the Lord. She thought of how even a small measure of light could change things, suffusing the window for just a few seconds before the clouds passed over the sun, and how a section of the hard wooden pew or the back of her hand would be bathed in brilliant colors—the vivid green of spring, the bright blue of a summer sky, the deep red of a rose—the sunlight refracted into a rainbow of colors.

After making her confession and being absolved of her sins, Mathilde knelt to say her Hail Marys and Our Fathers with the fervor of a true penitent, begging for clarity.

What did Antoinette's words truly mean? If Antoinette was right and Capucine and Bruno weren't so awful, after all, what did that say about Mami Yvette and Papi Auguste? Had they been lying to her this whole time?

Divine enlightenment eluded her, so Mathilde left Notre-Dame and, her knees still aching from the kneeling, decided to walk her bike home.

The streets of Paris were grim, the late-winter skies gray, the stone buildings streaked with dirt, water marks, and the occasional bullet hole that no one had tended to. Ornate knockers on tall wooden doors suggested tempting glimpses of courtyards. Pedestrians scurried along the narrow sidewalks, looking neither left nor right, their eyes cast down and shoulders hunched up about their ears. Their resolute refusal to engage with others reminded Mathilde of the three monkeys: see no evil, hear no evil, and speak no evil.

The Germans promised that when the war was over, Paris would rise like never before to become a beacon to the world, full of great art and entertainment. They had even invested in the film industry, pumping out one movie after another. These films were fine, moral art, they insisted, so unlike those of the degenerate jazz age.

But . . . Antoinette had painted such a different picture of the artists on Montmartre. Mathilde knew her parents had met in an art gallery where Roger was seeking representation for his sculptures, to his own father's eternal dismay. How differently might Mathilde see the world had her father lived and her parents remained together, had she grown up with them here, in Paris, instead of with Mami and Papi in Neuilly-sur-Seine? She would have been the daughter of two freethinking artists, rather than the daughter of a scorned woman of questionable repute. What would—

"You look like a plump little red cardinal in all this gray," said a handsome young man in a German uniform. His French was fluent but guttural, the harsh syllables of his native language coming through.

Mathilde froze. Her gloved hands gripped the bike's handlebars so tightly, they hurt.

Even before the war, she had never been comfortable flirting with boys. Unlike Simone, Mathilde had no idea what to say or how to react. The young man's attention would have embarrassed her even had he been French; that he was a German soldier, an occupier, left Mathilde speechless and she tasted something metallic, close to fear.

After a moment, he made a deep bow and handed her a rose the color of red velvet. "To match your coat."

She blinked. After a moment he tipped his hat, said, *"Auf wiedersehen, fräulein. Guten abend,"* and continued down the street, whistling.

Mathilde watched him leave, then quickly mounted her bicycle, dropping the rose in the bike's wicker basket as she pedaled in the opposite direction. It was later than she realized, and the daylight was fading. She would have to hurry to get home before the official curfew. When the Germans had taken over France, they had literally changed time, turning the clocks forward one hour so as to coordinate with the clocks in Germany, which meant that evening arrived earlier than ever before.

As Bridgette once remarked, the Nazis had brought the darkness with them.

On the way to her grandparents' big house on rue Pierret, she rode past the nuns' place and saw two little faces in the window peering out.

On impulse, she skidded to a stop, propped her bicycle against the iron railing, climbed the three stone steps, and reached up to the knocker shaped like a hand. She rapped. After a few moments, a nun appeared. Her habit hid her hair, but her wrinkled face and cloudy eyes seemed ancient.

She seemed to relax when she saw Mathilde.

"Yes, mademoiselle, may I help you?"

"Y-yes," Mathilde stammered. "I mean, no. I was hoping perhaps I could help *you*."

The nun's eyebrows rose.

"I mean," Mathilde clarified, "perhaps I could bring something for the children?"

"Something like what?" The nun tilted her head in question.

"Maybe . . . maybe some food or toys?"

"Anything would be appreciated, of course," said the nun. "Thank you."

Mathilde nodded, trying to think of what else to say. "I'll bring something, then. And—thank you for looking after the children."

"Go with God, my dear," the nun said with a sad smile, and closed the door.

THE TALL FRONT door of her grandparents' house featured a large leaded glass window with a design in the shape of a stylized tulip. The door creaked loudly when she pushed it open.

Inside, the foyer was dark, the blackout curtains over the windows deepening the shadows created by the heavy wood paneling. The house was always neat as a pin and smelled of lemon polish, yet despite the constant efforts of the housemaid, Cécile, and Mami Yvette herself, it always carried a hint of something else beneath it all: the dusty residue of things that once were but were no longer, of sorrow and anger and feelings without names.

During one of their early visits, Capucine had muttered under her breath that the house was sepulchral. Mathilde had looked up the meaning of the word in her dictionary: *relating to a tomb or interment; gloomy; dismal; melancholy.*

"*Ça va, ma fille?*" Mami called out from the parlor.

Mathilde swore under her breath. She had hoped to slip past her mami Yvette and run upstairs to her room, but as usual, her grandmother had been sitting next to the fire, working on her embroidery, an ear cocked for the rare comings and goings of the household.

"*Oui*, Mami," Mathilde responded. One foot was already on the first stair and her hand wrapped around the big newel post carved in the shape of a pineapple, the familiar slickness of the polished wood under her palm. "*Ça va.*"

She reached over to flick the light switch for the stairwell chandelier. Nothing happened.

"Wouldn't you know? The electricity is out again! I do hope Cook can manage," Mami Yvette clucked, patting her stomach, "though I suppose it wouldn't hurt me to go without. If I'm not careful, I'll need a whole new wardrobe, and just think what your papi will say about that!"

"It's fine. I'm not hungry," said Mathilde, hoping to fend off Mami's incessant advice to fill out a bit more in some places but not too much in others, for a woman must be ever aware of men's opinions.

"Don't tell me you forgot," said Mami Yvette.

"Forgot what?"

"Your young man is coming to dinner tonight."

"Victor? Not *tonight*," Mathilde said, realizing her words sounded like a plea.

"Sometimes I think you would forget your head if it wasn't attached," Mami said with an indulgent smile. "He'll be here in less than an hour. Hurry along, Mathilde, and do make an effort, won't you? You look a fright after all that exercise. Your papi thinks you should give the bicycle a rest before your legs become muscular. Men like a slender ankle, dear."

"*Oui*, Mami."

"The mauve gown looks lovely on you. Cécile sponged and pressed it this morning, so it's ready for you. And don't forget that Victor prefers that you wear your hair up."

"*Oui*, Mami," Mathilde said again, and blew out a long sigh as she took the stairs two steps at a time. *There go those leg muscles again*, she thought.

Victor. Mami and Papi assured Mathilde that Victor was a fine young man from a good family, and she would be respected and well cared for. Still . . . She thought about Antoinette saying that some people seemed one-dimensional, like cardboard cutouts. That described Victor to a tee: nice enough, good-looking enough. There was really nothing wrong with him. But neither was there anything to hold on to, anything of substance, as if he would blow over in a strong wind. Could she spend her life with someone like that?

The old concierge's voice rang in her head: What would it be like to imagine something different for herself?

On the stair landing, Mathilde paused in front of a nook that held a small bronze sculpture of a woman's torso. In a rare act of defiance, Mami Yvette had insisted on displaying the piece over Papi Auguste's strong, and loudly expressed, objections. The sculpture was carved with parts of the body missing, a partial carapace, as though it were still filling in. Sometimes it struck Mathilde as an empty shell; sometimes she thought of it as something with potential, with room for growth. Sometimes it looked to her like armor.

Mathilde's father, Roger, had sculpted it. As far as she knew, it was his only surviving work of art. It dawned on Mathilde that this nook was Mami Yvette's altar to her dead son, much like Antoinette's shrine to her lost children.

Papi Auguste had always planned for Roger to work with him at the factory, and he never missed the opportunity to point out that the artistic life had killed him. That wasn't strictly true, of course: Roger had died from a head injury sustained in a fall from scaffolding. But then, he had been working on a sculpture, so Mathilde supposed Papi was right. From the story she was told, he had been found still clutching his hammer and chisel.

Mathilde hurried along the hallway, her footsteps muted by the plush carpeting. Turning into her bedroom, she recalled the day she had come to live in Neuilly-sur-Seine, her little valise in her hand. The room had been newly remodeled to please a little girl, painted in soft pastels, with frolicking cupids carved into the heavy wood of a canopy bed fit for a princess. In one corner stood an elaborate Victorian dollhouse, which had utterly enchanted her as a child. She had spent hours playing with it, making up a tiny bed in a toy armoire, and painting rouge on one of the dolls, dressing her up with a little feather boa.

Mathilde looked at it now with distaste. Surely a grown woman had the right to a life that was different from what she had dreamed of as a little girl.

And then she took out of her bag the leather box with *La Maison Benoît* printed in gold foil. She sat on the side of the bed and opened the fan her mother had made for her birthday, running her hands along the soft ostrich plumes, studying the mother-of-pearl inlay on the carved stays, the burnished gold. The image of the ballerina dancing upon the sand. Had her mother painted it just for her?

Simone was right: It was very old-fashioned. No one used fans anymore.

Mathilde wondered if her mother had carried a fan like this when she went to those jazz clubs. Mathilde didn't remember much about those days, just her soft bed in the armoire, dancing with her mother around the room, her grandfather Bruno tickling her. . . . Her memories were vague, barely-there watercolor images that could well have been from a dream.

Tucked into the box was a folded piece of paper she hadn't noticed before. Mathilde took it out and read: *The language of fans . . . Some say the fan was the "woman's scepter," for a woman well versed in the language ruled through flirtation, cunning, and whim.*

She fanned herself, making gentle twirls around the room, watching herself in the dresser mirror.

Carrying in left hand, open . . . Come and talk with me.

Fanning quickly . . . I am engaged.

Drawing through the hand . . . I hate you.

Reluctantly, she set the fan aside. She was supposed to be making herself presentable for Victor. Was that to be her future? To marry Victor, or someone very much like him, and have children, to make a home of her own?

In school she had studied a few women who had followed their own paths: the scientists Madame Marie Curie and her daughter Irène, who were awarded Nobel Prizes. The American artist Mary Cassatt, who had come to Paris to paint with the Impressionist masters. But the Germans despised Impressionism, calling it *Entartete Kunst*, or degenerate art. Not to mention, Marie Curie and Mary Cassatt were immigrants, a group of whom the Third Reich did not approve.

Surely there were more examples. . . . What about Jeanne d'Arc, the most famous French woman of them all, a rebel in every sense of the word? But of course, Jeanne d'Arc was burned at the stake. That was a disturbing thought.

Mathilde's musings were interrupted by the clang of the doorbell, followed by the rumble of male voices. Papi and Victor were talking in the front hall, with Mami Yvette's high, piping voice, like that of a child, in marked contrast.

Mathilde quickly changed into the gown Mami Yvette had suggested: a mauve velvet with a sweetheart collar, puffed sleeves, and an appliqué of a stylized flower on one side of the full skirt. It was old-fashioned but pretty, and Mami and Papi liked it when she dressed for dinner. Mathilde's face was too strong for current fashion, but she received compliments on her hair. She brushed and pinned it up the way Victor liked, then added a string of pearls and earbobs.

She heard Mami calling her and started for the door, but at the last moment returned to grab her new fan.

"J'arrive!"

7

Capucine

As we neared the fourth floor, my nostrils flared at the reek of unwashed bodies.

Seven hundred of us prisoners were crowded into the store's attic, which lacked washing facilities. Add to that the detritus of meals that hadn't been particularly appetizing in the first place, and that we weren't allowed to open the windows, and that we wore and slept in the same clothes day after day and . . . well, it was a recipe for stench. We did the best we could to clean ourselves, our garments, and our dishes at the few cold-water spigots, but there was no getting around the fact that we, and our quarters, stank.

The attic was buzzing when Pettit and I walked in. The arrival of the new pod of ten men had spurred a flurry of activity as they were shown to available cots, and shelves were cleared to make room for the newcomers' paltry possessions. We peppered them with questions: *What was going on out on the streets? What have you heard? What was happening on the battlefields? Did you happen to meet my son / my daughter / my mother / my brother in Drancy? Do you know where they were sent?*

I remembered my first sight of the Lévitan attic: men and women, young and old, housed together, with no thought to modesty or privacy. The first prisoners to arrive, I was told, did not even have beds or cots, but over time they gleaned bedding from the Lévitan's inventory or the looted goods coming in on the trucks, and the men with woodworking skills managed to craft crude shelves and tables with lumber from discarded packing crates. As pods of prisoners were sent back to Drancy, new ones arrived and took their beds and shelves.

The attic's large arched windows let in light but no air. We heard rumors of a rooftop terrace, but it was *verboten*, lest the neighbors discover there were hundreds of French people being kept prisoner in the attic of the old Lévitan department store. In fact, the residents of the apartment building across the street had been instructed to keep their shutters closed at all times so they would not see.

The only truly pleasant aspect of our living space was the stacks of books piled here, there, and everywhere. Entire libraries had been pilfered from the homes of educated Jews, but the Germans were not especially interested in books written in French unless they were valuable antiques, so most were pulped or tossed onto the bonfire unless we begged for them. Reading kept us quiet and occupied, which made the guards' lives easier, so unless the guards were in a bad mood, they generally acquiesced.

Isedore was speaking with one of the new arrivals when she spied me and rushed over. "Capu! I'm so glad you're back! Tell me, what happened? What did the director want?"

"It was an interview of sorts. He wants me to go help someone with interior design."

"Interior design?" She blinked. "I don't understand. Why?"

I lowered my voice. "My father and I worked with some of the finest fashion houses in Paris. So apparently I'm to go through the store's inventory and pull together some nice pieces to furnish the apartment of a Nazi's girlfriend. Be her personal interior designer."

"That sounds . . . odd," she said, her big eyes wide with fear.

Several other prisoners had formed a ring around us to hear what had happened, why I had been summoned by Herr Direktor Kohn.

"She's to go help someone with interior design," explained Isedore. "But . . . you will come, back, won't you?"

Just last week a pod had been transferred from Lévitan to another Parisian prison camp, named Bassano, and we had heard nothing from them since. It was jarring to lose people; we held on so desperately to some kind of normalcy, to regular schedules and familiar routines. Some of the prisoners thought the situation at Bassano might be better—according to rumor, there were fewer prisoners, and the building was a more comfortable, beautiful old mansion—but as always, it was mere conjecture.

"Well, at least I will be out of here," I said, trying to keep my tone light. "Even if it's only for a day, I will be out on the streets of Paris."

But even as I said those words, I felt a frisson. Once upon a time, I had been an adventurous sort, up for anything new and different, but now? The past few years had taught me that change was frightening and potentially deadly. If I couldn't be back at La Maison Benoît, then I preferred to stay right here, in what the Germans called Lager Ost, or East Camp, surrounded by familiar faces, where I knew who people were and how things worked. Usually.

Being assigned to help Abrielle Garnier might well spell disaster.

"*Bonjour*, madame," said the man I had recognized from the *Kanzlei* in Drancy.

"*Bonjour*, monsieur." I nodded.

"It is a nice surprise to see a familiar face," he said. "But we have not been properly introduced: I am Ezra Goldman."

"Capucine Benoît," I said. We exchanged kisses, his stubble rasping my cheeks.

Conversation swirled around us as the newcomers introduced themselves: Jean-Marc Toussaint, Rolande Leroy, Didier Crémieux, Josquin Paul Cohen. . . . One had been a plumber, another owned a large shoemaking factory, and yet another used to be a banker. I let their names and occupations slip over me. Either we would have plenty of time to learn more about one another, in which case there was no rush, or we would not, in which case there was no point.

One of the odd things about our group was that we represented all social classes, educations, and backgrounds. We had been actors and shopkeepers, factory workers and traveling salesmen, artisans and wealthy industrialists. At least one elderly woman was whispered to be a marquise; tiny and birdlike, she was elegant despite her circumstances, and though unceasingly polite, she largely kept to herself. I was not convinced the rumor was true, because the gossip grapevine was constantly bestowing royal status upon new arrivals, as if we hoped the presence of a titled few in our midst might lend us commoners some protection.

We were not assigned to any specific cot or area but had divided into informal groupings that tended to stick together: the wives of

POWs, the older Jewish women, the wealthier Jewish men. Some of the internees were so well-off that, whether through outright bribery or simply in recognition of their social status, they occasionally received parcels of food, wine, and tobacco from their families.

"You really think you'll come back?" asked Isedore.

"Of course, I will!" I said with a confidence I did not feel. "It'll just be a chance to get outside."

"Paris is so gray these days," said Colette. Originally from Poland, she had committed two crimes in the eyes of the Nazis: She was an immigrant, and her husband had fought with the French forces and was now a prisoner of war. "It's not like it was, before."

"True enough," said Henri, a young man whose Jewish father had been deported to Bergen-Belsen. Henri's mother was from a prominent Aryan family, which had intervened on his behalf, and he was married to an Aryan, so he wound up here. "Still, it would be nice to breathe a bit of fresh air."

"Speaking of which, why aren't we allowed to open the windows?" asked one of the new arrivals. "No offense, but it smells a little ripe in here."

"Really? We hadn't noticed," Jean-Michel, the attic's resident wit, said wryly.

"I suspect it is for the same reason that we were brought in covered trucks to the loading docks in back," said Ezra. "The soldiers are afraid the neighbors will notice."

"Why would they care what the neighbors think?" asked Isedore, gazing at the handsome newcomer, a small smile gracing her pretty face.

"Because they want the French people in general, and the Parisians in particular, to cooperate with their plans," Ezra replied. "Little by little, the Germans are getting the French accustomed to our disappearance and eventual destruction. Eventually, they will be able to do whatever they want without fear of reprisal."

Everyone looked to Mordecai Krivine, who nodded in agreement and introduced himself to Ezra.

"I fear our new friend Monsieur Goldman is right," Mordecai said. "If they took us all immediately, the Parisians might well rise up against the occupiers. They are humanists at heart, after all. But when our freedoms are taken away little by little . . ." Mordecai trailed off with a shrug. "The heavy mantle of collaboration rests more easily upon their shoulders, as bit by bit we are erased from their memory."

That brought silence to the group. With so little information, we could only guess at what might be happening to our loved ones or what would eventually happen to us.

I held tight to the dream that the Germans would eventually run out of homes to loot and release us, that I would walk down rue Saint-Sauveur and return to the familiar yellow façade of La Maison Benoît, where I would find my father behind the counter, thin and disillusioned, wizened but alive. The shop bell would ring out with its familiar tinkle as I entered, and Bruno would look up with a smile and a wink and come around the corner of the counter to envelop me in a hug, smelling vaguely of pipe tobacco and chastising me for taking so long to come back to him.

I should never have let him go. I should have gone with him, done what I could to protect him. Why had I let him go without me?

"What was your profession, sir?" Mordecai asked Ezra.

"I am a teacher," said Ezra. Then he corrected himself: "I *was* a teacher. A lecturer in history at the Sorbonne."

"An intellectual! Excellent! I shall look forward to many discussions about the current state of our world and how we got here," said Mordecai, looking from one man to another. "The ten of you are replacing the previous pod, so I imagine you'll be assigned to their former duties of unloading the trucks and carrying crates. It is physically demanding work, but it will be easier if you cooperate with one another. Take it slowly at first, and you'll adapt. Are all of you married to Aryans?"

The men nodded.

Isedore seemed to deflate at this news. It both amused me and gave me hope that the young people among us were still interested in finding romance. It was a challenge to remember those sensations, but I cast my mind back to the alternating emotions of joy and distress, giddiness and desperation. First with Roger, and then ever more deeply with Charles: not just the physical attraction but the yearning for connection, for unspoken understanding.

Since letting Charles go, I seemed to have lost the ability, let alone the desire, to cleave to another.

After the introductions, we continued with our usual interrogation of newcomers, seeking any news from the outside world. In this, we inside Lévitan were not so different from the rest of the Parisians. Ever since France had been invaded and the radio and newspapers had been taken over by Nazi propaganda, only the search for food trumped the search for news and up-to-date knowledge.

"And the date is February twenty-seventh, correct?" asked Mordecai.

Mordecai had drawn a calendar on one wall of the attic, and whenever new recruits arrived, he asked them the date to be sure he was keeping the calendar correctly. It was too easy to lose track of time here in the Lévitan, where nothing but the faces ever changed, but it was essential to the Jews among us to know the proper date in order to acknowledge the holy days. The calendar was marked with two different dating systems: the one I had been raised with, in which it was 1944, and a second, Hebrew calendar.

"It is based on the lunar cycle," Mordecai explained when I asked him about it, "rather than the solar cycle, and dates much further back than the birth of your Christ. We're on year 5704."

That was reassuring. People had been around a very long time. Surely, we would survive the years of Occupation.

"Purim is coming," Mordecai said now as he looked around at the faces, some familiar and others new, as if searching for inspiration or confirmation. "It is celebrated on the fourteenth day of the Jewish month of Adar. This year that date falls on March ninth."

"What is Purim?" asked Colette.

"Usually, it is a grand feast, a huge party," said Mordecai with a small smile. "This year, alas, we will have to be satisfied with saying a few prayers in remembrance."

"I think we should at least make costumes," said Isedore. "I always loved dressing up for Purim."

This kicked off an animated discussion among some of the younger prisoners, who wondered if the guards would allow them to glean a few bits and pieces of materials from the incoming crates to make costumes.

"Mordecai," asked Isedore later, "is it a good thing that Capu has been asked to do this special task?"

"It's hard to say," he said, meeting my eyes with his old, wise ones. "Had they intended her harm, they would simply have taken her away, and we would not have seen her again. They don't feel they owe us any explanations."

"I think you're right," I said, forcing a smile. *Why did Abrielle ask for me?* "Herr Direktor was very specific: They want my help with interior design, that's all. But enough about that; let's concentrate on Purim. A party, you say?"

THE NEXT DAY I received permission to leave my pod to begin assessing and setting aside potential pieces of furniture for Abrielle Garnier and her Nazi officer, Herr Pflüger. Henri had been assigned to show Ezra the ropes, and both men had been "loaned" to me and tasked with moving the pieces that I selected.

We were working in the receiving area next to the loading dock. The concrete floor of our work area was covered in straw from unpacking the many fragile items, and we stuffed some of this straw in our shirts for added warmth. The area was jammed with all manner of household goods: sofas, tables, artwork, dishware, linens. Larger pieces of furniture, such as pianos and many armoires, were usually taken to the Gare du Nord.

"Let's take this, this, and that," I said, pointing to a marble-topped table with gold-gilt cabriole legs, a set of dining chairs with wheat-patterned carving, and an eighteenth-century side table with marquetry veneer.

"Where do they go?" asked Henri.

"Once I've seen her apartment and narrowed down the choices, we can arrange them up in the main showroom," I said. "But for now let's keep them over there in the corner. We'll need to position some crates in front to make them less obvious."

"You want to hide them?" asked Ezra.

"Sort of."

"From whom?"

"Fräulein Sigrid Sommer," I said.

Fräulein Sommer came to Lévitan only occasionally, but she had an unerring eye for the finest furniture and art. An officious woman in her thirties, she was always well-dressed and pretty in a severe sort of way, and she was quick to inform all and sundry that she had studied design in Vienna. Neither guard nor mistress, she was a rarity among the Nazis: a woman who appeared to have ambitions of her own, which she planned to fulfill by choosing only the very finest items for her clients among the Nazi elite.

So I faced a problem: Anything I selected might be appropriated by Fräulein Sommer. And since I hadn't yet met with Abrielle or seen her apartment, I had no idea what she had in mind or what would be suitable. Still, I wasn't about to complain about my new assignment.

In claiming to be an interior designer, I hadn't entirely lied. I did know a good deal about interior design, having worked for years alongside designers in search of fans to use as wall hangings, as well as other decorative featherwork. Making fans was a dying art long before this war came along. Changing fashions meant fans were no longer an obligatory ladies' accessory, while the economic collapse of the 1930s dried up the pool of customers who could afford expensive handmade products. By the time I started working in earnest at La Maison Benoît, business had fallen off dramatically, leaving us to make up the deficit through other methods: Bruno kept making fans for the few customers we still had and to maintain the façade of La Maison Benoît, which lent cachet, while I worked with dress designers, interior decorators, haberdashers, stage costumers—anywhere I could.

The work gave me insight into the world of designers and their exclusive customers. And I had a good eye, so whether a piece was signed or not, I could pick out the very best by the materials used— veneers versus solid wood, the rarest stone and inlay work, and most important, how the joints came together. The furniture sold by Lévitan in his department store was on the cheaper side, which meant the joints were glued or nailed, or fixed with the occasional dowel, where finer furniture used mortise and tenon.

Operation Furniture brought in items from fine country houses and Parisian penthouses, as well as ordinary apartments, so it was not unusual to find exquisite pieces from the Ancien Régime, such as Louis Quinze antiques, or Second Empire furniture, or neoclassical styles. I appreciated Art Deco—especially now that I was borrowing Ruhlmann's name—but it always struck me as a bit severe. Personally, I preferred the flowing, naturalistic lines of the Art Nouveau style.

I was guessing Abrielle would gravitate toward the shiny gold gilt and elaborate curlicue carvings of the rococo fashion. She seemed like a woman who liked to picture herself as Marie Antoinette in Versailles. Still, I wanted to select a variety of items in case I had misread her taste—or Herr Pflüger's.

Besides, it was a rare pleasure to spend an afternoon sorting through beautiful things, as if I were choosing them for myself. While I worked, I set aside a few useful items for the attic: candles, of course, as well as wallpaper and a few pots of paint from a ransacked hardware store.

Ezra and Henri did as I asked, moving the choicest pieces of furniture into one corner and placing in front of them an assortment of crates of inexpensive housewares that would eventually find their way onto a train bound for Germany.

By the end of the day, Ezra appeared winded. He was tall and thin, though apparently well muscled, but I doubted a career teaching history to university students had prepared him for the physical demands of a prisoner's work schedule. We were at our posts by seven or eight in the morning, usually fortified only by a breakfast of coffee and a slice of whatever passed for bread. Except for a half-hour lunch break, we were on our feet unpacking, sorting, repairing, cleaning, and repacking. Our workday ended only when there were no more trucks waiting at the docks to be unloaded, so it was not uncommon for us to labor until eight in the evening or later.

That was why we were at Lévitan, after all: to work, unceasingly, diligently, ploddingly, for the Nazis and the Third Reich.

"Thank you for your help today, gentlemen," I said after we had hidden as best we could a good selection of the finest furniture. "And for your discretion."

Henri and Ezra smiled, seemingly amused at the thought that they would betray this hiding place. Henri left to join the rest of his pod on the loading dock, but Ezra lingered.

"Madame—," he began.

"Please call me Capucine. Or better yet, Capu. We're in this together, after all. There's not much room for formalities here in Lévitan."

"True enough."

Once again, I was struck by the air of calmness that radiated from him. Despite the implicit violence of our lives, surrounded as we were by misery and uncertainty, he seemed to possess a deep well of quietude. It was a rare enough quality in peacetime, and almost unheard of these days.

He seemed to want to say something more, but hesitated. I realized with a jolt that Ezra reminded me of Charles.

"What is it?" I urged. "Go ahead. I won't bite. And I won't say anything to anyone, either."

"I was held at Drancy until coming here yesterday," Ezra said. "I felt you should know that your father was among a group of prisoners deported to Auschwitz. It's a camp in Oświęcim, Poland."

The breath caught in my throat. I knew Bruno had been marked for deportation, but having my worst fears confirmed was a blow.

"Are you sure?"

He nodded. "I am afraid so. I saw them leave with my own eyes."

"I've heard of that place," I said, trying to swallow my fear. "The director mentioned it, and the guards threaten us with it. What's it like, do you know? I mean, it's a work camp?"

He shook his head. "I don't really know. According to rumor, it's worse than here. Much worse. I am truly sorry to tell you."

We held each other's gaze for a moment. There was sympathy in his eyes, but something more.

"I should have gone with him," I whispered to myself more than to Ezra.

He frowned and shook his head. "No. You mustn't go down that rabbit hole, or you'll drive yourself mad. We're all doing the best we can, Capu."

"And what of your family?" I asked. "Do you have children?"

He shook his head. "My wife is Aryan, and for now at least, she is safe. I have one sister in Algeria, another in America, and my parents are in the unoccupied zone. I pray they remain safe. They are not in good health and would not fare well in a work camp of any sort."

"*Hey!* Get back to work," demanded Pettit. "New guy, where do you think you are, Baden-Baden? This is no spa vacation."

Wordlessly, Ezra nodded to me and headed to the loading dock.

"I asked him to help me," I intervened. "Remember? The director told me to select some pieces to decorate an apartment."

"Huh," she grunted, casting a jaundiced eye in my direction. "Be careful, 123. If Fräulein Sommer finds out, she'll take what she wants. She studied in Vienna, you know."

"So I hear."

"And she's one of Baron Von Braun's favorites. You don't want to make her jealous."

"Thanks for looking out for me, Pettit."

She snorted. "Back to work."

8

Mathilde

$\mathcal{M}$AMI YVETTE PERCHED on the side of the parlor divan, arranging the plate of hors d'oeuvres, while Papi Auguste stood at the walnut sideboard, pouring aperitifs into tiny crystal glasses. Victor lingered by the fire, dressed in a dark gray three-piece suit, one arm draped across the mantel as if he were having his portrait painted: *Young Parisian Gentleman.*

Mami Yvette's welcoming smile turned to a frown of disapproval when she spied the extravagant fan in Mathilde's hand, while Papi Auguste glowered.

"It's a fan," Mathilde said.

"I can see it's a fan," said Papi, his tone gentling slightly when he remembered they had company. "I suppose it does harken back to a more refined era, so at least there's that."

"It is lovely to see you, Mathilde, and your fan is beautiful," Victor said. "Your grandfather is right, you know: You are indeed an apparition from a bygone era. A more genteel era."

Mathilde appreciated that Victor was attempting to take her side and smooth things over. But could she ever grow to actually love someone like him? Simone had pronounced Victor "jaw-crackingly dull," while Bridgette thought he seemed nice enough—but she rarely said anything bad about anybody except the German soldiers, so her lack of enthusiasm spoke volumes. Still, as Mami Yvette liked to remind her, it was wartime and eligible young men were scarce as hens' teeth.

"Victor brought me the most beautiful bouquet of flowers," said Mami Yvette. "And I believe he has a gift for you as well, Mathilde. Why don't you join him by the fire? Papi will pour you a little eau-de-vie."

Mathilde joined Victor on the love seat, gathering her voluminous skirts about her. These dinners felt like a command performance, which she supposed was exactly what they were: She was playing the role of an obedient, well-mannered granddaughter auditioning for the role of an obedient, well-mannered wife.

The room was chilly, but since she was clad in her heavy velvet gown, the heat from the fireplace soon became too much. With one flick of the wrist, she snapped her fan open to cool herself, enjoying not only the breeze but the subtle barrier the fan created between her and the others.

"Mathilde, I have brought you something," announced Victor, presenting her with a flat black velvet box.

Feeling self-conscious, Mathilde removed the lid. Nestled in a bed of black velvet was a jewel-encrusted gold necklace in a starburst design.

"Oh, my, isn't that stunning!" exclaimed Mami Yvette. "Are those genuine . . . ?"

"Yes, indeed. Sapphires, an emerald, and a ruby. And that's not vermeil but true gold," said Victor, puffing out his chest in a manner that reminded Mathilde of a penguin she had seen at the zoological park at Vincennes.

"A very nice present, indeed," said Papi Auguste, handing Mathilde a glass of eau-de-vie from the private reserve he kept in the wine cellar. The dark cave scared her, smelling as it did of must and chill and lined with hundreds of dusty bottles, artifacts of a very different time, before this war and the last.

"It seems very extravagant," said Mami.

"It's a special birthday, after all. I purchased it from someone liquidating a jewelry store, so it was a very good value," Victor said as Papi Auguste nodded in approval.

"Come, my dear," Victor continued as he stood up and held out the necklace between his two hands. "Allow me to place it on your lovely neck."

Mathilde got to her feet and removed her pearls, setting them on the mantel. She turned her back to Victor and felt his hot breath on her skin as he looped the necklace around her neck and fastened it. She winced as the clasp caught bits of her hair at the nape.

The glittering starburst necklace felt like an unspoken promise. It looked rather garish to her, but by its weight, she knew it was valuable.

"Now, that is truly lovely," Mami Yvette sighed. "Mathilde, stand up straight. You look very regal, like a princess. Don't you have something to say to dear Victor?"

Mathilde's cheeks flamed in anger and embarrassment. She felt like a chastened little girl, a doll on display, an actor in the play of her own life.

"Of course," Mathilde said. "Thank you, Victor. It's beautiful."

For the next half an hour, Papi Auguste and Victor chatted while

Mami Yvette and Mathilde listened, nodding and exclaiming where appropriate, until at last the servant whispered that the dinner was ready, and they removed to the dining room. The long mahogany table was draped with an embroidered ecru linen cloth and set with Limoges china and sparkling silver cutlery. In the center of the table were a row of small nosegays and twin candelabra that cast an amber glow over everything.

Before assuming his seat at one end, Papi held Mami's chair as she sat at the other end of the table, while Victor helped Mathilde into her usual chair in the middle of one long side. When it was just the three of them at dinner, Mathilde faced the grand fireplace so that in winter she could enjoy the sight of orange flames licking at the logs and in summer the grand arrangements of flowers and greenery.

This evening, however, her ever-attentive "gentleman friend" blocked the view.

Mathilde thought of the soldier in the street this afternoon who had commented upon her red coat, then bowed and handed her a rose. He had frightened her, yet there was something appealing about the impulsive romantic gesture.

Mathilde tried to imagine the brash soldier at the table in Victor's place. For all his talk about collaboration with the Germans, what would Papi Auguste make of one sitting at his table, courting his granddaughter?

The thought made her smile, and she looked up to see Victor gazing at her, assuming her smile had been meant for him. She looked away.

Victor's necklace lay heavy on her chest, the clasp digging into the back of her neck.

Mathilde listened with half an ear as her grandparents and

Victor nattered on about the weather, speculating whether there was a change in the air that heralded the arrival of spring or if that was merely wishful thinking. Looking around the table at the sumptuous meal, she couldn't help but wonder what dinner was like for Madame Antoinette or her neighbors.

Or for her mother and *grandpère* Bruno—did they have anything to eat at all? And where had they been taken?

"I have a question," said Mathilde when there was a lull in the conversation. "What happened to Monsieur Lodska? He was a jeweler. Remember him?"

Mami, Papi, and Victor exchanged glances.

"He was a Jewish fellow, wasn't he?" asked Victor.

Papi Auguste grunted. "An immigrant."

"From where?" Mathilde asked.

"One of the eastern countries, I believe," said Mami Yvette.

"The name sounds Polish to me," said Papi.

"Was he sent back to Poland, then?" Mathilde persisted.

"How should we know, and why should you care?" said Papi.

"We used to buy from him, remember?" said Mathilde. "For my graduation you took me to his shop near the Place des Vosges and bought me a gold locket. He was very kind. I remember he had a funny little dog that he kept at the shop. What do you suppose happened to the dog?"

Papi Auguste's brows drew together, and he glared at her. "What's gotten into you?"

"I'm wondering where the people are sent, that's all." Mathilde almost brought up her mother, but her courage flagged at Papi Auguste's scowl.

"Our granddaughter is not happy with the presence of Germans in our city," Papi said to Victor.

"Understandable," Victor said diplomatically. "The soldiers can be raucous and do not always show young ladies the respect they deserve."

"True, true," Papi conceded. "But their officers keep them in line. The Germans understand discipline. I'll give them that. We are fortunate that the Germans respect our culture as they do. They—"

"The Nazi flag flies over the Hôtel de Ville, Papi," Mathilde interrupted. "I saw it just today, and there's another giant flag on the Eiffel Tower. Doesn't that disturb you? Where's our flag? The flag of our *patrie*?"

"Speaking of flags," said Mami Yvette, leaning forward with a nervous smile, "it is said that Paris is the beating heart of *la belle France*. Did you know the three colors of the flag mean something? The white field represents the king, while the blue and the red are the colors of Paris. Hence, Paris contains the monarchy."

"I didn't know that," said Mathilde. "Are you sure?"

"What did they teach you at that fancy school of yours?" asked Papi Auguste.

"That the three colors represent the revolutionary ideals of *liberté, égalité,* and *fraternité*." Mathilde lifted her goblet and murmured into her cup, "Though lately, I suppose those qualities are hard to come by."

Papi Auguste and Mami Yvette looked shocked at her implied criticism.

"Wartime makes everything more difficult, doesn't it?" Victor said smoothly, his tone affable. "Madame Duplantier, my compliments to your chef. That was a lovely côte de veau."

But Papi Auguste was not to be dissuaded and rapped his knuckles on the table to get everyone's attention. "We must remember what *Maréchal* Pétain says: It was the declining morals of the French people that made us vulnerable. Our defeat was due to our weakness as a nation, and the failings of our people in becoming more concerned with pleasure than with hard work and sacrifice."

He paused to take a long sip of wine, shook his head, and continued.

"We French—we *true* French—once were a proud and an upstanding race who attended Mass and lived according to the tenets of the Church. We have lost our moral fiber and become a nation of malingerers and skivers, intermixing with foreigners, listening to godless American jazz, dancing all night instead of going to bed that we might arise early and work hard. Even our painters have become degenerate! Look at the so-called Impressionists or the abomination that is 'abstract' art. The Germans have a name for it: *Gossenmalerei.* It means 'gutter painting.'"

"I like the Impressionists," said Mathilde. "I like the colors."

"Mathilde, you may find this interesting: I have read that the painterly qualities characteristic of Impressionism were the products of a diseased visual cortex," said Victor. "Also, that much of that sort of art is Jewish or communist in nature."

Mathilde stared at Victor, wondering if he could possibly be serious. Her mother had posed for artists at Montmartre and her father had literally died creating his art. Or perhaps Victor did not know her family story. But Papi Auguste certainly did.

"In any case," said Papi Auguste, looking uncomfortable, "France is occupied, Germany will surely win the war, and when it does, life will return to some semblance of normalcy."

"God willing," Mami Yvette said, nodding.

"But . . . if that happens, then France will be part of Germany, won't it?" asked Mathilde. "Isn't that Herr Hitler's ultimate goal?"

"France will have to submit to the changing balance of power in

Europe, as so many nation-states have done throughout history," said Papi. "Do you think France has always been as it is now?"

"Good point," Victor said, apparently eager to agree with everything the Duplantier patriarch said.

Mathilde held her tongue. Mami Yvette shared Papi's perspective, as did their priest, and their neighbors. Who was Mathilde to think that she knew better? She wasn't even sure what had started this war and who was on whose side. She knew from her history classes that the France into which she had been born had at one time been composed of several autonomous regions that had been united over the centuries, usually through war. So perhaps Papi was right: Perhaps being absorbed by Germany was simply France's next step.

"You met with your old school friends in town today," said Mami Yvette in a bid to change the subject. "Did you have a nice time?"

"Yes, it was very nice," Mathilde said primly, trying not to think about La Maison Benoît and her conversation with Antoinette Laurent. "It'd been too long since I'd seen them."

"I think this girl is not a good influence on you," said Papi. "What is her name?"

Mami Yvette answered for her: "One is Simone Bernard, the other Bridgette Caron. Isn't that so, Mathilde?"

"Yes, this is her name, Bridgette Caron," Papi Auguste said, nodding his head thoughtfully. "Her father has a tailor shop in Saint-Germain-des-Prés, does he not?"

And just that quickly, Mathilde's anger transformed to fear.

"She is a good friend, Papi. A very nice person. Very moral."

"That may be," he said. "But I hear her father is a malingerer. Just the other day, his name came up in conversation."

"I'm sure that's not true, Papi," Mathilde said, her heart pounding. "Monsieur Caron is a very hard worker. He and his wife both. They work hard to make the German officers happy."

To Mathilde's surprise, Mami Yvette came to her defense. "Bridgette Caron has always been a sweet, biddable girl, well-liked by the nuns. Isn't that right, Mathilde? And I'm sure her father is doing the best he can. It cannot be easy for him. After all, Monsieur Caron was severely injured fighting for France in the Great War. You remember, don't you, Auguste? And now his eldest son has been sent to Germany with the *Service du Travail Obligatoire*. Perhaps Monsieur Caron has some resentment toward our occupiers, but under the circumstances, we really can't blame him, can we?"

"I suppose not," Papi Auguste said. "Man's suffered. I'll give him that."

"Now, let us turn our talk to more pleasant things," Mami Yvette said, and looked around the table expectantly.

"I hear there is a new movie at the Louxor," said Mathilde, grateful for her grandmother's intervention.

"Ah, see there? That's another thing the Germans have been very good for," said Victor. "The film industry."

"Personally, I'm not crazy about moving pictures," Papi grumbled.

"I know you prefer plays, Auguste, but believe me, many of the films these days are very moral, very respectable," said Mami Yvette. "*Immensee* is supposed to have lovely music and German folk songs. And I am looking forward to Jean Grémillon's *Le ciel est à vous*. I do love the thought of flying, don't you?"

They all nodded, and the maid served small squares of ginger cake drizzled with plum sauce.

"What about *Le Corbeau*?" asked Mathilde. "It's about neighbors in a small village denouncing one another."

"That's the problem with country people," said Papi Auguste with a nod. "They do not have the benefit of culture and education."

Victor laughed and launched into a story about encountering a farmer and his flock of goats while driving on a country road. Mathilde nodded and smiled perfunctorily, listening with only half an ear. As she gazed around the dinner table, she kept thinking of what Antoinette had said about the one-dimensionality of cardboard cutouts. She rubbed the back of her neck where Victor's necklace dug into her skin, and she fought the urge to simply yank it off.

The fan her mother had made for her lay beside her plate. Mathilde reached over to flick the fan partway open, then snapped it shut, watching the feathers quiver and gleam in the honeyed light from the candelabra.

Mathilde always thought *she* was the problem, the one insufficiently thankful for her many blessings, the one who did not adhere closely enough to the commands of the priests, the one who dared to wish for something . . . different.

But now, with the nonsensical chatter of her dinner companions swirling around the table, Antoinette's words came back to her:

"Your mother has always been very brave . . . three-dimensional. . . . Have you never wondered what it would be like to embrace the life you desire?"

THE NEXT DAY Mathilde rode her bike to Notre-Dame to give yet another confession to yet another priest whom she did not know. As she knelt to perform her penance, she gazed up at the stained glass rosettes and tried to concentrate, to remain truly penitent in the presence of God.

But God did not speak to her.

Instead, her mind was filled with memories of her mother dressed in her sparkling flapper outfit, laughing, dancing, waving her fan. Mathilde thought of her grandfather Bruno getting down on the floor with her to build a castle with her wooden blocks. She thought of the fear in the pit of her stomach when Papi cast suspicions on Bridgette and her family.

A bright amber light reflected onto her hand, followed by a roseate glow, its intensity building as the sun emerged from behind the clouds and beams of sunlight illuminated the stained glass. She watched as the colored lights played upon her skin, then returned her gaze to the massive rosette windows, thinking this must be what heaven looked like and wondering how the glass artisan had known.

Upon finishing her prayers, Mathilde did not put her money into the collection box. Instead, she decided she would give it directly to the nuns sheltering the orphans.

And she would bring them her old dollhouse as well.

9

Capucine

*T*HAT NIGHT I lay on my cot, listening to Isedore's steady breathing. The unheated attic was so frigid that our breath came out in clouds, making my heart ache in nostalgia for the morning mist that rose from the pond in the Luxembourg Gardens in winter. Each of us wore several layers of clothes stuffed with scratchy straw for warmth.

It was not easy to become accustomed to sleeping in a vast, open attic among seven hundred others. I heard the soft sounds of snoring, a murmured discussion, the rustling of someone trying to get comfortable, an occasional cough.

But it was my memories that robbed me of sleep.

Bright silvery rays sifted in through the grimy arched windows like ethereal beams of grace from the heavens. *There must be a full moon tonight.* How I longed to turn my face up to the sky and bathe in its light the way I used to, walking home from Montmartre, arm in arm with Charles after a long night of music, exhausted, elated. Climbing into bed in the crisp golden light of dawn, serenaded by the birds.

I couldn't stop thinking how much Ezra reminded me of Charles, and thus couldn't stop thinking about Charles. About our life together in the before times. There was a saying that one didn't know what one had until it was gone, but I disagreed. I knew what I had. Even then I knew how lucky I was. How lucky *we* were.

What I did not know was how quickly it would be snatched away.

It was difficult now to think back to that time, to explain what we were thinking, how the art and music smashed through boundaries and cast their spell over us. I had barely entered my teens when *La Grande Guerre* of 1914 came to a close, but even as a young person, I could feel the palpable fear and heartbreak that permeated Paris. The scores of injured, lost men wandering our streets with vacant stares. Families devastated by the loss of sons, fathers, brothers. Nearly two million French soldiers and civilians had been killed in that hideous war, and hundreds of thousands more were grievously injured, mentally as well as physically. Entire towns had been wiped off the map, others simply abandoned because the land had been poisoned by gas. Railroads and roads, vineyards and farms, had been destroyed, the country's economy left in shambles.

We were hungry, broken, demoralized.

But then something miraculous happened. As we entered the 1920s, Paris began to remember who she was, to shake off the horrors of war and to embrace life, and art, and pleasure once again. We became infused with energy. We had survived; now we would thrive. We craved art and music and grabbed onto joy with both hands, declaring that the Great War was "the war to end all wars," secure in the belief that such wretchedness could never again plague our country.

Over the next few years, Paris rose from the ashes to become a beacon of culture to the world. That decade of the twenties became known as *les années folles*, the crazy years.

During the Belle Époque, before the Great War, the neighborhood of Montmartre had been discovered by the likes of Picasso, Utrillo, and Brissaud. Perched on a butte in the northern part of the city more than five kilometers from the Eiffel Tower, Montmartre offered low rents and a relaxed, bohemian atmosphere. And as often happens when artists colonize an area, cafés and bars and restaurants soon followed.

When the Great War finally drew to a close, many of those now-famous artists decamped to the neighborhood of Montparnasse, but still, the pulsing heart—the *jazz* heart—of the *années folles* remained Montmartre.

And the more intellectuals and artists flocked to Paris, the more the city attracted others. Soon Paris replaced Vienna as the cultural capital of Europe, if not the world. Montmartre and Montparnasse became not just neighborhoods but internationally known destinations for creative souls, shining beacons for artists and writers and thinkers from all over the world.

Foreigners were drawn to our city in search of sophistication and openness, a place where they could live as they pleased without being hemmed in by the dictates of tradition. Many African-American soldiers chose to remain in Paris after fighting in the Great War, unwilling to return to the racism and menial jobs that awaited them back home. The war hero Eugene Bullard worked in a famous nightclub called Zelli's before opening his own club, Le Grand Duc, and an American-style bar called L'Escadrille. The jazz cafés Chez Florence and Bricktop's thrived, and the notes of American music filled the cobblestone alleyways of Montmartre.

Dozens of American writers, thinkers, and artists were among those who were drawn to Paris: Langston Hughes, F. Scott Fitzgerald, Josephine Baker, Paul Bowles, Aaron Copland, Henry Miller, Louis Armstrong. Long ago, Paris had been dubbed *la Ville Lumière*, the City of Light, both because of its role during the Enlightenment, and then because it was one of the first cities to electrify its streetlamps. But now it earned the moniker through its artistic brilliance: Paris between the wars was incandescent.

To be sure, it was not a utopia. There were plenty of problems: clashes with the Parisian old guard, petty jealousies, and squabbles even among our own circles. Artists and musicians, not to mention their hangers-on, were justly famous for their volatility. The Japanese artist Léonard became known as Fou-Fou, "mad to the power of two."

But in the clubs and the cafés of Montmartre, men walked hand in hand, women kissed in public, atheists and anarchists felt secure expressing their beliefs, men wore women's clothes, and women dressed like men. People of different races and backgrounds met and mingled. "Strange" was no longer a synonym for "wrong"—in fact, the odder the better.

And Zelli's stayed open till dawn.

When I didn't have the fare for the train, Montmartre was an hour's walk through the city from La Maison Benoît; and when I was posing for artists in Montparnasse, it was a long walk in the opposite direction. Still, I never minded.

After Roger's sudden death, I felt adrift with my tiny daughter. Lost. We moved in with my father and we made do, but . . . I didn't fit. I tired of Bruno's political diatribes on the one hand, and my in-laws' incessant pressure to conform—and to move back in with them—on the other. Among the artists, I found my people, a tribe to which I did not have to continually explain myself.

And with jazz, I found my soul.

I was young and vain. Though I was not beautiful, I had the rather angular look popular among the Cubists and the Expressionists and even the occasional Postimpressionist. I had gained a small measure of local fame and was known for carrying exquisite fans that matched my bedazzled flappers' dresses. And after the marvelous Josephine Baker commissioned an extravagant feathered fan from La Maison Benoît, my reputation was made. It wasn't long afterward that I received an invitation to a soirée at Gertrude Stein's place in Montparnasse, and later I became a regular at R vingt-six in Montmartre.

By then I knew *everyone.*

I met Charles at Bricktop's nightclub. The first band had finished their set and we were waiting for the next, a band newly arrived in Paris and rumored to be fabulous. I was sitting at the bar with Django Reinhardt and Pierre Bonnard, relaxing after a modeling session. I wasn't really much of a model, but the artists liked me, my unique fans, and my willingness to get naked. And the fan business not being what it once was, I needed the money.

It is hard to explain what it feels like to remain absolutely still for hours at a time as artists attempt to capture a bit of one's soul. However keen the talent, what they apply to the canvas is never the essence, but merely one aspect of oneself filtered through their eyes.

Their very male eyes, usually.

There was a portrait of me on display on one wall of Bricktop's, painted by Fernand Léger. Léger was a Cubist, so even though the painting was a relatively realistic portrayal of me in the nude, it was so abstract that I did not feel shy about sitting not ten feet away as I drank and chatted with friends.

I noticed Charles the moment he walked in. He was a big man with an athletic build, beautiful sherry brown eyes, jet-black hair, and an easy, brilliant smile. But there was more. . . . There was something about him that resonated with me, as if we had known each other in a past life. Which was ridiculous, of course. But Charles felt it, too. *Chemistry,* he would say later.

He stopped in front of the Léger painting and stared at it so long that I abandoned my companions—who had started arguing about the relative merits of Fauvism versus Expressionism, so I was bored to tears anyway—and sidled up to him.

After a beat, he turned to me.

"It's you," he said, his voice deep and velvety.

"Is it?"

"Isn't it?"

I laughed. "It is. Not many people realize."

"The resemblance is quite strong."

"Well, it's an abstract painting. You're not supposed to make the connection."

He just grinned and held out his hand to shake, American-style.

"How do you do? I'm Charles, Charles Anthony Moore. From North Carolina."

"I'm Capucine Benoît." After losing my husband at such a young age, I had resumed my maiden name. His hand was large and his grip tight, but comfortably so. My palm tingled in response to his warmth. "From Paris."

"Capucine? I've never heard that name before."

"It refers to a hood or a cowl," I said.

"Is that because you keep yourself hidden?"

I gave him a small smile, and he smiled in return. We stood there for a long moment, our hands still clasped. Finally, we let go.

"It is a pleasure to meet you, Capucine. May I ask: Is it madame or mademoiselle?"

"It's Capu."

He nodded and turned to peruse the painting. "Imagine having such a thing of beauty at home to savor every day."

"Are you referring to the painting or to me?"

His laugh was a deep rumble, his accent charmingly American. "Both, I suppose. I very much doubt I could choose between the two at this point."

"Well, let me assure you, the painting's cheaper," I said. I heard a ruckus and saw Django and Pierre had been joined by Georges Joubin, and their argument was ratcheting up, exacerbated by the easy-flowing absinthe. "I should get back to my friends."

He held my gaze. "May I at least buy you a drink before I go onstage?"

"You're with the band?"

He nodded. "I play a little piano."

"A little piano" was, of course, an understatement. When Charles applied his long, lithe fingers to the keys, he unleashed a torrent of notes, a hurricane of sound, a swirling tornado of rhythm that lifted up the audience and swept us into his magical world. He liked to say that in a jazz band all the glory went to the trumpet, but that it was the *piano* that led the melody.

In all our years together, Charles and I never shared a home. I claimed I could not bring myself to leave my father and his business, but in truth, I feared the reaction of Mathilde's grandparents. Charles accepted my excuse, but I saw his disappointment in my capitulating to social expectations. My father looked at me that way as well. I liked to think of myself as a free spirit, as a flapper who embraced the new and the modern and rejected the outmoded restrictions of the past. But when it came to my daughter, I was a coward.

That Charles continued to love and to accept me was a mystery.

The 1920s ended with a crash, and the grim 1930s witnessed a worldwide economic depression, Hitler's rise to power in Germany, and the constant threat of another war. Paris, once a refuge for artists and iconoclasts from all over the world, was now imperiled by the winds of fascism. One by one, the jazz clubs were shuttered, and increasingly the bohemian lifestyle was denounced as immoral and degenerate. Most of the Americans in Paris left, including my Charles.

I missed him with a visceral yearning. The only consolation was our correspondence. When we were together, our lives were a whirlwind of music and dancing and lovemaking, but the physical distance between us now forced us to express ourselves in deeper and clearer ways through our letters.

In each missive, Charles offered to marry me, to come back for me, or he asked me to join him in America. He never married, did not even date, for he said he had no wish to. *I'm in love with my Fan Girl, and that is that.* Charles offered me an escape from the darkness descending upon Europe.

And I refused. Finally, I wrote and told him to stop. I could no longer bear reading his poetic letters, knowing we could not be together. It was better for him to make a life for himself in North Carolina.

His Fan Girl was no more.

ONE NIGHT AT Zelli's, I had been dancing with Charles, which was a rare treat since he was usually onstage. I relished nothing more than feeling his hands on my waist as we whirled to a jazzy tune or resting my head on his chest during a slow ballad, the sensation of my skirt brushing my legs, the vibrations of the music moving through me and melding with the beat of his heart.

As we were leaving the dance floor, I was stunned to spy Mathilde's godmother, Vignetta Jaccoud, sitting with her husband at a tiny table, sharing a bottle of wine. Zelli's was not the kind of establishment they frequented, and I could only imagine they had decided to go slumming in a jazz club.

Vignetta was a close friend of my former mother-in-law, Yvette Duplantier, who had never cared for me and who certainly would not care for jazz, or smoking, or drinking, or the fact that I was dancing in a club at three in the morning. Of course, the Jaccouds were here as well, but I imagined for them it was a rare naughty adventure, whereas for me it was a way of life.

"Vignetta! What a surprise. And Jean-Claude. It's a pleasure." We exchanged kisses, Vignetta's eyes never leaving Charles.

"And this is . . . this is my . . . Charles Moore," I stuttered.

"Nice to meet you, madame, monsieur," Charles said politely.

"He plays piano with the band."

I stumbled over my words in my nervousness. Vignetta and Jean-Claude stared at me with obvious disapproval, and I could practically feel Charles vibrating at my side, wondering what was wrong, why I was denying him. He did not react with anger, but rather with sadness and resignation. It cut through me, and yet I gave in to cowardice.

Two days later, I received a note from my in-laws, inviting me to tea.

Roger's parents had never approved of me—not when I married their precious only child, not when we lived with them for a while when I was pregnant, and not even after I delivered their cherished grandchild, my beautiful Mathilde.

I was not the woman they had envisioned as their daughter-in-law. I did not know the unspoken rules of formal dinner parties, and I didn't care to learn. I was at times unintentionally rude to their bourgeois friends and guests. I was so steeped in Bruno's radical view of the world that I dismissed as ridiculous their invitations to join them at Mass on Sundays and was never shy about expressing my views on the evils of capitalism. Bruno had taught me many things growing up, but diplomacy—and, perhaps, gratitude—was not among them.

I was glad for the Duplantiers' financial support and the offer of a place to live but was too young and self-centered to truly appreciate their generosity. They had more than enough, I reasoned. Why shouldn't they share it with their son and his wife and child?

Still, after Roger and I moved into a place of our own in Paris, and then after he had his accident, I allowed Yvette and Auguste to visit with Mathilde whenever they wanted. Their love for my daughter was undeniable, and I was glad of it for her sake.

So it was with mixed emotions that I heeded their call to tea. I sat on the uncomfortable horsehair sofa Yvette was so proud of, and listened as they explained why I was incapable of being a good mother.

My father-in-law loomed over me in his three-piece suit, a gold watch fob hanging from his vest pocket. I remember watching the chain as it swung and quivered with his every word, his deep, resonant voice sounding as if he were shouting, though he was speaking at a normal level. When his diatribe against the evils of American jazz fell on deaf ears, he moved on to a more salient point.

"Mathilde has the right to benefit from the social standing of her father's family," Auguste insisted. "What kind of life can you give her? Especially now, when France and, indeed, all of Europe appear to be plunging into an economic depression? Who will want to spend money on fans? And we have no way to know how long the hard times will last."

Yvette, for her part, looked at me heavyheartedly, her tear-filled eyes conveying her anguish as she spoke of her son. What Roger was like as a child, the bright future of which we all were robbed. Mathilde should not sleep in an armoire, which she would soon outgrow in any event, Yvette urged. She should have a room of her own. She would soon be of school age and deserved only the best education, with the nuns. Wasn't that what any mother wanted for her child? Besides, Yvette said softly, imagine how Mathilde would feel when she was old enough to appreciate what her mother's— Yvette took a delicate breath—choices meant for her. How she would be taunted by her schoolmates, denied entry into the social circles that were her birthright as her father's daughter.

I easily dismissed Auguste's economic arguments; after all, I was Bruno's daughter and had embraced his free and easy, creative outlook on life, no matter the economic ups and downs. The Benoîts might not have as much as the Duplantiers, but we had enough. But Yvette's words, spoken with the sincere passion of a mother's love, shook my faith in myself and my abilities. My own mother had left me when I was younger than Mathilde. What did I know about being a mother? What did I have to offer my daughter?

It pained me to admit that I had not given much thought to what school Mathilde would attend, and what her schoolmates—and their parents—might make of my relationship with Charles. What it meant to leave Mathilde in the care of Bruno or Antoinette while I went out at night, posing for artists and dancing in clubs. It was one thing while she was still young, but what about as she got older and grew capable of understanding more, demanding more, needing more—would she judge me, be embarrassed by me, suffer because of me?

And then Yvette played her trump card. "We would also be able to provide Mathilde with the best of medical care, of course."

For a moment, I wavered.

"It's settled, then," Auguste said in a tone of finality. "Should have done this when Roger died. Mathilde's a Duplantier, after all."

"*No*," I said. "It is not settled. My daughter is also a Benoît, and she belongs with me. I am her mother, and I will take care of her."

"But—," Auguste sputtered as I stood and gathered my things.

"Capucine, please—," Yvette began to say.

"Thank you for the tea. It was, as always . . ." Without bothering to finish my thought, I threw on my coat and hurried out the door. "Adieu."

Two nights later I came home very late from the club to find Mathilde's little bed in the armoire an empty, tangled heap of sheets and blankets. In a panic I awoke Bruno, who said she was with Antoinette, so I hurried into the courtyard and rapped on the concierge's apartment door. *"Madame? C'est moi, Capu,"* I called out softly.

"Entrez," a voice called out, and I opened the door to find Mathilde, rosy lips and pale cheeks, fast asleep in the older woman's lap.

"She's fine," said Antoinette. "She had a nightmare and began wheezing, and Bruno did not know what to do for her. I rubbed a bit of that ointment on her chest to ease her breathing and then made a cup of cocoa to put things to right."

"Thank you," I said, collapsing into a chair at the little table in front of the window. "I cannot thank you enough."

"You know that Mathilde is welcome here any time of the day or night. But . . . Capu, she does need her mother."

I suspected I smelled of cigarette smoke and probably of alcohol. I wasn't drunk exactly, but neither was I sober. In my feathers and sparkles, dancing and listening to Charles play in dim jazz clubs, I could lose myself and my worries in a world of music and joy and art. But the truth now hit me like an icy rain: I had been thinking of my own needs and wants, not of Mathilde. Not of my daughter.

"Roger's parents want her to live with them," I told Antoinette, my voice flat.

"Do they, now?" said Antoinette, her eyebrows raised. She remained silent for a long moment, then tilted her head. "That does make a certain kind of sense."

"Does it?"

Antoinette nodded slowly. "You know I don't cast aspersions on your late nights, Capu, much less on your love life. Charles is a treasure; I see why you like him so much. But your relationship will be a problem for a lot of people outside your artistic circle. It's not fair and it's not right, but it is the way of the world we live in." She paused to let her words sink in. "And though there are many more important things in life than money, her grandparents can offer Mathilde things you cannot right now: stability, a good education, and access to good doctors."

She reached out and placed her warm, soft hand on mine. Ever since Suzette had left, Antoinette had been the closest thing I had to a mother.

When next she spoke, it was in the gentlest tone, as though addressing a skittish mare. "It is not easy to raise a child on your own, *ma chérie*, and you are very young yourself. Maybe it would be better for her, and for you, if Mathilde went to live with them. It would not make her any less your daughter, or you any less her mother. It might even allow you to be more yourself if you no longer have to worry about her day-to-day well-being."

"I can't, Antoinette. She's my *daughter.* I just . . . can't."

For the next several weeks, I stayed home at night, refusing offers to pose for artists, even telling Charles I could not see him anymore. I denied him, and I denied myself.

Night after night, I lay sleepless in bed, staring at the ceiling and telling myself I was doing the right thing.

Then Mathilde suffered another asthma attack, the fourth in as many weeks, and we made another panicked run to the clinic, only to have them shake their heads and say they could do nothing more for her. I consulted everyone I could think of: the doctors at the hospital; an old woman in the Marais who produced tinctures and medicinal eaux-de-vie; Antoinette's sister-in-law, who claimed to have a connection in India with a new herbal product called ephedra.

Still, I could not cure her.

But then Antoinette's sister-in-law asked: If Mathilde was allergic to cats, might she also be allergic to feathers?

When I brought Mathilde to Neuilly-sur-Seine and saw how delighted she was to see the beautiful new bed draped in a pink canopy, the little Juliet balcony, the elaborate dollhouse, I almost managed to convince myself I was doing the right thing. Here, with her grandparents, she would be surrounded by plenty and cradled by the memories of her father. And far from the feathers of our fan shop.

But walking away from that big square house on rue Pierret without my daughter's little hand in mine was the hardest thing I had ever done.

At first, I visited every other day, but before long my visits became less frequent. It was excruciatingly awkward, sitting perched on that uncomfortable sofa in that gloomy house under Yvette's watchful eye. And each time I left, Mathilde would wail, my heart would break anew, and I would sob as I walked away, weeping the entire time it took to walk across Paris, all the way back home to La Maison Benoît.

Crying for my daughter and for myself. For what I lacked.

Auguste and Yvette and even Antoinette were right. Bruno had done the best he could, but my own mother had left me when I was younger than Mathilde. How would I know how to mother a child?

Everything that happened in the next several years—the decline of our business during the economic downturn of the thirties, the closing of the jazz clubs on Montmartre, the departure of so many of my artist friends, the German Occupation, the pervasive hunger—seemed to me to be divine retribution for my having failed my daughter.

My anguish even poisoned my relationship with Charles. Partly, I blamed him for the Duplantiers' inviting me to tea that dreadful day, for being an American, for not being socially acceptable.

But mostly I blamed myself for allowing all that to matter.

I deserved no better.

Isedore turned over with a loud squeak of her cot. Her eyes fluttered open, and she noticed I was awake.

"*Ça va*, Capu?"

"*Oui, ça va*. Go back to sleep, *chérie*," I whispered.

As I said it, I couldn't help but remember tucking Mathilde into her little bed in my armoire. The daughter whom I had abandoned. The daughter who had not spoken to me in years.

First Charles, now Mathilde. Surely next my mind would turn to Bruno and that final, cheery smile he managed for me in Drancy. I gave up on the possibility of sleep.

My ghosts haunted me at night. I wondered: Did I haunt them in return?

10

Mathilde

*T*ODAY WAS THE birthday of Mathilde's father, Roger. Mami Yvette always spent the anniversary of her son's birth upstairs in her bedroom crying, and Papi Auguste stomped about, more irascible than usual. It was a good day to leave the big square house.

Mathilde breathed a sigh of relief when she managed to lug the big dollhouse down the stairs without being seen. A bag filled with dolls and minuscule furniture and a small envelope of money hung off one shoulder, and she balanced the house on her bicycle seat as she walked several blocks to the nuns' house on rue Edouard Nortier.

This time a younger sister answered the door. She appeared surprised but pleased by the gifts of charity—and was enchanted by the charming dollhouse. Her profuse thanks embarrassed Mathilde. The residents of the neighborhood were well-to-do; had no one thought to aid the children?

And as she rode her bike into town, she wondered what else she could do, *should* do, to help.

The Eiffel Tower still sported the ugly red-and-black flag of the Third Reich. Below it a banner read *"Deutschland Siegt Auf / An Allen Fronten,"* which meant "Germany Is Victorious on All Fronts." But someone had altered the banner so that the "S" in *"Siegt"* was now an "L." Mathilde didn't know German well enough to understand what that meant but assumed the Germans would find it insulting.

Lately it felt as if something had shifted. It was hard to know what exactly—Papi had banned the BBC radio broadcast from his house and allowed them to listen only to the Nazi-controlled Radio Paris, which reported nothing but German victories on all fronts. But there was a feeling, a sensation in the air, that the Nazis were on the defensive, that they were losing control, that Parisians had just about reached their breaking point and were pushing back against the Occupation and the idea that their city should be a holiday resort for the Nazi *Herrenvolk*.

The Germans had attempted to win Paris by flattery instead of by heavy-handed repression, but Mathilde was not fooled. What had happened to the jewelry store owner? To the people from the Neuilly synagogue? To their children—they weren't really orphans, were they? After all, their parents had merely been taken away. Like her own mother and grandfather. They were still alive, weren't they?

She pulled her bike up to the *famille* Caron's tailor shop on rue Mazarine. Bolts of gray, black, and tan fabric were stacked up to the ceiling, the floor was covered in bits and pieces of threads and swatches, and dressmaker figures and mannequins wore fine men's suits in varying stages of completion, some covered in chalked markings awaiting alterations. Bridgette's father had always been soft-spoken and kind like his daughter, but lately he could barely summon a smile in greeting. Last night Papi Auguste had called him a "malingerer," but hunched over his workbench, shriveled and shrunken and looking about a hundred years old, Monsieur Caron was anything but a skiver.

Bridgette's mother emerged from the family's quarters in response to the tinkle of the bell over the shop door. Small and colorful and fluttering, she used to remind Mathilde of a butterfly, though lately she was more like a moth, wearing pieced-together gray serge no doubt left over from a man's suit.

"*Bonjour*, Madame Caron," said Mathilde.

"*Bonjour, ma fille!*" Bridgette's mother hurried over to plant gentle kisses on each cheek. Madame Caron used to have a signature scent, Guerlain's Vol de Nuit perfume, but these days she smelled only of the fabric size they used when they pressed the suits.

"It has been so long!" she exclaimed, standing back as if to look Mathilde over. "Why, you are all becoming such beautiful young women! Truly, even . . . under the current circumstances. It's quite astonishing. I'll always think of you as a little girl with skinned knees."

Mathilde laughed. "That was only the one time."

"It was Simone's fault, as usual," said Bridgette as she joined them, carrying two packages. She was wearing her old school uniform, with her hair in braids, and she looked much younger than her years. "Simone talked us into climbing that ancient maple tree at the cemetery. Remember, Mathilde?"

"Is Simone joining you today?" asked Madame Caron. "In school you were always *les trois Mousquetaires*! I'm used to seeing you three together."

Bridgette glanced at Mathilde and shook her head.

Mathilde hadn't invited Simone. Once upon a time, it was true, they had been like the Three Musketeers, their heads perpetually bent together over a game of jacks, a bit of gossip, a shared joke. Despite—or perhaps because of—their different personalities, they had been drawn together since they met in the third grade. Mathilde's mami Yvette had told her only the vaguest things about women's secrets, about periods, and especially about sex, and Madame Caron wasn't much more forthcoming, so free-spirited Simone filled in the gaps. Bridgette was straightforward and well-liked by adults and helped smooth things over whenever one of them got in trouble. Mathilde was the dreamy, artistic one who provided the glue to their trio.

But lately the realities of war had strained their friendship.

Bridgette shook her head and replied, "Simone's busy today with her young man."

"Ahhh." Madame Caron smiled and gently tugged one of Bridgette's blond braids. "I'm glad some are able to find romance, despite this wretched war. *Ne t'inquiète pas, ma fille.* Do not fret; it will be your turn soon enough."

Bridgette gave her mother a smile, but subtly rolled her eyes in Mathilde's direction.

Madame Caron handed Mathilde a small nosegay of flowers. "From my little garden to put on your father's grave. And, Mathilde, Bridgette told me the terrible news about your mother and grandfather. I am so very sorry. I will say a prayer for them."

"Thank you, madame." Mathilde wanted to say more, to thank the kind woman for always remembering to send flowers to her father's grave, for thinking about her mother. But as usual, nothing came to mind. "Thank you," she repeated.

They bid au revoir to Bridgette's parents and went outside to retrieve their bicycles. Mathilde set the flowers in the handlebar basket, while Bridgette added her packages to her bike's full panniers.

"What's all that?" asked Mathilde as they walked their bikes down the busy street.

"*Maman* fixed us a snack, and I have a few things to take to Claye-Souilly."

"You're going all the way to Claye-Souilly this afternoon? That's a long ride."

"I'm used to it. I'll spend a few nights but should be back by the end of the week."

"Why are you going?"

"Just to visit with family. And with luck, to bring back some fresh vegetables, maybe even a little meat." She gave Mathilde a sidelong look. "Most of us would starve to death without a little help from our country cousins. You must be receiving packages as well, yes? Or . . . perhaps your papi has enough money and connections to purchase food despite the shortages."

Mathilde knew Papi was somehow acquiring contraband, probably from the black market or perhaps through his business connections with the Third Reich. She thought of the coupon sheets Mami handed Cécile and Cook when she sent them to the market. Even then, even with coupons, the groceries hardly made a decent meal.

"Be careful, please, Bridgette," Mathilde said. "It doesn't seem safe for you to be riding around like that, given . . . everything."

"I'll be fine," Bridgette replied with a shrug.

They turned onto Boulevard de Ménilmontant and spotted the verdigris gates of Père Lachaise Cemetery. They propped their bikes against the high stone wall.

Their boots made crunching sounds as they trod the gravel

path, turning first left, then right on the vast labyrinth of pathways, finally arriving at the grave of Roger Paul Duplantier, "beloved son, husband, and father."

Mathilde always wondered why he hadn't been buried closer to her grandparents' home in Neuilly-sur-Seine, but apparently Roger had wanted to be laid to rest in Père Lachaise, famous for its many beautiful sculptures. She thought again of the torso her father had sculpted, the one Mami Yvette cherished but Papi Auguste loathed. Was it of her mother? Was that why Papi despised it so? Or was it because it was an example of modern art and thus unworthy, even degenerate?

"I wish I had known him," Mathilde said softly, placing Madame Caron's bouquet at the base of her father's headstone.

Bridgette stood by her side, silent and steady.

Mathilde wanted to confide in Bridgette about La Maison Benoît and the things Antoinette had said about cardboard cutouts; about her own doubts about the war; and about her anguish over her mother and grandfather's disappearance.

She tried to find the words, but before she could speak, Bridgette took a deep breath in through her nose and said, "What is it about this place? It has a particular smell, doesn't it? You could bring me here blindfolded and I bet I would know exactly where I was."

"It's funny how scents can bring back memories, isn't it? I was thinking earlier that your mother always used to smell of Guerlain's Vol de Nuit perfume, but she doesn't anymore."

Bridgette gave her a side-eyed look, and when she spoke, her voice had an uncharacteristic edge. "You do know that most people can't get luxury items anymore, right? There's no such thing as cosmetics and perfume and stockings. At least not for those who can't afford to pay the prices asked on the black market. For many people these days, like my family, just getting enough to eat is a challenge."

"But . . . your mother packed a lunch for us."

"She wanted us to enjoy ourselves. She's like that. Didn't you notice how thin she is?"

Mathilde stared at her friend. It was quite astonishing, Mathilde thought, how often she had no idea what to say. Even with one of her closest friends, someone she had known since they were children, with whom she had talked about school and boys and menstruation and the future. And how did one repay the kindness of a woman who prepared you a lunch when she herself was hungry?

"I'm sorry. I didn't realize."

"I know you didn't. It's not your fault," Bridgette said.

"Hey, you were always better in German class than I," said Mathilde, changing the subject. "You know the sign on the Eiffel Tower? On the way over here, I noticed someone changed the 'S' in 'Siegt' to an 'L.' Do you know what that means?"

Bridgette grinned. "Changing 'Siegt' to 'Liegt' changes the meaning of the slogan from 'Germany Is Victorious on All Fronts' to 'Germany Lies on All Fronts,' in the sense that Germany is 'lying down' in defeat."

"Oh," said Mathilde. "But . . . why would someone do that? I mean, why take the risk? They could be arrested or deported or worse. What's the point?"

"It's a symbol of the Résistance. It sends the message that the French people will not stand for the German Occupation. It's risky but it's happening more and more. I see it a lot in the countryside. I heard the Nazis hoisted their flag above the castle ruins in Coucy-le-Château-Auffrique, and someone tore it down and replaced it with the tricolor."

"Our flag?"

Bridgette nodded and smiled. "Not only that, but they wrapped the flagpole with barbed wire and removed the crampons used for climbing the tower, so the Germans couldn't get to it. The next day the *Wehrmacht* tried to shoot it down with a machine gun!"

Bridgette's laugh was one of Mathilde's favorite sounds: deep and throaty as if rising from her very core. It always made Mathilde imagine them as grown, confident women in their forties sitting on a café terrace, smoking and laughing and commenting on passersby.

"Did you know that in our flag, the white represents the monarchy, while blue and red are the colors of Paris? So Paris is hemming in the monarchy."

"I thought the colors represented *fraternité, égalité, liberté.*"

"I thought so, too."

Mathilde felt annoyed again and couldn't put her finger on why. She was always disgruntled these days, it seemed.

"I have to tell you something," said Bridgette. She looked around as if to make certain they were alone, and continued in a low voice. "There are rumors of French prisoners being held right here in Paris."

"What do you mean?"

"We have a family friend whose husband fought with the army. He's a prisoner of war, and now she's been interned as well."

"What did she do?"

Bridgette gave a humorless laugh. Unlike the laugh Mathilde loved, this one was bitter and sounded especially discordant coming from one who was so perennially soft-spoken. "She didn't *do* anything. You still don't understand, do you, Mathilde? She is married to someone who fought for France against Germany. There is no further 'crime' necessary. What crime did your mother commit, besides not living up to what others expected of her?"

They had arrived at the tomb of Victor Noir, and Mathilde gazed at the bronze sculpture of Noir fallen in death. Mathilde had heard of him because he was from Neuilly-sur-Seine. Was he buried here in Père Lachaise for the same reason her father was? Did Neuilly cast out its freethinkers?

"I'm sorry I spoke to you like that," said Bridgette as they continued walking. "The war, the Occupation, the suffering and uncertainty . . . they get to me sometimes. Oh, hey, I know. Let's check out Oscar Wilde's tomb. It's so unusual."

Mathilde found the outlandish sphinxlike creature strange and off-putting, so unlike the graceful angels of yore, or the cemetery's famous weeping woman, or the sculptures of the dead in beautiful repose or, like that of Victor Noir, captured in their last moments of life. Still, she had to admit that Wilde's tomb was distinctive, unlike any other she had seen.

"I like the inscription," Bridgette said, and read aloud:

AND ALIEN TEARS WILL FILL FOR HIM
PITY'S LONG-BROKEN URN,
FOR HIS MOURNERS WILL BE OUTCAST MEN,
AND OUTCASTS ALWAYS MOURN.

"My mother used to quote Oscar Wilde," Mathilde said. "She would say: 'We are all in the gutter, but some of us are looking at the stars.'"

Bridgette chuckled. "Your mother has always been fabulous. But I sincerely hope you don't quote Oscar Wilde to your papi Auguste. I can't imagine he would approve."

"You're right about that," Mathilde said. Papi had banned Oscar Wilde's writings from his house, pronouncing them inappropriate for a young lady. "He calls Oscar Wilde degenerate, but I've never understood why."

Bridgette looked surprised. "Probably because Oscar Wilde was . . . you know, a homosexual. Quite famously so."

"Oh. Isn't that against the law?"

"It is now, under the Occupation. It's one of the things the Nazis deport people for."

"*Père* Guillaume says it's wrong."

"'Wrong' is a relative term," murmured Bridgette. "It depends on who's doing the judging, I suppose."

Bridgette had such a quiet, gentle way about her that occasionally, especially lately, she could say quite radical things that snuck up on Mathilde without her realizing it. Mathilde thought of what Papi Auguste had said over dinner. Maybe Bridgette really *was* a bad influence.

Mathilde's eyes fixed on a bright red lipstick mark in the shape of a kiss placed near the carved sphinx's private parts—which weren't particularly private, hanging as they did right there overhead. She looked away, her cheeks burning.

"Shall we eat?" asked Bridgette. "Let's go find a spot under the old maple."

They laid out their picnic under the tree Simone had once dared them to climb, resulting in their skinned knees. Back when things were different. When they were young, and France belonged to France, and Paris was still Paris.

Bridgette unwrapped a square of floral material to reveal two biscuits, a small chunk of cheese, and an apple cut up into sections.

Mathilde tried to think how to tell Bridgette about what had happened with Antoinette Laurent and her visit to La Maison Benoît, but before she could speak, Bridgette said:

"Let me ask you this: Since you love movies so much, have you heard about the Cinémathèque Française?"

Mathilde frowned. "What's that?"

"An archive of sorts. They had maybe the largest collection of films in the world until the Nazis ordered them to burn everything made before 1937."

"Why did they do that?"

Bridgette shrugged and popped a piece of apple into her mouth. "Because the Third Reich said the films were 'degenerate.' I hear the owners have been trying to save what they can, smuggling films out so they may be shown again after the war."

"That sounds dangerous."

"Sometimes danger is worth it. Don't you think so? I thought you loved the movies."

"I do, but I wouldn't *die* for them."

The last time Mathilde had gone to the cinema, there was a newsreel that described a "glorious" meeting between "our most exalted leader" Adolf Hitler and "our nation's good friend" Benito Mussolini of Italy. People in the audience started whistling and shouting and stamping their feet to drown out the newsreel, and a shouted voice cursed the two fascist leaders with words Mathilde rarely heard and dared not repeat. The projector stopped abruptly, the lights came on, and the nervous, flustered theater manager begged the audience to show respect by being quiet during the newsreel.

Two German soldiers stood up and glared at the audience. Mathilde had been terrified, and when the lights went out and the film began rolling again, the noisemakers started to cough, clear their throats, and sneeze so loudly that they again drowned out the newsreel.

"Well, you should at least ask the authorities where they sent your mother and grandfather," said Bridgette. "They wouldn't dare kill you for that, especially given your grandparents' standing."

"And then what?"

"I don't know. . . . Maybe you could write to them. Send them food. I doubt they have enough to eat, and your family has plenty."

Mathilde felt her cheeks flame, the biscuit in her hand halfway to her mouth. She knew she was plump, with round, rosy cheeks that increasingly stood in stark contrast to those of the people she saw on the street. The lunch Bridgette's mother had packed might well have been the day's food for their entire family.

"I doubt my grandparents would be willing to help," said Mathilde.

"What about the money your father left you?"

"I told you—that's meant for my marriage."

"For your husband, you mean," Bridgette said.

"What if . . . I mean, if I could get hold of some of that money, where would I even start?"

"They say some of the Parisian prisoners are kept at Drancy, outside of town, not too far away," said Bridgette. "Others are sent farther, to camps in Germany and Poland. But the Germans keep good records. Someone should be able to tell you something."

Mathilde studied Bridgette's profile, her pretty golden hair plaited in old-fashioned braids, the high color in her smooth cheeks. Where did she learn these things?

"And what do the inmates do in these camps?" asked Mathilde. "Work for the Germans?"

Bridgette shrugged, opened her mouth to speak, then hesitated. "I suppose so. The Germans have sent so many of their own people to war that they need others to work the factories, like my brother in the STO."

The *Service du Travail Obligatoire* was the forced enlistment of French people to work in Germany to support the war effort. Hundreds of thousands of Frenchmen, and even some Frenchwomen, had been conscripted into the organization's ranks. Mathilde wondered why Victor had been spared but supposed his work at the Renault factory was considered essential. She made a mental note to ask him.

"You were going to say something else," said Mathilde.

"What? When?"

"Right then, you hesitated. Is it . . . Do you think it's worse than a work camp?"

"No one really knows," Bridgette said after another pause. "There are rumors, but we don't know anything for sure. It's just that the Nazis are . . . unpredictable."

"And if prisoners are being held here in Paris, where would they be?"

"In a department store."

"What are you talking about?"

"Do you remember the old department store Lévitan? On rue du Faubourg Saint-Martin?" she asked. "Your grandparents probably didn't shop there; its customers were mostly working-class."

"Lévitan sounds Jewish."

She nodded. "Yes, the owner was Jewish. What does that have to do with anything?"

"It makes no sense—the Germans don't like the Jews, so why would they use a Jewish store to hold prisoners?"

"Why do you keep insisting that everything make sense? Nothing about this war or the Occupation makes any sense because the Nazis don't make sense. The point is, there's a rumor that Germans are holding French citizens prisoner at Lévitan."

What am I supposed to do about it? Mathilde kicked at the dirt with the heel of her boot, feeling the gravel grind under her sole. Everything was just so uncomfortable these days, so awful.

"Your mother's not Jewish, and she knows a lot about the fashion industry, right? The Nazis want their mistresses to dress well, and they keep all the nice things they have looted for themselves. So it would make sense that your mother would be useful to them. What if she's being held right here in Paris?"

"What if she is?"

"You could go see her maybe. Or get a message to her."

"Are you suggesting I should go to this store? That maybe she's . . . working there?"

Mathilde thought about visiting the Galeries Lafayette with her mami Yvette, the counters holding sparkling perfume bottles and the shelves full of expensive handbags. She tried to imagine her mother standing behind one of those counters like an eager sales-girl ready to serve.

"Obviously it's not operating as a normal department store," said Bridgette. "I'm sure it must be some sort of work camp. I just thought maybe if you went there, you might be able to bribe some-one so you could see her. Maybe talk to her."

Mathilde remained silent. The biscuit was dry and tasteless in her mouth, probably made from something other than wheat flour, which was scarce. She'd heard that people were making baked goods from potatoes, ground-up tulip bulbs, and even sawdust. She washed down the lump of biscuit with a swig of water, wishing it were wine.

What if she *was* able to track down her mother? She remem-bered those painful afternoon visits in Mami Yvette's parlor, forcing smiles over tea, her mother looking as if she wished to be anywhere in the world but sitting on that uncomfortable divan. She supposed she could thank Capucine for the fan. It wasn't much, but it would be a start.

"It was just an idea," said Bridgette, her voice returning to its characteristic timbre: sympathetic, gentle. "Maybe I shouldn't have mentioned it. It's just that I hate the thought of you never . . ." She trailed off.

"Never what?"

"Never seeing her again."

11

Capucine

I FOUND MORDECAI reading on an old eiderdown mattress, propped up by a hodgepodge of worn pillows.

"I thought you might need these for Purim," I said, handing him the candle stubs I had squirreled away.

"Thank you, Capu. That is very thoughtful. We don't actually light special candles for Purim, but Hélène can use these for Shabbat."

Hélène was an older Jewish woman whom the others referred to as "Bubbe"; she filled the role of wise woman in the way Mordecai served as an informal rabbi. Each Friday at sundown, she lit the candles, waving her hands over them and reciting a prayer.

"She will be very pleased."

"Mordecai, could I ask you something?" I said.

"Of course, Capu," Mordecai said, closing his book. "Ask away."

"Isedore said you think none of her relatives—that none of the

Jews—will ever return. Where are they sent? Is there some kind of Jewish homeland? Where are your people from originally?"

He smiled. "That is a matter of great debate. We Jews are to be found in virtually every country on this earth, and yet we have no Jewish state, no place where we will be safe from persecution and pogroms." There was no laughter in his eyes now. "You mentioned Purim. Do you know why we celebrate it?"

I shook my head. "Not really."

"It is in remembrance of Queen Esther, who saved the Jews in Persia. My people have faced many previous attempts at mass murder."

"Mass murder," I repeated. The term felt foreign, wrong. "You think the Nazis are killing the prisoners? I thought they just wanted to deport the Jews from France."

"That is what they said. But think about it, Capu. Suppose the Nazis had admitted their true intentions. Would the Parisians, even the anti-Semites, have countenanced their neighbors being dragged off to their deaths? Paris is a sophisticated city that prides itself on art and culture and humanity. She likes to think of herself as a shining beacon of tolerance. When the Jews and those such as yourself simply disappear, Parisians can tell themselves everything will be all right."

"So you're saying the people who were deported are being murdered?" I asked, unwilling to accept such an unthinkable idea.

Mordecai gave me a look of sadness that seemed to reach beyond the centuries, as though he were imbued with the knowledge of the ages.

"I am merely a man, Capu. I cannot see beyond my line of sight. But listening to what the Third Reich has been saying, what the Nazis espouse, the language they use—referring to Jews as filth and animals and vermin—I believe their goal is to dehumanize us, which makes it easier to kill us. I do not believe the Nazis wish to allow a single Jew within their power to survive. I believe their goal is extermination."

I remembered an illustration from an old children's book about nightmares in which a feral-looking demon was sitting on the chest of a boy lying in bed. Our existence felt like that, like a suffocating, terrifying weight from which we could not escape.

"And . . . if someone were deported who is not Jewish?" I asked. "Would they likewise be put to death?"

"As I said, I don't know more than you or any of the others about what is happening beyond these walls. But the Nazis also despise many non-Jews, as you know from personal experience. Those caught helping the Jews are treated with a special kind of harshness."

"My father is a communist," I heard myself say. "Ezra Goldman saw him being deported to Auschwitz. Have you heard of it?"

Mordecai nodded slowly. "I am sorry to say that I have, Capucine. I believe many of my family members are there as well. But never forget, the story of Purim is the story of the triumph of personal courage over abject cruelty."

"Is personal courage enough?"

"Ultimately, it is all we have."

EACH DAY WE were given "coffee"—actually some kind of chicory-based substitute—and a bit of bread at seven and were at work by eight. This morning it was still dark because the electricity was out, which was not unusual. For the women, the lack of electricity was an inconvenience since we had to make do sorting through the crates by the dim light from the windows. But for the men, the darkness posed a much greater hardship. With the freight elevators out of service, the wooden crates had to be hauled up and down the stairs on the men's backs.

Jobs at the prison camp were strictly divided by sex. Male prisoners emptied the trucks of furniture, mirrors, art, and packing crates while we women unpacked the wooden crates and cleaned and sorted the items into yet more crates. Each crate sported a label: dishes and kitchen utensils, lamps, clocks, clothes, school supplies. Lightbulbs and towels. Record players and musical instruments. Children's toys, bed linens, shaving kits. We emptied desk drawers of office supplies, half-finished letters, manuscripts, drawings, photographs, the bits and bobs of life that composed a family's history.

Most paper items were of no use to the Germans and thus were destined for the bonfire.

At two thirty in the afternoon, we broke for lunch, usually a weak cabbage broth with a few chunks of potato or carrot; at dinner we received vegetables or "ersatzbrot"—a "bread" made of potato starch and sawdust—and powdered eggs. Saccharin replaced sugar; margarine replaced butter. Occasionally we were given a bit of meat, which was cause for celebration.

Even though the meals were wretched, there was a certain irony in our being provided with food every day. In the outside world, we had spent several hours a day, day after day, standing in line, determining what we could buy with our ration coupons, or trading or pooling resources with neighbors. Now we spent those hours working for the enemy.

In our department store prison, even the guards spoke incessantly of food. They were hungry, too, though the German soldiers seemed better supplied than the French jailers. The Vichyste French police were working for and with the Germans but were not granted the same privileges. It almost made their situation pitiable. Almost.

Some of the inmates in Lévitan were quite wealthy. Their money and the social status of their Aryan wives were among the reasons they wound up in a Paris prison camp rather than being held interminably in Drancy or deported to the camps in Germany or Poland. The families of these lucky ones occasionally sent packages that might include canned vegetables and meat and even confiture.

The more generous among them shared their bounty with those of us without connections to the outside, and every now and then we were able to go "out" to dinner, which meant sitting at the ends of our beds, the food set out on the makeshift table placed between the cots. Once in a while, the guards would allow us to set our tables with fine china and crystal from the looted items.

Every day except Sunday—though there were the occasional deliveries on the Christian Sabbath—truck after truck rumbled down the alley, loaded with goods looted from Jewish businesses and homes. The trucks were owned and operated by Parisians; their sides emblazoned with names like Maison Bailly, or Bedel Garde—Meubles et Déménagements, safe storage and moving. Each was a stark reminder that the Nazis relied upon the cooperation and collaboration of our fellow French citizens to accomplish their crimes.

One day a truck pulled up with plunder from a Jewish-owned factory. When one of our men popped open the top of a crate with a crowbar, we saw it contained dozens of gas masks.

"You think the army wants these?" Tremblay, the young pockmarked guard asked Pettit.

Tremblay was the one who had set aside the photo of Charles and me. Unlike most of our captors, he occasionally sat and conversed with us or shared a cup of what passed for coffee. He once confided in me that he had been bullied in school for his lack of athleticism, and how proud his mother had been when he was accepted into the police force. His father died last year, and his meager salary was her sole support.

"The soldiers could use these on the battlefield."

Pettit narrowed her eyes. "Maybe. But I hear the Jews sabotaged a lot of the gas masks when they realized we were going to confiscate them."

Tremblay slipped one over his head. "Looks all right to me," he said, his voice muffled. When he pulled it off, his hair stuck straight up. "How can we tell?"

Pettit shrugged. "I'll ask Herr Direktor what he wants to do with them. For now keep these crates together and make a note of where they are. And comb your hair, *ach du liebe Zeit*. You look like a fool."

Tremblay ordered several of the prisoners to mark the crates *"masques à gaz"* and stacked them in one section of the warehouse.

"In German, idiots!" Pettit yelled.

The men took down the stacked crates, wrote *"Gasmasken"* on the sides, and restacked them.

We turned back to our tasks. Hour after hour, we piled lamps in the lamp crate, shoes in the shoe crate, kitchen supplies in the kitchen crate. Jewelry went to the jewelry pod to be polished and assayed; clocks, working or not, were sent to the repair shop run by Mordecai; artwork and fine furniture were set aside to be evaluated by Fräulein Sigrid Sommer, who would swoop in ostentatiously and unannounced.

And when we'd emptied one crate, we opened another and unpacked, sorted, and repacked its contents. Figurines, saucepans, lightbulbs, even wastepaper baskets. From sunup to long past sundown, the crates never stopped.

I startled when Léonie, a young woman from my pod, suddenly cried out, her wail echoing off the ceiling-high stacks of crates. She held several photographs in her shaking hands.

"What is it? What's wrong?" I asked as I joined the others gathered around her.

"The things in these crates belong to her aunt and uncle," said Colette, shaking her head. "She thought they were safe."

"There's even a photograph of Léonie among their possessions. See here?" said Victorine, another woman from our pod.

"They've been arrested!" Léonie cried, her hands held out in front of her as if to ward off the blow. "No, no, no . . ."

Isolated as we were in our department store prison, it was easy to feel that time had stopped in the world outside, as if, once freed, we would resume our lives exactly where they had left off when we were arrested. We would be back in the arms of our loved ones, sharing meals and playing their pianos. When someone recognized the confiscated property of a friend or family member, the harsh reality of our situation broke through.

Léonie sank to the floor in a heap. Victorine crouched down to hug her.

Pettit approached, demanding, "What's going on?"

Victorine tried to explain but Pettit yanked her roughly by the arm and kicked Léonie in the thigh. "Get up, the both of you, and get back to work. Be happy you're not the ones being deported."

"I'll take over for her," I said. "Let her rest for a moment."

"You've got your own work to do, 123. There's no room for malingerers here," said Pettit, repeating Herr Direktor Kohn's favorite phrase. "You want me to deport your entire pod?"

"She's no malingerer," I said, willing Pettit to understand, to remember our shared humanity. Pettit was volatile and capricious, but she was not stupid. "She's had a terrible shock. Imagine opening one of these crates and finding your family's things."

"I don't need to imagine any such thing," said Pettit with a small smile. "*I* am not a Jew. Now get back to work!"

After she left, I noticed Victorine slipping a few of the photos into the pocket of her smock. I edged over to the crate and did the same. The other women followed suit, and soon we had saved the entire batch from the bonfire.

It wasn't much, but it was something.

12

Mathilde

O F COURSE I'LL see my mother again," Mathilde snapped at Bridgette. "If she and Bruno are prisoners of war, then they'll be released as soon as the war is over. And everything will go back to the way it used to be."

Bridgette did not respond. A few brave birds in the trees called to one another, signaling the return of the spring. A far-off car horn honked, and someone yelled. A popping in the street might have been a car backfiring or might have been a gunshot—there were more and more shots ringing out on the streets of Paris.

"Let's get out of here," said Mathilde, and packed up their things.

She loved the cemetery, but now it reminded her of Antoinette's altar, too full of death and sorrow. As they walked toward the cemetery gates, Mathilde studied the many sculptures that dotted the landscape and couldn't help but think of the sculpted torso on the stair landing in her grandparents' home.

"Do you want to go to the Jardin du Luxembourg? Or maybe catch a movie?"

"I can't," Bridgette said. "I told you, I have to ride out to the countryside. I don't have time for the movies—not that I have the price of a ticket, anyway."

"I could pay for us both. I don't mind."

They passed through the verdigris gate, retrieved their bicycles, and faced each other, gloved hands gripping the cold handlebars.

Bridgette shook her head and sighed. "Au revoir, Mathilde. Enjoy the movies."

"I . . . all right. Au revoir. Please promise to be careful, Bridgette."

"Don't worry," said Bridgette, throwing her leg over her bike. "They won't bother a girl on a bicycle."

Mathilde stood for a long moment, watching Bridgette pedal down the boulevard in her school uniform, looking like a schoolgirl with too many books in her overfull panniers.

Mathilde's stomach clenched uncomfortably, and the corner of her mouth twitched.

Everyone, it seemed, wanted more from her—most of all, perhaps, she herself.

She mounted her bike and put her feet to the pedals and, without quite meaning to, found herself in front of the lemon yellow façade of La Maison Benoît.

ANTOINETTE STOPPED SWEEPING and leaned on her broom.

"*Bonjour*, Mathilde!" she called.

"*Bonjour*, madame," said Mathilde, bringing her bicycle to a sudden stop.

Aha! I knew the child would come back, Antoinette thought, then chided herself.

Mathilde was not a child, but a young woman. Still, she acted younger than her years, a sure sign of a pampered life, a sheltered upbringing. It was a luxury few had these days. War made most people old before their time but suspended a fortunate few in eternal childhood.

Even knowing this, Antoinette found herself growing impatient. Bruno and Capucine had been arrested, their fates uncertain, yet Mathilde appeared curiously unmoved. Antoinette had made inquiries into their whereabouts but had been rebuffed. Had Mathilde asked her influential grandfather Duplantier to inquire? Did she not care, or had she become immune to tragedy?

But perhaps Antoinette was reading too much into Mathilde's silence. These days it was not safe to display any emotion except enthusiasm for the Third Reich.

"I've just come from the cemetery," Mathilde said, her nose and cheeks rosy from the exercise and the cold. "Today would have been my father's fortieth birthday. I laid flowers on his tomb."

Antoinette nodded. "That was very thoughtful of you. It is good to remember the dead."

"Did you know him? My father?"

"I did, yes, though not well. He and your mother had not been together long before—"

She stopped herself, remembering the day Capucine confided that she was pregnant, though there had as yet been no talk of marriage. Bruno, communist rebel that he was, was not nearly as upset by the idea of his daughter's unwed pregnancy as he was at the thought of her marrying into the bourgeoisie.

She continued. "—before they married and went to live with your grandparents. They moved back here when you were still a baby, and not long after that, your poor father had his accident."

Mathilde nodded. "I wish I could remember him."

"Roger was a very kind young man and quite a talented artist. He adored you and your mother." And he fought with his parents over his future, rejecting his father's demands that Roger join him at the factory.

"I've decided something," Mathilde said.

"Have you, now?"

"I would like to see the shop," Mathilde announced, her chin raised, as though this were an act of pure defiance.

Good for you, Antoinette thought, reaching for the heavy key ring at her waist. Taking it off the chain, she found the right key, a huge old-fashioned brass one, and fit it into the big lock on the front door.

MATHILDE HESITATED, UNSURE whether to attribute the pounding of her heart and the sweating of her palms to fear or anticipation.

"After you," said Antoinette.

Mathilde nodded and pushed the door open. A cheery bell rang overhead.

"I wasn't sure if I should clean things up," said Antoinette. "After they were arrested, I mean. Your grandfather was always so particular about where things went and how to store them, especially the feathers. I guess I was hoping he would be back and take care of it himself."

Feathers of every color and pattern were strewn around the

wood plank floor; seed pearls and beads had scattered everywhere, as though dozens of necklaces had been ripped apart; bits of carved ivory and wooden slats used for the structure of the fans had been flung here and there. One end of the glass counter had been shattered, and half of the slim, neatly labeled drawers lining the rear wall stood open, revealing their contents: fans made of feathers in every hue imaginable, some sleek, others fluffy.

As Mathilde walked slowly around the shop, feathers wafted up and scurried about her feet with each step, as though vying for her attention.

"They made the fans here, then?"

Even as Mathilde asked, a memory flooded back, of her grandfather hunched over his workbench carefully gluing and sewing feathers onto stays and weaving in bits of lace and fringe, while with delicate flicks of her wrist her mother painted the paper and silk fans. Mathilde remembered watching as they applied gold gilt, fragments of the tissue-thin metal flying as they brushed it on the fans before burnishing the gilt with a stone to a brilliant mellow sheen that would catch the light with each wave of the fan.

"Yes, they did all the fine finishes here," said Antoinette. "They used to have a small workshop across town for the basic carpentry and production, but they had to close that."

"Because of the war?"

"Before then, actually. That was in, oh, the thirties, I think. Yes, because of the Depression. Business had fallen off, even from the haute couture houses. So your grandfather moved everything here, which is why it's so crowded."

The wall to the left was occupied by a massive arched mirror, and straight ahead Mathilde saw a framed version of the printed language of fans that she had found in the box containing her birth-day fan.

> *Open wide . . . Wait for me.*
> *Carrying in the right hand in front of face . . .*
>   *Follow me.*
> *Presented shut . . . Do you love me?*

Her mother had sent her birthday fan in a slim box, presented shut. Had she meant anything by that? Was she asking Mathilde if she loved her? Probably Mathilde was reading something into nothing . . . but suppose her mother really *was* asking? How would she respond?

"Last time I was here you said these things belonged to me now," said Mathilde as Antoinette started sweeping up the broken glass from the display counter. "But when my mother and grandfa-ther are released, surely they'll want to set things up again, won't they? It is their livelihood, after all."

The old woman gave her a searching look.

"Yes, of course," Antoinette said after a moment. "I'm sure you're right. They might well come back and reestablish the business."

"But you don't think so," said Mathilde. "Why is it that no one thinks the deported people will return?"

Another long hesitation. "We are at war, child. We are occupied by our enemy. Many of us are old enough to have suffered through the last war and remember well how hard it was not to know what was happening, much less why. I still do not understand why my son Richard was killed, what it was all for." She shook her head. "And now with the Third Reich—things are different. The Nazis have invaded our country, our city, and made themselves at home. It's almost as though they are deporting people to make more room for themselves."

"But that doesn't mean those people won't come back. I mean, they could return any day now, couldn't they? A friend of mine said my mother and grandfather might be in a work camp right here in Paris. Have you heard of such a thing?"

"A work camp in Paris?" Antoinette shook her head. "Where?"

"At the Lévitan department store. Do you know it?"

"Yes, I bought my dinette set there years ago, as a matter of fact. You think there might be prisoners in the store?"

"A friend said she'd heard some people were being interned there. They're doing something with furniture and objets d'art, and since my mother and grandfather worked in fashion, perhaps they are there?" Mathilde heard the hope in her own voice.

"My sister-in-law lives on that very block, but she's never mentioned anything about the Lévitan being used as a work camp. I know the store was closed early in the Occupation."

"It sounds far-fetched, doesn't it?" Mathilde said, pulling open one long, slim drawer after another, peeking within. The contents had been riffled through, but apparently the fans were deemed not worth stealing. "I mean, what would the Germans want with a department store? Surely they have more important things to worry about."

"The Nazis are greedy," Antoinette said. "They ransacked one of the apartments in this building after the family fled. Stripped it bare."

Mathilde noticed a single fan box on a wooden chair near the door. It looked out of place, sitting there all by itself. She opened the lid. The fan nestled within looked very old. "What is this one doing here?"

"According to Bruno, when his wife, Suzette, left, she forgot her favorite fan. He found it right there on that chair. In all these years, Bruno and Capucine never moved it."

"Bruno's wife? You mean my other grandmother?"

Antoinette nodded.

"I never met her, either."

"I don't suppose you would have. Suzette left when your mother was only five or six. She sent the occasional postcard, but I don't think your mother ever saw her again."

"Why did she leave?"

Antoinette let out a long sigh. "That's an excellent question. It was during the Great War. Such a terrible time. Bruno's brother was killed in battle, and it changed your grandfather, made him more political, more outspoken in his beliefs. And your mother was not the easiest child. Bruno doted on her, but Suzette struggled. She missed her family and was not happy as a wife and a mother. She was a very sophisticated woman, not beautiful but extremely fashionable. She liked to do what she wanted, to have her needs seen to, and she wasn't happy that Bruno paid so much attention to his political causes—and to Capucine."

"I've never heard of a mother jealous of her own daughter."

"It happens."

"What were the soldiers looking for that they made such a mess?" Mathilde asked, nodding at the papers that were scattered everywhere.

"Money maybe? Anything of value," Antoinette suggested.

"Maybe evidence to use against Bruno and Capucine at their trial."

"What trial?"

"If they've been arrested, there will be a trial, won't there? I was thinking if I could get access to my inheritance, maybe I could hire a lawyer."

The old woman shook her head. "There will be no trial, and no evidence of guilt is required. And even if it were, Bruno would never deny being a communist, and he would tell the Nazis exactly what he thought of them and their French puppets, *Maréchal* Pétain and the Vichy. Bruno is who he is without apology."

"Oh. Then . . . why did the soldiers tear the place up? What were they looking for?"

"Like I said, anything valuable. They took a few of the most precious fans, no doubt to send to their wives and girlfriends in Germany, but the only other thing Bruno had of value was the feathers."

"Feathers are valuable?"

"The rare ones are. Or at least they were before the war. I doubt you could get much for them now. They were precious to Bruno, though," she said with a long sigh. "The man adored his feathers."

"Oh." Mathilde wandered around the shop as if trying to dredge up memories of the brief time she had lived here. In a small voice, she finally put words to what had been eating at her, and asked, "Antoinette, did my mother send me to Neuilly because she was jealous of me?"

"No, *chérie*," Antoinette said. "Your asthma attacks were getting worse, and the physician thought perhaps the feathers were part of the problem. Capucine had to be convinced to let you go live with your grandparents. Believe me when I say, it broke her heart. Oh, she put on a good face but . . . I don't think she ever forgave herself."

"She sent me away because of these stupid feathers?"

"You were struggling to breathe, Mathilde. That was no small thing," Antoinette said dryly. "But it wasn't just that. I thought you would be better off with your father's parents, and I told her so. And

I thought . . ." Antoinette blew out a long breath and shrugged. "Capucine was such a free spirit; she was so young and had such potential. . . . I thought she would be better off if she did not have to worry about you day to day. But I was wrong."

AFTER CAPUCINE'S MOTHER returned to her family in Italy, Antoinette had stepped in to help Bruno care for the young Capucine, as did other neighbors and friends. His few relatives were distant, not only by blood but by miles. Most lived in the south of France, near Marseille. Bruno gave his daughter an unconventional education, filling her head with ideas of freedom and beauty, partly in response to the grim reality of life during and after the Great War. He fostered her creativity and open-mindedness but had very little idea how to raise a daughter.

Antoinette remembered finding Capucine sitting on the steps one day, crying. She had stopped eating and was growing thin and wan. When Antoinette finally persuaded her to talk over a cup of rich cocoa, she discovered Capucine thought she was sick, perhaps dying. The poor child had never been told to expect a monthly flow and thought the blood coming from her "bottom" was related to some kind of deep, shameful disease that surely must be a punishment for something.

Bruno adored his little Capucine, but he was flawed, as were they all.

Although Bruno taught his daughter the craft of fan making, Capucine's heart was not in it. She preferred drawing and painting, and found the painstaking detail required to make a fan frustrating. More than once they loudly debated the difference between "art" and "craft," with Capu insisting that creating something with the goal of selling it inevitably eroded its pure artistry, and Bruno arguing that in the capitalist society in which they lived, art must necessarily bend to the market.

When Capu had found her niche in the ateliers of Montparnasse and the jazz clubs of Montmartre, there was no holding her back.

Antoinette wondered whether the same could be said for Mathilde. Once she found her path, would she be strong enough to follow it? She watched Mathilde poke around the shop, her hands clasped behind her back as they had been while she was looking around Antoinette's apartment, as though she was afraid to touch anything.

"Why don't I leave you to look around while I finish sweeping outside?" Antoinette suggested. "Give you a chance to become re-acquainted with your old home."

"*Merci*, Antoinette."

"*Je t'en prie.*"

MATHILDE RAN HER hands along the counter, then wandered through the door at the rear of the shop, which opened into a small hallway and the suite of rooms where the family had lived: a tiny galley kitchen and parlor, two small bedrooms, and a bathroom. Mathilde's bedroom in Neuilly was nearly as large as the entire apartment, save for the shop in front.

Here, too, everything had been searched, the cabinets and drawers ransacked and their contents dumped onto the floor.

Mathilde stepped carefully, trying not to tread on anything of value as she made her way across her mother's room to the old armoire, where she used to sleep. The doors were hanging open, and as she gazed at the space, she was surprised to find it was so much smaller than she remembered. No wonder her grandparents had been horrified.

Several garments still hung from the bar: old-fashioned flapper dresses covered in multifaceted beads and sparkly sequins. Mathilde held one dress up to her nose and inhaled, closing her eyes and letting her body, her heart, remember what her mind could not.

Appalled by the sensation of tears burning the backs of her eyes, she turned to a small vanity and picked up a tiny vial of the perfume her mother used to wear, Habanita de Molinard. She sprayed some on her wrist and breathed in deeply. This was no subtle perfume of lilac and bergamot, like her mami Yvette wore.

Oh, no, it was bold, loud, exciting. She picked up notes of tobacco, overlaid with the slightest aroma of talcum powder and roses. According to the label, it had been inspired by the "Beautiful Cigar Girls of Havana," and it put Mathilde in mind of smoky rooms, of the kind of music that reached into your chest and grabbed your soul . . . the kind of music she was not allowed to listen to. *Entartete Musik.*

The music of temptation. Of seduction.

Mathilde shook herself and stood up straighter. She was being ridiculous. It was just perfume. It meant nothing; every woman in Paris had a bottle or two squirreled away somewhere—or at least she had before the wartime shortages.

Her eye was caught by a bundle of letters on the floor near the bed, tied together with a violet satin ribbon. The return address on the top letter indicated it had come from North Carolina, in the United States, from a man named Charles Moore.

She sank onto the edge of the small bed, which, ironically

enough, was still neatly made with a patchwork quilt in bright colors: deep purple, royal blue, vivid orange.

She carefully untied the ribbon and looked through the envelopes, all of which were from the same Charles Moore. She opened the letter on top and found to her surprise that it was written in French. The spelling was slightly flawed, a few of the tenses and accents were off, but by and large, it was fluent. The letter had been written in a hand quite unlike the carefully measured script taught in her lycée—this one was bold, with occasional loopy flourishes and even little cartoons. She read:

> *My dearest one, I know full well that many years have gone by, that Zelli's and Bricktop's have long since closed, that you are no longer the same young woman I saw that first time, standing at the bar wearing your feathers, a beautiful and oh-so-exquisite bird. Still, I imagine you walking the streets of Paris, strolling along the Seine, perusing the old books at the stalls on the quay near the bridge to Notre Dame. Not thinking of your poor American admirer in the least, except perhaps for a faint memory of my devotion—and my American accent! Whereas I miss you more than I could ever have expected, and I had braced myself to miss you a good deal. So these letters are really just cries of pain, a cri de coeur, sent into the void.*
>
> *I suppose you are accustomed to people saying such things to you. Capucine, la femme à l'éventail. The Fan Girl. As rare and unique as the feathers in your hair.*
>
> *I will end this letter with my usual plea: Come, my dearest, and join me in North Carolina, and I will play*

my mother's piano for you. And then I will cook what
you call my "exotic" American cuisine: collards and
yellow yams, beans and corn bread. And perhaps when
this is all over, we will return together to Paris to
reclaim our Ville Lumière, our City of Light.

Mathilde's heart thudded. She turned the envelope over in her hands, looking for clues. Who was this man, this Charles Moore?

The letter was dated February of 1938, before the war began. He was asking Capucine to join him in America. But she had stayed in Paris, where she eventually had been arrested. Why would she have remained rather than join him in safety? Perhaps Capucine was not as fond of Charles as he obviously was of her. But if that was the case, why would she have kept the letters bound together like this, tied with a beautiful ribbon? They seemed . . . special.

The sound of a slamming gate startled her out of her reverie. The window in her mother's room overlooked the courtyard, and she watched as a tired-looking gray-haired couple walked arm in arm, steadying each other as they slowly negotiated the stairs to their apartment, helping each other up the steps. Old-couple love.

What would it be like to have someone care for you like that—or the way the man in the letter, this Charles Moore, seemed to cherish her mother? She tried to imagine Victor penning her such a fervent, passionate note. *Non. Ce n'est pas possible.* Impossible.

Mathilde returned the letter to its envelope, and after a moment of indecision, she took the entire bundle with her. *For safekeeping,* she told herself.

Back in the shop she began collecting feathers from the floor and counter and shelves, wondering which were the most valuable, assuming they were the prettiest ones: the ostrich plumes and iridescent peacock feathers; the mottled, striped, and spotted ones she could not name.

For a moment Mathilde considered taking the fan that the grandmother she had never known had left on the chair by the door when she abandoned her husband and child, but decided to leave it where it was. If Bruno and Capucine did come back—*when* they came back—they should find at least one thing just as it had been.

Mathilde found the old concierge on the sidewalk, leaning on her broom and chatting with a little girl who was showing off her toy pinwheel. The little orange tabby, Croissant, sat on the windowsill of Antoinette's apartment, her amber lamplike eyes staring, unblinking. When Mathilde tapped on the windowpane, the cat gazed at her and meowed so loudly she could hear it through the glass.

"Did you find anything of interest?" Antoinette asked Mathilde as the little girl ran home, her pinwheel spinning in the breeze.

"I found . . . a few things," said Mathilde. "It's strange, like walking into a place I've never been, yet is very familiar. I remember it, but as if it were a dream. The way I remember you."

The moment Mathilde said the words, she realized that they might be construed as insulting or dismissive. But the old woman just smiled.

"You were happy here, Mathilde, and very much loved."

"They sent me away."

"Your mother wanted the best for you. She made the best choice she could at the time."

Mathilde felt herself twisting her lips in a gesture Mami Yvette had tried very hard to rid her of. "I was wondering—"

A middle-aged man approached, removing his hat and bowing. "Pardon me, Madame Laurent, mademoiselle," he said. "I'm sorry to interrupt but I noticed you were in Monsieur Benoît's shop. Any news?"

"Monsieur Dervin, this is Capucine's daughter, Mathilde."

"It's an honor to meet you," said Monsieur Dervin, his lined face breaking out in a large smile, which quickly faded. He leaned toward her, eagerly. "We've been so worried about your mother and grandfather—have you any word of them?"

Mathilde shook her head.

"Nothing yet," said Antoinette.

"If you find them, please let them know their neighbors are thinking of them," he said. "Your mother and grandfather have many loyal friends, mademoiselle. Please, let us know if there's anything we can do."

"I— Thank you, monsieur," said Mathilde.

Monsieur Dervin shuffled off, shaking his head.

"Your mother and grandfather were well-known in the neighborhood, and generally very well-liked," Antoinette told Mathilde. "Bruno could be a bit caustic at times, but he gained the eternal gratitude of the neighbors when he sacrificed his pigeons so they could have a little protein."

"His carrier pigeons?"

Mathilde remembered Bruno kept a coop on the roof; she used to help him gather the fallen feathers to use in his fans. Whenever the birds flew, he would point and smile: *Look, Mathilde! Just imagine what it would be to soar over the rooftops of Paris!*

"He loved them like pets. It pained him terribly to sacrifice them. I had never before seen him cry." Antoinette shook her head, as though ridding herself of the memory. She handed Mathilde a slip of paper. "I've written down the address of my *belle-soeur,* my sister-in-law who lives on rue du Faubourg Saint-Martin, not far from the Lévitan department store. You could ask her if she's noticed anything unusual going on there."

"Do you think I should?"

Antoinette smiled. "Only you know the answer to that, *ma fille.*"

It took only a few minutes for Mathilde to bicycle to the tenth arrondissement. Nothing looked out of the ordinary, and there were still displays in the department store's large windows: a child's bedroom set, a man's office desk. The store was closed, most of its windows shuttered, but that wasn't surprising these days. Few businesses had managed to stay open during the Occupation, and none that was owned by a Jew.

Near the front door was a sign with the store's slogan: *"Un meuble signé Lévitan . . . est garanti pour longtemps."* Furniture from Lévitan is guaranteed for a long time. And the tiled façade carried the inscription *"Aux classes laborieuses."* The store specialized in affordable, sturdy furniture for the working class.

She crossed to the far side of the street so she could peer up to the upper windows. Nothing seemed amiss. The building simply looked abandoned. The nearby apartment buildings appeared forlorn as well, with their shutters closed and no signs of life.

Where had Bridgette gotten the notion that this old department store was a prison camp, of all things? Her friend must have been listening to tall tales, that was all.

Mathilde considered looking up Antoinette's sister-in-law, but it felt so awkward. How would she even begin the conversation?

Bonjour, *madame! I wonder if, by chance, you've seen any prisoners working in the big department store down the street? You see, my mother was arrested, along with her communist father, so I wondered whether they might now be living in Monsieur Lévitan's store.*

A woman walking in the opposite direction down the sidewalk followed Mathilde's gaze, craning her neck as if to see what Mathilde was searching for.

Mathilde's cheeks flamed. She decided to leave the address of Antoinette's *belle-soeur* in the box in her basket, nestled amid the feathers, and ignore it. At least for now.

She mounted her bike and slowly, thoughtfully pedaled across Paris, to Mami and Papi's big square house in Neuilly.

13

Capucine

*O*NE TWENTY-THREE!" PETTIT barked.

I had been unpacking a crate of old worn shoes with holes in their soles. Dutifully I located each shoe's mate and tied the pairs together with twine. Perhaps the pod of talented cobblers at Lévitan could work their magic.

"You have an appointment," Pettit continued.

Abrielle.

"How long will I be gone?" I asked. "Should I bring my things?"

Pettit gave a crooked, enigmatic smile. "Just a coat."

The decent wool coat I arrived with had long since been confiscated, no doubt sent to a more deserving German. We prisoners shared a few warm coverings we had pieced together from the cheapest materials—black like the work smocks, as if we were all in mourning. Which, I supposed, we were.

My eyes locked with Ezra's as Pettit led me out into the freezing wind in the alley and ordered me into the back of a small canvas-covered truck. A young, bored-looking police officer climbed in next to me and reminded me to stay quiet, but allowed me to peek out a slit in the canvas.

I breathed deeply, vowing never again to take fresh air for granted.

Paris was gray and sad-looking, patches of dirt and *pétanque* courts left untended, a few anemic winter vegetables growing in flowerpots. People on the street scurried along, arms folded and heads bowed, or waited stoically in line outside shops. I noticed much more graffiti than before, large "V"s for "Victory" painted willy-nilly on walls and bridges. The "V"s had originally been signs of the Résistance, but according to Bruno, the Nazis were determined to appropriate the symbol, so now it was impossible to know whose victory the letters were calling for.

Even in my former life, March had always struck me as a cruel month, overly long, with the tentative signs of spring and the promise of new life dashed by sudden turns in the weather. The temperature rarely rose above a frigid twelve degrees, and Charles and I and our friends used to shiver at the sidewalk cafés, even with the outdoor heaters. But we sat there anyway, smoking and drinking espresso, chatting and laughing, watching the passersby.

Now the tiny café tables were mostly occupied by uniformed *Wehrmacht* soldiers, seemingly without a care in the world.

The truck bounced over a bump in the road, nearly tossing me off the wooden bench. I righted myself and realized my fingers were turning numb. I shoved them under my armpits for warmth, wondering where we were going and how much longer it would take to get there. I peeked out once again and saw we were passing the Palais Garnier, better known as the Opera House.

Abrielle used to like to claim a connection to the Palais Garnier, though in reality she had none. In our Montmartre days, she was, like me, an occasional artist's model who enjoyed the nightlife. Abrielle's petite stature and breathy manner seemed to inspire in men the desire to take care of her. In contrast, I was of average height but broad shouldered and strong-looking, more fashionable than beautiful, and I seemed to inspire in artists the desire to paint me, in poets the desire to write about me, and in others the desire to sleep with me.

Abrielle never could understand why I was more in demand as a model than she. Charles said that Abrielle had a hard time understanding the idea of substance: that artists strove to capture on canvas not just surface prettiness, but what resonated in their heart. It was like jazz, he continued: the search not for a sweet, straightforward melody, but for something deeper, for something truer. The artist's eternal search for magic.

Charles. How could I have denied him?

Finally, with a shriek of the brakes, the truck lurched to a stop in front of a traditional six-story Parisian apartment building. The façade was creamy white stone, punctuated by terraces with black wrought iron balconies. Here, everything looked well tended, and several of the flower boxes had actual flowers in them.

Pettit threw open the truck's canvas flap and jerked her head. "Out."

The young soldier and I obeyed.

"Move."

I followed her through the doorway and into a dark lobby. There was a desk with a phone, but no attendant.

Pettit flicked the light switch. Nothing.

"*Scheisse*," she swore, slapping the elevator button repeatedly, though there was no response.

"The electricity must be out," I said, looking up at the many stories of steps in the stairwell.

"No kidding," she said.

"Shall we climb?"

"It's on the top floor."

After a moment, Pettit let out a sigh, and we started up. By the third flight, she was breathing hard.

"Are you okay?" I asked.

She frowned. "You go on up. I'll watch from here. Have her call the lobby when you're done. And remember, if you try anything funny, much less try to escape, your entire pod will be immediately deported. And the girl, too, the one who follows you around like a puppy. I'll throw her in for good measure."

"What do you have against Isedore?"

"Reminds me of my kid sister."

"And that's a bad thing?"

"Wouldn't mind putting *her* on a slow train to Auschwitz or Dachau."

When I didn't react, she added: "That's where they're being sent, you know. To the camps. Very special camps."

She said this last with a sick smile that reminded me of the Drancy guards and their references to lighting special candles for the Jews.

I knew that many of the German troops were ordinary men who had been drafted into a war they had no control over, as had soldiers through the millennia. But the ones who called themselves Nazis were a special breed: They held mystical beliefs based on blood purity that seemed a bewildering puzzle of riddles and innuendo and fear. The more I got to know some of them, like Pettit, the less I understood them.

"Go on, then," Pettit said, giving me a hearty shove.

I continued up the stairs, relishing the freshness of being anywhere except the Lévitan, but wary of what awaited me in the penthouse. Round and round the flights of stairs I went, taking my time, pausing on each landing, looking down the elevator well at Pettit, who stood by the railing, watching me. The elevator hung halfway down the center of the stairwell, and I wondered if someone might be trapped within it. Given how frequently we lost power, I doubted I would willingly step into an elevator even if I lived in Abrielle's apartment, six floors up.

I arrived at last at the penthouse, whose large paneled door was painted in a shiny black lacquer. I peered down the center of the stairwell, gave Pettit a thumbs-up, and announced my presence by banging the brass door knocker. Within seconds, the door was flung open.

"*Capu!* Oh! Thank you for coming!" Abrielle gushed as though I were a highly anticipated date.

"Did I have a choice?" I said, then bit my tongue when I caught a glimpse of Herr Pflüger over her shoulder. "I . . . I mean, I'm here to help. What can I do for you?"

"You always had such magnificent taste in clothes and, well, everything, really, and this apartment is *desperately* in need of a designer's touch. When I saw you at Lévitan, I remembered how talented you are, and I said to Otto—didn't I, *Bärchen?*—that I had known you before the war and trusted your taste, so dear Otto asked Herr Direktor Kohn about you, and your papers confirmed you were trained in interior design. Isn't that fortuitous! Please, do come in."

The apartment was large and sunny, painted an aged creamy yellow. Huge windows framed a marvelous view of the Eiffel Tower and the rooftops of Paris. But the furnishings were atrocious, a hodgepodge of old and new—not in a devil-may-care way, but like a random collection of hand-me-downs.

Herr Otto Pflüger was jovial enough when he looked at Abrielle, but there was a harsh gleam in his eye when his gaze turned to me.

"You are trained in design?" He looked skeptical.

"I am, yes," I lied.

"Do you know Fräulein Sommer? She is so gifted. She trained in Vienna, you know. Unfortunately, her expertise is in high demand."

"I imagine it is. We've not met officially, no."

I had seen Fräulein Sommer many times when she came to peruse our fine art and furniture; she strode about self-importantly, with a clipboard in one hand and a pencil tucked behind her ear. But we had never been introduced, of course.

"But I know her impressive reputation. Still, I'm sure I can do a good job for you, Herr Pflüger. I was not so fortunate as to study in Vienna, but here in Paris, I worked with the likes of Émile-Jacques Ruhlmann."

Both of them stared at me blankly.

"The father of Art Deco . . . ?" I said.

"*Ach*, of course," Pflüger said. "Ruhlmann is very famous, no?"

"The father of Art Deco!" Abrielle chimed in. "Marvelous."

"Do you like Art Deco?" I asked. "We have all sorts of things coming into the Lévitan every day. I've seen some inlaid ebony furniture and some exquisite pieces of Limoges geometric designed dishware in a stylized morning glory motif. I could set some aside for you if you'd like."

Again, I was met with blank expressions.

This should be easy enough, I thought. Neither of them appeared to know the first thing about furniture or design.

As we spoke, I couldn't shake the sensation that we were taking part in a bizarre sort of experimental theater, the likes of which Fou-Fou or Toklas might have foisted upon me during *les années folles.* But this job might be my ticket out. If Abrielle was pleased with my work, she might recommend me to other women who had attached themselves to Nazi officials and enjoyed their privileges. I could envision fine dinner parties taking place here, officers walking through that door with their French mistresses on their arms, gulping champagne, reveling in all that Paris had to offer, asking who was responsible for the beautiful interior design.

And who was I to judge the women? Might I have done the same thing if it meant saving myself and my father—or even my daughter?

"Great windows," I murmured as I went over to the far wall. "With the northern light here, this would be the perfect wall to form your highlight. There's a concept of emphasis in design that states that a central piece of furniture or art should grab the attention upon one's walking into a room. Why don't we begin by creating a focal point? And only once that is completed will we add other pieces. Such an approach will increase the sense of balance and harmony in this beautiful apartment, don't you agree?"

I was blowing smoke, of course. In addition to teaching me the craft of fan making, Bruno had schooled me on how to sell to clients. *It is all about having a list of key words at the ready, Capu. "Balance, harmony, glamour." People strive for such things in their lives, and they like to reflect them in their choice of style. They will also pay much more for them.*

"Oh! Yes, indeed. Isn't that something?" Abrielle said in her breathy, high-pitched voice, and actually clapped her hands together like a little girl waiting for her turn on a carousel. "She really is something, isn't she, Otto?"

"Where did you train?" he asked.

"In addition to working with Ruhlmann, I also trained with Louise Boulanger." I was betting they wouldn't know Boulanger was a dress designer, not a decorator. "And of course, I worked with my father in his shop making fans for haute couture designers and customers. As I am sure you know, *mein Herr*, there is considerable overlap between the fashion world and interior design and decoration. And now that I work with *Möbel Aktion*, I am in the perfect position to handpick the best pieces for you."

He raised an eyebrow. "You will compete with Fräulein Sommer, then?"

"I would not dream of such a thing," I said, careful not to overstep. "But there are so many beautiful things coming and going, I'm sure we can find enough to please everyone."

"Well," he said, eyeing me but seeming mollified, "I shall leave you to your decorating. Abrielle, be ready with dinner at eight."

"*Ja, ja, mein liebe Herr,*" said Abrielle, smiling at him coquettishly.

The moment the door closed behind him, Abrielle seemed to relax, and her fluttering and breathiness lessened. "I'm so glad you're here, Capu! This is gonna be fun!"

I gave her a thin smile.

"Let me give you a tour of the place. Down here are the bedrooms. . . ."

Abrielle led the way down a narrow hall, and we stuck our heads in a large room being used as the master bedroom, a smaller room that was clearly Pflüger's study, and a guest room. In the cramped kitchen, something had been baking in the oven, filling the air with a yeasty aroma that made my stomach growl and my mouth water. A dour-looking woman was hunched over a wooden table, cleaning up bits of dough.

"Zelia, this is Capu, my decorator!" Abrielle gushed.

The middle-aged woman nodded in my direction and cast us both a surly look. She wiped her hands on a towel and reached behind her to untie her apron.

"I must do the shopping, madame," Zelia said.

"Of course." Abrielle went to get the ration coupons while Zelia glared at me as if I were a collaborator.

I didn't know whether to be embarrassed or offended. Me, a prisoner of the Nazis, in my worn clothes and work smock adorned with a red triangle—a collaborator? *You're working for them, too*, I felt like saying. But I bit my tongue. The war had made us all sour, ugly, suspicious of one another.

"Here they are!" Abrielle sang out, and handed the ration coupons to Zelia. "Now, we went over the menu this morning, so you know what to buy and what to do if you can't find what we'd planned for. Run along, and don't dawdle! Herr Pflüger expects his dinner promptly at eight."

"*Oui*, madame," Zelia said, heading out.

Abrielle shut the apartment door behind her and leaned on it for a moment, closing her eyes and letting out a long sigh. "Oh, *merci à dieu*, she's gone. I swear, that woman hates me. We're lucky she hasn't poisoned our food."

I had to smile. "Maybe she will yet."

She made a breezy wave, and I caught a whiff of her perfume. "Otto says he's going to bring a girl from Germany so we can be more comfortable in our own home."

"It's tough to occupy a country, isn't it?" I asked.

She tilted her head as though wondering if I was kidding. "Anyway, now we can have a good talk," she said, moving over to an uncomfortable-looking sofa covered in what appeared to be some kind of animal fur dyed a grayish purple, as if with wine must. "Come sit, and tell me true: How are you doing?"

I stared at her, incredulous. How did she *think* I was doing? But I bit back those words and instead said, "What am I doing here, Abrielle? What is it you want from me?"

"Well, I think you have to admit I've done well for myself," she said, gesturing at the view out the living room windows. "Can you imagine *me* living in a penthouse like this one?"

"Congratulations."

She smiled, nervous. "The last time I saw you at La Maison Benoît, I couldn't afford even your least expensive fan!"

"Things have certainly taken a turn for the better for you," I said in a neutral tone.

Not long before Bruno and I were arrested, Abrielle had come into La Maison Benoît to inquire about a fan. I told her that our handmade fans were far too expensive for her, which I had not meant as an insult—they would have been out of my reach as well, had I not been creating them. I remembered how her face had fallen and the way her gaze had landed upon the pamphlets my father had written, calling on his fellow Parisians to defy the Nazis and embrace communist ideals. She picked one up, read a little, then tossed it aside with a sneer.

A few days later the dreaded *Schutzstaffel* showed up at our door, ordered us to pack a single bag each, and dragged us off Drancy.

Her face fell again. "But, Capu, tell me—what happened? It was the shock of my life when I saw you there in that awful department store. Is that where you live now?"

"I'm a Nazi prisoner, Abrielle. It's not as though I have a choice. Surely you understand that."

"Still, living in a *department* store! What will they think of next?" Abrielle shook her head, as if the absurdity of the situation was just too much to comprehend. She gazed at me a moment, then leaned forward and lowered her voice. "Listen, Capu, I was thinking: I could get a message to your daughter for you. Does she even know where you are?"

My breath caught in my throat. *Hope is the thing with feathers*, Charles used to say, quoting an American poet. But in my current circumstances, hope was the thing that hurt. The day-to-day grimness of my life could be endured, but hope—and the threat of hopes dashed—could destroy the soul.

Besides, I wondered again, could sending Mathilde a message put her in danger? Might it be used against her to prove that we still had a connection, that she might have been polluted by my "antisocial" thoughts and manners?

"You don't trust me," Abrielle said when I did not respond. Her mouth twisted into a pretty little pout that I was willing to bet Herr Pflüger found adorable. "Capu, I'm offering to do you a favor. For old times' sake."

"Like the 'favor' you did me when you turned us in to the S.S.? My father and me?" My heart pounded with barely suppressed rage.

"What are you talking about?"

"The last time you were in La Maison Benoît, you read a pamphlet my father had written. Just a few days later, the S.S. arrested us."

"Communism is evil, not to mention godless," she said, pursing her lips.

"And the Nazis aren't?" I blurted out.

My mouth had gotten me into trouble more than once in my life, but now I was playing a dangerous game. The cherished mistress of a Nazi commander might have enough power to have me sent to one of those camps Pettit liked to threaten us with—or even summarily executed.

"I'm doing what I have to to survive," she said in a flat tone, echoing what I had been thinking just moments ago.

Abrielle had always grated on me, though I never could put my finger on exactly why. Back when we rubbed shoulders in Montmartre, she liked to tell people we were the "best of friends" when clearly we were not. Still, though I found that irksome, it did not explain my distaste.

One night, long ago, I had confessed my aversion to Abrielle as Charles and I lay in bed, our hands entwined. He chuckled and said his grandfather used to train dogs in North Carolina. Sometimes, for no apparent reason, the dogs took an instant and intense dislike to a person. Even the most docile animal might snarl or snap at a man who smelled wrong to them.

Chemistry, Charles said, adding with a seductive smile, *It brings some people together and drives others apart. How else do you explain you and me, two people from such different backgrounds?*

"Anyway, I didn't turn you or your father in," Abrielle said, looking surprised. "I wouldn't do that."

I nodded, but remained unconvinced.

"It's true! I did see the pamphlet that day, and you know I've never agreed with atheism. I'm a good Catholic," said Abrielle. "But I didn't go to the secret police! We were such good friends not so very long ago! How could you even think I would do such a thing?"

As if on cue, the gold cross she always wore at her throat caught a shaft of afternoon light and gleamed.

I did not know what to think. I had vowed to seek revenge

against Abrielle, but as I sat here with her now . . . she seemed silly and shallow, not calculating and evil. And, of course, anyone who came into the store could have seen Bruno's newsletter and alerted the S.S. Or perhaps my in-laws, the Duplantiers, had seized on the opportunity to be rid of me once and for all.

"We all have our own cross to bear, Capu. And I have to keep Otto happy. You think that's easy?"

I shrugged. *I certainly wouldn't find being Herr Pflüger's mistress easy.*

Abrielle apparently misinterpreted my shrug, for she seemed to relax. "I knew you'd understand! A big part of making Otto happy is presenting myself and our apartment in just the right way. We'll be entertaining some very important people here, Capu. Why, Otto tells me *Reichsminister* Speer sometimes comes to Paris to check on *Möbel Aktion*! Can you imagine entertaining Herr Speer himself?"

"No, I can't," I said, meaning it.

"And . . . I hate to admit it, but I've never had the best taste. Everything I like, Otto says is, well, tacky. You always had great taste, and you ran around with all those fancy designers. . . . I envied you that." She sighed and patted the couch. "Otto *hates* this couch. Absolutely despises it. Please, I need your help."

"All right," I said as if I were doing her a favor. "But I want a few things in return."

"Don't take this the wrong way, Capu, but you're not exactly in a position to make demands. This isn't Zelli's, and you aren't the famous Fan Girl anymore."

"We can agree on that, at least," I said. "But, Abrielle, I know a few things that I suspect you'd rather no one else knew."

Abrielle looked uncertain. "Like what?"

"For one thing, you're not twenty-nine years old. Far from it. I wonder what Herr Pflüger would think if he knew you were nearly middle-aged." I let that sink in for a moment, then continued. "I also have lots of fond memories of us in the good old days, at Zelli's and other 'degenerate' clubs. What if your boyfriend and his Nazi colleagues knew about your past?"

"You can't tell him, Capu! Otto is good to me, but he's . . . prickly. These men, these officers, they're under a lot of stress, you know."

"I know they turn on their own at the drop of a hat," I said. "I'd hate to think what would happen if Herr Pflüger turned on you."

She let out a quick, harsh breath. "You would tell him?"

I stared at her for a long moment. "I wouldn't want to, no. But desperate times call for desperate measures. And I'm desperate."

She sat back in a huff, her cupid-bow mouth settling into a hard line.

"What is it you want?"

"For now? A hot bath," I said. "Oh, and something to eat. Meat. And paper—I'll need some nice paper to make sketches."

I FELT SELFISH, lolling in the sheer bliss of the hot bath, sipping a glass of wine. I probably should have asked for something more important, or relevant to my situation. But there was only so much Abrielle had the power to give me, and at the moment, I felt the closest I had to "normal" since Bruno and I were arrested.

My big toe played with a drip from the faucet as I recalled the horror of that day. It had begun like any other. My father and I were in the shop organizing the feathers. Ever since the war began, the demand for anything nonessential had fallen precipitously, and folks were scraping by with whatever they had. Still, the women of Paris were known for their sense of style, and now that permanent waves and salon dye jobs were out of reach, they wore more hats.

That day Bruno and I were sorting through our supply, deciding to dye the cheapest chicken and pigeon feathers. The rarest and most valuable feathers we set aside, hoping that one day soon, when the war was over, business would revive.

The shop door burst open and the *Schutzstaffel* poured in, guns at the ready.

Terror swamped me. I could feel my bowels liquefy.

I should have gone with Charles. I should have escaped when I could.

My father tried bargaining. *I can get you money,* he said in that low, "trust me—I'm sincere" voice he used when trying to talk someone into buying a fan that cost far too much.

A pink-faced soldier, probably younger than Mathilde, picked up the fan box my mother had forgotten when she left; he opened it, then snorted in derision and tossed it aside. Oddly enough it landed on the rush seat of the same wooden chair where it had sat for more than thirty years.

"We have rare feathers here," Bruno said, holding up a handful of egret plumes and a box of tiny iridescent hummingbird feathers. "These are worth more than gold. I apprenticed in London, and I can tell you—"

"London," the man spat, and knocked the boxes out of my father's hands, the plumes scattering into the air and slowly zigzagging down to the floor.

The gleaming hummingbird feathers were crushed under bootheels as the soldiers ransacked the store, stealing the money from the cash register and searching for anything else of value—

feathers, apparently, did not count. Bruno and I were given five minutes to pack a single bag each under the watchful eye of a soldier.

We were dragged outside and loaded into a truck half full of Parisians in various states of shock. A mother held her young son to her chest, weeping. An old man on the opposite bench seemed resigned, his face settled into lines of fatalistic expectation. A teenage girl sat frozen and silent, only her huge dazed eyes signaling her distress. A shaft of light passing through a slit in the canvas shone on her face in a bold, gleaming stripe, reminding me of a Modigliani painting. The last time I saw that girl, she was standing next to Bruno, clutching a purple ticket. No doubt they had both been sent to Auschwitz and its unnamed horrors.

And here I was, soaking in a hot bath in the penthouse apartment of a Nazi officer.

I was a coward. In my Fan Girl days, I had been bold and brash, quick with a laugh and a quip. I had tempered my grief and confusion after my young husband's death into a sort of blithe optimism. What more could happen? We had art and music and joy.

But then I let Mathilde go, and then Charles, and finally Bruno.

I felt small, diminished. Deep in my heart, I thought that my being a prisoner made a strange sort of sense.

ABRIELLE PULLED TOGETHER a meal of bread, olives, and a bit of cheese and cured meat, which I ate off a wooden cutting board, every bite ambrosia.

I consumed a generous dose of guilt with each glorious morsel, thinking of my fellow prisoners at Lévitan eating their meal of thin gruel. But just as I could not share my bath with them, it would not be possible to bring food back with me. Even if I was to ask Abrielle to pack me a picnic, I would surely be forced to surrender it to the soldiers when they searched me upon my return. I had no inclination to feed my prison guards.

"Good?" Abrielle asked, sitting on the other side of the dining table as I tried to take measured bites so as not to make myself sick.

I nodded.

"You will help me, won't you? It will be good for both of us, Capu."

I nodded again and spoke around a mouthful of chicken. "Like I said, it's not as though I have much choice, Abrielle."

"But—"

"It's fine." I waved off her concern. "No reason why we both can't benefit from this relationship."

"That's what I was thinking!"

I used one hand to feed myself some cheese and, with the other, sketched a general plan for the front room. "I'll need to take some measurements so that I can pick the right pieces for the room. Do you have a tape?"

"A tape?"

"A measuring tape. It's a little doughnutlike thing, and you pull out the tape . . . ?"

She shook her head.

"I'll see if there's one at Lévitan. In the meantime, I'm thinking of something like this." I drew the windows, the hallway off to the side, the wall I had suggested as a focal point. "I wasn't kidding about the importance of balance and making a first impression. We should look for a really bold painting to go there."

"Oh, yes. You are so clever! I knew you were the one to help me."

"I'm glad you like it." I feasted on some cured olives, taking a moment to savor their saltiness. "I've already pulled some nice pieces, and you—and your German—can come by and see if they're to your taste. Have you considered putting a piano in that corner? A full grand would be too big, but a baby grand should fit and would lend the room a delightful air of sophistication."

"A delightful air of sophistication," Abrielle repeated with a sigh. Then she shook her head, a pretty flush staining her cheeks. "I never learned to play, though."

"You could probably hire a pianist. I'll bet there's someone at the Lévitan whom you could force to play for his supper."

Her big eyes widened, and her mouth made a little "O."

"Sorry, bad joke," I said.

"I hate to think I'm *forcing* you to be here, Capu. I thought I was doing you a favor."

"I was being ironic, Abrielle. The situation is peculiar for both of us. I'm . . ." Fresh and clean from my bath, with a full belly. "I am grateful. Thank you."

"I'm so glad!" She flashed me a huge smile as she placed a hand over her heart. A diamond bracelet sparkled in the afternoon sun streaming through the main window. "I can't tell you how much that means to me. And this place will be beautiful, won't it?"

I nodded. "It has great bones."

"Great bones," she repeated thoughtfully, as though she'd never heard the term. "Hey, speaking of pianists, whatever happened to your fella?" she asked, her voice dropping to an irritatingly earnest pitch. "The piano player. Did he get out?"

Why could I not even think *of Charles without wanting to cry?* I stopped chewing, the food suddenly dry in my mouth. I had to force myself to swallow.

I nodded. "He left years ago. When things . . . when talk of war first started."

"Oh, *good.*" She seemed to catch herself. "I mean, I'm sorry. You two always seemed so . . . close. I'm surprised you didn't go with him."

The last time I saw Charles, he had asked me again. *Marry me, Capu. Even if you don't believe in such a bourgeois institution, the immigration officials do. Come with me.* He looked at me in that special way of his, as if intrigued and amused and fascinated and protective, all at the same time. He pushed the hair from my eyes, let out a low chuckle. *I can't guarantee you'll love life in my humble hometown, but the Fan Girl will sparkle no matter where she is.*

A lot he knew. I had lost anything resembling a sparkle.

I downed the rest of the wine, fighting nausea.

"I—," Abrielle began, but stopped at the scrape of a key in the lock.

Zelia walked in, her bags heavy with groceries.

"Ah, perfect timing!" Abrielle said as if the woman were a long-awaited guest. "Thank you, Zelia! We were just finishing up our session."

The maid glowered at her, met my eyes for a brief moment, then passed wordlessly into the kitchen.

"That woman scares the daylights out of me," Abrielle whispered.

"Me, too."

We shared a small smile. Abrielle handed me a pile of nice stationery I could use to make drawings, then picked up the telephone and called downstairs.

"We're finished here. She's ready for you."

14

Mathilde

$\mathcal{T}$HE TELEPHONE IN the front hall rang, the shrill sound bouncing off the wood-paneled walls and filling the foyer. Mathilde heard Mami Yvette's footsteps, followed by her voice conversing in that clipped, excruciatingly polite tone she used with those with whom she did not wish to speak.

It couldn't be Victor, or Mami Yvette's voice would have been warm and engaging. Mami and Papi were eager to launch Mathilde into adult life through marriage to a Fine Young Man with a Respectable Job in Manufacturing.

"Mathilde!" Mami Yvette called out, craning her neck to look up the stairwell. "Mathilde, please come to the telephone."

Mathilde hurried downstairs and shot Mami a questioning look as she took the heavy receiver, its solid metallic weight still warm from her grandmother's hand.

"Allô?"

"Mathilde?" came a woman's voice.

For a moment Mathilde's heart skipped a beat, as she thought it might be her mother calling.

"This is Madame Caron, Bridgette's mother. Have you seen her?"

"No, madame, not since the day I was at your shop," Mathilde said, "when we went to the cemetery."

"That was the last time?"

"Yes. She said she was on her way to Claye-Souilly."

"She was supposed to be back today," said Madame Caron, a note of panic in her voice. "She hasn't arrived."

"But I'm sure—" Mathilde hesitated. She couldn't help but remember listening to her grandparents talk, in hushed whispers, of the Résistance groups, and recall how Bridgette's eyes lit up at stories of French defiance. "Perhaps she was delayed by road conditions or . . ." She trailed off, wondering what innocuous event might have been the cause of the delay.

She heard a soft whimpering, and Madame Caron said: "Please, if you hear from her, let me know. And would you contact Simone and ask her? I haven't been able to find her, and Bridgette spoke of her not long ago."

"What do you mean?"

"I think they were going to get together. In any case, I haven't been able to get Simone on the telephone, so perhaps the lines are down. Please—please, let me know if you hear anything?"

"Yes, of course. I'll speak with Simone right away. I'm sure Bridgette's fine, madame. Please don't cry—"

The only answer was the click as Madame Caron hung up the phone.

Mathilde tried telephoning Simone but could not get through.

The telephones, the electricity, the mail, the trams . . . all had become unreliable to the point of exasperation.

"Mami," she called into the parlor, "I have to go to Simone's house. I won't be long."

"But it is so late, Mathilde. Is that wise?" Mami asked. "What about curfew?"

"I'll be quick. Anyway, they won't worry about a girl on a bicycle."

She paused, recalling Bridgette saying something similar when she left for Claye-Souilly.

"What's going on?"

"Bridgette went to visit relatives in Claye-Souilly and hasn't gotten back yet," Mathilde said, gathering her coat and hat. "Madame Caron is very worried and thinks Simone might have heard something, but can't get in touch with her."

Even as she spoke, Mathilde realized how unlikely it was that Simone would know anything about Bridgette's whereabouts. Whether due to the war or simply to growing apart, the girls were no longer the Three Musketeers. These days, Bridgette and Simone got together only when Mathilde was there, too, as if she were the bridge connecting them. Why would Bridgette and Simone have met without her?

"*Attends, ma petite fille,*" said Mami Yvette, looking nervous. "Your grandfather does not think Bridgette is a good companion for you. I know she is a sweet girl, but these days especially, we must be careful with whom we associate."

Mathilde froze, her arms half in and half out of the coat sleeves. Slowly, she shrugged the coat onto her shoulders.

"What are you saying, Mami? I should turn away from my

oldest and dearest friend? And anyway, I promised her mother I would go."

"I . . ." Mami Yvette trailed off, then shook her head with a little smile. "Of course, you're right. You go on, then, and see if you can find out anything from dear Simone. I'm sure Bridgette's plans simply changed, and she wasn't able to call. You know how the telephones are these days. Just promise me to be careful, *ma petite*."

Mathilde nodded. "Don't hold dinner for me."

Simone lived in Boulogne-Billancourt, about a twenty-five-minute bicycle ride through the Bois de Boulogne, a park that once had been Louis XVI's hunting preserve. It would have been much faster to go by car, but even Mami and Papi did not have reliable access to petrol. Everything went toward the war effort, and what little petrol was available on the black market was too precious to waste on casual trips.

Arriving at Simone's house, Mathilde came to a quick stop, shocked to see Simone leaving with a German officer, apparently her date. He was older, probably in his thirties, and though Mathilde did not know the meaning of the braid and insignia on his uniform, the eagle looked very posh. Tall and blond with a square jaw, the officer might have stepped out of one of the posters of Hitler's ideal Aryan man.

Simone looked flustered to see Mathilde. "Mathilde! What are you doing here? Is everything all right? Excuse me one moment," she said to the German officer, pulling Mathilde aside and lowering her voice. "Is it your mother? Did you find out something?"

"No, it's . . . Have you seen Bridgette or heard from her in the last few days?"

Simone's mouth tightened. "No, of course not. Why do you ask?"

"Her mother just called. Bridgette went to Claye-Souilly a few days ago and hasn't returned. Her mother expected her back earlier today."

"Well, I wouldn't worry about it. You know how the roads are these days," Simone said, flashing a smile and winking at her date, who was waiting impatiently by a car, its motor running. "I'm sure she was simply delayed and hasn't been able to find a telephone."

"But—"

"I'm sorry, Mathilde, but we're expected for drinks before dinner, and Manfred simply *hates* it when we're late. I swear, the man is ruled by his watch. And after, we're going to a show at the Moulin Rouge—I do believe it's my favorite place in all of Paris! But don't worry. Bridgette will turn up. You'll see. She's like a bad penny."

"Okay, thanks." Mathilde's gaze shifted to the man in uniform. "Who is he?"

"His name's Manfred. Manfred Wolff. Isn't he dreamy?"

"He's . . . very handsome," Mathilde said.

Simone stuck one arm out of her wrap, holding a pale wrist out to Mathilde. "Smell. He brought me a new perfume, Femme Rochas. It's very exclusive."

Mathilde leaned over to sniff Simone's wrist. "Mmm, nice. But really, Simone? A German officer?"

"There's no reason why we can't get along, Mathilde. You should know that better than anyone."

"What do you mean by that?" Mathilde said, but Simone was already returning to her date, leaving a trail of perfume in her wake.

Mathilde watched as Wolff helped Simone into the shiny black car. It roared down the street, the rear red lamp glowing in the waning light of the day.

Mathilde tried to think of someone else who might know something about Bridgette, but no one came to mind, so she pedaled, defeated, back to Neuilly-sur-Seine. As she passed the now-shuttered Synagogue de Neuilly, with its rounded front and columns, she noticed new slurs marring its walls. Before the war, men wearing black skullcaps and fringed prayer shawls would come and go, often gathering near the synagogue's entrance. Not all of them wore special garb, of course; some of the Jews dressed like everyone else. Like the orphans living with the nuns, wearing hand-me-down clothes.

How did the Nazis even *know* who was Jewish? The devout were obvious, but what of the others? That must have been why they had ordered the Jews to stitch the yellow Star of David onto their clothing, to make them stand out. To set them apart.

The big square house smelled of roasted meat and potatoes. Mathilde arrived just as her grandparents were sitting down to eat.

"Good of you to join us," Papi grumbled as he poured the wine.

"Did you have any luck, dear?" Mami asked, and signaled Cook to serve the first course.

Mathilde shook her head. "I was wondering: What happened to the people from the Synagogue de Neuilly?"

"Don't you worry about them," Papi said, glancing at Mami. "They're not our concern."

"But I do worry, Papi," Mathilde said. "When they are deported, where do they go? What happens to them? Don't you remember the synagogue's priest—"

"Those men are most certainly *not* priests," Papi Auguste interrupted. "They're rabbis, and that's an entirely different kettle of fish. Among other things, unlike a priest, who is loyal only to God, the rabbis marry and set about having dozens of children, whom they inflict upon society."

"Of course, I forgot they're called rabbis," Mathilde said. "But the rabbi there, Monsieur Meyers, and his wife were always very kind. They took in children in need, remember?"

"That was very generous of them," Mami Yvette said, "but not necessary. There are plenty of nuns to care for needy children. The nuns on rue Edouard Nortier are housing more than a dozen."

Mathilde nodded. "I see them peeking out the window sometimes when I ride by. In fact, I brought them my old dollhouse."

"You did *what*?" Papi demanded.

"I'm far too old for it, Papi. Why shouldn't they be able to play? They're just children."

Papi Auguste grunted. "Jewish children right here in our neighborhood. It's a damned shame."

"But what I don't understand is what's so bad about being Jewish," Mathilde persisted. "I mean to say, in and of itself, why is that wrong? Don't we pray to the same God?"

"They don't believe in Jesus."

"Actually, they do. They just don't believe he's the son of God."

"Which is blasphemous!"

"Auguste, Mathilde, please!" murmured Mami Yvette. "We're supposed to be enjoying our dinner. Bickering promotes indigestion."

There was a long pause. When Papi spoke again, his tone was thoughtful. "The Jews think differently than we do. They are not true French, and they do not belong in France. Most are immigrants, bringing foreign ways. They should go back to where they came from."

"By that logic, so should the Germans," said Mathilde. "And here's another thing: Where was my mother taken? And *Grandpère* Bruno? Is there any way you can help me find them?"

"Is that what this is really about?"

"I don't think it's too much for me to want to find out where my mother is."

Auguste and Yvette shared a glance but did not respond.

"If you won't help me, could I have access to my inheritance? It was legally mine upon my twenty-first birthday. I was thinking I could use it to find them."

"That money has been set aside for your marriage, which, by the way, I've been meaning to speak to you about," said Papi.

He smiled and his tone became gentle, jovial, the way it had been when Mathilde was a child. With a pang, she remembered how she used to love to look through his huge atlas, to listen to his stories about his boyhood adventures and the time he traveled to the French colony of Algeria.

"Mathilde, you know how fortunate your mami Yvette and I feel to have you in our lives, to see you grow and flourish into a young woman."

"I have been very fortunate as well—," Mathilde began.

"Yes, indeed you have," he said, cutting her off but patting her hand. "This war—any war, really—is not easy for anyone, least of all for young people such as yourself. So many young men have been conscripted by the *Service du Travail Obligatoire* or even imprisoned. You are fortunate to have found someone like Victor, who is so attentive to you. You do not remember the last war, Mathilde, the misery it entailed. It took many years for France to get back on her feet. It's just as *Maréchal* Pétain says: We lost our way as a nation, as a people, not only economically but also morally, when pleasure became more important than hard work. Your mother . . . your mother was part of all that. I know I sometimes sound harsh—your mami Yvette reminds me of this often. But you must believe this, Mathilde: We want only the best for you."

"I know you do, Papi, and please know that I am very grateful for everything you and Mami have done for me. It's just . . . doesn't the Bible say we must love our neighbors?"

"Our true neighbors are those who share our beliefs and values, Mathilde. I have nothing against the Jews, but they will be happier among their own kind. Like must stick to like. It is simply the way of the world. Now, I am sorry to spoil the surprise," said Papi, "but Victor has requested to speak with me in private. I believe he intends to ask my permission to take your hand in marriage."

"But—" Mathilde's breath caught in her throat. "But I barely know Victor. We've never even been alone, just the two of us."

"It is proper for a young woman of good family to have a chaperone," said Papi.

"This is 1944, Papi. And I don't . . . I hardly even know Victor as a person, much less as a potential husband."

"What is there to know? He is a good man from a good family. He respects you and will treat you well."

"But I'm not even sure . . ." Mathilde trailed off as she met her grandmother's gaze. How could she say she might want to follow another path, a different way of life?

"Mathilde is right," said Mami Yvette, addressing Auguste. "She and Victor should be allowed to spend a little time together by themselves. Don't you remember when we were courting? Why, I remember one time—"

"That'll do, my dear," Papi said, smiling at Mami. "You've made your point. Mathilde, you have my permission to spend an evening or two alone with your young man so that when he proposes, you will accept happily. But as your mami Yvette likes to say, it is high time for you to put away childish things."

It wasn't until she was preparing for bed that night that Mathilde realized she had not received an answer about helping her mother, or her inheritance.

Or perhaps she had.

15

Capucine

$\mathcal{T}$HE LAST TIME I had approached Lévitan, I was coming from Drancy, stupefied and shaking like a leaf. I literally could not stop my body from trembling.

This time I saw everything much more clearly. Peering out the small gap in the canvas, I could make out the quiet streets. There was not a soul on the sidewalks, and I wondered whether the residents were hiding within their shuttered apartments or had themselves been deported. Was this a Jewish neighborhood surrounding the Jewish department store?

Before the Occupation, I had never paid much attention to which Parisian neighborhoods were filled with immigrants or those espousing one religion or another. Back then we all got along. A least that was what I thought. That was what I had wanted to believe.

The lorry pulled up to the rear of the store, and Pettit banged on the side of the truck. I climbed out, carrying in the crook of my arm the sketching paper Abrielle had given me.

In my absence, the work had continued as usual. A long line of trucks waited to be unloaded; men hoisted and moved heavy wooden boxes onto the loading dock; rows of women leaned into the crates to sort through the plunder. A small group of bored-looking guards watched it all.

"What's this for?" Pettit snorted as she took the stack of paper from me, flipping the pages to be sure there was no contraband hidden within.

"To make sketches," I said. "Interior design doesn't just happen, you know. It requires planning."

"Whatever. Get back to work," Pettit said, and I took my place in the sorting line with my pod.

I felt self-conscious, wondering if I smelled of Abrielle's bath salts, my belly full of meat and wine and good bread. Prisoners weren't supposed to talk while we worked, so my associates shot curious glances at me as we sorted through boxes for the next two hours, until the last truck was emptied and it was finally time to return to the attic.

My thighs burned as we mounted the stairs, still tired from climbing the six stories to the penthouse. The evening's meager meal had already been brought to the attic and I found the smell nauseating after my feast at Abrielle's.

Isedore abandoned the dinner line and rushed over, kissing me on both cheeks.

"*Capu!* I am so relieved! *Baruch HaShem!* What happened? You smell wonderful!"

Others gathered around, excited to see me back, for any change in routine that did not involve deportation.

"It's good to see you," said Ezra in his quiet voice.

"You, too."

"You look . . . refreshed."

I smiled. "Believe it or not, I had a bath."

His eyebrows rose. "That sounds nice."

"It was wonderful. Get your dinner, and I'll tell you all about it."

"You're not hungry?" Isedore asked.

I shook my head. "You can have mine."

They left to join the people shuffling slowly along the food line.

Isedore returned with her plate, and we sat at the ends of our beds. She leaned forward, taking a big bite of stewed cabbage. "Tell me, Capu. What's the city like? What did you do?"

I kept the story lighthearted, describing the building, the apartment, the grim-faced maid. And Abrielle, fluttering about, simultaneously friendly and threatening. Others joined us in our little sheltered cot area to hear what I had seen on the streets and done in Abrielle's penthouse.

Everyone laughed at my stories, especially when I described asking for a bath.

"You didn't!" Isedore gasped, wide-eyed. "You asked a Nazi for a bath?"

"I *did*. But Abrielle's not a Nazi, Isedore."

Her expression hardened and she shrugged, scooping a bite of boiled carrots into her mouth before she announced, "She might as well be. She's a Nazi's whore."

Her ugly words surprised me. Isedore looked so young and innocent, but the war, the imprisonment, the grief, and the fear were having an effect. I noticed several others nodding in agreement, but most kept their thoughts to themselves.

"She's . . . ," I began, then wondered how to explain it. "I'm by no means Abrielle's biggest fan, but she's just doing the best she can to survive."

"Really? You're *defending* her? You're saying her Nazi would have had her arrested if she hadn't agreed to be his mistress?" Isedore frowned.

Her plate was empty, nothing left but a greasy smear on the Limoges china. One of the strange things about living in a department store was our access to a never-ending supply of household items. The guards didn't want to bother with requisitioning items for us, so they sometimes let us take what we needed from stock: sheets, pillows, dishes. They ordered us to choose only the cheapest items, of course, but every once in a while, a piece of fine china snuck in among the inexpensive dishes. At times, prisoners didn't want to bother washing dishes, and instead tossed them to the floor "by accident" so they were simply swept up with the garbage.

"What I mean is, it's wartime. People are hungry and desperate," I said, choosing my words carefully. "I find it hard to condemn anyone, really, for doing whatever it is they need to do to save themselves. Just as you and I and the rest of us did when we traded our skills to come here to Lévitan."

"You're saying *I'm* a collaborator?" Isedore demanded, her color high.

"No one is saying that, sweetie," said Hélène.

"No, of course not!" I said. "I'm just saying that we all make compromises. We do what we can—"

"Like sleeping with Nazis?" demanded Léonie, a bitter note to her voice.

"I'll admit that one is hard to take," I said. "I just find it hard to condemn anyone out of hand these days."

"I don't understand you," said Isedore, fixing me with a suspicious, searching look. "You're apologizing for them now? For these Nazis, these *murderers?*"

"*Quiet down!*" yelled one of the guards from across the room.

"I'm not apologizing for anyone," I whispered, feeling a weariness down to my bones.

The sun had long since set, the attic was freezing as always, and I pulled a blanket around my shoulders. It was a handmade crazy quilt, too threadbare to tempt the Germans, but I loved how soft it was and liked to think of the grandmotherly hands that might have stitched its delicate pieces together.

"But these days, everything is . . . complex. I've lived a lot longer than you, Isedore, experienced a lot. It puts things in perspective."

"And we should trust the opinions of a woman who abandoned her own daughter?" Isedore demanded.

I had confided to Isedore about my estrangement from my daughter, sharing my shame and regret, because she reminded me of Mathilde. That she would say this to me now was a dagger to my heart.

Abruptly, Isedore stood and let her plate crash to the floor. Shards sprayed our ankles, and small beads of blood welled up along a cut on her shin.

"Isedore—," I began, but she interrupted me.

"Every day those damned trucks pull up, trucks driven by *French* people, and every day we are guarded by *French* police and ignored by the *French* collaborators," said Isedore, her voice shaking. She addressed the group. "What if our neighbors had stood up against these invaders, each and every one of them? What might have happened then?"

They would have been shot was my first thought.

My second was: *She is right.*

I remembered Bruno in that line at Drancy saying, *How can you deny what has been happening these past few years, Capu? Have you not seen what the Nazis have done to Paris?*

His words had stung. It was true. I had done my best to ignore the changes in my beloved city. After the initial bombings, the "war" seemed so far away that we even called it *"la guerre drôle."* The phony war. There were shortages of food and other necessities, we had to buy everything—from socks to groceries—with ration tickets, and uniformed German soldiers began to fill our streets and frequent our nightclubs and cafés, but otherwise life carried on.

We heard whispers of things happening elsewhere, in Poland and beyond, but it wasn't until two years into the war, in 1942, that Jews in Paris were forced to wear the yellow Star of David on their clothing. And then their businesses began to be sprayed with graffiti and boycotted; a bomb went off at a jeweler's shop in the rue des Rosiers. Synagogues were abandoned, Hebrew schools shuttered, and some were burned.

Since my favorite haunts in Montmartre had long since closed, and my artist friends—and Charles—had already fled the city, I kept my head down, helped my father in the shop, and spent my time and energy searching for enough food to keep us alive. The reality of everyday life in Paris, the grimness that was creeping up on us all, seemed only to echo my own dour outlook on life, like a personal penance for everything I had done wrong.

Why hadn't I stood up to the Nazis? Why hadn't we all?

Even now my biggest act of defiance was squirreling away a few family photos. Surely I could do more, *should* do more. Bruno used to say that merely surviving was an act of resistance, which was true. But was it enough?

All I knew for sure was that I had no answer for the young woman standing in front of me, trembling with anger.

After a moment of silence, Isedore turned on her heel and stalked away, her boots crunching on the shards of china. The crowd dispersed, leaving me to my thoughts.

Ezra appeared with a broom and wordlessly swept up the pieces of Isedore's dinner plate.

I thanked him, then grabbed the stack of paper Abrielle had given me and ran my hands over it. It was thick linen parchment, high quality. In the fan business, I had become almost as much of an expert in paper as I was in feathers. And speaking of feathers . . . a softly curled down feather had escaped from Isedore's pillow. I stroked it between thumb and forefinger, remembering. Thinking. Wondering.

I had so little to offer and so much to atone for.

I started folding the paper. I would make Isedore a fan, the most beautiful fan I could manage under the circumstances.

It was the very least I could do.

THE NEXT DAY I had permission to leave the sorting line to find items for Abrielle's apartment. Like yesterday's outing, it was a welcome change from the everyday tedium.

It was so pleasant to be left to my own devices, matching fabrics and colors and playing with form and texture. It seemed a million miles away from the reality of being a prisoner. Until I was reminded that all of the things had been stolen, pillaged from the homes of Jews. Who had sat on these couches? Slept in these beds? Eaten off these plates?

Henri and Ezra were again assigned to help me, and we were also assisted by a young, eager man named Jérôme. Jérôme had been studying at the yeshiva before it was closed, and he had been sent here because his father was a furrier, and he knew how to safeguard stolen furs from mold and insects. Jérôme loved to talk about, and to debate, anything and everything. He was good-natured but never walked away from an argument.

Together we moved upstairs everything I had chosen, as well as several pieces that had come in yesterday. The main showroom of the Lévitan had been laid out with partitions, some complete with mantelpieces, so we could arrange little groupings of furniture as if one were sitting in a living room or parlor. That way the items could be properly shown to Baron Von Braun during inspection or to Nazi elites looking to spruce up their lodgings or, in this case, to Abrielle and her protector.

We laid out two nice bedroom sets: bedsteads, mattresses, chests of drawers, bureaus. The furniture had the sleek, curved lines of Art Deco, and I found some beautiful linens and duvets to dress the beds. We completed the room by placing an assortment of crystal perfume bottles and vials on the vanity and rolling out plush silk Turkish carpets to pull everything together.

At long last, I collapsed into a soft armchair covered in green silk brocade, while the men gratefully sank onto the couch.

"Thank you, gentlemen, for your help," I said. "I feel as though I should bring out a tray with an aperitif. We have the glasses. All we need is the liquor."

"My bubbe used to love her aperitif," said Jérôme with a sad smile.

"Maybe the guards would like to share," I said, craning my neck to be sure no one noticed that we were quite literally sitting down on the job. There were no guards in sight, so I relaxed back into the armchair, grateful for the stolen moment of rest and normalcy.

"Fat chance," said Henri.

"So, Capu, how do you know this woman you're designing for?" asked Ezra. "I hear she asked for you by name."

"We used to haunt the jazz clubs of Montmartre way back when."

He raised his eyebrows. "Why do I feel there's more to that story?"

I met his eyes and smiled. "It was a different time."

"In so many ways."

"I prefer klezmer music to jazz," said Jérôme. "No offense."

"None taken," I said.

Not long ago a broken violin had arrived at the dock, its body no doubt having caved in during its owner's arrest. A prisoner named Claude asked to keep it and did his best to repair the once-beautiful instrument. It was far from perfect, but he coaxed some lovely sounds from the strings, and when Claude began to play, others joined in, thumping on pots and whistling, keeping time by rapping their knuckles and clapping their hands. A group of women started dancing in a circle.

It was raucous, jubilant music that at its heart reminded me a lot of jazz: celebratory and euphoric, with just a touch of sorrow beneath the joy.

"Did you hear?" asked Jérôme. "Mordecai says we have been granted permission to have a celebration of Purim."

"Really?" I asked, surprised. "Why would they allow that?"

He shrugged. "Perhaps they grow weary of pounding us down at every opportunity."

"More likely they want to keep us occupied so we don't cause trouble," said Henri. "Also, I suspect they hope to drive a wedge between the Jews and the non-Jews. They want the wives to resent us for the privilege."

"The wives" was the term used for the women who were married to prisoners of war, only a fraction of whom were Jewish. Most of the wives came from humble backgrounds, which contributed to the tension between them and some of the more fortunate Jewish prisoners. Still, I couldn't imagine anyone coming to blows over a religious festival, especially since Mordecai had described it as a party, which usually meant the better-off internees would feel compelled to share their packages of supplies from family.

"So, what is Purim exactly?" I asked. "Mordecai said something about escaping a disaster?"

"Literally, Purim means 'lots,'" said Henri, "as in the lots cast per the order of Haman to decide which day the Jews in Persia were to be executed."

"Who was Haman? And why did he order the execution of the Jews?" I asked.

"I think Jérôme ought to tell the story," said Henri, "unless Ezra wants to take a turn. For me, Purim is mostly about the cookies and costumes."

"Haman was the prime minister of King Ahasuerus, who had a beautiful wife named Esther," said Jérôme, picking up the story. "Haman demanded that Mordecai, a Jew who was one of the king's ministers, bow down before him. Mordecai refused because Haman wore an image of a pagan idol on his robes. Because of his refusal, Haman decided the Jews were a threat to all of Persia, and they should all be hanged."

"That turned dark fast," I said. "One man refuses to bow down, and an entire people is condemned?"

"It's not an infrequent occurrence for our people," Ezra said softly.

Jérôme continued. "Haman argued that since Jews believe in the one and only God, instead of idols, this meant they believe in the equality of all people."

"A radical idea," I said.

Ezra nodded. "Back then, certainly. Anyone questioning the divinity of a king was clearly causing trouble. But it was more than that, wasn't it, Jérôme? Haman said that since the Jews were devoted to our one God, who is not of this earth, they could not be governed by an earthly king."

"Exactly." Warming to his story, Jérôme grew more animated. "Fortunately, Queen Esther managed to convince the king not only to rescind the order, but to execute Haman instead."

"She sounds quite persuasive," I said. "How did she manage that?"

"There's a lot more to the story," Ezra said with a smile, "involving dinner parties and dances and other entertainments."

I returned his smile. "Isn't that always the way?"

"When we celebrate, we have kazoos and noisemakers, and whenever Haman's name is said aloud, we're to make noise to obliterate it. We throw candy, and people dress up as Queen Esther or as Mordecai, the wise old man with a white beard, or as King Ahasuerus."

"Do you dress up?" I asked Ezra.

"Not usually," he said with a shake of his head. "My favorite part is the hamantaschen. It's a jelly-filled cookie in the shape of a triangle that is said to be Haman's ear or hat, depending upon whom you ask. When you bite into it, you're ritualistically decapitating him."

"Ha! Good for you."

"My bubbe used to make the most amazing hamantaschen," said Henri, closing his eyes as if tasting them in his mind.

Ezra replied, "My mami would give yours a run for her money."

"It sounds wonderful," I said. "But isn't it an awfully lighthearted response to the threat of mass murder?"

"Well, you get used to it," said Jérôme with a shrug.

"Our people have learned to celebrate when we can," added Henri. "There's nothing quite like persecution to make you happy for—"

"What's going on here?" a woman's voice demanded.

Relaxing in the comfortable furniture, we had gotten so caught up in the story of Purim that we had not noticed someone approaching. We jumped to our feet and faced none other than Fräulein Sigrid Sommer.

As usual, she was nicely dressed, wearing a fine, slightly flared skirt and a fitted jacket, her chestnut hair topped with a black fur pillbox hat and snood. She carried a clipboard in one black-gloved hand and a tape measure in the other.

"I—um," I stammered. "It's my fault, mademoiselle. These men were helping me to move the furniture, and I suggested we take a break and make sure the sofa was comfortable enough for the clients. I apologize."

She twisted her mouth a little in thought, assessing first me, then the furniture arrangement in the "parlor" area. Fräulein Sommer walked over to the sleek credenza with mirrored doors and opened it. Then she ran one gloved hand along the top of the striking ebony chest and crouched down to inspect the ivory inlay in the shape of a stylized chariot. At long last she straightened and turned to me.

"What is your name?"

"Capucine Benoît, number 123."

"Where did you study?"

"Here, in Paris," I said.

"Where? With whom?"

"Do you know Émile-Jacques Ruhlmann?"

"Of course I do."

Fräulein Sommer was not going to be as easy to snow as the others had been. She looked me up and down, and I imagined how I must look to her, dressed in my headscarf and old clothes, sitting on the handsome furniture.

"You're saying you apprenticed with Ruhlmann?" she demanded.

"I did some work with him. My father and I made very intricate fans for the haute couture houses, so we were—"

"I studied in Vienna," she declared, cutting me off, "the true heart of European sophistication."

"Indeed," I said, then added, "Vienna is without peer, especially in this sort of thing."

She looked me over again, as though trying to decide whether I was making fun of her. Then she spared her first glance for the men, who were standing stock-still, trying not to be noticed. She again perused the furniture grouping and nodded.

"Well chosen," she said, and strode away.

I looked at Henri, Ezra, and Jérôme, widening my eyes and puffing out my cheeks to make a *phew!* expression.

Ezra cocked his head. "If I were a betting man, I'd wager half this stuff will be gone by morning. Not sure your friend Abrielle has enough clout to outbid Fräulein Sommer."

I smiled. "True. But tomorrow and the next day, more trucks will arrive."

"Well, well, well, what do we have here?" Pettit demanded. "A nice little *kaffeeklatsch*?"

"Pettit! Pull up a chair, won't you?" I said. "Join us."

"Cute. You three men, back to work. What do you think this is, summer camp?"

Ezra, Henri, and Jérôme wordlessly complied, heading across the showroom to the stairwell.

"What did Fräulein Sommer want?" asked Pettit.

"To tell me she was trained in Vienna."

"You knew that already."

"I did, yes. I imagine she would also like to steal—I mean, requisition—that ebony chest. She seemed quite taken with it."

"You think you're awfully smart, don't you?" Pettit sneered.

"I don't, not really. After all, I'm the prisoner."

"That's exactly right."

"I'm curious, Pettit. How do you speak French so well?"

She flashed me a suspicious side-eyed look. "Why?"

"I just wondered. I feel like—I don't know—like if things were different, maybe we would have been friends."

She sniffed in disbelief. But after a moment she said, "I grew up in Alsace. My father fought for Germany and was killed in 'seventeen. And when Alsace was ceded to France after the war, we had to leave our home and move. We lost everything: first my father, then our home. My mother never got over it, used to lie in bed crying and let us kids starve."

"I'm sorry."

She shrugged. "War is war. If you're not a victor, you're a victim."

"I hear you gave the Jewish prisoners permission to celebrate their holiday of Purim."

She gave me a genuine-looking smile, and I saw her as she might have been as a younger woman: hopeful, interested. Pettit was quite ordinary-looking, with her broad face and stocky build, but it was her meanness that made her ugly.

"I have my reasons."

"Well, it was kind of you," I said.

"Don't you know? I'm kindness itself," Pettit said. "Now, get back to work."

16

Mathilde

THE TAPPING AT her bedroom window wouldn't stop. Was that rain? Or some annoying night bird? Last spring a pigeon had pecked incessantly at the window, and it went on for weeks. Mami Yvette told her it was reacting to its own reflection in the window, perhaps thinking it was a romantic rival or a potential conquest.

But at this hour?

Snick . . . snick. Mathilde finally threw off the warm covers, climbed out of her cozy bed, and went to investigate.

She opened the window and stepped out onto her little balcony. The metal was icy beneath her bare feet, the frigid night air cutting through her thick nightgown. In the dim light of a waning moon, she had to squint to make out a dark figure below on the lawn, a barely-there silhouette, black against gray.

Victor? Surely not. That would be far too outrageous, too romantic a gesture for his quiet, composed character. For a brief moment she thought again of the soldier in the street—the one who had commented upon her red coat and handed her a rose with a grand sweep of his arms.

"*Mathilde?*" a familiar voice whispered.

"Bridgette?"

"Can you help me?"

Mathilde's heart thudded, her pulse pounded at the base of her neck, and her chest tightened. Mami and Papi's rooms were on the other side of the house, and she prayed they had not heard anything.

"I need help."

"*Kitchen door.*"

Mathilde closed the window, grabbed her robe and slippers, and ran down the dark stairs, through the hall, and into the kitchen. The stove was always lit, and the room was the warmest in the house. Despite the darkness, she didn't dare turn on a light.

She undid the latch on the back door and Bridgette practically fell into her arms.

"Bridgette! Where have you been?" Mathilde demanded in a fierce whisper, holding her old friend. Bridgette felt cold and smelled of smoke and something acrid, metallic. "What are you doing here? Are you all right?"

In the soft moonlight streaming through the open door, Mathilde saw the strain on Bridgette's face. The fear.

"Come in, come in," she said, closing the door as softly as she could. "Take a seat. I'll put the water on for tea, get you warmed up."

Wordlessly, Bridgette settled into a chair at the farmer's table in the center of the large kitchen.

Mathilde lit a penny candle and placed it on the table. Bridgette's face was so pale, she appeared ghostly in the mellow glow of the flame. She still wore her schoolgirl's uniform, but there were dark stains on her gray serge coat.

"What's that on your coat?"

"Blood."

"Bridgette! You're *hurt*?"

She shook her head. "Not mine. I'm not hurt."

"Talk to me, Bridg," said Mathilde as she filled the heavy copper kettle and set it on the burner. "Your mother's frantic with worry. Where have you been?"

"Hiding."

"Hiding from whom?" Mathilde slid into the chair beside her old friend.

Bridgette held her gaze for a long moment. "From the Nazis."

"I—I don't understand."

"I know." Bridgette's mouth remained open as though she had more to say, but she hesitated.

Mathilde lifted the glass dome off a plate of biscuits Cook had left on the table for tomorrow's breakfast. When the water in the kettle came to a boil, she arranged some of Mami's precious tea leaves in a strainer and made them each a cup of tea with a dollop of cream. It felt like an absurd parody of Mami's afternoon teas in the parlor with her friends, or of her mother's long-ago visits, when she would drink tea and sit stiffly on the uncomfortable sofa.

Bridgette wolfed down a biscuit as though she were starving, and Mathilde handed her another. In the morning she would have to explain the missing baked goods, but at the moment, all she could think about was helping her friend. Bridgette was always so calm, so steady, so comforting. It felt odd to be the one assuaging her friend's fear, trying to help.

"I'm— I could get you in trouble just by being here," said Bridgette.

Mathilde shook her head. "As long as we keep our voices down, I doubt we'll be discovered. Mami and Papi sleep like the dead, and they're on the other side of the house. And the servants don't live in."

Bridgette gave Mathilde an odd look, and Mathilde felt ashamed of having two servants when most people were barely getting by.

"I'm not worried about your grandparents, Mathilde. It's the *Boches*. If they followed me here . . ."

"What . . . what did you do, Bridgette?"

Mathilde thought of what Bridgette had told her, about raising the French flag over the old castle, about the small acts of defiance she had seen throughout the countryside as well as in Paris. Suddenly Mathilde wasn't sure she wanted to know what Bridgette had been up to. If she knew, wouldn't that make her complicit?

"I . . . They shot him," Bridgette whimpered. "Just like that."

"Who? Who shot whom?"

"His blood spurted onto my coat. He was so close to me. . . . Just like that."

"Good Lord, Bridgette! What in the world happened?"

Bridgette covered her face with her hands and started to cry. The weeping ratcheted up into a wail that she muffled with the arm of her bloodstained coat. Mathilde didn't know what to do, so she just leaned over and held her old friend.

"Let me have your coat," said Mathilde after the sobs subsided. "I'll see if I can get the stains out."

After a moment Bridgette stood and, like a child, allowed Mathilde to take off her coat before sinking back down onto the chair. Mathilde pushed her teacup toward her.

"Drink, Bridgette. It will make you feel better."

Mathilde poured a little cold water into the washbasin, picked up the big bar of strong lye soap Cook used to scrub the most difficult pots, and rubbed it on the bloodstained coat, horrified at the sight of the water turning pink. This was a person's lifeblood?

And . . . shouldn't blood be more permanent somehow, not wash out so easily?

Mathilde knew the battlefields ran red, had seen many families receive the death notices of their kin, understood the suffering of so many. But she had never actually witnessed the blood, the shooting. What had Bridgette been doing? What had she seen?

When Mathilde was satisfied that the coat looked better, if not completely stain free—she lacked Cécile's wondrous talent at getting stains out of laundry—Mathilde hung it to dry on the back of a chair, which she placed in front of the stove. She smoothed the fabric as best she could, returned to the table, and leaned toward her old friend.

"What happened, Bridgette? Tell me."

Bridgette took a sip of tea. "I've been doing a few things to help the cause."

"What cause?" Mathilde asked before realizing how stupid that sounded.

"Mathilde, please," said Bridgette, her blue eyes still shiny with tears, rimmed in red against the ashen paleness of her face. "Don't pretend you don't understand. It's been years, *years*, that we've lived under this yoke, this oppression. The Nazis have closed our businesses, killed our people, deported our neighbors. They arrested your mother and grandfather, for heaven's sake. Aren't you furious?"

"What have you been doing?" Mathilde heard herself ask, though she wasn't sure she wanted to know.

There was a safety, a haven, in ignorance, in simply agreeing with her papi when he counseled acceptance. On the other hand, it pained her to see what was happening to Paris. The one emotion she could identify was a frantic kind of anger, born of fear. What would happen to her friend?

"I'm not supposed to tell anyone, not even my parents," Bridgette said, and let out a sudden breath. "Mathilde, you can't tell a soul. Not a *soul*. Do you swear upon the lives of your papi and mami, of your mother and her father?"

When they were children, Mathilde and Simone and Bridgette had sat in the maple tree in Père Lachaise Cemetery and pricked their palms to make a blood promise: friends forever. *Toujours et encore.*

"I promise," said Mathilde. "Friends forever, still and always."

"Friends forever," Bridgette said, smiling sadly. "I've been doing things for the *maquis*, the French Résistance in the countryside. Sometimes it's as simple as typing up pamphlets and passing on messages. Sometimes I help people to escape."

"What kind of people?"

"Anyone the Nazis are hunting. Communists like your grandfather. Labor organizers, Jews, even aviators who have been shot down."

"Aviators? You mean, Allied pilots?"

"And soldiers." Bridgette nodded. "I help get them provisions and fake papers."

"How?"

"A few of us wait near the village *mairies*, the city halls, and when someone leaves a door open or a desk unattended we search it for anything of value: ration tickets, stamps, identity cards. It's like finding golden tickets."

"That's why you go to the countryside so often," said Mathilde.

Bridgette nodded. "A lot of the rural folk support the *maquis*, and there are fewer Germans out there to notice what's going on. I transport all kinds of things in the panniers of my bike: eggs, meat, but also weapons, fuses, dynamite."

"Dynamite?" Mathilde exclaimed. "Bridgette, are you serious?"

"It has to be done, Mathilde, and who better to carry it? I look young, and in my schoolgirl's outfit, I'm the least likely person to be stopped. When I *am* stopped, I pretend to flirt, and most of the young soldiers just wave me through because they think I'm smuggling food for the black market, which they don't really care about. It doesn't occur to them I'm part of the Résistance."

"But it's not always so easy, or you wouldn't have blood on your coat," Mathilde said.

Bridgette slumped. "This time was different. I was working with a man I knew only by his code name, Sébastien, and we were stopped by three young soldiers. We pretended we were a couple on our way to a romantic rendezvous. They were about to wave us through when one of the soldiers found the timing device in Sébastien's bag. Sébastien stepped in front of me to try to explain it away, and one of the soldiers pulled his gun and shot him. Just like that, no warning, no questions. Just . . . shot Sébastien. He staggered backward, and we both fell to the ground, and they shot him again, and I guess the soldiers thought I had been shot, too, or maybe they got scared, because I heard them swearing and arguing, and then they just . . . left."

Bridgette shook her head and took a shaky breath, then continued. "I lay there for what felt like hours, though it was probably minutes. We were taught to count slowly to two hundred before moving, but I didn't make it past one hundred before I heard Sébastien let out a slow groan, and the breath left his body. I—I knew I had to leave him there. I ran and hid and traveled at night to avoid the German patrols and so no one would see the blood on my coat. Finally, I made my way here."

The steady candle flame reflected in the tears in Bridgette's clear blue eyes as though she were lit from within.

"How do you do it?" Mathilde asked. "Aren't you frightened?"

"Frightened? I'm petrified. It keeps getting more dangerous. The *Wehrmacht* has started unannounced inspections in the villages. Now, each time I go, I feel my life is hanging by a thread. I could be the next one shot, just as easily as Sébastien. Or maybe even worse, I could be arrested by the Gestapo and subjected to the bathtub torture. As I ride my bike along, it's all I can think about. Would I be able to withstand it, or would I break down and name others?"

"What do you mean, bathtub torture?"

"The *Boches* call it *Verschärfte Vernehmung*, or enhanced interrogation. They put you in a bathtub, tie your ankles to a pole, and hoist the pole up until your head slides underwater. They pull you out when you're about to drown, and then do it again and again until you tell them what they want to know."

Mathilde was horrified, not only at the description of torture but also at what her friend had been doing, the risks she was taking. Bridgette had always been so kind, the first to stand up for a classmate getting bullied at school, the one who tried to see all sides of a situation, of a person. She was so gentle that it was easy to think of her as soft and malleable, but clearly that was wrong. Mathilde grasped only now that Bridgette's innate kindness was a manifestation of a core of inner strength.

Mathilde thought about Mami and Papi and Victor at the dinner table the other evening, how they had seemed so one-dimensional, like the movie cardboard cutouts the old woman Antoinette had talked about. Not so her courageous friend. Bridgette was entirely three-dimensional.

The nuns had taught them how light passing through a prism was refracted, displaying a rainbow of colors previously hidden. Being with Bridgette felt like that now, and Mathilde doubted she would ever again see Bridgette without an array of color around her.

Mathilde was terrified.

She was exhilarated.

Mathilde knew that she, too, had just passed through a prism, never again to exist in that pale pink innocence of the past.

17

Capucine

"ISEDORE? I HAVE something for you," I said.

"What is it?" she replied, refusing to meet my eyes.

Since our argument the other night, Isedore had been avoiding me, which was no mean feat, considering our cots were only three feet apart.

"I made you a present."

I held out the fan. It consisted of pleated paper with cutouts shaped like stylized lilies and leaves, overlaid with netting. I had edged the fan with some fluffy feathers from our pillows and a few of the precious ones I had brought from La Maison Benoît: spotted pheasant and striped eagle. I glued them down with lace and finished it off by painting an abstract design along each side.

"You made this for me?" she asked, holding out her hands for the gift. She splayed it open and looked at it as though it were the most precious thing she had ever seen. "I thought you only made fans for barter or for people when they're sick."

"And for my best friends. Anyway, it's not exactly haute couture, but it's the best I could do under the circumstances. And it will go great with your Purim costume—you're dressing as Queen Esther, right?"

"Queen Esther, yes."

"Did you know there was a language of fans?"

"Really?"

"Let me show you. Drawing it across your cheek means 'I love you.' Snapping it shut means 'I want to talk with you.' Drawing it across your eyes means 'I am sorry.'"

She smiled, then snapped it shut. "Like this?"

"Exactly. You're a natural. What does this mean?" I drew it across my eyes and then my cheek.

"Um . . . you're sorry, and you love me."

I smiled and nodded.

She returned my smile. "Thank you, Capu. It's beautiful. I'll cherish it. Listen, I—I'm sorry for all that stuff I said, too. It's just this place—"

"There's no need to apologize, Isedore. I understand. Truly."

"We're friends, then?"

I wanted to say more, to explain how I felt about her, how she brought out all my maternal tendencies and to thank her for giving me a chance to make amends in a minor way for how I had failed my daughter. I wanted to tell her what she really meant to me.

But all I could manage was: "Always."

THE NEXT DAY, a group of us went "shopping."

A pair of guards leaned against the wall in one corner of the showroom while we had the run of the place. Pettit had not only given the prisoners permission to celebrate Purim but even allowed a few of us to select items from the department store for the party: china and cutlery and crystal, even a snowy white tablecloth for the feast.

We were also allowed to gather things to make costumes. There wasn't much actual clothing to choose from; the Lévitan featured furniture and housewares, not clothes, and most of the looted apparel—especially the nice stuff—went to the Bassano satellite camp for alterations or was sent by train directly to Germany. Still, enough passed through Lévitan that we had a few crates to look through.

All the others in today's scavenging group were Jewish, but Isedore had insisted I accompany them.

As we pawed through pillowcases piled high on one shelf, Hélène looked around the showroom and said: "I remember coming here to buy a bedroom set for my son." She had a faraway look in her eyes, a sad smile on her lips. "Do you remember the store's slogan? *"Un meuble signé Lévitan . . . est garanti pour longtemps."*

"Yes!" said Léonie. "I remember it, too!" She launched into the old Lévitan advertising jingle.

Hélène chimed in, and then Isedore and two others.

The guards glanced over at the commotion, shrugged, and went back to their chat.

"I remember we came here to buy a dresser for my brothers," said Isedore, her eyes suddenly cast down, shiny with tears. The last time she had seen her family, her two young brothers were being torn from the arms of her anguished mother and father.

What use did the Nazis have for children too young to work?

"Isedore, these gold brocade curtains could be repurposed as capes, don't you think?" I said, hoping to distract her. "And this satin counterpane would make a nice dress. The burgundy color would look wonderful on you."

"You think so?" she said, stroking the material.

"I know so. Madame Schreyer is pure magic with a needle. Now that she's feeling better, I'm sure she could help. And Madame Savanier has volunteered her services as well."

"That's a great idea!" said Hélène, looking through the bedspreads for other likely candidates.

And for the next half an hour, we amused ourselves as so many had over the years, shopping at the Lévitan department store.

WE PASSED THE next few days in the high spirits of a people for whom being lighthearted was a thing of the past.

No matter how tired we were after our workday, we gathered together to sew and contrive costumes from what we had scavenged. We made hats of black fabric scraps and capes out of tablecloths. A bit of cotton wool would serve as a beard for anyone who dressed as the historical Mordecai—though our actual Mordecai needed no such makeup to approximate an older bearded gentleman. Ezra fashioned a crown out of some wire that he wrapped in paper and that I painted to look like jewel-encrusted gold. Along with an improvised cape and beard, it was a perfect costume for Jérôme's interpretation of King Ahasuerus.

As Queen Esther, Isedore wore a long tunic made from the burgundy counterpane, topped by a jacket fashioned from bits of several old coverlets—including a piece of my own precious quilt. We draped her dark hair with a pillowcase repurposed as a scarf, which was held in place by a leather band across her forehead. I drew upon my years as a flapper to come up with an elaborate headdress, adding a few of my precious feathers. The fan and the feathers weren't genuine to the era, but we were going more for effect than for historical accuracy.

On the day before Purim, several of the internees observed the fast of Esther, including the elderly marquise, who was already so thin and frail that she seemed likely to blow away in a stiff breeze.

Fasting seemed a bit much to me, given how close we all were to starving. But one thing I had learned from Mordecai and Hélène and many of the other Jews in Lévitan was their commitment to faith, to tradition, and to remembrance. I wondered what Bruno would have made of such fierce devotion despite war and hunger and circumstances. Despite everything.

Finally, the day of Purim arrived. We created a banquet "table" by laying tablecloths and white sheets in a long line on the floor. We had only a few chairs, which we reserved for the elders among us. Most of us perched on our cots or sat cross-legged on the floor. Some of the wealthier folks had agreed to share food and treats sent by their families, and the regular meal service included some squash as a treat. A few of the young women brewed a concoction they called punch from wine dregs, packets of saccharin, a very little bit of grape juice, and a few mystery ingredients.

It was a grand feast for all, including those of us who weren't Jewish. The prisoners even brought plates of food to the guards. Tremblay, who always seemed as hungry as we, was particularly appreciative and finished his plate with gusto.

Half our number were costumed as Queen Esther, Mordecai, or the king, and everyone was laughing and eating, lamenting only the lack of hamantaschen. The violinist brought out his salvaged instrument, and men and women arranged themselves in separate circles and began to dance.

I settled in on the floor, my back against the wall, and closed my eyes to let the music wash over me.

It was impossible to keep my mind from drifting back. I remembered sitting on Charles's lap for want of a chair in the crowded brasserie one night, his strong arms wrapped around me as I leaned back against him. The flowing wine, the shared food, the easy laughter filling the air. Our carefree joy.

Charles's brother, Freddy, occasionally filled in on drums with the band, but mostly he tended the bar. He was a few inches shorter than Charles, but stockier, and did not put up with what he called nonsense in the club. As a veteran of the Great War, Freddy liked to say that he did not back down from a just fight.

Freddy stood and held up his glass. "Let's have a toast to jazz, the greatest music ever made."

Everyone raised their glass and we toasted.

"I agree with you, Freddy," I said. "But *why* is it so amazing, do you think? It feels like—I don't know—as if it has the power to actually change things."

"It's the best, that's all. It's everything," said Freddy.

"Here's how I see it," said Charles. "Jazz isn't just *music*. It's something more. It lifts us out of depression, out of grief. The first time I played in public was at my grandfather's funeral, and even as a young boy, it helped center me. Jazz is like a proclamation to the world: Open your heart, open your heart, truly *listen* to the notes, to the improvisation. The way the musicians come together, negotiate the music, create a musical dialogue, a conversation with notes. It's individual and yet collaborative, which is why the music is brand-new every night. . . ."

"Enough already, Poet," groused Freddy, signaling the waiter for another pitcher of wine.

I laughed. "Freddy, I've been meaning to ask you, why do you call your brother Poet?"

"I like to read," Charles volunteered.

"He's a college boy," said Freddy at the same time.

Charles seemed almost embarrassed, but he inclined his head. "That I am—or was for three semesters. North Carolina College for Negroes."

"I didn't know that," I said. "Why only three semesters?"

He shrugged. "Ran out of money."

"Poet here found out it's a lot easier to earn a living as a mechanic than as a poet."

"True that," said Charles with a grin. "Or as a piano player, for that matter."

"At least it's easier to make a living as a musician here in Paris than back home," said Freddy. "Another thing you have to thank me for, Poet."

"That's something else I've been meaning to ask you, Freddy," I said. "What brought you to live in Paris in the first place? Wasn't it hard to leave your country?"

The tone turned more serious.

Freddy nodded. "I served my country—and yours—in the war. I fought. I was wounded. And then I went back home and was denied any kind of skilled job. I was spat on even while wearing my uniform. And then a man in the next county was lynched. Another veteran."

"I'm . . . I'm so sorry," I said, trying to think of something more profound, but words failed me.

"But in some ways what hurts on par with the threat of violence," said Freddy, "is not being seen as a full human being. Don't get me wrong. You Parisians are far from perfect, but at least I feel like people *see* me here. They see *me*."

There was a long moment of silence.

"Anyway, after a few months at home, I decided, 'Enough with this. I'm going back to Paris.' I could never forget how comfortable I felt here—not to mention the food! And so I wouldn't get lonely, I brought my baby brother with me. Figured he'd like it as much as I did, plus he's a natural with languages."

"He just can't live without me," said Charles with a smile.

Freddy punched him playfully in the arm. The two men tussled in the friendly way of brothers, laughing over their pastis and wine.

"Can't believe he made it through the Great War without me," Charles went on.

"Remind me again why you didn't volunteer?" Freddy teased.

"I tried, remember? Wouldn't take me because I was too young."

"Excuses, excuses," said Freddy. "Anyway, Capucine, I'm not as philosophical as my baby brother, but I know this: Jazz is all about improvisation, and throughout history, we Negroes have *had* to improvise to survive, much less thrive. Right, Charles?"

"Can't keep a good man down." Charles nodded.

It was heartbreaking to think back on that discussion, yet heartwarming at the same time.

Ezra came to sit beside me.

"I like the dance," I whispered, nodding toward the revelers.

"It's called the hora."

"Why do the women and men dance separately?"

He shrugged. "Tradition, I suppose. You should ask Mordecai or Hélène. My parents were not very religious."

"Did you go to synagogue?"

"We went on High Holy Days, and my mother lit candles on Shabbat, but other than that, we were secret Jews."

I smiled. "Secret Jews?"

"That's what my mother called us. She liked to say we didn't need to rub it in everyone's face. We could keep it to ourselves. And lately, of course . . ." He tilted his head back to rest on the wall. "Well, I suppose I should have taken her words to heart, shouldn't I? I probably should not have sewn that Star of David onto my jacket, but I was overtaken by a sense of pride in my own heritage."

I had always wondered why more Jews had not attempted to "pass," to avoid Nazi scrutiny. But many had, fleeing to the country-side and hiding their children within the broods of sympathetic Aryan families.

"I like some of your Christian traditions," Ezra continued. "My wife used to put up evergreen branches and wrap ribbons around them and light candles for Christmas. Perhaps I should have pre-tended to be a good Catholic. Perhaps I could have skated by."

I studied his face as he spoke. In homage to the Mordecai from the story of Purim, Ezra had let his beard grow for the last week, and the black whiskers highlighted the planes of his face and his hooded romantic eyes. I still marveled at the deep stillness that seemed to radiate from him no matter the circumstances.

"But then"—Ezra closed his eyes and hung his head—"I don't know if I could have lived with myself. It would have felt as though I was renouncing my people, my heritage, whether or not I frequent temple."

"I like watching Hélène light the candles on Shabbat," I said. "And how she says a prayer to bless the household. It's beautiful."

Ezra nodded. "On the High Holy Days, there's a part of the service where the rabbi reads that God is opening the Book of Life, and we have until sunset to truly repent and seek a closer relationship with him. As the day closes, as the sun sets, the Book of Life is closed and those who have sincerely repented and sought a closer relationship with God will have their names inscribed for another year of life."

"I like that."

"In another part of the service, the rabbi bows down to the floor to beg God for mercy and forgiveness on behalf of the entire congregation. Sometime there is a rope tied to the rabbi's leg just in case he gets pulled in by God." He chuckled. "As a kid I always hoped he would be, just to see the struggle that might ensue, though I could not imagine God losing such a tussle."

We shared a laugh.

"How about you?" Ezra continued, turning his head toward me. "What was your favorite part of going to church? I always thought it would be amazing to hear Mass at the Cathédrale Notre-Dame. Those stained glass windows are astonishing."

"I've never been to Mass. My father taught me that religion was the opiate of the masses."

His eyebrows rose in surprise. "You are . . . a communist?"

"My father was—is," I corrected myself, appalled at my slip of the tongue.

"You don't believe in God at all, then?"

I shrugged. "I was raised to believe that religion—any religion—was just another way to control people's minds and spirits so that they won't demand justice in this life because they think they'll get it in the next one."

Ezra nodded and remained silent so long that I feared I might have offended him. But at long last, he spoke. "In most cultures, religion offers hope for the hopeless, an explanation for the unexplainable. Ever since humans began to lift their eyes from the incessant struggle for survival, they have wondered about their own reason for existing. Religion can indeed be a tool for oppression, something we Jews know only too well. But it is also . . . the essence of hope. And it is human to hope, beyond hope."

"That, I agree with. My father also believed—fervently—in the human spirit. In literature, and poetry, and science. He had quite the library, and even when I was young, he would read to me from various writers and philosophers: Oscar Wilde, René Descartes, Marcel Proust, Mary Wollstonecraft. I remember him quoting Voltaire: 'A hundred years from my death the Bible will be a museum piece.'"

Ezra grinned. "Voltaire died when? In the late 1700s? I guess he got the dates wrong. Seems to me the Bible is still in use."

"Well, the Nazis claim to love the Bible," I said, my voice bitter, "though from what I know of its teachings, they either haven't read it, or they have a very twisted interpretation of 'love thy neighbor.'" I leaned my head back against the wall. "Really, the closest thing my father had to faith was a belief in Karl Marx, Sigmund Freud, and Charles Darwin. He used to call them the Big Three, the modern thinkers who held the keys to a future beyond superstition and tradition."

"Are you calling my religion superstition?"

"Oh, no! Not at all. I—" I cut myself off when I saw he was smiling.

I poked him in the ribs with my elbow and he laughed.

"Well, we got two out of three, anyway," he said.

I gave him a questioning look.

"Marx and Freud were Jews. And who knows? Maybe Darwin was a secret Jew."

"Wouldn't that be something?"

"I find Freud's concept of the subconscious fascinating, but doesn't he seem a bit obsessed with sex?"

"No more than the average middle-aged man," I murmured.

Ezra threw back his head and laughed, and I joined him.

"But then, I suppose I was a bit obsessed myself," I said. "Back in my youth."

He gazed at me. "You talk as though you're a hundred years old, Capu."

"I feel like it sometimes. Especially lately."

"You're not all that much older than I am, you know."

"It's not the length of the road. It's how rocky it is," I said. "I was younger than Isedore when the Great War ended, and the twenties were a revelation. The artists, the musicians, the writers, the American military heroes who remained in Paris after the war. It felt like everyone was there, from Eugene Bullard to Louis Mitchell to Gertrude Stein. . . ."

"You were friends with Stein?"

I chuckled. "I wouldn't say we were friends, though she tolerated me, which was compliment enough—an invitation to her salon was coveted."

At her salons, Gertrude Stein would hold forth like a stout, grumpy queen, with her consort, Alice Toklas, by her side. I had never before seen two women openly living together and loving each other like that. It just seemed right; at that time and place, the world seemed open to possibility, to art, to beauty.

"But then, Gertrude seemed to adore Ernest Hemingway," I said, "and he always struck me as something of an ass."

"Americans are a rather odd lot, though, aren't they?"

"No more than any of us, I suppose." I shrugged. "And the Americans in Paris back then were different. Many came to France to fight in the Great War and stayed on because they felt more accepted here. Others were drawn by the idea of open minds and hearts, and Paris was where they could be who they wanted to be. It was . . . astonishing."

"And you fell in love."

Charles.

"What?" I asked, startled.

"You speak of that time as if you were in love—with Montmartre, the salons, the people. . . ."

"Oh, yes! But don't forget the music," I said, closing my eyes as I summoned the memory. "The jazz. I can't convey the kind of electric excitement we felt, in those dark clubs, smoking, drinking, dancing. And the clothes! I never used to go anywhere without sparkling and shimmering. Although now . . . it all sounds so trivial. I suppose it was a good thing we didn't know what was coming, isn't it? We wouldn't have been able to enjoy it."

When I opened my eyes, Ezra was gazing at me.

"What? What'd I say?"

"Rest assured, madame, you still sparkle and shimmer, though perhaps more mutedly than before. It comes from within now, not without. That is the beauty of growing older."

Our eyes met and held for a long moment.

"Punch?"

Isedore held out a tray filled with cups. Her costume made her look even younger than she was, like a little girl playing dress-up in her mother's clothes. With her dark eyes and pink cheeks, she might have stepped from the pages of a storybook.

"Thank you," I said. "But I don't think I could eat or drink another thing."

"It's marvelous, isn't it?" Isedore asked. "It may sound strange to say, but this might be the best Purim of my life. Punch, Ezra?"

She held out a cup to him, which he took with a polite thank-you. She smiled and blushed, then moved on.

"Isedore likes you," I told Ezra in a low voice.

"Isedore?" His eyebrows rose in surprise. "What is she, twenty?"

"She turned eighteen a few weeks ago. We had a little party for her."

I had made a deal with Tremblay, bartering a fan for his mother in exchange for a small cake and candles. The cake was made of potato flour, and the candles were ridiculously large, but they were appreciated nonetheless.

"She seems very sweet," said Ezra. "But she's still a girl. Besides, I'm married, remember?"

We watched as a few of the younger women began another hora, and some of the older women joined in, singing, chanting, and smiling. It amazed me that they could celebrate, however briefly, given everything that had been taken from them.

"What bothers me most about our work here is not the theft of furniture and art," said Ezra as though reading my mind. "Ultimately those are simply worldly goods. They come and go, are bought and sold. What breaks my heart is the loss of history—a family's letters, correspondence, photographs, and writings. Those words, those traces of lives lived, plans made and broken, thoughts and dreams . . . those are the truly precious things. They're irreplaceable."

"The very items destined for the bonfire."

"Exactly."

"The other day I found a manuscript by a playwright whom I'd never heard of, Jules Romains. One of the lines was 'The world is an enormous injustice,' which struck me as a tremendous understatement."

"Were you able to save it?"

I nodded. "Mordecai's been reading it, and I'm sure he'll pass it around to anyone who's interested."

"What if you could do more than that? Now that you're able to leave the building occasionally, maybe you could sneak a few things out."

"Out? As in . . . *out*, out?"

"Maybe your friend could help hide things for you."

"Abrielle is at best an old acquaintance. And I might be more sympathetic to her situation than Isedore, but she does live with a Nazi, so I doubt anything given to her would be safe. She is a collaborator."

He nodded thoughtfully. "Were there not ways in which you collaborated? Or I?"

I shifted uncomfortably. I had not spoken up when the synagogues were bombed or when Jews in Paris were forced to sew golden Stars of David on their clothes. I continued to buy from our local baker, but when he was arrested, I did not protest, did not even ask questions when the boulangerie closed. When one of the families in my apartment building disappeared, I told myself they must have evacuated to the south like so many others. I had not wanted to believe there was more to it.

"You were not the only one," Ezra said, as if reading my thoughts. "I was a lecturer at the university. I had an Aryan wife, Aryan friends. I thought I would be spared. I wanted to believe that it was only the most devout and outspoken Jews who infuriated the powers that be, that French society—and our government—would not countenance the removal of those of us who were so interwoven, so much a part of life in Paris, so French. An English philosopher, John Stuart Mill, once wrote, 'Bad men need nothing more to compass their ends, than that good men should look on and do nothing.' I regret that I have lived to see the truth of these words. Even now I want to believe that those of us in Lévitan who do as Herr Direktor Koch commands will eventually be released, that we are luckier than our relatives who have been sent to camps elsewhere. Does that kind of thinking not condemn me as well?"

His voice was as calm as always, yet the clenching of his fists revealed his anguish. His knuckles went white.

"Do you agree with Mordecai that those sent to the foreign camps will never return?" I asked.

He let out a long shaky breath but did not answer.

"*L'effacement,*" I said.

"Pardon?"

"That's what it feels like—the Nazis are seeking to erase us as if we never existed at all. All of us prisoners, but especially your people."

"They are terrible words, but they ring true." Ezra kicked his leg out, ran the heel of his boot along the floorboards.

"Suppose I *did* save the personal papers," I said slowly. "What purpose would it serve? Surely you're not suggesting they would be helpful to the Allies in some way?"

"It is hard to imagine how it would help the war effort, true enough. But if Mordecai is right, just think how much those papers would mean to those who survive. Like—like the family photographs you saved for Léonie. Can you imagine what it would be like to hold in your hand a letter written by your father, or your wife, or your child, whom you will never see again? When a loved one dies, we Jews say: 'May their memory be a blessing.' Those papers would help keep that memory alive."

"Help keep them from being erased," I responded, my mind made up.

18

Mathilde

"YOU'LL STAY HERE tonight, get some rest," whispered Mathilde as she placed an extra pillow on her bed. The two young women had tiptoed up the rear servants' stairs and snuck into Mathilde's room. "Tomorrow Papi will leave early to go to work, and Mami has her weekly luncheon with her church friends. I'll distract the servants and you can slip out."

"I can't sleep there," said Bridgette, staring at the comfortable bed with its crisp white sheets and shell pink coverlet. "I'm filthy."

"I can't risk running a bath for you. Besides, after what you told me a few minutes ago, I doubt you'll ever relax in a tub again!" Mathilde let out a nervous giggle, but Bridgette remained silent. "No matter. The water pitcher's full, and you can use the basin to wash up. And anyway, it's not like we haven't both been filthy before, remember?"

Bridgette smiled. "That time we tried hunting for frogs at the pond?"

"We looked like we were made of mud! Mami was furious."

"We just wanted a nice dinner of frogs' legs!"

The young women shared a laugh, which faded quickly.

"Those were good days," said Bridgette, picking up the fan Capucine had made for Mathilde and waving it around.

"They were," said Mathilde. "Oh, Bridgette, don't look so sad. There will be good days ahead. You'll see."

Bridgette said nothing, just put down the fan, scrubbed her hands and face, and passed a washcloth under her arms. When she was done, Mathilde handed her a clean nightgown made of soft white lawn with lace at the neckline and wrists. Bridgette slipped it over her head and ran her hands along the supple fabric with reverence.

"This is lovely. You've always had such nice things."

"I've been lucky. Papi and Mami have provided for me."

But at what cost? Papi had said that he expected her to accept Victor's offer of marriage. Her stomach clenched. Try as she might, she could not conceive of being married to the young man. As she crawled into bed, Bridgette on one side and she on the other, she tried to imagine sharing a bed with Victor, his leaning over to embrace her. She pushed the image from her mind. It seemed unnatural, like kissing a brother.

Bridgette sank into the downy bed with a long sigh.

"Remember our sleepovers?" Bridgette asked.

Mathilde nodded, lying down facing Bridgette. "Staying up all night talking."

"It's funny. I'm weary to the bone, but I don't think I can sleep," Bridgette said.

"Maybe you need something to read. I have a nice book of poetry Mami Yvette gave me. . . ." Even as Mathilde suggested it, she
realized the book would probably be boring. "Wait. I've got a better
idea. How about we read some love letters?"

"Oh, I don't know, Mathilde. Don't take this the wrong way,
but . . . I'm not up to reading Victor's love letters. I'm not sure I want
to know his private thoughts."

"I thought you liked Victor."

"I like him well enough. I mean, I don't *dis*like him. He's a traitor
to his people, working where he does, but I do understand that collaboration takes many forms, and everyone must decide for themselves
what they're willing to do. How far they're willing to go."

Mathilde let that sink in for a moment. If Victor was a traitor to
his people for working for the Germans at the Renault factory, then
Papi Auguste was as well. She knew Papi Auguste loved his country
fiercely, but just how far would he go to accommodate the Germans? At what point would collaboration be too much? She didn't
know how she would answer that herself. She did know she loved
her papi, the man who had taken her in, cared for her, protected her
from want and hunger—and from the enemy.

"These letters aren't from Victor," said Mathilde. "They were
written to my mother."

"To Capucine? From your father?"

"No, from her lover. Her *American* lover."

Bridgette's eyebrows lifted in surprise.

"*Now* would you like me to read them to you?"

"*Mais oui, s'il te plaît!* Where did you get them?"

Only then did Mathilde realize that she had not yet shared with
her friend her visits to La Maison Benoît. So she told Bridgette
about Antoinette and what it felt like to see her grandfather's ran-

sacked shop, to linger in her mother's bedroom, to smell her perfume. She scattered the feathers she had collected atop the duvet. The bright, patterned plumes looked like a work of modern art against the muted shell pink of the counterpane.

"They're so pretty." Bridgette picked up one after another, running her hand along the edges. "I've always wondered, do the birds shed their feathers, or are they killed for them, like animals are for their hides?"

"I hope not. I would hate for birds to be slaughtered in the pursuit of fashion."

"Maybe someone follows them around and harvests the feathers as they fall out naturally." Bridgette let out a low chuckle. "Imagine chasing an ostrich! I've heard they're quite fast."

"I saw one at the zoo once," said Mathilde. "It seemed on the cranky side."

They shared a smile, then gathered up the feathers and put them back in the box, and Mathilde set the bundle of love letters on the bed.

"I found these in my mother's old room. See how they're bound with a violet ribbon? They must mean something to her, right?"

"It would appear so," said Bridgette, settling back against the pillows. "Read to me *un billet-doux*, my good woman. I command it."

"As you wish, my lady."

Outside, the wind picked up and the rain began to fall, fat drops bouncing off the balcony and tapping softly on the windowpane as Mathilde read aloud the letter she had first read in La Maison Benoît. And then she opened the next one:

> *These days I have become a man beset by desire tinged*
> *with regret. I wish that we could remake our ruined*
> *lives together, that our friendship—our love—would*

have a different meaning to the world. I wish I could
have been frozen in time that night we met in Paris, and
so many nights afterward.

I know well that many would not understand us,
would condemn us. Your people, and mine. But I
suppose it comes down to this: I love Capucine. I need
Capucine. I yearn for Capucine. I simply miss you, in a
straightforward, human, desperate way. I can't bring
myself to give a fig what anyone else thinks. As you said
in your last letter, they don't know our love. They don't
know what true love is.

Bridgette sighed. "That's so romantic. Can you imagine loving someone like that?"

"I really can't," said Mathilde.

Bridgette gave her a searching look. "I take it you don't feel that way about Victor."

Flopping over on her back, Mathilde stared at the ceiling and let out a long groan.

Bridgette chuckled that deep belly laugh of hers. "Sounds like that's a no."

"Papi says Victor's going to propose."

Bridgette nodded, and after a pause said, "And what will be your answer?"

"I don't know. . . ." Mathilde searched for the words. "I mean, he's nice enough. Papi and Mami like him, and they want the best for me. And they're older and wiser. It's just that . . ."

"It's Victor," Bridgette suggested. "And you don't love him."

"Even if I did, I keep thinking, is that all I'm good for? Getting married?"

"What else would you like to do?"

"I don't know that, either. That's the problem. I like drawing, but that's hardly a vocation, and I'm not even that good. And even if I were, my grandparents would not be willing to support me while I pursued a life in the arts."

"You'll have your own money soon, won't you? What if you used it for yourself instead of for marriage?"

"It wouldn't be enough to live on for very long."

"Maybe long enough. You could go to school, become an artist."

Dare to follow in her mother's—and father's—footsteps? And then what? *Look how things turned out for them.*

But Mathilde stopped herself—that last was her papi speaking.

They held each other's gaze for a long moment. Mathilde couldn't help but notice the closeness she had always felt with Bridgette and how easy it was to be herself around her. The sheer terror in her belly when she saw the blood on Bridgette's coat. Mathilde tried to think of Victor in the same light. If he had come, appearing wounded, to the house in the middle of the night, of course she would have let him in and tended to him as best she could, but would she have felt such dread at the thought of what might happen to him? Would she have felt even a fraction of what she felt when she was with Bridgette?

She reached out to the end of Bridgette's braid, the little tassel curling slightly. It felt like silk and reminded her of the fluffiest plumes in Bruno's shop.

"I was so jealous of your hair when I was little," said Mathilde. "It's like liquid gold."

"You're one to talk. In the sunshine, you glow like a redhead, but in the candlelight, your hair looks like spun honey."

Mathilde chuckled. "We're quite poetic this evening, are we not?"

They smiled at each other.

"I have a question," said Mathilde. "When your mother called here looking for you, she said Simone might have seen you. Have you gotten together with her lately?"

The smile left Bridgette's face. *"Simone,"* she said in a flat tone.

"I take it you know about her new gentleman friend?"

"He's no gentleman. He's a Nazi and ten years her senior, if not more. He's trouble, Mathilde. I—I tried to tell her, but she wouldn't listen." Bridgette seemed to be debating whether to say more. "He's part of *Möbel Aktion*, or Operation Furniture."

"What's that?"

"The Nazis are emptying out the homes of the Jews they've been deporting."

"They're stealing their furniture?"

"Not only that. From what I've heard, they take *everything*. One of the men in the Résistance used to work for a moving company, and he reported that's all they've been doing lately: stripping one home after another, taking all a family's possessions, down to the lightbulbs and dustbins. That's where I heard about people being held at the Lévitan department store, and apparently there are a couple of other Parisian camps as well."

"You told me you heard it from an old friend of yours, the wife of a prisoner of war."

"I lied. I'm sorry, Mathilde. I lie to my parents as well. It's necessary when working with the Résistance. At this point, it's become a way of life."

Mathilde nodded. Of course Bridgette had to lie. So, the Germans were seizing everything belonging to those whom they deported, as if to obliterate any record of their existence. Clearly, the occupiers did not intend for the Jews to return. Ever. What did that mean for her mother and her grandfather Bruno?

Should she go back to the Lévitan department store? But Bridgette had mentioned a couple of other Paris work camps. How was she to know which one her mother was at? And what if Capucine wasn't in Paris at all, but had long since been deported somewhere far away, to Germany or beyond?

"Let's read more letters," Bridgette suggested.

She snuggled down under the warm counterpane as Mathilde read aloud, her voice accompanied by the patter of rain and the rumble of distant thunder.

Very soon, they slept.

THE NEXT MORNING, Mathilde left Bridgette asleep in bed and crept downstairs, where she found Mami in the kitchen scolding Cécile the housemaid.

"If you didn't eat them," Mami demanded, "then what happened to all Cook's biscuits?"

"It was me, Mami," Mathilde confessed. "I'm the culprit, not Cécile. I got so hungry in the middle of the night and couldn't help myself."

"Mathilde!" Mami Yvette looked her up and down as if to determine if she had gained weight from the late-night snack.

"I'm sorry, Mami. I was reading and lost track of time and got hungry."

"That's all right, my dear," Mami said. "But do take care to protect that pretty figure of yours! Victor expects nothing less."

Mathilde forced herself to smile. "Of course, Mami."

After Papi Auguste had left for work and Mami Yvette went out to her luncheon, Mathilde brought coffee, a plate of scrambled eggs, and more biscuits up to her room for Bridgette.

"What will you do now?" Mathilde asked.

"My contacts can smuggle me out to a safe place in the country-side," said Bridgette as she polished off the scrambled eggs. "The only problem is that, now that my cover has been blown, the Germans will be looking for a blond schoolgirl. Maybe I should—I don't know—change my clothes, at least."

"Not sure how much of a disguise that will be," Mathilde said. "Wait. I have a better idea! Come with me."

Checking to be sure the servants weren't nearby, they scurried down the hallway to her grandparents' en suite bathroom, where Mathilde started searching a tall cabinet.

"What are you looking for?" Bridgette whispered.

"Mami Yvette dyes her hair brown. I'll bet she has some dye squirreled away."

"Won't she miss it?"

"If she does, I'll tell her I used it to paint a picture or something. She'll be disappointed in me, but then, she usually is. You should have seen the look on her face this morning when I told her I ate the missing biscuits."

"I'm sorry, Mathilde," said Bridgette, looking crestfallen. "I'm already causing trouble for you."

"I'm kidding, Bridgette! Please don't worry about it. Disappoint-ing my grandparents is nothing new. Imagine what they'll say if I turn down Victor's proposal of marriage."

Her stomach clenched at the thought, but she shoved it aside. Right now her friend's safety was paramount.

"*Aha!*" Mathilde said, holding up a large brown carton.

"What is that? *Juglans nigra*?"

"It's the name of a plant, the black walnut. Mami Yvette used to have her hair colored at the salon, but when the war began, L'Oréal hair dye became scarce, and anyway, Hitler denounced the use of hair dye as immoral. So she started using this instead. It's made of the husks of black walnuts from trees that grow in the Americas."

"Where in the world does she get it?"

"Of that, I'm not certain. But the black market is a marvelous thing. The point is, it should do the trick on that blond hair of yours. Also, I think we should cut it."

"Really?"

Bridgette looked so discomfited by the idea that it made Mathilde smile.

"You face down Nazis but quail at the thought of a haircut?"

"I like my hair."

"So do I. But it's not worth your life, is it? Now sit down and let me get to work."

"Do your worst," Bridgette said, resigned. "I always wondered what I'd look like as a brunette."

They took the dye and a pair of scissors back to Mathilde's bedroom and locked the door. It took a while, but at long last Bridgette's golden tresses were a decided brown. Then Mathilde cut them into a short bob, inspired by the memory of Capucine in her flapper days. Finally, they brushed her hair dry.

"What do you think?" asked Bridgette, sounding nervous.

"Honestly? You look like a movie star. Exotic, with your blue eyes and brown hair and old-fashioned hairstyle. But even still, you might be recognized if they're looking for you, right? We need to get you out of Paris."

"Only after I deliver the papers. That can't wait."

"Let me do it," Mathilde offered. "I promised to help Mami Yvette this afternoon, but I could go tomorrow. Would that be too late?"

"Tomorrow's fine. But . . . ," said Bridgette, shaking her head, "I can't ask that of you."

"You didn't. I volunteered."

"And I appreciate that, but— No, it's out of the question."

"What option is there? And anyway, most of the time nobody even notices me, much less gives me a second glance."

"Don't be ridiculous, Mathilde. You're beautiful."

"Only to those who already love me. To the world, I'm quite ordinary." She laughed when she saw Bridgette's face. "I'm really quite fine with it. So, where do I go?"

After another moment of hesitation Bridgette said: "There's a butcher in the twentieth arrondissement. He has a shortwave radio and is in touch with the British."

"What's in these papers?"

Bridgette shook her head. "I haven't looked at them. Usually they contain information about troops and equipment, sometimes coordinates. Sometimes it's all in code. It's best not to know too much, in case . . ."

"In case you're arrested and tortured?" Even as Mathilde said it, it sounded like part of a movie plot, perhaps one of the British Hitchcock movies she had seen with her mami Yvette. The situation was so absurd and yet so very real and terrifying. Mathilde wondered whether she would ever be able to relax in a hot bath again after hearing about that particular form of torture.

"I know it's a lot to ask," said Bridgette. "But Sébastien, the man who was killed . . . I feel like I have to do it for him. To at least accomplish this much of our mission."

"Then let's not waste any more time," Mathilde said. "Tell me what to do."

For the next hour, Bridgette gave Mathilde lessons in Résistance work.

"Most of the time, it's pretty simple," Bridgette explained. "The worst part, believe it or not, is waiting in the long queue at the butcher shop. That grates on your nerves. But when you get in, you simply ask the butcher for the special flank steak that your grandmother loves so much, especially with flageolets."

"Is that a code?"

She nodded. "It lets the butcher know you're there on behalf of the Résistance. Then, while he's preparing your order, you set your bag down on the floor at the end of the counter, and after you pay, you leave it there and walk away with the package of meat he'll give you."

"That doesn't sound too hard."

"It's not. The hardest thing is to act natural, as if you're just there to buy meat like everyone else. If you're nervous or you start sweating, you'll give yourself away. Most of the customers won't pay any attention to you, though. You'll see. They're busy thinking about themselves and their own worries. It's not like they're expecting another customer to be a spy—and even if they did, it's doubtful anyone would say anything. I'm telling you, Mathilde, we French are getting fed up with the Occupation."

"What if there's a soldier there?"

"There won't be. But should you encounter one on the street or anywhere, relax and smile—a lot of the *Wehrmacht* are our age and more interested in flirting with you than anything else. The ones to look out for are the men in trench coats, because they're often undercover. So try to relax, but be aware of everyone."

"What . . . what if I'm caught? What do I do?"

"Don't give them my name—not for my sake, but to protect my parents. Instead, make up a school friend. Let's call her . . . Béatrice. Tell them who your grandparents are, act young and stupid and scared—that last won't be hard—and say Béatrice asked you to hold the package for her uncle, but didn't tell his name."

"Won't they find out there was no Béatrice in our class at school?"

"Perhaps, but that will take time, and if you act silly enough, it's unlikely they'll bother. And if it comes to that . . . your grandparents will vouch for you, won't they?"

"You mean, will they say I'm naïve enough to carry an unknown package for a friend? I'd say the answer is a decided yes."

Bridgette smiled. "There's power in being underestimated, Mathilde. A surprising strength in softness."

"You're quite the philosopher."

"I've had a lot of time to think. You know how long it takes to ride a bike from Paris to Claye-Souilly and back again?"

Mathilde laughed, then sobered. "How do we get in touch with the people in the Résistance who can get you out of Paris?"

"We have a rendezvous point for emergencies. I just have to let them know I'm coming and when. Would you be willing to make a telephone call?"

"Of course."

Bridgette gave Mathilde a number and a code phrase to say to the woman who answered the phone. Mathilde went downstairs to the big front hall, picked up the receiver, and performed her first official act of resistance.

WHEN COOK AND the maid left to do the shopping, the young women went down the servants' stairs and out the back door. It was cold enough to see their breath, and everything was wet and washed clean from the storm. A large branch had fallen on the lawn, a smaller one in the birdbath.

"I feel bad taking your bicycle," said Bridgette.

"Don't be silly. You need it more than I."

"Thank you, Mathilde."

"You're welcome."

Mathilde felt like she should say more, something profound, knowing it was only too possible she would never see her friend again. But as usual, nothing came to mind.

"Please, tell my parents what has happened," said Bridgette. "Let them know that I'm all right, that I'm safe but in hiding. But you must tell them in person, not over the telephone."

"I will."

"With my brother being sent to work in Germany, it's all so hard on them. Tell them . . . Just tell them that I love them."

Her big eyes filled with tears, and Mathilde had to resist the urge to brush them away.

"I will. I promise," Mathilde said. "But you must promise to be careful. I couldn't bear it if . . . Well, I couldn't bear it."

"You, too, be safe. And . . . if you change your mind about delivering the papers, I'll understand."

Mathilde nodded, standing back as she watched her old friend throw her leg over the bike as she had so many times since they were children. But this time she carried Mathilde's old knapsack on her back, and her now-brown hair was bobbed. Bridgette rode quickly down the gravel drive, turned left onto rue Pierret, and disappeared behind a line of trees. She did not look back.

Mathilde turned to go back in the kitchen and stopped cold.

Mami Yvette stood in the doorway.

"What on earth are you doing in the garden without a coat?" Mami demanded.

"I didn't realize how cold it was," Mathilde said, fighting panic. What had Mami seen or heard? "I was . . . checking on my bicycle. I thought the tires felt a little flat yesterday."

"When I returned from my luncheon and found the back door open, it gave me quite a start, I must say. Are Cook and Cécile back from the market yet?"

"I don't think so. *Brrr*, you're right. It's cold out here. Let's get inside."

"Where's your bicycle?" asked Mami Yvette.

"It—it's the strangest thing. I can't find it. I think it must have been stolen."

"Stolen? Are you certain?" Mami Yvette shook her head and clucked as she turned to go back into the kitchen. "What is this world coming to?"

19

Capucine

$\mathcal{P}$ETTIT STOOD TO the side, observing the dancers, a small smile on her face. As I watched, she accepted a glass of punch from Isedore, holding her pinkie up like a guest at a fancy party.

She made me nervous.

The behavior of all the guards was starting to put me on edge. Some were more lenient than others, but all were eager to please their Nazi masters. Something had shifted.

When I met Pettit's eyes, she smiled and nodded. Then she made an announcement. "I need one women's pod, and one men's pod." She looked straight at Ezra and me. "You two, get your pods and come with me."

"Where are we going?" I asked.

"Where I tell you to go." Pettit looked around. "Where's the girl?"

"What girl?"

"The one that follows you around—there she is!"

Isedore had been chatting with one of the young men on the other side of the room. He was dressed as Mordecai and she as Queen Esther, making it easy to imagine them in another time and place. When Isedore looked over, her hands holding the tray shook so violently, the remaining glasses of punch clattered and crashed to the floor.

"You, too, *mon amour*," Pettit said to her, and several guards snickered.

Our two pods, plus Isedore, gathered near the door of the stairwell. Tremblay looked flushed—was he excited or uncomfortable? Two other guards followed, urging us down the steps.

"Let's go," Pettit said. "All the way down to the basement."

Lugging things up from the basement to the showroom floor was a job typically assigned to the men. Maybe we women would be sorting through some newly arrived crates? But when we reached the basement, we were herded toward two open crates of gas masks.

"Everyone grab a mask," Pettit said.

We exchanged glances but did as we were told, each taking one as we passed by the crates.

"Very good, children. Now go down to the end of the hall to that storage room straight ahead."

We shuffled down the hall, masks in hand. The narrow corridor, like the one that led to Kohn's office, was decorated with Nazi propaganda posters calling on "good people" to fight for the Fatherland and ignore the British lies.

The storage room at the end of the hall had an exterior door and a hallway door with a small window. Like the director's office, it was disconcertingly warm.

Pettit pushed all twenty-one of us into the small room, where we stood shoulder to shoulder.

"Put on your masks," she ordered.

"What is this all about?" I demanded.

"These are from a Jewish manufacturer, remember? We need to know whether they work before sending them on to the *Herrenvolk*. We can't have our brave boys dying because some Jew at the factory sabotaged the gas masks."

I must have looked uncomprehending, because she laughed and said, "Don't worry. You'll be fine. Probably. Oh, and don't bother trying to open the other door. It's bolted from the outside. Take deep breaths now!"

Pettit slammed the hallway door behind us and threw the bolt. She peered at us through the small window, grinning.

"She's a madwoman," growled Henri.

"Do you think the masks really have been sabotaged?" asked Isedore, her voice high with fear.

"If they were," said an older man named Philippe, sounding resigned, "they'll have twenty-one corpses to haul out of here. Could have proven the point with half as many."

It was only then that it finally sank in. We were the subjects of a deadly experiment. Several men tried shoving open the exterior door, but as Pettit had said, it was blocked.

"Masks on, everyone," Ezra said, but it wasn't as easy as it seemed.

"I don't know how!" cried Léonie. "How do I put it on?"

"Me neither!" said Isedore.

"How do we put these on? Does anyone know?" said Jérôme.

"*Everyone*, pipe down and listen," said Ezra with his usual calm

243

resolve. "Take a deep breath and hold the mask in front of your face, like this." Ezra demonstrated with his thumbs inside the straps. "Thrust your chin forward and pull the straps over your head as far as they will go. Once it's on, run your finger around the facepiece to be sure the straps are not twisted. Turn up your collar if you have one to keep gas from drifting down your neck. Women, use your headscarf if you have one. Everyone, help your neighbor."

There was a commotion as we tried to follow Ezra's directions, our hearts pounding and our hands shaking.

"How do you know all of this?" I asked him.

"My father brought home a gas mask from the Great War, and I used to play with it when I was a boy. Different design, of course, but close enough." Ezra was helping Isedore put on her mask. "Try not to cry," he said quietly. "The tears will make it harder to get a proper seal."

My own hands were shaking as I pulled my mask over my face. The masks were made of black rubber that emitted a gassy odor, mixed with the strong scent of disinfectant. The rich Purim feast backed up on me as my nausea grew.

I fought panic, feeling as though I could not inhale enough air through the filter. A rubber flap below my chin flipped up and hit my face each time I took a breath. The lens misted up, blinding me and increasing my terror, and when I exhaled, the edges of the mask blew an absurd raspberry against my cheek. My face grew hot and sweaty, and the bottom edge of the mask became damp with saliva.

I wanted to scream.

Was this *it*? Was this the end, just this stupidly, this unceremoniously? Twenty-one people murdered for no good reason? And why had we obeyed, so bovinelike, allowed ourselves to be herded down the stairs and into this little room? There were more prisoners than there were guards—why hadn't we fought back? Better to be felled by a bullet than poisoned with gas, especially if it gave others a chance to escape, perhaps to melt into the city streets.

But . . . then what? How would we evade all the military patrols, the members of which would happily shoot escaped prisoners on sight? And if we appealed to friends and family for help, they would be at risk of the same punishment.

Our survival had been predicated on keeping our heads down and doing what we were told. It had worked up until now.

Pettit's eyes were shiny with excitement as she observed us through the small window in the door.

Several of the women, and some of the men, were weeping, their shoulders shaking. Ezra was trying to say something to me, but I could not hear his words.

He reached out and squeezed my hand.

Suddenly, Pettit opened the door, yanked me by the arm into the hallway, and tossed a gas canister into the room. It clattered to the ground at the prisoners' feet and began spewing a faint mist, making a horrid hissing sound.

She banged the door closed again and shoved me aside, ordering Tremblay to apply tape around the door to prevent the gas from escaping the storage room.

I tore off my mask and lunged at the door. Pettit backhanded me so hard, I tasted blood and my head slammed against the wall. I fell to the ground, dazed, my cheek and head throbbing.

"*Idiot*," she snarled. "I may have just saved your life, and this is the thanks I get?"

She held out her hand as if to help me up. Stunned and dizzy, I grasped it and got to my feet.

"They'll be fine," Pettit said, then shrugged. "Unless the masks *were* sabotaged. How ironic would that be? Jews causing the death of Jews. Anyway, your little girlfriend there took your place. Be thankful."

Through the window in the door, I saw only the foggy outlines of my friends and fellow prisoners engulfed by the mist.

I vomited.

"You'll have to clean that up," announced Pettit.

HALF AN HOUR later, Pettit and the other guards escorted me back through the building and outside, then around to the exterior door of the storage room turned gas chamber. The guards looked nervous and held their guns at the ready. My ears still rang, I couldn't stop shaking, and my head ached, but all I could do was stare at the door.

Tremblay undid the latch, and everyone streamed out, a few running, others stumbling, all tearing off the gas masks and taking great gulps of the evening air.

Pettit laughed and pointed. "Look at 'em run!" she said.

The guards guffawed—even Tremblay, the man who knew the pain of being bullied as a boy. When I caught his eye, he blushed and looked away. Who was the bully now?

The prisoners' faces were red and sweaty, and several were retching from the sheer terror of what had just happened. But they were alive. The masks had not been sabotaged.

"What's the matter, 123?" Pettit frowned. "I thought you had a sense of humor. No? Well, we'll let this room air out and then you'll all clean the gas masks. I don't want to see any traces of disgusting Jewish vomit."

Our two pods, plus Isedore, spent what was left of the evening cleaning the masks of our tears, spit, and vomit. The next day we would load the *Gasmasken* into crates to be shipped off to Germany, to help safeguard the soldiers of the Third Reich.

EZRA AVOIDED ME during the cleaning of the room and the gas masks, but as soon as Pettit left, he reached out and enveloped me in a long hug. He whispered something unintelligible, and when I asked him to repeat it, he shook his head, lifting one hand to trace the ugly swollen bruise on my face left by Pettit's hand, and he gave me a sad smile.

After we returned to the attic and told everyone what had happened, the aftermath of the Purim festivities turned subdued as we finished cleaning up the dinner dishes and folding costumes.

"If that is how our captors responded to Purim, I wonder what might be in store for us on Passover," Mordecai said.

"When is Passover?" I asked.

"April eighth to fourteenth in the Gregorian calendar; Nisan fifteenth to twenty-first are the Hebrew dates. If Purim had gone well, I thought we might ask permission to hold a Seder on Passover Eve, but now . . . what price might our captors exact for the privilege?"

"What is a Seder?" I asked.

"It is a celebratory dinner that commemorates Exodus, the freeing of the Jews from slavery in Egypt."

"Ah. First mass murder and now slavery. Very appropriate holidays, then."

"Indeed."

"How are things these days in the watch factory?"

"Busier than ever. It's as though they're in a race against time. . . . Pardon the pun."

"Do you have any really nice pieces? I would love a mantelpiece clock for the apartment I'm decorating."

"Come see us on Monday, if you can get permission."

Mordecai worked with Isedore and a small group of men to clean and repair valuable clocks, watches, and jewelry. Isedore liked to bring leftover gears, clockfaces, hands, and other paraphernalia to the attic to use as decorations; the ones from the watches were minuscule. Ezra had cobbled together several to make a wind chime to hang from the shelf over her bed, though there was never so much as a slight draft in our stuffy attic.

That night I lay awake, watching the clockwork wind chime, wishing for a breeze to make it dance, thinking about Roger. My husband.

It was a Tuesday morning. I remember Mathilde was cooing in her basket and I was making an asymmetrical fan of swirling cock feathers that looked black but gleamed a deep sapphire blue in the light. The socialite matron who had ordered the fan was so very prim and proper that it had seemed an oddly daring choice for her, and Bruno suggested perhaps she simply enjoyed saying *"coq"* because in English it meant something risqué.

I was laughing at the silly off-color joke when a man in a red cap walked into La Maison Benoît and informed me that Roger had fallen and struck his head.

"Where is he?" I asked, untying my apron strings to rush to the hospital.

"I regret to tell you that he is at the morgue, madame," he said.

I froze, made him repeat it. Made him tell me thrice that my husband was dead.

And just like that, my young life changed.

How could the man who had been warm and sentient in my arms just a few hours ago now no longer exist? Roger was not perfect; he was sometimes impatient and, when it came to social niceties, too often sided with his parents or traditional conventions. It irritated me when he wanted me to go along with his bourgeois ideals, to tone things down—after all, as he had told me many times, it was my "free spirit" that had attracted him to me.

But he was loyal, he stood up to his parents when it really mattered, and he was insanely in love with his daughter. Whenever he was at home, he insisted upon carrying Mathilde constantly, so much so that I teased him, saying she might never learn to walk.

"That's my little angel," he'd say. "She's my very own little angel."

Bruno accompanied me to the morgue to view Roger's body. The man with the red cap had not lied: My husband was, indeed, dead. His eye sockets were swollen and blackened; his face seemed distorted. The man who had lain with me, married me, loved me and our Mathilde, was gone. He had disappeared. I no longer had a husband. Mathilde would never know her father.

I heard a loud wail and turned to see Auguste supporting Yvette as she keened, a horrific, agonized sound unique to a mother who had lost her child.

And I read the dread in Yvette's and Auguste's eyes as they realized the babe I held in my arms was all they had left of Roger, and that meant they had to deal with *me*.

Now, I wondered, had they succeeded in erasing me from my daughter's thoughts, from her life? If I had died in that gas chamber, would they have been notified? Or would I have disappeared without notice, just . . . *gone*? Were the Nazis unintentionally aiding my in-laws in their desire to expunge me from Mathilde's life?

Ever since Roger's death, I had been afraid. I covered it up with quips and sass, but down deep, I was afraid. A particularly astute judge of character would have painted me crouched in a corner, my arms wrapped around my head.

It would have been entitled *The Cringing Woman*.

THE CALLOUS DISREGARD for human life Pettit and the other guards had displayed down in the storage room made up my mind: better to die quickly by a bullet on the loading dock for a good reason than to be gassed for simply complying with orders.

So the next time a large shipment arrived that included documents from what appeared to be a home office, I approached Tremblay.

"You know I'm doing work for Herr Pflüger now, right? Paper is so hard to come by these days. . . . May I keep these and use them for my sketches?"

"I guess so. . . . I mean, I don't really know. . . ."

I swore under my breath when Tremblay called Pettit over and explained what I wanted.

"The lady gave you some paper the other day," said Pettit. "Why do you need more?"

"That paper is for the finished sketches. In the creative process, I need to make a number of preliminary sketches to try out ideas, and I don't want to ruin the good paper with that sort of thing."

Pettit snorted. "What are you designing, the Sistine Chapel?"

She shuffled through the papers: letters from a daughter to a mother, family budgets, grocery lists. Nothing of any obvious importance. "Looks like junk to me. All right, take them if you want them."

"Thank you," I said, gathering as many as I could before she changed her mind.

From that point on, I amassed any and all papers without regard to topic. There were random notes, professional and personal correspondence, real estate papers, and receipts. Children's drawings, nonsensical doodles, and a note from a mother to her child away at school. Love letters, informative missives, and friendly notes between neighbors.

The other women unpacking crates noticed what I was doing and followed suit, hiding papers in their smocks until they could give them to me.

I tried to think of other small acts of defiance we might be able to manage, given our constraints. Although I was enormously relieved the manufacturer hadn't sabotaged the gas masks, I wondered why it hadn't taken the opportunity to do so, and I tried to imagine something we might do to the furniture to cause the Nazis harm. Apart from loosening the joints—which at its worst might cause someone to fall to the floor, and in any event could be easily remedied by anyone with a screwdriver—I could not think of anything.

"I was wondering . . . ," I said to Isedore one night while we lay on our cots. "Is there a way to rig clocks or watches so that they work well for a short time but then fail?"

"You mean . . . so they stop working for the Nazis?" She grinned. "They are so tied to their clocks and schedules, it would drive them nuts! I could use defective springs maybe, or cut partway through the gear shaft. . . . Let me think about it."

"It would have to be subtle, though, Isedore. You can't have them trace the sabotage back to you."

"Don't worry. I'll be careful. But Mordecai might catch on and I'm not sure what he would say about it."

"Why's that?"

"He's very attached to those clocks. Even if they're meant for Nazis, he wants them to run perfectly. He says his people have dealt in the finest jewelry and watches for generations, and that tradition is all we have left."

ON FRIDAY, JUST before sunset, I was sitting on the floor in my usual spot, my back against the wall, watching as Hélène lit the Shabbat candles.

The Jews in Lévitan were forced to work on Saturdays and given the day off on the Christian Sabbath of Sunday. But that did not keep them from lighting the candles on Friday evening, which, I had learned, was the beginning of Shabbat. Our collection of candles was a motley one, scraped together from the crates of stolen goods, but lighting the flames was far more important than the aesthetics.

Ezra came over to sit next to me.

"I love this ceremony," I said. "No idea what it's all about, of course, but . . ."

"The lighting of the candles is said to have a dual purpose: to honor Shabbat, and to create *shalom bayit,* or peace in the home.

Lighting Shabbat candles is mandated by rabbinical law. It's traditionally done by the woman of the household."

"Why does she wave her hands like that?"

"After lighting the candles, the woman moves her hands over them and toward herself, as if guiding in the Sabbath. Then she covers her eyes and recites a blessing."

"That's really lovely. I know in the Christian church when people light a candle it's a symbol of sending a prayer out into the world—or, I suppose, up into the heavens."

He nodded.

"And you don't take part?" I asked.

He shook his head.

"Does that have to do with being a secret Jew?" I teased.

"No, my mother used to do it, and my wife, Fayette, as well."

"I thought your wife was Aryan."

There was a long pause. Ezra stuck one long leg out in front of him, crooking the other so he could rest his arm on it. "Fayette was my first wife. She was a devout Jew, so I tried, for her sake."

"What happened to her?"

"She died in childbirth, along with our baby. Almost five years ago. We had been so excited to begin our family, and then the two of them were gone"—he snapped his fingers—"just like that. It is hard. . . . It is beyond difficult to imagine how that kind of senseless loss and pain could be countenanced by any higher being."

"I am so sorry, Ezra." After a pause, I asked, "Are you angry at God?"

He shrugged. "Let's just say we're taking a little time off."

"I'm probably not the right person to say this, given my own views, but it seems to me that now is not the best time to be on the outs with the Lord."

He chuckled softly and met my eyes, and I realized our hands were on the floor, palm down, next to each other. I could feel the heat of his hand so close to mine. I edged my hand over just a fraction of an inch to touch his.

We stayed there like that for a long moment.

"Does your current wife come to visit?" I asked.

"How do you mean?"

"I've heard that some of the spouses linger out on the sidewalk. Jérôme managed to toss a note to his girlfriend not long ago."

He shook his head. "She sends packages when she can. But . . . Michelle and I have an unconventional relationship."

"What do you mean by 'unconventional'?"

"I thought you of all people would understand the meaning of the word," he said with a smile.

I gave a humorless laugh. "I've discovered lately that being unconventional is a sin the likes of which can cause a person to be arrested."

He nodded again in that slow, thoughtful way.

"Ours is not a love marriage. Michelle and I are good friends. She's a very bright woman, also a lecturer at the university. She saw what was happening in our country and thought I would have a better chance if we were married."

"That was good of her."

"It was. I was very grateful, and pleased that our marriage could protect her as well."

"How so?"

"She lives with her friend. Her very good woman friend."

I stared at him for a moment, understanding dawning. *"Ah."*

"Ah," he said with a nod.

"So you both benefitted."

"Her family was happy she was marrying, even to a Jewish man."

"Way back when," I said, "I knew a lot of people who lived openly with the person they loved, no matter their sex or religion or skin color."

"That must have been in Montmartre." He smiled and nudged me with his elbow. "When you were the Fan Girl."

"Did Isedore tell you about that?" I chuckled. "That was back in my wild days."

"You aren't wild anymore?"

"No, not anymore."

But the truth was that Ezra's hand next to mine, the scent of him, the heat of his presence, made me think of things . . . secret yearnings I thought had died for good when I lost Charles. *Chemistry*, I thought to myself.

"My first wife, Fayette, was a very optimistic person. She used to say that to dare to love is to dare to hope for the future."

"She sounds wise."

"I've been thinking of how I felt in that room with the gas. Not knowing if it might be the last for me, for us all. I was glad— profoundly so—that you weren't in there with us."

My eyes filled with tears. Words failed me.

"And I think that perhaps the experience was a strange sort of gift," Ezra continued. "I think I needed to be reminded."

"Reminded of what? That the Nazis think we're trash? That they're just as happy if we die?"

"I never forget *that*." Ezra shook his head. "But when we are stripped of all things, we are left with nothing but our humanity. *Nous sommes dépouillés*: no property, no pride, no ambition, no pretense. Not even family connections. It's as though we are melted down and all that is left is who we are deep within, at our core. Our essence. And we are forced to accept it, to acknowledge our essential truth. That is the gift."

He placed his hand over mine.

"One of my truths," he said, "is that I love you, Capucine."

20

Mathilde

EVEN BEFORE THE shortages and the coupon system made shopping a full-time endeavor, Cook seemed perpetually harassed, despite the assistance of Cécile the housemaid. So when Mathilde offered to pick something up for dinner at the butcher's, Cook happily handed over the family's ration tickets.

Without her bicycle to take her into the city, Mathilde waited for nearly half an hour for a streetcar that never came before she gave up and started walking. It would take at least an hour to get to the butcher shop in the center of Paris on foot, but she was young, she was wearing good shoes, and she had plenty of time. What else did she have to do? The embroidery sessions with Mami could wait—forever as far as she was concerned.

Although Mathilde regularly ventured into the city, this time her heart pounded as she walked along the sidewalks and traversed cobblestone streets. She felt intensely aware of the illicit papers in her tote, hidden under an old sweater and a boring history book. Hoping to strengthen the ruse that she was an innocent young girl, she had topped these items with a few sprigs of pink cherry blossoms she found along the way. The bag's weight tugged at her arm with every step, a constant reminder of what she was carrying.

Mathilde had been sorely tempted to read the documents last night, but ultimately followed Bridgette's suggestion that it was better not to know.

When she reached the butcher's shop, Mathilde took her place at the end of the line of customers queued on the sidewalk. Only then did she fully appreciate what Bridgette had meant when she warned her this part could be tricky. In some ways, it seemed the easiest thing in the world, standing in line with everyone else, inching forward bit by bit. It was how most Parisians experienced this war: as a long, tedious wait.

But every person she saw seemed suspect, every glance a potential betrayal. As she neared the head of the line, she saw in the shop's window the reflection of a man in a trench coat, and she nearly keeled over from fright. But he simply glanced at his watch, then looked up and down the street, as if searching for someone who had failed to arrive, and after a few more minutes, he left.

At long last, it was Mathilde's turn to step up to the counter. "*Bonjour*, monsieur," she greeted the butcher, and recited the line Bridgette had taught her. "I would like flank steak, please. It is my grandmother's favorite, especially with flageolets."

The unsmiling man in a bloody white apron was younger than her grandparents, but his deep-set eyes looked ancient. He gazed at her with sadness, and she wondered whether he knew what it meant that Bridgette was not here to deliver the package herself. She wished she could reassure him that her friend was safe, but of course she had to remain mute. After an excruciating moment, the butcher nodded and turned to the meat display, grabbing a hunk of flesh and wrapping it in brown paper.

Mathilde set the big tote bag on the floor at the end of the counter as she rooted through her reticule for her ration tickets.

"*Merci*, monsieur," she said, handing the coupons to the butcher in exchange for the package of meat.

"Mademoiselle." He nodded and added in a gravelly voice: "*Bonne journée.*"

"*À vous de même. Au revoir.*"

And with that, Mathilde turned toward the door, leaving the tote bag and its secrets behind as though she'd forgotten it. She worried that someone in line might notice and kindly remind her, but they all appeared to have learned the lessons of the Occupied: *Keep your eyes down and your thoughts to yourself. Do not notice or be noticed.*

Exiting the shop, Mathilde took a deep breath of cold fresh air and started down the street, glancing over her shoulder to be sure the man in the trench coat hadn't returned. But no one paid any attention to her. She was simply a young woman walking along in her red coat, her reticule dangling from her wrist, a package of meat in one hand. As she put more distance between herself and the butcher shop, a feeling of elation bubbled up inside her. She was almost giddy with relief, and with a sense of . . . What was it?

Accomplishment. She had done something important. She hoped.

But self-doubt quickly returned. When the Occupation began, her grandparents had counseled her to cooperate, to accept the situation. She was young; she did not understand the ways of the world. She must trust them and do what they said. They knew best. And until now she had.

If she was caught, would her grandparents suffer for her sins? What was that phrase Bridgette had used—"guilt by association"? And if Papi and Mami were wrong about cooperating, and Bridgette was right in declaring that they must resist, must defeat the Nazis . . . then what had Mathilde been doing the past few years, spending her time and money going to the cinema, losing herself in the fantasy of films?

The business with the butcher completed, Mathilde headed to rue Mazarine, to the *famille* Caron's tailor shop.

Monsieur Caron looked even more gaunt than when she had been here last. Mathilde cursed herself for not thinking to bring them something to eat, some bread or fruit at least. She couldn't give them the meat, or her ruse would be uncovered.

"Mathilde!" said Monsieur Caron, looking up from the fabric he was pinning, and managing a ghost of a smile. "*Ça va?* Have you heard anything?"

Bridgette's mother came out from the back of the shop and rushed over, taking Mathilde's hands in hers. "Mathilde, tell me. Where is my baby? Is she . . . ?"

"Are we alone?" Mathilde whispered. At Madame Caron's nod, Mathilde said, "I don't know where she is now, but she spent the night before last with me. She was very tired, but she was fine. She asked me to tell you that she has to go away for a while and can't be in touch, but she will be safe, and she loves you."

Like a puppet whose strings had been cut, Madame Caron collapsed on the shop's thread-strewn floor. Mathilde thought she had fainted until she realized Madame Caron was weeping silently, her shoulders heaving.

Her husband hurried to her side, crouched down, and hugged her, whispering words of comfort. After a long moment, he looked up at Mathilde. "Thank you for telling us. She is working with the *maquis*, then?"

Mathilde nodded.

"I had my suspicions," Bridgette's father said softly. "Such a headstrong, foolish girl. Where did you find her?"

"She came to my house the night before last," Mathilde said. "No one saw her. We cut her hair and dyed it brown, and I gave her my bike and a knapsack with supplies. She was going to meet a contact who could take her to a safe house in the countryside. That's all I know."

Madame Caron looked up, her face streaked with tears. Her husband helped her to her feet, and she reached out to Mathilde and enveloped her in a long, tight embrace, then stepped back and stroked her cheek.

"Thank God for you, *ma fille. Merci à dieu.*"

"I haven't really done anyth—"

"Oh, but you have," said Monsieur Caron, limping back to his workbench and picking up his shears. His jaw was tight, and Mathilde thought she caught the glint of tears in his eyes as he returned to his work. "Make no mistake, Mathilde—you have done something very, very brave and important. We will never forget it. I know you come from a fortunate family, but please know you always have a place in our home."

Mathilde felt embarrassed by their gratitude, like a child who has been congratulated too heartily for completing a simple task. It was almost as if no one had expected her to do anything useful, anything brave. Anything at all.

"Are you all right, my dear?" asked Madame Caron, looking at her anxiously.

"Yes, of course. It's just . . . I've been thinking about my grandfather's fan shop, where he and my mother used to work."

"Was it ransacked?" Madame Caron asked. "The Nazis do enjoy destroying things."

Mathilde nodded. "The concierge says the shop is mine now. And I . . . I suppose I have no idea what to do with it."

"Perhaps you could start by cleaning up the mess," said Madame Caron with a sympathetic smile. "Mathilde, you are a sweet girl. I know that you haven't had an easy relationship with your mother, and that your grandparents never cared for her. But trust me, your relationship with your mother, however imperfect, is important. Your grandparents raised you and love you, but your mother will always be a large part of who you are." She tapped her chest. "In here, where it counts."

"That is right, Mathilde," Monsieur Caron said. "Children often do not appreciate how much they are like their parents—even if they would like to think otherwise."

Mathilde left the shop, mulling it over. Was she like her mother? Maybe it was time to find out. And so even though she was tired from the long walk, the anxiety of her covert mission, and the emotional encounter with Bridgette's parents, Mathilde did not head back to Neuilly-sur-Seine but instead walked to rue Saint-Sauveur, to La Maison Benoît.

It took much longer to get there on foot than by bicycle, of course, but the slow pace gave Mathilde the opportunity to study the city: the blackened façades of buildings, the many shuttered homes and businesses, the pinched countenances of those whom she passed on the street, save for the hale German soldiers. The more she allowed herself to take it all in, to realize what it all meant, the more certain she was that she had done the right thing in delivering that package to the butcher.

It was a tiny contribution to the cause, but a contribution nonetheless.

As Mathilde strolled along the Seine, her gaze rested on the grand winged buttresses of the Cathédrale Notre-Dame, and she peered at the roofline, hoping to spy the gargoyles perched high above the city. With a jolt, she realized that perhaps for the first time in her life, she had no inclination to confess her many recent lies to a priest, or indeed to anyone.

She would keep her own secrets, Mathilde vowed. And she would keep Bridgette's secrets as well.

Mathilde at length arrived at her grandfather's shop and had stood outside only a few minutes when Antoinette tapped on the windowpane, waved, and gestured for her to come in. Mathilde went around to the gate and let herself into the courtyard.

"*Bonjour*, Mathilde! What a lovely surprise," Antoinette called from her doorway.

"*Bonjour*, madame," said Mathilde, and they traded kisses on the cheek.

"What brings you here today?"

"I think . . . I think I want to start cleaning up the shop."

Capucine

I HAD NO IDEA how to respond to Ezra's stunning admission.

According to the dates written with care on the big wall calendar, Ezra and I had known each other only a short time. But here in the attic, everything was heightened: Minutes became elongated, days stretched into weeks, and a week felt like a month or two. On the other hand, given the uncertainty of our current reality, time was too precious to waste. If a Nazi officer didn't like the way you looked at him, he might well send you to Drancy and, from there, to your death. If a madwoman decided to lock you in a small room and fill it with gas, each breath could well be your last.

Ezra's marital status did not bother me, since his wife, Michelle, had no romantic interest in him and would not have married him except for an admirable desire to save him from the Nazis. And besides, things were different here in Lévitan. Inside these department store walls, friendships, love affairs, and alliances were forged that would rarely, if ever, have been pursued on the outside. When— *if*—we were released, I doubted many of those relationships would survive the transition back to real life.

Ezra said his first wife told him that "to love is to dare to hope for the future."

But I knew something else: To love is to invite loss. I thought of Roger, Mathilde, Charles, Bruno. . . . I had tried to stuff my feelings for them into that old fan box in my heart, but their memories haunted me still.

Did I dare hope for a future?

ABRIELLE ARRIVED ON the arm of her officer, Otto Pflüger, to assess the furniture I had selected and arranged on the main floor. We had the showroom to ourselves, and I felt as if I were a shopgirl giving an after-hours showing to a client.

The fine inlaid ebony chest I had chosen was gone, replaced by one that, while quite nice, was not nearly so special. Fräulein Sommer's work, I suspected.

"Ooh, I like this!" said Abrielle. "What do you think, Otto?"

"It's a bit . . . severe," he said. "I like a little more class."

"In what way?" I asked.

He flashed me an irritated glance, and I clarified: "What I mean is, the more specific you can be about what you prefer, the better able I am to find something that will please you. Do you like the wood in these pieces, for instance? Or do you prefer painted pieces or gold gilt—something reminiscent of Versailles perhaps?"

His mouth kicked up on one side in what passed as a smile. "I hardly think our apartment qualifies as Versailles," he said, gazing down at Abrielle, "though I wish I could offer you that, *Maus.*"

I smiled. "I speak only of styles, *mein Herr.* Cabriole legs covered in gold, with a marble top—such a piece would make quite a statement. Like that one there." I gestured to one of the pieces we had set to the side just in case. "You could place one on your highlight wall, topped with a fine work of art. Perhaps a small sculpture or something bright on canvas? Like the painters we once knew, Abrielle."

Abrielle's mouth gaped open as though she was shocked. *Didn't she tell her Nazi where we met?* I wondered. Had it never occurred to her that some of the paintings she had posed for might well pass through my hands here at the Lévitan?

"I detest modern art," he said.

"Oh, I do, too, *Bärchen,*" Abrielle eagerly agreed.

"Of course. I'll just make a note of that," I said, and jotted it down on a piece of paper for show. "We have hundreds of canvases in storage here. They're all jumbled together, so it may take a while to find just the right one, but many are true antiques or painted in a classical style."

"I believe I would prefer such a thing, yes. Perhaps a nice landscape." Herr Pflüger took a seat on the couch. "It's comfortable, certainly a step up from that purple atrocity you inflicted upon me." He chuckled and patted the seat next to him, and Abrielle sat. "Do you like it, *Maus?*"

"I do," said Abrielle. "But . . . perhaps we could see it in another fabric? Something a little . . . classier?"

I swallowed my annoyance with Abrielle's cluelessness. Did she think we had several of the same model in the back, like a regular department store?

"*Mein Herr*, Mademoiselle Garnier, I regret to say that here at Lévitan we have only a basic tailoring shop, and many of our finest seamstresses have been moved over to Bassano," I said. "But I believe there might be upholsterers at the camp at Gare du Nord. If you like the structure of the couch, you might inquire with Herr Direktor Kohn."

"I like this carpet very much," said Herr Pflüger, rubbing the soles of his shiny black boots on the plush wool Aubusson carpet.

"Oh, I do, too!" Abrielle exclaimed.

"I'd like to"—he leered at her—"relax on it with you, once it's at home."

She giggled and I tried hard to think of other things.

"Shall I show you the rest?" I suggested.

As I led the way through the other "rooms" I had arranged with the help of Ezra, Henri, and Jérôme, I tried to see it through a client's eyes: The antique mantel clock I had gotten from Mordecai, the fine Turkish carpets, the carved and polished end tables—everything was stylish yet not pretentious.

Abrielle and Herr Pflüger were stuck together, arm in arm, the entire time, occasionally exchanging sweet nothings. I distracted myself by thinking of the purloined letters and papers I had been collecting. To the Third Reich, even attempting to smuggle out a love letter could qualify as treason. How could I convince Abrielle to help me?

"*Guten tag*," said Fräulein Sommer with a cool nod as she entered the showroom.

Herr Pflüger, Abrielle, and I turned, surprised. The Nazi and Fräulein Sommer greeted each other, shaking hands.

"It is so nice to see you here, Fräulein," said Herr Pflüger, giving her a big smile. "Since we were not so fortunate as to have you design our apartment, we have accepted an inferior model."

"That's me. The inferior model," I mumbled. When they all looked at me, I hurriedly added, "*Désolé.* I wasn't thinking. Please pardon me."

Fräulein Sommer seemed amused, but then frowned. "What happened to your face?"

"A, um, misunderstanding," I said, touching my cheekbone.

It was still swollen and had turned a sickly yellowish green. It was the bump on my head that really hurt, however, and woke me up every time I turned over at night.

"Hmm," she murmured, clearly suspecting there was more to the story, but she let it go. "The truth is, Herr Pflüger, I wanted to apologize to you—and to Capucine—for having stolen from you."

"Stolen from me?" he asked, puzzled.

"Capucine discovered an exquisite chest, made of ebony inlaid with ivory. As I am sure you know, Baron Von Braun is particularly fond of the work of Ruhlmann, and as such, I requisitioned it for his new flat. I hope you do not mind."

"Mind?" Pflüger said. "Certainly not. Anything for the baron."

"Indeed," she said. "Do you find the substitute piece acceptable?"

"I . . . er . . . ," Pflüger sputtered.

"I think I might have gone in the wrong direction when I selected these items," I suggested. "I do believe Herr Pflüger's taste runs more to the rococo."

Fräulein Sommer tilted her head and smiled. "Of course, it does. Well, isn't that always the way? Rarely are discriminating clients pleased on the first try. May I suggest the design process would be strengthened were Capucine to spend more time in your apartment so that she might get a better feel for the space? After all, that is how it is done in Vienna."

"What a good idea!" Abrielle said.

"Fräulein Sommer is very clever," I murmured.

"Certainly, certainly," said Pflüger. "That's how it's done in Vienna, is it?"

"*Ja, mein Herr*," Fräulein Sommer said.

"Excellent, then," Pflüger said, looking pleased. "I shall speak to Herr Direktor Kohn about it."

"I assure you, Herr Pflüger, you and your"—Fräulein Sommer paused as she ran cold eyes up and down Abrielle's curvy frame—"lady friend are in very good hands with Capucine. I have been impressed with her taste and her abilities. I have been tempted to steal her from you to work with some of my clients, since I am so overbooked. I am sure you consider yourselves very fortunate, indeed."

"Yes, quite so." Pflüger looked me over as if seeing me for the first time.

"Oh, we do feel fortunate, don't we, *Bärchen*?" said Abrielle, her voice breathier than usual. "We certainly do. Very fortunate, indeed."

I FOUND IT amusing—but not surprising—that Fräulein Sommer had requisitioned the ebony chest, just as Ezra had predicted. If it was from Ruhlmann's workshop, then it was worth a small fortune; some of his pieces took an entire year to produce. And even if it wasn't an authentic Ruhlmann, it was a superbly crafted copy.

Before leaving, Pflüger assured me that he would speak to Herr Direktor Kohn about having me return to the apartment "as often as it takes to get it right."

I spent the rest of the day going through hundreds of paintings that had been stolen from homes, museums, businesses, and galleries. The canvases were wrapped in brown paper and leaning up against the wall, some framed, others not. Each carried an inventory reference number on its stretcher bars and the outer wrapping. Some of the elaborately carved and gilded frames were probably worth more than the paintings themselves.

I was sure Fräulein Sommer had already picked out any well-known artists; for all their talk of disdaining modern art, the Nazis had an eye for the most valuable items. A prisoner who transferred to Lévitan from Austerlitz claimed that the entire contents of the Louvre, as well as the inventory of many other museums, were being packed up and shipped out to Germany to be added to the personal collections of Göring and Hitler.

It was hard to imagine France stripped of its historical and artistic legacy. We had rebounded after the Great War, but this time felt . . . different.

What would Paris be without its art?

It was a painstaking process to unwrap each painting, assess it, make notes to myself, rewrap it, and move on to the next, but I savored every moment. I leaned into one after another, inhaling the familiar scents of varnish and linseed oil, and thinking of my old life, of entire days and many nights spent in artists' ateliers. Happier days.

Remembering Charles, and jazz, and art, and joy.

Remembering who I used to be.

LATER THAT EVENING, after a meager meal of vegetables cooked in fat, I started sorting through the papers we had been collecting. Ezra joined Isedore and me in our little "room," sitting beside me on my cot.

"There's so much here," I said in a low voice so as not to attract the guards' attention, a stack of papers clutched in each hand. "How are we to know which documents are the most important?"

"I think we can rule out the grocery lists," Ezra said, "though I suggest you draw some sketches on the back of several, to keep up the ruse."

"Good idea."

"Why don't we help you?" suggested Isedore. "I'll ask Hélène and Léonie to join us."

Reading was one of our favorite pastimes in the attic, and now there was a purpose for it other than to take us off our present situation. We sorted the papers by household when we could and made notes if we found any information about the family. An address and a family name were the ultimate goals, but at least we could indicate the approximate date the papers arrived at Lévitan and often from which neighborhood or town. We found memos, personal lectures, bills, a handwritten musical score, notes to a gardener, a partial manuscript—Ezra especially enjoyed reading that one—and the loose-leaf diary of an exhausted young mother with a colicky baby. That one made Hélène cry.

"Oh, look," said Hélène. "Here's a letter about the family's Seder. They write: 'Our feast reminded us of the holiness of the season, that from slavery we were set free.' Isn't that timely?"

Léonie let out a sigh. "I remember our last Seder—my bubbe was still with us. She passed right after."

"May her memory be a blessing," said Hélène, reaching out to squeeze Léonie's shoulder.

"At least she was spared what came after. All of this," said Léonie.

"Oh, I love Passover," said Isedore, her tone wistful. "Seder at our house was always so much fun; my mother said that when she was young, her parents were very somber, and she vowed that when she had a home of her own, she would make it fun."

"My parents were pretty serious, too," said Léonie.

"I wonder if we could have a Seder here," said Hélène.

"Is it simply a feast?" I asked.

The memory of what had happened on Purim was still raw, but the Jewish prisoners found so much comfort in their traditions, it was hard to suggest another celebration would not be a good idea. And the marking of time, the recognition of heritage, was a crucial tether to normalcy for all of us, no matter our religion.

"More important than the feast itself is the Seder plate, set with the symbols of the service," Hélène began, looking at the two younger women. "Do you know them all?"

"There are three matzahs, or matzot, representing the three groups of the Jewish people: the Kohen, the Levi, and the Yisroayl," said Léonie as if reciting a lesson learned in childhood.

"And there's a roasted lamb shank," said Isedore, "representing the paschal lamb that was sacrificed, and a roasted egg, which was a festival offering brought to the high temple in times of holidays."

"The charoset represents the mortar used by enslaved Jews while building the pyramids," added Léonie. "And the chazeret and maror are bitter herbs, representing the bitterness of slavery."

"Very good," said Hélène. "And finally, karpas, representing spring and the earth's bounty."

"The karpas is dipped in salt water to represent the tears of our ancestors," said Léonie softly.

"And of course," said Hélène with a smile, "there is no Seder without wine."

"Well," said Isedore, blowing out a breath. "We might not have wine, but we have enough tears to fill a trough."

"True," said Hélène. "But don't forget the true message of Passover: Our ancestors endured slavery and were freed."

Léonie and Isedore exchanged a glance, and I imagined they were thinking what I was: that none of us was free at the moment.

"It sounds like a beautiful ritual to welcome spring, at any rate," I said.

"It is. Still, there's usually a lot of kvetching about the work involved and how we tend to overeat," Hélène said with a chuckle. "But then, that's part of the tradition as well."

"Shouldn't be a problem this year," Isedore murmured.

We turned back to the piles of papers, and resumed reading to ourselves and sharing snippets aloud, our concentration interrupted by an occasional hoot of discovery.

The guards seemed perplexed but, as usual, bored with our antics.

Still, I was glad the project seemed to bring a little lightheartedness to us all, especially the young women. The pile of "important" papers was growing, and along with it my certainty that I was doing the right thing. These seemingly trivial bits and pieces added up to intimate family portraits. They must not be erased.

The next step, though, made my heart flutter: convincing Abrielle to help us smuggle the papers out.

22

Mathilde

ANTOINETTE WAS NOT surprised to see Mathilde again, and so soon. How could she stay away?

"I'm glad you're here. Come along. I have some supplies you can use."

"Thank you," said Mathilde, and followed the old woman to a utility closet that opened onto the courtyard.

"Oh, by the way," Antoinette said as she handed Mathilde a broom, "I spoke with my sister-in-law. She says she hasn't seen any prisoners at the Lévitan department store, but the immediate neighbors were ordered to keep their shutters closed, and trucks pull up behind the building throughout the day. At first, they assumed the Germans were confiscating the store's inventory, but it's been going on for some time now. So perhaps there is something to what your friend said."

"Thank you for telling me," Mathilde said, grabbing a dustpan and a handful of rags while Antoinette took a metal bucket and some soap. "You don't think Bruno and Capucine will mind my being here, do you? You said Bruno was particular about where things go, and I can only guess. I wouldn't want to misplace anything."

"I imagine they would be delighted to return to an orderly shop instead of the disaster it is now," said Antoinette as she closed the closet and they walked to the gate. "And besides, you're their precious Mathilde. You can do no wrong."

"What do you mean?"

Antoinette gave her a gentle smile. "You really don't remember how much you were loved, do you, *ma fille*?"

"I guess not," Mathilde said. Then she straightened her shoulders as they approached the shop door. "But you're right. It's far better that they find a few things out of place but the shop put aright in general."

Neither woman gave voice to her real concern: that Capucine and Bruno would not care what Mathilde did with the shop, because they were never coming back.

"I spoke with the landlord. It seems Bruno had some good luck not long ago and paid the rent for several months in advance. And when I explained what happened with Capucine and Bruno, the landlord agreed not to ask you to vacate the premises anytime soon."

"That is kind of him," said Mathilde.

"He's a kind man and a very good landlord. In that, at least, we are lucky." Antoinette located the correct key on her ring and opened the door. "Besides, he is unlikely to be able to rent it anyway. There are so many empty shops in Paris these days. Here, why don't you keep the key? That way you won't have to wait for me if I am not here when you come by. It's your place, after all."

"Thank you," Mathilde said, staring at the large brass key, cold and heavy in the palm of her hand.

She entered the shop, Antoinette close on her heels.

"Well, child, you've got your work cut out for you, that's for sure," Antoinette said with a sigh as she stared at the destruction.

"Why did you include the key for the language of fans?" said Mathilde.

"Your mother tucked it into the box. As a child, you were an expert in the language. Don't you remember?"

"I was?"

"You wielded the fan like an expert."

When she was a child Mathilde had gone for hours, even days, at a time without speaking except by using her fan. But now the young woman shook her head, that puzzled look on her face, as though Antoinette herself was speaking a foreign language.

"Ah, well," Antoinette said, waving it away. "It was child's play, right? You were very young when you left here."

"Where do I start?" Mathilde asked, looking around at the mess.

"Good question. If it were me, I'd begin by gathering up everything you don't want further damaged, such as these drawings. I've always loved these," said Antoinette, picking up a few intricate fan designs sketched in graphite and colored in delicate gouache and colored pencil. Some of the designs included materials lists, while others seemed to have been drawn simply for the joy of it. Several had been marred by partial boot prints. "These are your mother's designs. I always thought them pretty enough to be framed just as they are."

"I never knew my mother drew so well—I thought she was mainly a model," said Mathilde, taking one in her hands and running her fingers gently over the painting.

"She was an artist in her own right, though I don't believe she realized it until she began working here with Bruno."

"I like to draw, too."

"Do you, now? I'm not surprised. Your father was quite gifted as well. It would have been a surprise had you no aptitude for art."

The bell on the courtyard gate sounded, and Antoinette craned her neck to look out the window.

"I'm so sorry, my dear," said Antoinette. "But I'm expecting a plumber to fix a sink in one of the apartments. I believe that might be him now."

"I'm fine," said Mathilde. "I wouldn't mind a little time here by myself."

Antoinette smiled. It wasn't her place to say, but she felt proud of the young woman.

"Good, then. Call if you would like a little company or need some assistance. Oh, by the way, your grandfather keeps a phonograph there on the shelf, and there is a stack of old records next to it. The Nazis didn't destroy those, at least. Take it from an old woman who has mopped more floors than she can count: Music helps to lighten the load."

LEFT ALONE IN the fan shop, Mathilde fought the sensation that she really shouldn't be here. She kept hearing Mami's and Papi's voices in her head warning her that Capucine and Bruno might mean well, but they were trouble.

Maybe they're right, Mathilde thought. But even if they were, she couldn't just walk away from the shop. So she did as Antoinette suggested, plugged in the phonograph and put on the first record she put her hands on even though the word "jazz" was in the title: *Louis Mitchell and His Jazz Kings.*

Next to the records was a large book: *Feathers: A Compendium.* She took that as well.

The music was fast-paced and fun. It made her smile and gave her the urge to dance. Was this a sign of the degeneracy Papi Auguste consistently attributed to jazz?

No matter. The music energized her, and she turned the volume up. At first, she felt awkward, self-conscious. But after all, who would see her? The grumpy fruit monger across the street, the paperboy? So after a few minutes Mathilde allowed herself to sink into the music, to swing and bop around to the rhythm in a way she rarely felt free to do in her grandparents' big house. Here, in this crowded, devastated Parisian fan shop, she let herself relax and flow with the beat.

Time to get to work. But where to begin? *I'd begin by gathering up everything you don't want further damaged,* Antoinette had said, so step one was to pick up the scattered feathers and fans. Then Mathilde cleared off a section of the counter that was still intact and opened the big book on feathers. She started to sort the plumes by type: fluffy marabou, striped turkey, and spotted partridge. There were silver pheasant feathers and steel blue goura feathers with white tips. She collected all kinds of dyed ostrich plumes and pink Moluccan cockatoo quills. Feathers from eagles and spotted owls, blue-black swirling *coq* plumes.

Some were stiff, others full and fluffy and soft, others so spare it was hard to imagine they could move the air at all.

The needle had reached the end of the record. Mathilde turned the record over and set the needle back down, and the sounds of trumpets and drums filled the shop.

Once she had sorted the feathers, more or less, Mathilde placed them in sturdy boxes and stowed them away on a shelf. Next up: the fans. She pulled open drawers and found more variety than she ever would have imagined: Some fans were made of feathers, others of silk; there were folded paper fans and fontange and balloon shapes, as well as "fixed" fans made of feathers attached to a single stick, usually tied with a big satin ribbon that reminded her of the violet one around the letters from Capucine's American lover.

Where some fans had feathers, others were decorated with tassels and spangles, black Chantilly lace laid over ivory silk, hand-painted cartouches, gold gilt, or something called brisé, made of thinly sliced bone, horn, tortoiseshell, or mother-of-pearl.

Each fan had a little tag with a description and the price; most of the prices made her gasp. Who would pay so much for a frivolous "woman's scepter"?

One fixed fan was meant for a wedding: made of pure white feathers mounted on blades tipped with white peacock feathers on a carved ivory monture. Another was made of brown turkey feathers, tufted peacock and ostrich at its base, with a white straw stick handle. Yet another had black iridescent feather blades with scattered red and green tufts, brown silk connecting ribbon, and a black tassel. One was made of gold and red pheasant feathers, highlighted with blue and green "eyes"; it was mounted on tortoiseshell monture blades, with a cream silk tassel.

None of the fans was signed. The tags read only: *La Maison Benoît.*

But the fans that most intrigued Mathilde were those she guessed had been painted by her mother. They had a distinctive style: figurative but sketchy, the paint used in a form more of drawing than of painting.

The first record having finished, Mathilde put on another and turned to cleaning in earnest: righting a fallen chair, picking up the scattered papers and the big leather sales ledger, gathering pencils and pens and scissors, and sorting all the other accessories necessary to the art—lace and ribbons and silk and carved ivory and ebony stays. Under the counter she found an undisturbed box of colored pencils, brushes, watercolors, and gouache. She swept up the broken glass and straightened the posters on the wall, then wiped down the windows and the glass counter, taking care not to cut herself on the smashed bits. She carefully cleaned the elaborate framed mirror, surprised at her reflection. She looked determined, and there was a small smile on her lips.

At last, Mathilde paused and looked around at her handiwork. The shop floor was clean, and most of the shelves were at least more orderly. She had not touched the apartment behind the shop, but it could wait. Right now she wanted to study her mother's sketches of fan designs. She brought the box of artist supplies to the counter, stroking the brushes with her fingers and imagining her mother doing the same.

And then she laid out a big sheet of paper and started to draw.

BY THE TIME Mathilde locked up the shop, it was already growing dark. She would have to race against the curfew.

She thought about what Antoinette had said about the Lévitan department store. She could try going there again—it wasn't far and was more or less on her way home. But if she did, then what? Knock on the door of the closed store and demand entry? Go around to the loading dock and ask the truckers what they were doing?

What if it really *was* a prison camp, a part of Operation Furniture? Wouldn't that mean it would be guarded by Nazis? The memory of the man in the overcoat outside the butcher shop made her shiver.

No, she would focus on La Maison Benoît for the time being and figure the rest out later. She just hoped she reached Neuilly in time for dinner.

Only then did she remember that she had the meat for their meal. Cook—and Papi Auguste—would not be pleased.

She sighed and picked up her pace. Dinner was going to be late tonight.

23

Capucine

*T*HE NEXT DAY, I was summoned not to the penthouse apartment Herr Pflüger shared with Abrielle, but to meet with Fräulein Sommer on the showroom floor.

I was surprised to find she had set up an office space in one of the display areas, using a crate as a table. I wondered why she didn't simply requisition one of the store's offices or at the very least choose a nice desk. In her fine sage green tweed skirt suit, with an orange felt tam topped by a flat bow on her head, Fräulein Sommer resembled a stylish woman of means who had come to shop at the humble Lévitan and was awaiting her personal shopper.

"Ah, Capucine. May I call you Capucine, or do you prefer Madame—"

"Capucine is fine," I said, surprised to be asked. Most of the guards referred to us by our armband numbers. "Thank you."

"I find myself in need of an assistant."

I waited.

At my silence, she continued. "There are many respected officers of the Third Reich in desperate need of my services but only one of me."

The corner of my mouth kicked up at the idea of anyone in wartime being in desperate need of interior design services, but I held my tongue.

"You say you worked for Ruhlmann?"

"I worked with my father in his fan-making shop," I said, choosing my words with care, for Fräulein Sommer was not as easy to impress, or to fool, as the others had been. "Through the course of that work, I came to know many designers and did small jobs for them, though I was never an employee."

She looked me up and down, then nodded.

"Would you like me to inform you when particularly nice pieces come through our doors?" I suggested.

"That would be helpful. But I had in mind more of an actual assistant. For instance"—she checked the face of a delicate, expensive-looking timepiece on her slim wrist—"in an hour I am to meet with a client at a manor house in the countryside. I would like you to accompany me, to make notes and write down my thoughts and suggestions. You won't speak, of course, but afterward you will share your thoughts with me."

"I . . . Of course, Fräulein. As long as Herr Direktor Kohn—"

"Leave Herr Direktor Kohn to me."

"Indeed." It was frustrating to have to delay my talk with Abrielle, but I had no choice.

"Good. Meet me by the loading dock in twenty minutes," she said, getting to her feet and gathering a few things. "Wear your black smock but leave the headscarf. Take a moment to fix your hair, if you would. And cover up that bruise on your cheek."

"Cover it how?"

She looked surprised, then reached into her purse and handed me a compact. "This should help."

Upstairs, I brushed my hair and pinned it up, then pulled on my smock. I did the best I could with the powder from the compact, but the results would not win any awards. It wasn't just the ugly bruise that marked me as beaten down: There were dark circles under my eyes; my cheeks were sunken; my skin was ashen, my hair limp and dull. Back in the day, I used to diet to keep my figure. Now I understood what near-starvation did to a person. I was not only thin. I was dulled and diminished. *No Fan Girl in sight.*

"You're beautiful," said Ezra as though reading my mind.

He stood behind me; our eyes met in the mirror.

"I'm not. I never was, not really. Distinctive maybe, but never beautiful."

"I don't believe you."

"Ezra." I turned to face him. "I—I still don't know what to say."

"You don't need to say anything."

"I . . . You know I feel for you, too. But I've told you about Charles. And I fear that you and I . . ." I searched for the words. "That our feelings are a product more of our circumstances than of reality."

He smiled and tilted his head. "Isn't everything circumstance in the end?"

I took a shaky breath and caught a glimpse of Pettit glaring at me from the door to the stairwell.

"I'd better go."

Ezra nodded and stood aside to let me pass. "Good luck."

At the loading dock, I had expected to climb into the back of a truck but spotted only a shiny black Mercedes. The driver had been leaning against the hood, smoking a cigarette, but he tossed it aside when he saw me and opened the rear passenger door.

"Madame," he said with a nod.

"*Merci*," I said, and joined Fräulein Sommer in the car.

"That word is about the extent of our driver's French, and he speaks very little German, either," she said. "He's Russian, part of the Vlasov guard. So don't worry about being overheard. He won't understand what you say."

I nodded, unable to imagine what confidences Fräulein Sommer and I might share that should not be overheard by a driver.

Her eyes fell on the red triangle sewn to the front of my smock.

"Your file said you were a communist. Forgive my ignorance, but I was surprised to find a communist so well versed in design."

"I was *accused* of being a communist."

"Were you falsely accused?"

"That is not for me to say," I replied.

Certainly Bruno had done his best to turn me into one, but I didn't know enough about economics or sociology, much less politics, to know exactly *what* I was. I believed in art, and music, and literature. And at this point, I would support anyone who could put an end to war.

"Well, no matter," she said. "You are an enemy of the Reich. That is enough."

The drive was glorious. The car rode smoothly; the seats were plush. The driver smelled vaguely of tobacco, and Fräulein Sommer wore a delicate, earthy perfume. My eyes hungrily took in everything I saw through the car windows: the little shops and the umbrellaed sidewalk cafés, a small but colorful produce market, men getting their shoes polished at a shoeshine stand. Street signs in German had been erected at busy intersections, and the ugly Nazi flag hung from public buildings, either alone or above our French tricolor. A familiar coffeehouse had a new sign that read, *Soldatenkaffee Madeleine*, and the Parisiana cinema was draped with red-and-black banners featuring the swastika.

But there were other signs as well: posters calling for the citizenry to rise up against the occupiers. Many had been ripped as though someone had tried to tear them down, but there were many studding the walls and lampposts. Graffiti was everywhere calling for the same thing, and there were multiple "V"s for "Victory." Could it be true? Could the tide be turning?

Soon the city fell away, and the sights of nature filled my soul: the early-spring wildflowers, the bright green grass beginning to thrive. And the fresh air! I opened the window and let it blow on my face until Fräulein Sommer ordered me to close it because the breeze was mussing her hair.

At last we pulled up to a fine house reminiscent of Claude Monet's famous home in Giverny but on a grander scale. I had been invited to lunch at Monet's shortly before he passed away, and I remembered the lush and verdant gardens, and especially the ponds full of *nymphéas*, the water lilies he had immortalized on canvas.

This estate was larger, but the formal gardens did not compare to Monet's explosion of texture and color, nor did the rooms rival his pure yellow dining room or charming blue-and-white tiled kitchen. Instead, everything here—from the floors to the few pieces of furniture that remained, and the walls, the trim, and the ceilings—was in varying shades of off-white and beige. Elegant but boring.

We were met not by the Nazi officer but by his wife, Frau Ursula Wolff, who was thirtyish, plump and pretty, blond and blue-eyed.

She greeted Fräulein Sommer enthusiastically and dismissed me with a glance.

Fräulein Sommer strode through the house, haughtily suggesting a chaise longue here and an étagère there, speaking to Frau Wolff mostly in German. I did not understand the language well enough to recognize their accents, but it was clear that Frau Wolff spoke a more guttural form of German, and I wondered whether there was a class difference. Frau Wolff appeared rather nonplussed at the prospect of running a country estate in France. *Perhaps it was hard to feel at home in an occupied country,* I thought to myself, *living in a residence stolen from a Jewish family.*

I tagged along as Fräulein Sommer whipped out a leather-covered tape measure and instructed me to write down the measurements of this and that. I took notes when I understood a phrase in German, and made quick sketches of each room, jotting down whatever Fräulein Sommer said in French: an Aubusson rug for the sitting room, long velvet curtains for the study—garnet red perhaps?—and a grand gilt-framed mirror in the entry hall, sandwiched between amber sconces.

"And clocks?" suggested Frau Wolff. "My husband simply adores clocks. One must always be on time, he likes to say. Punctuality is the sign of a disciplined mind."

"Indeed. Write that down, Capucine," Fräulein Sommer said to me while smiling at Frau Wolff. "I'm a great believer in lists. Aren't you?"

"*Ja, ja,*" Frau Wolff agreed. "*Was auch immer Sie am besten denken.*"

Frau Wolff had her servant prepare a small tea, and I was surprised to be invited to join them. I perched uncomfortably on a formal chair in the exceedingly formal dining room, trying not to embarrass myself by gorging on the finger sandwiches Frau Wolff had set out "in the English fashion."

Although my work at the Wolffs' commandeered manor house was much easier than my typical labor at Lévitan, I was exhausted by the time Fräulein Sommer and I climbed back into the car to return to Paris. In Lévitan I was surrounded by comrades who had become friends, but spending a day with the Nazi elite, maintaining a serious, attentive face and taking care not to give offense, was grueling. Add to that the heartbreaking knowledge that the legitimate owners of this lovely home had at best fled, at worst been deported.

As I relaxed on the comfortable car seat, I felt unaccountably emotional and weary. . . . *"Verklempt"* was the term my Jewish friends would have used.

I kept playing with the tape measure, pulling it out a bit and letting it snap back. I remembered Bruno telling me that when women's hoopskirts went out of style, someone had had the brilliant idea to repurpose the springy metal straps as self-winding tape measures. Was that a true story, or had he made it up? Bruno was always so full of stories.

We rode in silence for a while, each lost in our thoughts, but as we approached the city limits, Fräulein Sommer said, gazing out the window, "Frau Wolff is a very lonely woman. Her husband does not hide his young Parisian mistress, whom he escorts to nightclubs and dinners while poor Ursula rambles about in that big old house."

I remained silent, wondering if I was supposed to feel sorry for the pampered wife of a Nazi.

"She's a simple woman from the countryside," she continued. "She's a good Nazi, I suppose, but she knows almost nothing about furniture or design, so she'll be easy enough to please."

"I'm sure we can find some nice things for her in our inventory at Lévitan," I replied.

"I wonder, Capucine: Have you heard the rumors?" Fräulein Sommer continued in exactly the same tone. "They say the Allies are gaining the upper hand. Everyone expects them to invade France soon."

I stared at her, agog.

"No, I had not heard that," I said after a moment, playing it safe. "In Lévitan, we have no radio, and the only newspapers are the ones that sometimes arrive in the crates. But even those are usually burned before we get a chance to read them."

"I think perhaps you know more than you say."

"I assure you, I do not."

"I am not loyal to the Third Reich, and Hitler is an ass," Fräulein Sommer said in a loud voice. I glanced at the driver, who gave no sign he had understood. She smiled. "See? He doesn't speak a word of French."

"Was that a test, or is what you said true?"

"What if it were true?"

"I—I don't know." Exhausted from our day, drowsy from the unaccustomed food in my belly, I was finding it hard to mentally spar with this woman.

"I'm no fan of the Jews," Fräulein Sommer went on. "But I don't appreciate the world-conquering attitude of those in charge. And I despise the ugliness of war. I want things to go back to normal."

"What is normal anymore?"

She let out a laugh. "Excellent question. I knew I liked you, Capucine. Number 123." Her eyes raked over me. "Tell me, what is your life really like as a prisoner?"

"You're welcome to come up to the attic, see how we live. It's not comfortable, but I've heard there are much worse places to be."

"I believe you're right," she said, a grim set to her mouth. "There are rumors of atrocities. . . . Never would I have believed it would have gotten so bad, so fast."

Her words again reminded me of Bruno, and I wondered: Were some German loyalists wearying of the war as well? Might they be turning away from the preachings of Adolf Hitler and the Third Reich? And if so, what would that mean for France?

"In the beginning, I appreciated that the Third Reich admired art and culture, that Germany was rebuilding after the hard times. The years following the Great War were so hard on us all. But now"—she shook her head—"things have changed. And given my relatively privileged position, I feel as though I should do something more. Something to help."

"Like what?" I asked.

She met my eyes. "There are many people, you know, who are working to bring this war to an end. Working to liberate Paris."

"Are you saying you're working with the"—I lowered my voice to a whisper in case the driver understood more than she thought—"*Résistance*?"

She did not confirm it. But neither did she deny it.

"I need to know," she said, "what would it take for the prisoners in Lévitan to be involved in an uprising? What about the prisoners' families? Are they involved in anything? Are any of the guards sympathetic?"

My heart thudded. "I really don't know."

"Maybe ask around? Are the prisoners in a position to sabotage items heading to Germany, anything along those lines?"

"I can't imagine any such thing," I said. "Of course, I'll keep an ear out."

Fräulein Sommer was scaring the hell out of me. If she was working with the Résistance, then why was she asking about the prisoners and guards at Lévitan? Sommer's entrée to the homes of high-ranking Nazi officials would give her access to all kinds of potential intelligence; who cared about the internal working of Lager Ost? If she was lying—for what reason I couldn't imagine, but then, I could never have imagined a lot of what had happened these past four years—then it behooved me to play dumb, to protect myself and my fellow prisoners.

But . . . maybe Fräulein Sommer was in a position to help us, at least in some small way.

"The prisoners might be more willing to confide in me if I had something to offer them," I suggested.

"Something like what?" she asked, a frown marring her forehead.

"Nothing extraordinary. But maybe a daily walk on the rooftop terrace? It would be good for our spirits to have a little fresh air, and no one would be able to see us up there. All the neighboring buildings have their shutters closed anyway."

She nodded thoughtfully, and I decided to push a little more.

"Also, the prisoners want to hold a Seder."

"What's a Seder?" she asked. "Is it Jewish?"

"It's a special meal to celebrate the eve of Passover," I said. "It commemorates freedom from slavery in Egypt, I believe."

"How is it you know so much about it? Being in there turning you Jewish?"

"I'm a communist, remember? My papers say so."

She rolled her eyes.

"The other prisoners are my constant companions these days," I said. "Hard not to pick up on a thing or two. Anyway, last time we were allowed to celebrate a Jewish holiday, Pettit tried to gas us all, so I was thinking maybe we could have a nice dinner just to make up for it."

She looked appalled. "What do you mean, someone tried to 'gas us all'?"

I wondered if I should say anything more, if I had perhaps already said too much. Pettit was clearly subordinate to Fräulein Sommer, so I might be able to make trouble for her. But unless Pettit was reassigned, she would almost certainly make trouble for *us* in revenge.

"It's a long story and not worth going into," I said. "Suffice it to say that we all survived but I think the Jewish prisoners—all of us, actually—would benefit from a nice evening. What could it hurt?"

"I don't know that I can influence the food delivery."

"I'm not asking for that—a Seder's officially a dinner, but I think it's more about the occasion than the food."

"When is this Seder?"

"If I remember correctly, Passover starts April eighth, which means the dinner is the evening before, April seventh. If we could use some of the nice china and silverware from the store, that kind of thing . . . A lot of the inmates try to keep kosher, so they can't use the same plates and utensils for meat and dairy."

She rolled her eyes again.

"But really, just access to some of the items in the store, and a few nice tablecloths, would be fine," I said. "I'm sure the prisoners can come up with whatever else they need."

She made a note on her clipboard.

"I'll see what I can do," she said, her eyes focused on the tape measure I kept playing with. "And go ahead and keep the tape. It was part of a shipment from a hardware store. Plenty more where that came from."

AT NIGHT, EZRA joined Isedore and me to read more papers. The three of us had become a sort of little family, eating together, relaxing together, sharing passages when we found something particularly poignant or poetic in the papers we were sorting through. When we wearied of our task, we took turns reading aloud from the French translation of a novel by the American Sinclair Lewis, *Impossible ici*, or *It Can't Happen Here*, until we decided it was too eerily prescient of what had happened to our country.

Even though I had not returned Ezra's words of affection, he did not push me and did not appear to take offense. This was one of the many ways in which he continued to remind me of Charles: that quiet acceptance. Still, I appreciated our closeness, the way things were allowed to remain unsaid and yet were still understood.

I considered confiding in Ezra about what Fräulein Sommer had told me on the drive back from the countryside, and how I wondered whether I—we—could possibly trust her and what she might be able to do to help us. It could have been some kind of trick, but perhaps the tide really was turning, and she was searching for a lifeboat in case Germany was defeated. No matter what, it seemed dangerous.

Ultimately, I kept it to myself, remembering Bruno's reminder to treat the enemy like an unpredictable and deadly wild animal.

"You said you read Gertrude Stein's book in English. Did you ever read Hemingway?" I asked Ezra.

"Yes, I read *L'Adieu aux armes*, or *A Farewell to Arms*, in the original English."

I nodded. "I never really cared for Hemingway's writings—or the man, actually—but I liked the line *Le monde brise tout le monde et après, beaucoup sont forts dans les endroits brisés.*"

"I know that one. In English, it reads: 'The world breaks everyone and afterward many are strong at the broken places.'"

"Do you believe that?" I asked.

"Maybe." Ezra paused, and then added: "But Hemingway goes on to say, 'But those that will not break it kills.'"

24

Mathilde

ON SATURDAY EVENING, Mathilde sat in the parlor, waiting for Victor to arrive.

Given everything that had happened with Bridgette and at La Maison Benoît that week, the last thing she wanted was to spend the evening at a restaurant making small talk with Victor. But she had already agreed to go and could not think of a graceful way out of the date.

So she sat waiting on the parlor sofa in an ice-blue silk dress, black gloves, and a black coat with a nice fur collar borrowed from Mami, who had insisted Mathilde's red coat did not "go" with the dress, and was too flashy, besides.

"Please, *ma petite fille*," said Mami. "Give Victor a chance. He is such a nice young man."

"Play your cards right and you'll be a married woman this time next year," Papi said from behind his newspaper.

Papi was in a good mood; he had gotten his hands on some precious tobacco, and over Mami's protests, the parlor was filled with smoke from his carved ivory pipe.

"Your papi's right, as usual," Mami agreed. "Wouldn't that be something!"

"Whatever you do, smile—and don't talk about politics," Papi warned.

Victor arrived, looking blandly handsome in a dark blue three-piece suit, and Mami greeted him as if he were visiting royalty. He handed Mathilde a wrist corsage of sweet-smelling pale pink roses with a spray of baby's breath.

"My, isn't that beautiful!" Mami sighed as Mathilde slipped the corsage on her wrist.

"*Merci*, monsieur," she said, feeling oddly shy now they were going on their first official date.

"*Je vous en prie, mademoiselle*," Victor answered. "My pleasure. Shall we? I was able to borrow a car for the evening, so we shall be quite comfortable."

"Good man," Papi said.

"Have fun, you two!" Mami called after them.

The upscale brasserie in the eighth arrondissement was patronized by the military elite, and as the maître d' led them to their table, Mathilde noticed the restaurant was full of German officers and their wives or French mistresses, dining cheek by jowl with Vichy officials and their wives or French mistresses. Everyone was dressed smartly and looked well-fed and healthy. There was clearly no shortage of food and wine here. In one corner a woman played soothing music on a harp, and waiters wearing short black jackets and long white aprons rushed to and fro between the kitchen and the tables.

Mathilde wondered how Victor had secured such a reservation,

how he could even afford it, but assumed it was because he collaborated with the Germans at the Renault factory to produce airplane
parts for the *Luftwaffe*.

A traitor to his people. But she benefitted as well. What did that
make her?

Victor offered to order for both of them, and Mathilde acquiesced.

During dinner Victor was . . . fine. Courteous and polite as always. She asked a few questions about his work, but though he
seemed happy to answer, the conversation went no further, and after
several attempts, she realized that Victor asked no questions of her.
Guess I'm not interesting enough, she thought, and was surprised to
feel a spurt of anger. She was trying to avoid politics and was not
about to confide what she had been up to recently. But nattering on
about the weather seemed insufferable.

The waiter brought the first course: a pâté de campagne with
cornichons for him and a petite cheese soufflé for her. Silence pre-
vailed at the table. Out of nervousness, and for something to do,
Mathilde kept sipping her wine, and before she realized it, she'd
finished the entire glass. The group at the next table shared a laugh
and the room was full of the low buzz of conversation, the clinking
of glasses raised in toasts, the clatter of silverware, the mellow
notes of the harp strings.

Victor gazed at her and smiled but said nothing. So she decided
to ask some "getting to know you" questions, the way she did to get
small children to talk. *Do you like animals, and if so, do you prefer cats
or dogs? City or countryside? The mountains or the sea?* She knew Victor's family was in the south, near Avignon, and she asked what had
brought him to Paris.

He spoke of coming to study at the Sorbonne and how he fell in love with the city's architecture and bridges, the Seine and the cafés. "And of course, the Louvre," he said with a smile, refilling her wineglass as the waiter brought their *plats principaux* of confit de canard and coq au vin. "The Louvre is an attraction in and of itself. A national treasure."

"The finest pieces were evacuated, weren't they?" Mathilde asked.

In 1939, as war loomed on the horizon, the Louvre's curators had proven themselves more prescient than many of their contemporaries and closed the museum for a few days, ostensibly "to make repairs" but in reality to empty the Louvre of its most famous works of art. No one knew where they went, though it was assumed they were hidden in châteaus and country estates, wine cellars and champagne caves, where, with luck, they would be safe from the devastation of war and from the Nazis' famously voracious appetite for France's treasured artwork.

Victor nodded. "They'll be back. Once the war is over, you'll see. Things will go back to normal. More or less."

As if they could all pretend the war had never happened. As if the missing people, the closed businesses, the lives destroyed were momentary inconveniences.

She took a long pull of her wine.

"You mentioned the other day that Impressionism might be the result of some sort of physical problem," she said. "You truly don't find some of the paintings beautiful?"

"I suppose I prefer the classics, that's all. The chiaroscuro of the Italian Renaissance, the elegant, elongated lines of a Raphael, or even the intense colors and complex compositions of the Pre-Raphaelites. To me, that is true talent, incredible talent. Just imagine what it must have taken. Promising young boys were apprenticed to great masters and spent years perfecting their skills."

"You sound quite knowledgeable on the subject. Do you paint yourself?"

He shook his head and chuckled. "I leave that to those with talent. No, I enjoy a bit of sport, and I often read in the evenings. But there again, I prefer the classics over the modern novel."

"Because modern novels are degenerate?" she asked. "That's what my papi says."

Victor laughed. "With all due respect to your papi, I would not go that far. But I prefer classical literature. I find it very . . . soothing."

Mathilde wondered what this perfectly fine but not terribly interesting man found so agitating about his life that he needed to soothe himself by reading a classical book.

"I like to draw and to paint," Mathilde said, and felt emboldened by confessing this simple truth. "Honestly, I've tried not to do so very much, because Mami and Papi do not care for anything that reminds them of my mother and father. Especially my mother."

Victor nodded, then reached across the table and placed his hand upon hers. The wine had helped Mathilde to relax and warmed her cheeks, and she found Victor's touch surprisingly nice, his skin soft on hers. *Maybe he's not that bad,* she thought. *Maybe Mami and Papi are right. Maybe I should give him more of a cha—*

"I want to assure you that I don't hold her against you," Victor said.

"Hold *who* against me?"

"Your mother," Victor said. Then, as she bristled and yanked her hand away, he added, "I understand that you hardly knew her, after all. And I've never been one to believe it is proper to visit the sins of the father—or in this case, the mother—upon the child."

"Is that right? Does that apply to Jewish children as well?" Mathilde demanded.

"Shhh." Victor glanced around, but relaxed when he saw that everyone was absorbed in their own conversations, laughing, savoring their wine. He leaned forward and, in an earnest whisper, said: "Keep your voice down, Mathilde, please. The people at the very next table are very important Nazi officials."

Mathilde craned her neck to catch a quick glimpse of them: three men in officers' uniforms, each with a pretty young woman at his side.

Victor sat back and resumed his normal tone of voice. "Anyway, let us speak of something more pleasant. I am very glad to know we share a love for art."

They both sipped their wine, and now that Mathilde was aware of the group at the neighboring table, she overheard a few words from their animated conversation: *"Möbel Aktion,"* then "Drancy" and "Lévitan." She leaned back to try to hear better.

"What is it?" Victor asked.

"I . . . It's nothing," Mathilde said, shaking her head.

The waiter appeared, wordlessly whisked their plates away, poured more wine, and brought small plates with a few lettuce leaves: the salad course.

"Sorry. Do go on. Tell me more about your favorite artists."

"Yes, art!" Victor spoke of a trip he had made to the Uffizi in Florence.

Mathilde nodded but listened with only half an ear, trying to catch more of what the men at the next table were talking about. Not for the first time, she cursed her limited German language skills.

"I also adore Versailles, of course," Victor was saying. "It's an amazing work of art in and of itself."

"Mmm," said Mathilde.

Now the women at the next table were chatting excitedly in a mixture of French and German, so Mathilde understood more. They seemed to be making plans to go shopping for furniture and dresses. Again, she overhead "Lévitan," as well as "Bassano."

So Möbel Aktion *is real.* And Bridgette was right: Her mother and grandfather would have been well suited to work with such an effort, given their experience with fashion and design. How could Mathilde find out for sure whether they were part of it and thus being held right here in Paris? Whom could she ask? And then . . . what would she do about it?

"You don't care for Versailles?" asked Victor.

"I'm sorry. What?"

"I say, you seem suddenly distracted."

"Sorry."

The conversation with the Nazi officials had moved on to a discussion about which nightclub they would go to after dinner, so Mathilde returned her attention to Victor. The truth was that Mami and Papi had taken her on a tour of Versailles a few years ago, and while the palace was undeniably impressive, Mathilde found the garish gold baroque finishes overwrought. Besides, knowing of the widespread deprivation that had made such luxury possible for a fortunate few had made it hard for her to enjoy.

But in response to Victor, she simply said, "I preferred the gardens to the château."

"Perhaps we could visit one day," he said, "and ride bicycles around the palace grounds."

"My bike was stolen."

"Truly?" Victor frowned and shook his head. "Crime is on the rise in our fair city, I'm sorry to say."

The sentiment was as ludicrous as when Mami expressed it. The

Germans had invaded their country, plundered whatever they wanted, deported those whom they didn't like for any reason or for no reason at all—but Mami and Victor fretted about the implications of a stolen bicycle.

"Anyway, it's no matter. We can rent bicycles there. Or better yet"—he paused and took a sip of wine, and his voice dropped as he leaned forward—"I'll buy you a new one. In fact, Mathilde, I would like to be in the position to buy you a great many things. Speaking of which, Mathilde, I wanted to ask you—"

"*Don't.*"

"Don't what?"

"If you're going to ask me what I think you're going to ask me, please don't. I mean . . ." The hurt look on his face surprised her. "I'm sorry, Victor. It's not you. I'm just very . . . Well, you know, I've been wrapped up with everything going on with my mother and grandfather. And well, just . . . everything. This horrid, never-ending war."

"*Hush,*" Victor hissed. "Honestly, you must not speak of such things, Mathilde."

And in that moment, she realized who Victor really was: a young Papi Auguste.

EVEN THOUGH THE date was a disaster, Mathilde could not bring herself to reject Victor outright. She had been drinking more wine than usual, so perhaps she had misjudged him. And the conversation she had overheard had distracted her. Maybe Victor had more depths to him than a single awkward dinner could reveal.

Also, there was that small nagging voice in her head: *This might be your one chance.* If she rejected a perfectly nice offer of marriage from a perfectly acceptable young man, then what? Would she become an old maid, living forever in Neuilly-sur-Seine, caring for her eternally disappointed mami and papi in their dotage? If she married Victor, perhaps children and a home of her own would make up for a lack of deeper feelings for her husband.

Mathilde tried to focus on how nice Victor's hand had felt on hers, and as she read through Charles Moore's love letters to her mother, she wondered what it would be like to have someone want you like that, need you like that.

So she asked Victor—and later, her papi and mami—for more time.

She blamed the tensions of the war, the stress of the unknowable future. After all, she said, what was the hurry? A proper wedding would not be possible until life returned to normal anyway.

Surprisingly, they all agreed. Mami, in particular, was persuaded by the idea that a formal wedding reflective of their social standing would have to wait. She had been robbed of the opportunity to give her own son a lavish wedding when Roger and Capucine married in haste.

Mathilde's days fell into a pattern. She spent each morning with Mami in the parlor practicing her embroidery and mending garments but claimed the afternoons for herself. Spring had arrived at last, and though there were frequent rain showers, the sun shone much of the time, the trees and flowers budded out, and the birds kicked up a loud and lyrical fuss.

Upon learning of Victor's offer to replace Mathilde's "stolen" bicycle, Papi insisted upon doing so himself, and one morning she came downstairs to find him standing next to a shiny bicycle with an absurd red ribbon on the front wicker basket. Though it was a smallish women's bike, Papi climbed on and took it for a spin in the garden, his big knees splayed, pretending he might at any moment crash into Mami's prized hydrangeas. Mami called out in mock outrage, and Mathilde joined in the laughter. Papi's antics made Mathilde nostalgic for the time when the deep rumble of his laughter had frequently filled the halls of their big home.

Now that Mathilde again had easy transportation to the heart of Paris, she told Mami that she yearned to meander through the Jardin du Luxembourg and smell the spring flowers, to peruse old books at the *bouquiniste* kiosks along the Seine, to meet a friend in a café.

In reality, she returned several times to rue du Faubourg Saint-Martin, riding by the Lévitan, seeking any clue about any potential prisoners within. Occasionally there were soldiers patrolling the streets in front of the store, but then there were *Wehrmacht* all over the streets of Paris, so that did not signify much.

And then, disappointed and afraid and unsure of what to do next, she went back to La Maison Benoît.

Once Mathilde had put to right the apartment's bedrooms, kitchen, parlor, and lavatory, she spent the majority of her time sketching and reading about fans and feathers in the compendium she had found. She even tried her hand at making a fan, playing with the materials, folding a big piece of paper on which she had painted a scene of children playing in the Trocadéro fountain, putting their little sailboats out to "sea."

She quickly discovered that, like most things, making a fan was much harder than it looked. She found it nearly impossible to keep the folds all the same size, to bring everything together properly, to glue the paper to the monture blades without creating a mess. Mathilde shared her frustration with Antoinette one afternoon over a cup of tea, while petting Croissant the cat.

"Have you been listening to your mother's records?"

Mathilde nodded. "Music helps the cleaning go more swiftly, but how can it help make a stinking fan?"

"Next time, listen to the music carefully. Hear how the musicians come together, not in search of perfection, but in joyous abandon. I remember Charles saying that this was what he most loved about jazz: that oftentimes, the greatest beauty is found in imperfection."

"Well, if he's crazy about imperfection, he would love my fans," Mathilde said tartly.

But she took the old concierge's advice, and listened, and learned. The more time she spent at La Maison Benoît, the closer Mathilde felt to Bruno and Capucine, and she came to appreciate what it must have cost her mother's father to cater to the very wealthy. Bruno the communist shopkeeper was no hypocrite, she realized. He was a man with a family to support.

And her mother, Capucine, was a gifted artist who never signed her work and was the recipient of beautiful, eloquent love letters from an American named Charles Moore. Why hadn't her mother accepted his proposal and gone to be with him?

When Mathilde asked Antoinette what she thought, she responded, "Your mother didn't want to leave you."

"Me? But . . . I was already living with Mami and Papi, wasn't I?"

"You were. But she was not willing to put an ocean between you."

"So I'm the one who kept her from the man she loved?"

"Not at all. Capucine made her choice."

"But—," Mathilde said, feeling awash with shame. "I've barely seen her these last several years. I refused to see her."

"I know, Mathilde. One of the hardest things for young people to understand is that everyone makes their own choices, according to their character. She did what she had to do to be true to herself. That's not your burden."

"I don't understand."

"I know you don't," Antoinette said, not unkindly. "You are young, and though you have experienced loss, you are still fighting it. Believe me, once you choose to embrace it for what it is, you will begin to deepen."

Mathilde frowned and scratched the cat's neck. "You speak in riddles, old woman."

Antoinette let out a hearty laugh. "Do I? Well, now, I suppose I do. Isn't that the right of an old woman?"

Mathilde shook her head but gave Antoinette a reluctant smile.

"I think of life as a kind of braid, of choice, chance, and character entwined," said Antoinette. "Every decision involves those three strands, and the longer and more intricately they are braided, the more beautiful and multifaceted the life. Your mother made her choices according to her character, and she was overrun by chance. As we all are."

THOUGH MATHILDE HAD long since read all of Charles Moore's love letters, in bed at night she sometimes brought them out to reread them, hoping to glean a better understanding of her mother, of this mysterious American, and of a world of passion beyond her ken:

> *I wish I could better express myself, but even in my*
> *native language I doubt I could convince you how every*
> *time I put my arms around you, I felt that I had come*
> *home. Despite Paris, despite being thousands of miles*

*from the place of my birth, across an ocean. Despite
everything.*

*Now I play my emotions, punishing the keyboard
with my anger at being apart, with my frustration. I do
believe my poor instrument cries as much as I do.*

*Since I left, I have found no contentment. My
happiness is to be near you. Incessantly I relive in my
mind your caresses, your kisses, even your tears. The
feeling of holding you in my arms as we danced, the
charms of the incomparable Fan Girl, Capu, who
kindled a burning, glowing flame in my heart. I
remember feeling so proud, so special to have been
chosen by none other than the glittering, sparkling
Capucine Benoît.*

*But if I had you here, would you be mine? Would you
allow me to display my affection in public, allow me the
happiness of loving you and saying so—and proving so?*

And another:

*I know we are both growing older. Perhaps if you saw
me, you would be put off by the gray that is stubbornly
showing up in my once-black hair, the wrinkles I see in
the mirror when I catch myself with a rare smile. I no
longer stay up until four in the morning, dancing,
drinking, laughing. Of course, the times no longer lend
themselves to such activities, but still . . . when I lay
myself down in my soft bed long before midnight, I think
of holding you, cradling you in my arms, the scent of
your hair, the feel of your skin. . . . I would adore what*

age has done to your body just as I would respect what experience has done to your broken heart.

I am a simple man, and I do not claim to know much. But I know this: Nothing compares to your hands. There is nothing like the rich earth brown of your eyes. My body is filled with you for days and days. You are the thunder and the lightning, the birds and the fireflies, and most of all, the diamond stars. You are the dampness of the grass after the rain. The wine in my goblet. When my fingers touch your skin, I can feel the rushing of your blood. All my joy is in your hands.

My body is simply crazy with wanting you, mon amour. I wonder if your body wants mine the way mine wants yours, the kisses, the heat, the melting together, holding each other so tight that it hurts. Do you remember the first time? I thought I should die for holding you, and now I think I should die for wanting you.

Mathilde felt her face grow warm, her heart pound. In some ways she was embarrassed to be privy to such intimate thoughts— about her mother, no less. Her grandparents had always described Capucine as immoral and degenerate, a lost woman who was lured by art and jazz and foreigners into a world of sin. But . . . this was so much more than that.

Mathilde carefully folded the crinkly onionskin paper and re-placed it in its envelope. The letters made her wish she had a mail-ing address for Bridgette; she would like to be able to share her jumbled thoughts with her old friend. But, of course, it wouldn't be worth the risk. Better they both remained quiet until they could be reunited safely. They could tell each other their stories then.

Mathilde realized she might not see her old friend until after the war had finally come to an end, and the thought left her feeling desolate. She thought about calling Simone and suggesting they get together for a coffee or a walk in the Jardin du Luxembourg, but after what Bridgette had told her about Simone's Nazi boyfriend, she reconsidered. Mathilde would have to watch what she said and did for fear of giving something away.

There was a tapping sound at her window. *Bridgette?* Had Mathilde conjured her?

Mathilde got out of bed, pulled on her wrapper, and went out onto the balcony.

But this time it was a young man out on the dark lawn. She scurried down the back stairs and met him at the kitchen door.

"Take this to the same place," he said, handing her a package wrapped in brown paper.

He turned and left before she could react, his form dissolving into the darkness of the moonless night.

This time Mathilde did not think twice. She would take the package to the butcher.

Like a light through a prism, refracted, never to be the same.

25

Capucine

*I*T WAS ANOTHER week before I made it back to Abrielle's apartment.

Herr Pflüger was there when I arrived, so I mimicked the way Fräulein Sommer strode through the large country manor, commenting on the moldings or lack thereof, noting the way the light struck the mantelpiece, suggesting items go here and there. I made a show of taking measurements with my new tape measure, recording the numbers, and making quick sketches that I would elaborate upon later.

As before, it was only after Herr Pflüger left, and Zelia went to shop for dinner, that Abrielle seemed able to relax.

My heart pounding, I plunged in before I lost my nerve.

"Abrielle, I need your help."

"With what?"

"I want to get some papers out of Lévitan."

Abrielle shook her head and opened her mouth in a silent gasp. "Capu, are you crazy?" Although we were alone in the apartment, she lowered her voice to a fierce whisper. "I can't work with the . . . the *Résistance*!"

"I'm not asking you to," I said. "Honestly, Abrielle, it's nothing like that. These papers aren't important to the war—they're personal notes, even love letters. The guards just burn them. I don't know what France is going to be like when the war is over, but the families might want their personal papers. And, of course, the photographs."

"What difference would it make?"

"That's the sort of thing that matters to a family, Abrielle. Think about it. They've already lost so much. Imagine what it would mean to have some sentimental items, like family letters."

She had a worried frown but asked, "But I don't understand. What am I supposed to do with them? I can't have them here. . . . What if Otto found them? How would I explain why I had a bunch of Jewish papers?"

"You're right. It's too risky to hide them here. I thought maybe you could take them to a friend of mine."

"What friend?"

"Her name is Madame Antoinette Laurent. She's the concierge at my old apartment building, where La Maison Benoît is located. She's extremely trustworthy, and I can't imagine she'd run afoul of the authorities—she's elderly, a devout Catholic, minds her own business. She could keep them hidden somewhere until after the war."

"What's so important about the papers? Are the people famous or something?"

I shook my head. "They're just ordinary people so far as I know."

"Let me get this straight: You want me to take letters and photos from a bunch of Jews I've never even met, who aren't even important, to an old woman across town? Why would I?"

I should have thought this through before talking to her. Abrielle had been friendly to me, but she wasn't motivated by the same sorts of things I was. So how could I convince her to do something like this for me, for people she didn't even know?

"Because we all need to make amends, Abrielle," I said softly. "You and I did not speak up when the Nazis came here and did terrible things to our city, to our neighbors, to our fellow Parisians. What I'm asking of you won't take much. No matter how this war ends, think about it: You could make a real contribution, be a very important person."

I could tell by the set of her mouth that appealing to her honor was a losing strategy. And then inspiration struck.

"Also . . . if the shop hasn't been emptied out, you could have your choice of fans. Any one you want. I'll write a note to Madame Laurent, tell her that you may help yourself to any fan in the place."

Her eyes lit up. *"Any* fan I want?"

"Any fan."

WHETHER DUE TO Fräulein Sommer's influence, as a sort of apology for the gas mask incident, or because the guards were increasingly demoralized—whatever the reason, Pettit announced we would be allowed to set a makeshift "table" of crates with tablecloths and nice china and silverware to hold a Seder dinner. As with Purim, the wealthier inmates received packages from family, a portion of which went to the guards as bribes, which allowed us to assemble the ingredients necessary for the Seder plate, plus a little wine and matzoh for the "feast." The food service had also sent unleavened bread and a form of gefilte fish.

April 7 landed on a Friday, so it was also the welcoming of the Jewish Shabbat, and two candles were lit.

The long table was laid out and dressed, and Hélène used little demitasse cups on a platter to hold the special ingredients on the Seder plate.

Mordecai poured tiny amounts of wine into espresso cups so everyone could have a taste and said the blessing: "Blessed are you, Adonai our God, Sovereign of all and Creator of the fruit of the vine. *Baruch Atah, Adanai Eloheinu, Melech haolam, Borei pri Hagafen.*"

And over the candles: "Blessed are you, Adonai our God, Sovereign of all, who hallows us with mitzvoth, commanding us to kindle the lights of Passover. *Baruch Atah, Adonai Eloheinu, Melech haolam Asher kid'shanu b'mitzvotav, v'tzivanu l'hadlik ner Pesach.*"

Isedore, as the youngest person at the table, asked the traditional four questions, and Mordecai and Hélène took turns answering, telling the story of the liberation from slavery in Egypt.

Given what happened after the Purim celebration, we were all a bit on edge, but it was a beautiful ceremony. I sat at my usual place on the floor, leaning back against the wall, watching.

Ezra joined me.

Our hands rested flat on the floor next to each other. Ezra edged his over and placed his pinkie over mine.

I DID NOT understand the rankings of the various factions of the German military, but it became clear to me that Herr Pflüger did not wield as much influence as others, which meant my work on his penthouse apartment could wait and I was assigned to Fräulein Sommer almost every day.

But at long last Pettit told me I would work with Abrielle on Thursday morning. The challenge now was figuring out how to justify bringing so many papers with me to Abrielle's. I had drawn on the back of many items, and had mixed them in with other papers, but there were just too many. I needed a way to bring as much as I could without arousing suspicion.

"I don't know how many times I'll be able to get Abrielle to help me," I explained to Ezra when we were alone in my little cot area.

The blankets were drawn, and Isedore had not yet returned from her work with the clockworks pod. Still, I kept an eye out for her arrival, not wanting her to overhear our conversation. Our rift over Abrielle had long since healed, but I did not want to create any more bad feelings.

"After all, how many fans does one woman need?"

"Couldn't Abrielle have helped herself to any fan she wanted, anyway?" he asked. "I mean, as the mistress of a commandant . . . ?"

I let out a long sigh. "To her credit, Abrielle doesn't have a particularly devious mind. And in her own way, she's rather . . . honorable."

"Well, then," said Ezra, "let's make this batch the best of the lot."

We decided to prioritize personal letters with known addresses or family names, plus the precious loose-leaf diary of the young mother.

"That still leaves the problem of how to transport them. I can't carry a big pile of papers to the apartment. Pettit would be suspicious—not to mention Herr Pflüger, if he's there."

"You'll have to smuggle them in, then."

"How?"

"I have an idea but it's a risk," he said, holding my gaze.

"Everything's a risk these days," I said.

"All right. Let's give this a try."

Ezra's hands were warm and gentle as he wrapped some papers around my upper arms and secured them with twine, then did the same with my thighs and waist. I felt equal parts frightened and excited, and could not decide if my reaction was due to the risk of smuggling the papers out or the strange intimacy of Ezra's hands on my skin.

To camouflage the reason for my newly bulky appearance, we stuffed straw into the front, back, and sides of my dress. I looked as if I had gained thirty pounds, but I could explain it away by claiming the straw kept me warm in the back of the truck on the ride to Abrielle's apartment.

"How do I look?" I asked Ezra with a smile, holding my arms out, feeling very much like a stuffed scarecrow from an illustration in a children's book.

He gave me a slow smile.

"Like a plump little pigeon, sparkling from within."

He pulled me to him very slowly and kissed me.

I kissed him back.

26

Mathilde

MATHILDE WAS BEHIND the counter, swaying to the music and working on a fan—that was what she told herself, anyway; in reality, she was playing with feathers, seeing how they went together, the textures, the shapes, the colors and patterns—when the little bell over the shop door rang out, and a blond woman entered La Maison Benoît, wearing a luxurious fur coat and hat in sharp contrast to the drab neighbors.

Mathilde froze for several seconds before gathering her wits enough to say, "I'm sorry, madame, but the shop is not open for business."

The woman smiled and winked one big green-gold eye. "No problem, sweetie. I'm not a customer. I'm supposed to meet someone here, a Madame Laurent?"

"She's next door, the concierge. If you ring the bell at the courtyard gate she should answer."

"Oh, good, then. I'll do that," she said, gazing at the large poster of the language of fans. "I heard about this—there's a language to them. Isn't that somethin'?"

"Yes, there is," said Mathilde, warming to the subject. "Fans used to be called the woman's scepter, because it was said that women ruled so subtly, and so well, using their beautiful fans."

"You know a lot about 'em, huh?" she asked.

"I'm still learning. But"—Mathilde wondered if it was wise to reveal her connection to Bruno and Capucine, then decided it probably was not but she was going to anyway—"this shop belonged to my grandfather. He and my mother made the fans."

The woman's big eyes widened; then she gave a huge smile and slapped her hand to her heart. "Well, in that case, you're just the girl I want to see! I know your mother."

"Y-you do?"

"She's the one who sent me. I'm Abrielle Garnier, your mother's best friend in the whole wide world."

"SO, YOU'VE BEEN cleaning this place up?" Abrielle asked after Mathilde had summoned Antoinette to join them. "I'll tell Capucine next time I see her. I'm sure she'll be pleased to hear it."

"She's here in Paris, then? Is she at the Lévitan department store?"

"Yes. Don't you know? I thought they told the families where their people went."

"Not in this case," said Antoinette.

"And how are you in contact with her?" asked Mathilde.

"She's helping me to redecorate my apartment, in the ninth arrondissement. It's such a lovely place. You should see it! We thought about getting a place in a Haussmannian building, but my fella loves looking out over the city, so we have a *penthouse*. Capucine tells me it has great bones. You ever heard of such a thing?"

Antoinette and Mathilde exchanged glances as Abrielle meandered around the shop, and picked up a fluffy fan with rather garish pink ostrich plumes that was tied with a chocolate brown ribbon. She batted it in front of her face, then laughed.

"Too silly?" she asked.

"It looks nice with your hair," said Mathilde, trying to decide if this woman was truly her mother's friend.

Given how she was dressed, and that she had "hired" Capucine to do some interior design, Mathilde assumed Abrielle was mistress to yet another Nazi officer. She wondered whether Abrielle's "fella" might know Manfred, Simone's date the other night.

"What about Bruno, my grandfather?" Mathilde asked. "Is he there as well?"

"Oh, I don't know anything about that," said Abrielle.

"What brings you here today, madame?" asked Antoinette.

"Mademoiselle, actually," Abrielle said with a simpering smile.

Inclining her head, Antoinette said, "Of course, Mademoiselle."

Abrielle let out a little sigh and finally stopped examining the merchandise. She turned to face them, as if about to make an announcement.

"*Madame et mademoiselle*, I have in my possession . . ." Pausing dramatically, she looked over her shoulder as if to make sure there was no one else in the small shop, and it seemed to Mathilde that she was acting as if she were in a play. Abrielle lowered her voice and said, "I have some papers. I'm supposed to give them to Madame Antoinette Laurent, but I suppose if Capucine knew you were here, too, Mathilde, she wouldn't mind your knowing."

"What kind of papers?" asked Antoinette.

Abrielle gave a dismissive wave. "Bunch of nonsense if you ask me. I insisted on looking through them, you see, before I agreed to help Capucine smuggle them out."

"My mother smuggled these papers out of the Lévitan?" asked Mathilde. "For what purpose?"

"Beats all heck out of me. Like I said, they really don't seem like much." She brought a bundle of papers, tied together, out of her bag. "There are letters to parents, real estate deeds, notes to lovers, even a manuscript of a play—why anyone would care about such things, I have no idea. But she asked me to bring them to you and I'm doing so out of friendship."

"Just friendship?" Antoinette asked.

"Well . . . Capucine did say I might help myself to one of the shop's fans," said Abrielle. "She even sent along a note. It's right in there, see? She kept it real vague just in case someone saw it."

Antoinette set the bundle on the counter and snipped the twine.

At the top of the pile, an unsigned note addressed only to *A* seemed to be intended for Antoinette:

> *I hope these can be kept somewhere safe for posterity.*
> *If it is impossible or too much of a risk, I completely*
> *understand. Please allow her to take any piece she'd*
> *like in return for this favor.*

Antoinette and Mathilde started looking through the correspondence, the documents, and the play manuscript. Mathilde was disappointed; though there was no way Capucine could have known Mathilde had found her way to La Maison Benoît, she had hoped there might have been a note addressed to her.

"Did she say what we're to do with these?" asked Mathilde. Did the papers contain some sort of code? Would she be making yet another trip to the butcher or somewhere similar?

"Far as I can tell, she wanted Antoinette to keep them safe until after the war. They belonged to families that were taken away, and she thought if they came back, they would want the papers to remind them of their relatives or something like that. I told her it was silly. Who wants old letters? And besides, from what I hear, it's not as though those prisoners will ever be returning. I mean, after all . . ."

She clapped a hand over her mouth, noting Mathilde's crestfallen expression. "There I go again. My mouth outpaces my mind, as my mother always said. Anyway, these are for you. Capucine and I are friends, and she is choosing some nice furniture for my penthouse from the items at Lévitan. She even comes occasionally to my apartment."

"Could I meet her there?" asked Mathilde.

Abrielle gasped. "Oh, no, I'm sorry, darling. That's not possible. No one can know I've reached out to you, no one. You wouldn't want me to get in trouble, would you?"

Mathilde shook her head.

"Certainly not," Antoinette said, looking up from the papers. "You may rely on our discretion. Right, Mathilde?"

"Of course," Mathilde murmured.

"We thank you for your kindness in letting us know Capucine is all right, mademoiselle. I will keep these safe, as she requested. Was there anything else she wanted me to do with them?"

"Nope, just told me to ask if you wouldn't mind squirreling them away somewhere. She said this way the people wouldn't be erased.

I remembered the term because it seemed sort of funny. They're going away. They're not erased like a pencil mark!"

"I see," said Antoinette. "Thank you, Abrielle. It was good of you to bring them here."

"Well, I like to do what I can for my friends," Abrielle said, adding, "Now, about that fan Capucine promised me?"

"You will have to ask Mathilde," said Antoinette. "Until Bruno and Capucine return, she is in charge of the shop."

"Oh," Mathilde felt herself blush. "Um, of course. If my mother said so."

"She did! Do you know, I came in here once, not so very long ago, but I couldn't afford a single thing! And now I have my choice of any fan in the shop. My, how things change. Am I right?"

Mathilde and Antoinette watched as Abrielle wandered around, looking at this and that. Near the front door, she stopped and picked up the fan box that sat on the chair.

"What's this one?" she asked as she removed the lid.

"Oh, that's . . ." Mathilde's instincts told her to play it cool. If she suggested it was among the most valuable fans in the shop, not just in materials but also in sentiment, Abrielle might well insist on having it. "That's an old one. Very old-fashioned. Allow me to show you something more appropriate to a woman of your youth and beauty. What about this one? These feathers are very rare: orange and tan grebe, with iridescent teal feather insets."

"Well, now, that is awfully pretty. But I don't know. . . ." Abrielle held on to Suzette's fan. "I really like these pastel colors. It looks so classy, don't you think?"

"It *is* an antique," Mathilde agreed. "But because of that, it's very delicate and shouldn't really be used or it'll fall apart."

"Wouldn't want that," Antoinette said.

"No, indeed—it would look as if you were molting!" Mathilde agreed. "*Wait*. I've got just the thing. It would be exquisite with your coloring, and it's very, *very* special."

Mathilde moved the step stool over to the rear wall, climbed on top, and reached up high, where the finer fans were stored. "Voilà!" She climbed down and returned to the counter, where she snapped open the fan. It was made of fluffy white marabou plumes interlaced with pink-dyed silver pheasant feathers. The monture was of gleaming white mother-of-pearl, and there was a tiny silver-framed oval mirror on the left side, attached with a white ribbon.

"This one is extremely rare and *very* valuable," Mathilde said.

"Lemme see." Abrielle dropped Suzette's fan on the counter and took the extravagant one from Mathilde.

"Just look at that little mirror! Very handy, in case you need to check your lipstick," said Antoinette.

Abrielle held it at arm's length, then peered at it up close. "Looks nice. Now for the real test." She held the fan in front of her face and studied her reflection in the large mirror on the wall, turning this way and that, preening and batting her eyelashes.

"I *love* it," said Mathilde.

"Oh, my," said Antoinette. "That suits you very well, indeed. Mathilde, I declare you have the touch! Look how you've chosen the absolute best fan for mademoiselle's coloring and disposition. A rare and lovely fan for a rare and lovely woman."

Mathilde held her breath, afraid Antoinette was laying on the flattery too thick. But Abrielle appeared thrilled with the compliment.

"Think so?"

"I don't *think* so," Antoinette said. "I *know* so."

"I believe you're right," said Abrielle. "This is much nicer than that old one."

"Much nicer, indeed," agreed Mathilde.

ANTOINETTE WATCHED AS Mathilde blossomed into a shrewd woman right before her eyes.

Abrielle was quite a character, and it was hard to know if the mistress of a Nazi officer could be trusted. But if Capucine had asked her to bring papers here for safekeeping, she must have considered it a safe bet. And in any case, it wasn't as though they had that many choices.

Antoinette made a decision. "Wait one moment," she said. She returned to her apartment, snatched the letter from Charles off the mantelpiece, and handed it to Abrielle.

"What is it?"

"It wouldn't be right to open it," said Antoinette. "It's addressed to Capucine. Would you be sure she receives it?"

"It's from the United States," said Abrielle, studying the envelope. "Is it something . . . *verboten*?"

There were so many things forbidden under the Occupation that the German word had become part of everyday speech.

"No, of course not," said Mathilde. "It's from her former boyfriend."

"It is?" Abrielle looked more closely at the return address. "This is from her fella, Charles?"

Antoinette nodded. "Yes, yes, it is."

"Did you know him?" Mathilde asked.

"Oh, I tell you, we were all the *best* of friends back in the day." Her smile slipped, and she looked troubled, as if suffering from a rare moment of self-doubt. "His older brother was a military hero, a Harlem Hellfighter in the Great War. Charles joined him here after the war and played the piano. We were all friends. We made such a gay party! But that was back when . . . when things were different." She fanned herself with her exquisite new fan. "It's best not to think of such things anymore."

Mathilde hurriedly scribbled a note to her mother and asked Abrielle to give it to her.

"This is such a kindness," said Mathilde.

"I could get in trouble if anyone found out."

"Why should anyone find out!" exclaimed Antoinette.

"You were out for a lovely day of shopping, that is all. Goodness, it's not as if you're involved in *espionage*," Mathilde said with a laugh.

Abrielle still looked a bit unsure but returned Mathilde's smile. "I suppose you're right. If anyone discovers I was carrying that correspondence, I'll say I found it and thought I'd use it to start a fire."

"Excellent thinking!" said Antoinette.

"ANTOINETTE, COULD I ask you a question?" Mathilde said after Abrielle left. "Abrielle said Charles's brother was a Harlem Hellfighter. Weren't they *les Hommes de Bronze* from America, who fought in the Great War?"

"Yes, they were quite heroic. It was the Germans who gave them the name Hellfighters. I read that they spent more time in the trenches than any other American unit. And apparently, a lot of them liked it in France so much that they stayed after the war."

"*Les Hommes de Bronze* were Negroes," said Mathilde.

Antoinette nodded.

"Does that mean Charles . . ."

"Are you asking if Charles is a Negro as well? Is that what you're worried about?"

Mathilde shrugged. "Do you . . . Don't you think it's . . . unusual? I mean, my mother's white."

"Unusual or unthinkable?" Antoinette smiled. "'Different' isn't another word for 'wrong,' you know. And personally, I'm not sure we have that much control over whom we fall in love with."

"Did I ever meet him? I wish I could remember more."

"No. He wanted to meet you, but your mother insisted he was not to be part of your life. I believe they argued about it. He was such a sweet soul and so talented! Played the piano like a dream. I heard him a few times when Capu dragged me along to the club."

"Why didn't my mother want him to know me?"

Antoinette looked at her with the sad, knowing expression Mathilde was becoming accustomed to.

"Think about it, Mathilde. What do you suppose your mami and papi would have made of that? Would they have welcomed him into their home—or welcomed your mother—if they had known?"

"Probably not," Mathilde said. "Papi doesn't like Americans of any kind."

"Capu could not bear to give you up completely, which was what she feared would happen should she be open about their relationship."

Antoinette had been hesitant about their relationship at first as well. She liked Charles immensely, but she feared Capucine did not recognize the challenges they would face as a couple in broader society. Capucine had been raised by Bruno to scoff at tradition and polite society, but denial did not necessarily impart immunity. Antoinette had feared for them both.

"And yet he still writes to her?"

"She told him to stop, and he did for a while, but that letter I gave to Abrielle arrived just last month." She smiled. "He's a stubborn man."

"He's in love."

"That, too."

Mathilde made up her mind.

"I'm going to Lévitan. I'm going to ask to see my mother."

Antoinette opened her mouth as if to protest but said simply, "*Bonne chance, ma fille*. Just . . . be careful."

MATHILDE GRABBED THE fan she had been making most recently—the imperfect, crooked fan—and headed to rue du Faubourg Saint-Martin.

On the way, she noticed posters urging citizens to take up arms against the "German oppressors." One called for a general mobilization of Parisians, saying that *"The war continues."* Others called on the Parisian police, the Republican Guard, the gendarmerie, the Garde Mobile, and *"all patriotic Frenchmen, from 18 to 50 years old able to carry a weapon"* to join the struggle against the invader.

Maybe Bridgette was right; maybe the tide truly was turning. Throughout the city, Mathilde had been seeing more and more "V"s for "Victory" graffitied on the sides of buildings, on Métro stops, and even on Nazi propaganda posters. Could Germany hold on to France if Parisians as a group rose up against them? She didn't know enough about politics or the war to be sure, but she knew one thing: It would be demoralizing for the well-fed Nazi elite who enjoyed crowding into restaurants and drinking fine champagne.

When Mathilde stood on the street in front of the Lévitan department store, just as before, she saw nothing amiss on the façade.

She peered up at the top floor but could no more spot prisoners in the attic than she could catch a glimpse of Notre Dame's famous gargoyles from the sidewalk.

There were no soldiers on the street today, but halfway down the block, she saw two women with a young child. They were also looking up as though searching the façade of the building. After a moment's hesitation, Mathilde approached them.

"*Bonjour.*"

"*Bonjour,*" they replied.

"Are you . . . looking for someone?"

They stared at her but remained silent.

"I . . . I think my mother may be in there," Mathilde continued.

"There are some prisoners," said the younger of the two quietly. "Sometimes you can catch a glimpse, but not often. They're not allowed to go near the windows."

"Not officially, anyway," said the older woman. "But they dare sometimes."

Mathilde did not know what else to say. The older woman began to cry; the younger one tried to comfort her. The child started to fuss, and they headed down the sidewalk, away from the Lévitan.

The younger woman looked back at Mathilde and said: "*Bonne chance, et bon courage.*"

Good luck, and courage. That was what she needed. After a moment, Mathilde straightened her shoulders, took a deep breath, and walked her bike around to the alley that led to the store's large loading dock.

Five lorries were lined up, apparently waiting their turn. Men with numbered armbands, sweating from exertion despite the cold, were unloading crates from the truck parked at the dock. At least a dozen large wooden crates sat on the concrete slip, and through the wide bay door, Mathilde saw what looked like hundreds more stacked within. In addition, there were chests and armoires, bedroom sets and mattresses, suitcases and side tables.

Several uniformed guards stood on the far side of the loading dock, but they were smoking and talking, and none had noticed her.

A small group of workmen glanced in her direction. Two men set down what appeared to be a very heavy crate and paused to stretch their backs, watching her.

"Do you know Capucine Benoît Duplantier?" she asked in a whisper she hoped would carry over the sound of the idling trucks.

The men nodded and glanced at the guards. One held his finger against his lips in warning.

A tall, dark-featured man replied, "I am Ezra Goldman. Is Capucine your mother?"

"How did you know?"

"You look much like her. Except for the hair, of course. She speaks of you often."

"Hey!" A woman in a guard uniform shoved Ezra aside. Strong and unpleasant, with a square face and a nasty expression, she was exactly what Mathilde would have pictured as a prison camp guard. "You know the penalty for speaking to civilians."

"I—I'm Capucine Benoît's daughter," Mathilde stammered, her heart hammering so fast, she wondered if the others could hear it. "May I see her?"

"What do you think this is, the Hotel Ritz?"

"But . . . she's my mother."

The guard's mouth settled into a flat line. "Word to the wise, kid. Be careful whom you claim as family."

"I was raised by my grandparents," Mathilde clarified, though her own words made her feel like a coward. "My Catholic grand-parents."

The guard nodded, but said, "No visits. *Keine Besuche.*"

"But—"

"Scram, little girl," said the woman. "If you know what's good for you, you'll go away and never come back. Forget about this place. Forget about your mother. And as for you," she said to Ezra, "no dinner for you tonight."

Ezra gave her a little mock salute.

Mathilde felt awful to have robbed this kind man of his dinner but feared she would only make things worse if she said anything further.

She met Ezra's eyes, hoping he would understand. She touched the fan to her heart, and as she turned to leave, she let it fall to the ground.

27

Capucine

"CAPU, I HAVE something for you," said Ezra that evening. "Something special."

"Oh, Ezra," I said, shaking my head. I knew it was wrong to encourage his advances, but I had not been strong enough to turn away the comfort of his arms. "I don't . . . I mean, I can't . . ."

I had spent that morning with Abrielle. She laughed at my scarecrow appearance when I arrived but sobered when she realized what I had hidden beneath the straw. When she fretted about being caught carrying the papers to Antoinette, I suggested she claim to have found them in the street and thought they would make good kindling for the fireplace. To my mind it was a preposterous explanation that no Nazi would believe for a second, but it made sense to Abrielle, and she agreed to do as she had promised.

It was draining to jolly her along, keeping up the pretense and trying to ignore Zelia's dirty looks when she returned from the day's shopping. Worst of all was the very real possibility that Abrielle would back out and confess all to Herr Pflüger.

But when I left her apartment that afternoon at one, Abrielle walked me out, the papers in her bag, and insisted she would go straight to La Maison Benoît to pick out her fan.

"It isn't from me," Ezra said with an understanding smile, and handed me a fan.

The body of the fan featured a charming sketch of a cherry branch in blossom with a bird perched upon it. The folds were uneven, and there were obvious clumps of dried glue under the lace along the edges. The work of an amateur but delightful nonetheless.

"Where did you get this?" I asked, turning it over in my hands, enjoying its weight in my palm. "I thought I was the only one in Lévitan who made fans. Don't tell me I've started a trend."

"It was dropped out at the loading dock this afternoon," said Ezra, "by a young woman who looks a lot like you, but with lighter hair."

"I don't understand."

"Your daughter, Capu."

"Mathilde?" I was simultaneously petrified and elated. "She was *here*? How did you know she was my daughter? What do you mean, she dropped the fan?"

Ezra patiently answered my flurry of questions, telling me what Mathilde had said, how she looked, what Pettit had said to her.

"She really asked to see me?" I asked.

Ezra nodded. "She dropped the fan on purpose, Capu. Her message was clear, even to me, unversed though I am in your language of fans: She touched the fan to her heart, then let it fall to the ground when the guards weren't looking. She was sending it to you."

Touch to heart . . . You have my love.

SPRING WAS TOO brief. It felt as if summer arrived early, turning our once-freezing attic into a sweltering sauna.

Whether through Fräulein Sommer's intervention or the mercy of the guards who were forced to spend time in the sweltering attic with us, we were allowed to go out on the rooftop terrace after work.

We oohed and aahed as we emerged into the orangey early-evening sunshine, blinking in the light of day as if we were creatures of the night. Turning our faces upward, we breathed the fresh air and felt the warmth of the sun on our skin. The half dozen potted plants that ringed the terrace had long since perished from neglect, the shutters on the buildings across the street were tightly shut, and the staccato sound of gunfire rang out frequently in the distance. But there were benches, and we could pretend, just for a moment, that we were taking in the sunshine in one of Paris's ubiquitous parks, the Parc Monceau or the Jardin du Luxembourg or even the Place des Vosges.

The simple act of spending half an hour outside revived and enlivened us, helped us remember that there was a world on the outside, a world to which we might one day return.

Bruno once told me, when I attempted to plant tulips indoors at La Maison Benoît, that it wasn't right to "force" bulbs, that they must be allowed to follow the schedule of nature. Looking around now, I wondered whether I and the other inmates were like those tulips, waiting for the signal of spring before we arose from the frozen ground and reached upward toward the sun.

FRÄULEIN SOMMER KEPT me so busy that I was rarely on crate duty anymore. Instead, I joined her on visits to various houses and apartments, and spent hours, days, weeks sorting through inventory and making elaborate design sketches for her high-ranking clients. I was taken to the two other satellite camps in Paris, Bassano and Austerlitz, to review the inventories there as well.

Though working with Fräulein Sommer and traveling around the city was preferable to being confined in Lévitan, I itched to return to Abrielle's apartment and learn what had happened. Had she taken the papers to Antoinette? What had Antoinette said? Had she sent a note for me with Abrielle perhaps? Was that how Mathilde knew I was here in Lévitan?

I lobbied Fräulein Sommer, and even Pettit, for the chance to work on Abrielle's stil-unfinished apartment, arguing that while some of the items I had chosen had already been delivered and set up, I hadn't seen them in place. The apartment still needed a number of pieces of furniture and miscellaneous items such as mirrors and artwork, a few tchotchkes, the sorts of things that would make the apartment a real showcase.

At long last I was summoned to Abrielle's apartment, but now I faced another problem. The heat of the season made it impossible to get away with stuffing my clothes with straw to hide the smuggled papers, so I had to make do by sketching on the backs of fewer papers. There were far too many sketches for a simple three-bedroom apartment, but I relied on the guards' ignorance of the process of interior design.

"It's been forever since I've seen you!" Abrielle gushed upon opening the door. She held a fan in one hand and sported an aigrette in her yellow hair. "Don't I look amazing? Come in, come in!"

Zelia was in the foyer pulling a straw cloche hat over her mousy brown hair. Abrielle said to her, much more subdued, "Thank you again for doing the shopping, Zelia."

Zelia nodded, glowered at both of us, grabbed her shopping bags, and left. As before, Abrielle closed the door and leaned against it with a sigh of relief.

"I have *so* much to tell you, Capu! I thought I should burst if Zelia did not leave! Wretched woman."

Abrielle's beautiful marabou-feather fan summoned a vivid memory of Bruno hunched over the worktable, telling me a funny story about his apprenticeship in London as he carefully threaded pink-dyed silver pheasant plumes through the delicate monture of carved white mother-of-pearl.

"Well, what do you think?" she prompted, annoyed by my silence. "Don't I look amazing?"

"You do, indeed," I said. "Stunning, in fact. Sorry. I was remembering when Bruno made that fan. Excellent choice, by the way. It is very precious."

"Isn't it, though? Speaking of precious," said Abrielle, her voice as breathy as when she was flirting with men, "I have something for you."

"What is it?"

"Hold on, silly! I've hidden it," she said.

I followed her into her bedroom. She stood on tiptoe to reach a hatbox on a high shelf in her closet, then set it on the bed and opened it with a flourish.

The feathered chapeau nestled within also reminded me of

Bruno, and I tried to stifle the now-familiar pang. I remembered Isedore telling me she was sure her parents were already dead, and at the time, I had held out hope, not wanting to entertain the possibility that Bruno might have been killed. But now I understood what Isedore meant. Bruno had been sent to Auschwitz, which meant he might well already have passed, already joined my husband, Roger, not to mention the hundreds of thousands of war fatalities, in the world beyond. It was becoming almost impossible to think otherwise.

"Here it is!" Abrielle handed me a letter with red and blue markings along the edge indicating an airmail envelope.

From America.

From *Charles.*

"What— How—," I stammered. "How did you get this?"

"From your concierge, of course. Henrietta or whatever her name is. There's a note from her as well. And one from your daughter. I have *so* much to tell you. Let's sit and talk!"

"My daughter?" I said, fear lancing through me. As if the shock of the letter from Charles weren't enough, Abrielle had apparently also met my daughter. "Where did you see Mathilde?"

"At the shop, silly. I went there, and she was behind the counter, just like you and your father used to be."

"Mathilde's minding the shop? La Maison Benoît?"

"I wouldn't go *that* far. She told me the shop was closed for business, so I doubt she's making any money for you, I'm sorry to say. But the place looks real nice, except that part of the counter glass was shattered. Guess she had an accident, huh?"

"Come, sit with me and tell me everything," I said, dropping onto the side of the bed and patting the coverlet. "Don't leave anything out, not one single thing."

I OPENED THE note from Mathilde, and cried at her simple words:

> *Maman, I love you. Take care of yourself, and come back*
> *to me.*

But I waited until I was in the lorry, heading to the department store where I was imprisoned, to open the letter from Charles. Abrielle had begged me to open it in front of her so she could hear my news, but I wanted to read it by myself.

The lumbering truck jostled and bounced so much over the cobblestones and potholes that it was hard to make out Charles's sometimes messy script. I had read only *To my dearest, loveliest Fan Girl* when the sound of gunfire startled me. The truck screeched to a stop, throwing us forward, and a bullet ripped through the canvas.

In an oddly gallant move, the young guard assigned to ride with me yanked me down to the floor of the truck, protecting me with his body.

We lay so close, I could see that he had no trace of whiskers on his face. He was probably Isedore's age, maybe even younger. I felt his heart pounding as fast as mine.

After several minutes, he told me in broken French to stay down, and hopped out.

I gathered up the two sheets of delicate onionskin paper that had fallen to our feet, and still lying on the floor, I read:

> *Dear Capu,*

> *I know that you told me not to write anymore, that*
> *we were done. But I had to tell you this: Though I may*

be too old to be of much service, I can no longer sit this war out.

I am volunteering for the army. I want to defend la Belle France from fascism, not to mention England and Belgium and all those other countries, and help determine the fate of the United States as well. I want to do what I was too young to do in the Great War. A number of us older recruits have joined up recently—I suppose we're the dregs, but as my French friends would say, "The dregs are good for your health!"

Of course, I will have no control over where the army chooses to send me to fight. With my luck, I will next write to you from the Pacific Theater of war! But regardless, I will dream of returning to Paris and to you—if not as part of the contingent of conquering heroes marching down the Champs-Élysées, then afterward, to help with the cleanup, to help Paris come back to herself, if she'll have me. I believe she will; she was in the past so unexpectedly, unabashedly welcoming. Please tell me she has not lost that in all the misery of war.

North Carolina will always be my home, but Paris will always be my heart. As Josephine Baker would say, "J'ai deux amours: my country, and Paris."

I know you say you've moved on, and I won't interfere in your new life. But I must see my beloved Paris, at least, one more time.

Charles was coming to Paris. If he survived the battle.

If *I* survived, I would find him. I let him go once. I would not do so again.

28

Mathilde

$\mathscr{A}$S THE WEATHER heated up, Mathilde made several more trips to the butcher and spent most afternoons at La Maison Benoît, drawing and working on her fan designs—which were still a mess, but improving. Abrielle came by the shop a few more times, carrying bundles of papers and photographs from her mother. Capucine had written Mathilde several tiny unsigned notes that she had mixed in with the correspondence from Jewish families: *Je pense à toi*—I am thinking of you. *Tu me manques*—I miss you. Each one included small drawings of flowers and ballerinas and ribbons. Mathilde saved them all in the box where she kept Charles's letters.

Abrielle was initially reluctant to carry messages from Mathilde back to Capucine, but was bribed easily enough with baubles and aigrettes and the occasional new fan.

One night a young man came to the back door of the house in Neuilly and handed Mathilde a stack of posters.

"What am I supposed to do with these?" she asked. "Take them to the butcher?"

"Of course not. Put these up with a little paste or some tacks. On the sides of buildings, on benches, on church steps, everywhere. Leave a few, secured by a rock, anywhere the public might see them."

"What if someone sees me?"

He rolled his eyes. "Do it after dark. That's one good thing about the lack of electricity, right?"

"What about curfew?"

"Don't get caught," he said, and disappeared into the night.

The posters were similar to those she had seen all across Paris, calling on the populace to rise up against the oppressors. Some declared, "Victory is near," while others promised "Chastisement for the traitors," meaning Vichy loyalists and collaborators.

As usual, it gave Mathilde pause to condemn out of hand those who had tried to appease the Germans. After all, her grandparents had taken care of her, had sacrificed and worked with the Germans in part for her sake so that she could remain safe in their comfortable home. But what else was she supposed to do? She was now part of the Résistance, however unlikely that seemed. Even just a few months ago she had thought of the Résistance "spies" and "rebels" as brave, organized people committed to a political cause—not unfocused young ladies who didn't know what they wanted to do with their lives.

Choice, chance, and character, Antoinette had said.

Fear wasn't a choice, but bravery was. A daily choice. Mathilde supposed her fate would be up to chance, but she wasn't sure what any of it said about her character.

She told Mami Yvette she was going to meet up with an old

school friend, Béatrice, in the afternoon, and perhaps they would spend an evening in town, and if it got late, she would sleep over. Mami and Papi were beginning to worry she might be betraying Victor by indulging in a romance with another young man, but she assured them such was not the case.

"I just like being outside, that's all! It's been such a long and dreary winter. And oh, you know how I love the city."

She brought her things to La Maison Benoît, stowed them in her mother's bedroom, and then played with the feathers for a bit, her agitation mounting as darkness fell. In the evening, Mathilde changed into her old school uniform and braided her hair, hoping to look younger. She placed the posters, some tacks, and a jar of paste from the shop at the bottom of a woven shopping bag, then covered them with blank paper, an old sweater, and a piece of cake she had purloined from under the glass dome in the kitchen at home.

Could she really bring herself to do this—to pepper the city with posters calling on the citizenry to rise up? Standing in line at the butcher's was one thing, actively plastering posters around the city quite another.

Choose bravery, she told herself.

The nearly empty streets were illuminated only by moonlight. Paris was one of the first cities in Europe to be fully lit with electric streetlights, but electricity was scarce these days, and the Germans did not want to give Allied aircraft a clue as to where the cities were. The war had brought darkness in more ways than one.

Mathilde tried to work up the courage to stop and put up some of the posters, but it was hard to know when. She tried once at a bus stop, but thought she heard footsteps and chickened out at the last minute. She kept walking, trying to calm her heart, staying in the shadows. She felt safer leaving small stacks of posters here and there, on benches, on the steps in front of the Square Hector Berlioz at the Place Adolphe Max . . . and only then realized she had walked all the way to the Quartier Pigalle.

She turned a corner onto the Boulevard de Clichy and came face-to-face with a soldier. He was young and sweet faced, but wore a fierce expression.

"Show me your papers," he demanded in broken French. "Why you are here?"

She gave her *carte d'identité*.

"Where do you go?" he asked.

"Neuilly," she blurted out.

"Neuilly?"

"Ja, ich wohne in Neuilly-sur-Seine," she said after taking a deep breath. Yes, I live in Neuilly-sur-Seine, she said in his language, hoping to curry favor.

Her plan backfired when the young man continued speaking to her in German. Mathilde had never paid much attention in German-language class, unlike Bridgette, or even Simone. She had always preferred English.

"Entschuldigung bitte, ich verstehe nicht," she said, remembering the useful phrase: Excuse me. I don't understand.

He repeated slowly in French. "Why you are here now? Where you go?"

"Oh, I'm visiting my grandmother." Bridgette's lessons on what to do when encountering a German patrol returned to her, so Mathilde flashed the young man a smile and batted her eyelashes. "My grandmother is the sweetest little old lady. She's not feeling well, so I'm bringing her some cake. She lives just down the street."

He held his hand out for the bag.

"Perhaps you would like some cake?" Mathilde suggested,

reminding herself to breathe, to pull herself together. Her life might depend upon it.

Still, her hand shook as she held out her bag. Would he look beyond the cake and under the sweater? If he did, how could she explain the posters? Bridgette's "uncle of a school chum" cover story wouldn't make much sense this time. Her mind was blank.

Just as he started to open the bag, a well-dressed couple came walking down the street toward them.

Simone. And her Nazi officer boyfriend, Manfred Wolff. Only then did Mathilde realize they were not far from the Moulin Rouge, the famous nightclub Simone mentioned frequenting with her handsome Nazi.

Simone seemed shocked to see Mathilde and whispered something to Wolff. He nodded, and asked the young soldier, "What's going on?"

"Sie scheint mir misstrauisch," said the soldier.

"Warum? Weshalb?" said Manfred.

Mathilde watched the exchange, not understanding what was being said. She locked eyes with Simone.

Wolff took her *carte d'identité*, frowned, and in fluent French asked Mathilde, "Why are you out so late at night?"

"I was visiting my grandmother," Mathilde said. "She's sick and lives not far from here. I was bringing her cake."

Simone intervened. "Darling, this is Mathilde, an old friend of mine from a fine, upstanding Catholic family. We went to school together, and her grandfather is a very respected director at the Renault factory. Come, *liebling*, let's go. We don't want to be late to the show."

Wolff cast a suspicious glance at Mathilde. "You were the one who came to Simone's house looking for your friend. Did you find her?"

"Nein, mein Herr," she said.

He handed back her identification card and glanced at his wrist-watch. "Run along home, mademoiselle. It's well after curfew."

"Ja, mein Herr." Mathilde thanked him. *"Danke schön. Guten abend."*

Run Mathilde did, all the way to rue Saint-Sauveur and La Maison Benoît, stopping only twice: once to vomit in the gutter, and a second time to toss the remaining posters in the doorway of a government building. She could not bear the thought of being caught with them.

Mathilde let herself into the dark fan shop, crawled into her mother's bed, and wept with fear and relief and disappointment in her own lack of courage.

If bravery was a choice, she had chosen fear.

MATHILDE SPENT A restless night plagued by nightmares. In one, the butcher's shop was filled with men in trench coats watching her in eerie silence; in another, the eagle on Manfred Wolff's uniform came to life and chased her through the city, demanding its feathers back. She listened to the unfamiliar sounds of the neighborhood and yearned for the comforting safety of her old bedroom at her grandparents' house.

Mathilde shared the cake with Antoinette for breakfast, and the old woman made some sort of strong chicory-roasted dandelion root concoction that passed for coffee. It wasn't great, but the sustenance, the affection of Croissant the cat, and her chat with Antoinette about fan designs made her feel more herself. Mathilde sorely wanted to tell Antoinette what had happened last night, but remembering what Bridgette had said, she kept her secrets to herself. She would never forgive herself if the kind old woman was put in harm's way because of her.

Mathilde spent the day in the shop, which also helped. Listening to jazz records on the phonograph, spending hours drawing and playing with feathers and design ideas for fans . . .

The shop bell tinkled, and Simone walked in.

"*Here* you are!" she said, looking around. "I stopped by your grandparents' house in Neuilly, and according to the maid, you're hardly ever home these days and didn't come home at all last night—which, I don't mind telling you, gave me quite a fright. What happened?"

"It was late, and I was tired, so I decided to spend the night here instead," said Mathilde. "How did you know where to find me?"

"I went by Bridgette's family's shop, and Madame Caron informed me Bridgette's still missing, for weeks now. She and her husband both look *dreadful*, by the way, don't they? She suggested you might be here. You could have knocked me over with a feather," she said. Then looking around at the fans and plumes, she smiled. "Pardon the pun."

She meandered around the small shop, admiring a fontange-shaped fan made of blue ombré-tinted silk leaf with sequined and painted butterflies, and another made of painted silk gauze and black net with Art Nouveau stylized leaves and edged with silver paillettes.

"These are so fantastic, aren't they? Wouldn't it be nice if they came back into fashion? I came here once before a long time ago," said Simone, "when your mother and grandfather were here."

"Really? When was that?"

"When we were in the lycée. I remembered how fashionable

your mother was, and I was curious. But of course, I couldn't afford anything."

"Their clientele was mostly the wealthy," said Mathilde. "And haute couture, of course."

Simone smiled. "Your mother took pity on me and made me a little feather bauble to attach to my hat. Do you know, I still have it?"

"I'm glad. Why didn't you ever tell me about that?"

Simone shrugged. "You were always so touchy whenever the subject of your mother and grandfather came up. Your grandparents got into your head, I think."

"That's probably true."

Simone came to lean on the counter, and asked, "Mathilde, what's going on?"

"What do you mean? I've cleaned up in here, that's all, and it's fun to play with the fans and feathers. And I mean . . . what else do I have to do with my time?"

"I meant last night, when Manfred and I met you in the street. You were 'bringing cake to your sick grandmother'? Why did you lie?"

"I . . ." Mathilde trailed off, realizing she should have given this some thought, should have realized Simone would find her and ask questions. They were old friends and had once made a blood promise: friends forever. Mathilde was almost positive Simone wouldn't betray her to her German officer boyfriend, but still . . . as everyone kept reminding her, this was war, and nothing was certain.

"Hey, did I tell you Victor wants to propose marriage?" Mathilde said to distract her.

"He *does*? What did you say?"

"That I wasn't sure. There's just too much going on right now with this war and everything. . . . I asked him to wait, and he agreed."

"No wonder, since you're wearing your hair in braids and running around in your old school uniform," Simone continued. "He might just change his mind if you're not careful. You remind me of Bridgette, but you don't have her excuse."

"What do you mean?" Mathilde asked, her heart pounding. Did Simone know Bridgette was working with the Résistance?

Simone shrugged and stroked a long white ostrich plume. "A tragic lack of fashion sense, combined with poverty. So, are you going to tell me what's going on?"

"I . . . Tell me more about your officer, why don't you? He's very handsome but seems a little . . . old."

Simone smiled a "cat and the canary" smile. Leaning forward, she whispered, "Manfred's thirty-two, which is old but not *that* old. And he's a darling who treats me like a queen."

"And it doesn't bother you that he's a Nazi?"

"Now you sound like Bridgette, too," she sighed. "I am so tired of all this war talk! I wish it was over already and we could get back to normal life. Although I have to say, I do have a weakness for a man in uniform. . . ."

"Are things serious with Herr Wolff?"

"Who can say? For the moment, I'm having fun. See, you're acting like Bridgette now—why can't a girl have a little fun? He takes me to the nicest restaurants, and of course the Moulin Rouge, and the other night we went to the opera! Are you going to tell me what you were doing last night, running around Paris after curfew? Oh, wait! You were meeting a fella, weren't you? Come on, admit it."

"Yes," Mathilde said, happy to be handed an excuse. "You found me out."

"I knew it! Okay, tell me all about it. How did you meet?"

"Believe it or not, I met him in the street," Mathilde said, surprised at how easily the lie slid off her tongue. "He liked my red coat. He bowed and offered me a red rose, and now he's writing me love letters."

LATER THAT EVENING Mathilde returned to Neuilly-sur-Seine.

When she let herself into the house, her grandparents were sitting in the parlor by the radio, listening intently. Papi Auguste looked ashen.

"What is it?" Mathilde asked, looking from one to the other. "What's happened?"

"The Allies have landed," said Mami Yvette, glancing at Auguste, who remained silent.

"Landed where?"

"On French soil. On the beaches of Normandy."

29

Capucine

*M*ORE AND MORE I spent my days at the homes of various Nazi wives and mistresses, helping to arrange and rearrange their furniture, as well as giving advice on fabrics and paint colors. It seemed absurd to spend hours haggling over just the right blush of apricot for the walls of a sitting room, given there was a war going on, but the work was easy, and I counted myself lucky to be able to leave the Lévitan.

Especially because the women, more accustomed to servants than to prisoners, sometimes fed me.

Each time I returned to the department store attic, I gave a report to the other prisoners: where I had gone, what I had seen, what I had heard. I rarely had much pertinent news to share—not only was I constantly in the presence of clients or soldiers, but the conversation focused exclusively on interior design—but from time to time, I was sent to requisition items at the other Paris prison camps,

Bassano and Austerlitz, where I occasionally saw former inmates from Lévitan. There were a mother and son who had been split up when the most talented seamstresses were moved to Bassano, and I was able to pass messages between the two, as well as from other friends.

The higher-ranking clients often sent a car to pick me up, and since on these occasions I was not accompanied by a guard, Pettit would give me another stern warning about what would happen to my pod if I did not return. One day I climbed into a shiny Mercedes driven by a stooped old man. He did not speak to me beyond a gruff *bonjour,* and when he started driving, he switched on the radio.

And then he tuned the channel to the BBC. I met his rheumy eyes in the rearview mirror. He gave me a little nod and turned up the volume, though I still had to strain to understand the broadcast over the static. Leaning forward, I cursed my lack of fluency in English, but I caught a few stunning words:

Prime Minister Churchill. General Eisenhower. Général *de Gaulle. Operation Overlord. Paratroops . . . series of landings . . . Allied landing . . . coast of France . . . Four thousand ships . . . aircraft. Tactical surprise. Complete unity . . . Allied naval forces on the northern coast of France . . . British, Canadian, and American . . . liberation of Europe . . . the French Free Forces . . .*

The beaches of Normandy.

"*C'est vrai?*" I asked the driver if it was true.

He nodded again. "It won't be long now. The Allies are advancing. Do you understand English?"

"Only a little."

"Too bad you missed the broadcast in French. *Général* de Gaulle says to remain patient. We French must rise up, but only when the time is right."

"How will we know when that is?"

"We will know. . . . The French Forces of the Interior are amassing and will join the Free French Forces under the direction of *Général* de Gaulle, and the rest of the Allied forces. It is happening. It is finally happening."

He pulled up to an apartment building.

"Your appointment is on the second floor. Do you have the number?"

"Yes, thank you," I said.

He nodded again. "Do not despair, madame. You are surrounded by friends. We have to be careful, but it won't be long now."

I was beyond excited to tell the prisoners at Lévitan this news, but when I returned from my outing that evening, several women were crying, and many more in the dormitory were upset.

"What's going on?" I asked.

"They took the wives away!" said Léonie. "Colette and the others. Didn't even let them pack their things."

"All of the wives of prisoners of war?"

"Pretty much," said Jérôme.

"Madame Schreyer and Madame Savanier, too," added Isedore.

"But . . . are they coming back?" I asked. "Where did they take them?"

"We were hoping you might be able to find out," said Isedore. "Maybe you can make Pettit tell you."

"I'll ask, but I doubt she'll tell me anything. Maybe they were just transferred to Bassano like the seamstresses were."

Henri shook his head. "Tremblay said they were going to Drancy, supposedly to 'clarify' their papers."

"I overheard the guards talking about quotas," said Jean-Claude.

"They have to fill the convoys to Bergen-Belsen and the other camps."

"But we're still getting deliveries," said Léonie. "I mean, the trucks keep coming. It's not like they don't need workers right here in Lévitan. They're not going to take the rest of us, are they?"

By now everyone was talking at once, and I kept thinking about what I had heard on the radio, that the Allies had landed on the beaches of Normandy. I glanced at the guards—I certainly did not want to shout this news over the din—and went to find Ezra, who was helping Hélène and a few others to distribute the possessions of the deported women among the prisoners before the guards could requisition them. We would keep them for the women, in case they ever made it back.

"I have news," I murmured, and told the small group what I had heard on the radio.

"The driver tuned the radio to the BBC?" said Hélène. "Why would he do that?"

"He was French. He says that we are surrounded by friends and should not despair, that it won't be long now."

"Can this be true?" Hélène whispered.

"I think it is," I said. "I hear a few things when I'm outside. I think the tide is turning."

IT DID NOT take long for the news of the Allied invasion of France to spread along the attic grapevine, and I must have repeated my story a dozen times as inmates came to my cot, seeking more information. We were abuzz with excitement, with hope, while also grieving the prisoners who were now gone.

That night I lay on my cot, unable to sleep, thinking of the letter from Charles. I had read and reread it so many times, the delicate onionskin paper was already fraying.

If the Allies were on the offensive, did that mean the war would be ending soon and that Charles would come to Paris? And what about Ezra? Were our feelings for each other simply the result of our strange existence, stolen moments of human connection that reminded us that we were still alive?

If Charles really came back to Paris, and I could find him . . . would I tell him, *Yes, I will marry you*? Considering how much time had passed, how much had happened since we were last together, we were not the same people we had once been. Could we recapture what we once had?

Or . . . what if the unthinkable happened? What if Charles was cut down on the battlefield, like so many others? Fear knifed through me at the thought. My handsome American always loomed so large in my imagination, so dynamic and vital, that it was easy to forget that he was as mortal as anyone else. As vulnerable to bombs and bullets. Not made of bronze, in fact.

I thought again of an argument we had when I denied that his race mattered.

"You cannot believe that, Capu," he had said. "At times, it means everything."

"Not to me."

What I meant was that to me, Charles was simply Charles. The man who made me feel wanted and alive, understood without explanation. The man I wanted to be with, to cleave to, to grow old with. A beautiful spirit, a gentle soul, a passionate heart. That was how I saw him.

He gazed at me, his beautiful sherry brown eyes full of sorrow.

"When you deny someone's reality, you are denying a piece of them. I know you don't mean it that way, but that's what it means; that's how it feels."

"But—"

"There is no *but*," Charles said, cutting me off in a rare gesture of impatience. "Listen to what I am saying, Capu. Denying the color of my skin, denying what that means to society, how it affects the way I have been treated and seen my entire life, would mean denying a part of myself. Denying a big part of the man I am. And what's more, I think you know that, or you would have married me long ago."

I opened my mouth to protest, but I could not.

"If I were white," Charles continued softly, "you would have allowed me to be a part of your daughter's life. You would not continue to deny me to your in-laws."

He was right, of course.

I had denied his reality, and then I had denied *him*.

My shame at what I had done to him, to us, spilled out of the fan box in my heart, no matter how hard I tried to stuff it down.

If we both survived, and if I managed to find him, I vowed I would never deny him again.

THE NEXT DAY the men finished unloading the last truck early, and we were allowed to go up to the rooftop terrace. We were enjoying the last rays of sunshine when we heard a clatter from across the street.

Someone dared to open their shutters and unfurl a banner out the window: our beautiful tricolor flag. The blue, red, and white stripes of France.

Very quietly, Hélène started singing our national anthem, *"La Marseillaise"*:

> *Allons enfants de la Patrie,*
> *Le jour de gloire est arrivé!*

Léonie and Henri joined in, the singing growing louder.

I felt a shiver run down my spine, and tears burn the back of my eyes. Dared we hope?

In a deafening blast, a soldier on the street below opened fire on the flag, the bullets ricocheting off the walls of the residential building in a hail of stone chips and mortar.

The singing stopped. We froze in horror, watching as a hand inched up over the windowsill and slowly pulled the shutters closed.

The flag remained.

30

Mathilde

"B UT THE INVASION is good news, is it not?" Mathilde asked that night at dinner. Victor had stopped by, and his unexpected arrival sent Mami Yvette into a flurry of activity. She had ordered Mathilde upstairs, insisting she change into an evening gown and put on the starburst necklace Victor had given her. "The British and Canadians and even the Americans are coming to save us, like they did in the last war."

"What are you going on about?" Papi Auguste had been distracted and irritable ever since they heard the news. "What are you saying about Americans?"

"They came all the way over here to help us in the last war, didn't they?" Mathilde asked.

"They did, and we were grateful for it. But afterward, they were meant to return to where they came from, not to linger with their modern art and wretched music. There is something"—he cast a

glance around the room as if searching for the right phrase—
"something inherently corrupt about Americans. They don't have
enough history, enough tradition, to keep them on the proper path."

"What about *les Hommes de Bronze*?" Mathilde asked.

"Oh, I believe I've heard of them," Mami Yvette murmured.
"They were very brave, were they not?"

"They were. And a lot of them stayed on in Paris until they were
forced to leave out of fear of being imprisoned, or worse, under the
Occupation."

"Americans should stay in America, and Negroes in Africa," declared Papi.

"I daresay I agree with your grandfather, Mathilde," said Victor.
"These are complex issues, and—"

"But they're from America, Papi," Mathilde said, cutting Victor
off. "They aren't from Africa."

"They once were. And I've had quite enough of this discussion.
If I've told you once, I've told you a thousand times: Leave the phi-
losophizing to men who know what they're talking about."

There was a brief pause in conversation, and Mathilde surprised
even herself when she said: "No, actually I won't hold my tongue. Have
you seen the signs in the streets? Parisians are fed up with the Occupation. They are ready to rise up against the Nazis, and if the Allied
troops arrive to help, then that's it, is it not? The Allies have landed
on French soil, so very likely this war and this Occupation will soon
be over."

Her grandparents and Victor stared at her as if she were a painting suddenly come to life.

"What has gotten into you?" Papi demanded.

"I've been thinking. On my own. So, here's my real question:
What's next for us?"

But even as she said it, Mathilde realized she could guess what would happen if the Germans were defeated and the Vichy government fell. The posters she herself had put up around the city made it clear: The collaborators—people like Papi Auguste and Victor, who worked for the Germans at the Renault factory—would pay.

Papi Auguste banged his fist on the table so hard, it rattled the dishes, and he slowly rose to his feet. "I will not have this kind of talk at my dinner table, young lady."

Mathilde stood as well. "I apologize, Papi, Mami. May I be excused from the table? And, Victor, may I speak with you alone for a moment, please?"

Papi nodded, sat back down, and took a bite of his black-market pork chop while Mami signaled Cécile to bring more wine.

Mathilde led Victor into the parlor, closing the pocket doors for privacy.

"Mathilde," said Victor, "I'm sorry to side with your grandfather so consistently, but you simply must understand—"

"I understand more than any of you realize, Victor. Really, I do." Mathilde reached up to unlatch the clasp of the starburst necklace. Cupping it in her hands, she held it out to him. "It's beautiful, and you were very generous to offer it to me, but I can't accept it. I can't accept anything from you."

Victor looked stunned. "Whyever not?"

"Because we are wrong for each other."

"I'm sorry to say, Mathilde," Victor said, gazing at the necklace in his hands, "that I do not believe you are the girl I thought you were."

"I daresay I'm not," she said, and then in a gentler voice: "I tried, Victor. I really did. For their sake and yours. But I'm not the woman any of you thought I was. I truly believe you will be happier with someone else."

"You've been seeing someone, haven't you?" he said, his eyes narrowing. "That's why you've been spending so much time in Paris."

"There *is* no one else, Victor," Mathilde said. "That, at least, you must believe."

"I *don't* believe it," he said, his voice full of disdain. "I was willing to overlook your disreputable mother because I thought you, at least, were a respectable woman. Well, I am a respectable man and you have made a fool of me and disgraced your grandparents. Good luck finding someone else to ask for your hand in marriage." He gave a humorless chuckle. "You'll end up just like your mother."

"We'll just have to wait and see. And I am proud to think I take after my mother even the littlest bit. And as it turns out, Victor, you are exactly the man I thought you were."

31

Capucine

"WHERE WERE THE wives of the POWs taken?" I asked
Pettit the next morning. "Were they transferred somewhere or sent
back to Drancy?"

The guard shrugged, not as communicative as she used to be. I
wondered: Had she heard the news of the Allied invasion from the
BBC, or however it might have been filtered and presented to the
German audience? If the Third Reich was losing its grip on France,
did that mean it was failing on all fronts? And what would that
mean for the guards? Would Pettit be sent home in disgrace to an
impoverished Germany suffering yet another massive defeat?

Pettit, at least, had a country to return to. What about our
French jailers, like Tremblay? What would happen to Abrielle or to
Mathilde's grandparents, the Duplantiers, who had collaborated
with the Nazi and Vichy forces? How would they fare with their

war-maddened neighbors, at least some of whom would be bent on revenge?

And most important, what would this mean for Mathilde?

"Herr Pflüger is impatient for you to finish their apartment," Pettit said.

"But—" I cut myself off. I should have known by now that there was no logical explanation for much of what happened at the Lévi-tan. Why were we continuing to decorate the city flats and country estates of the Nazi elite if the war was going badly for them?

"But what, 123?" Pettit demanded, her eyes narrowing. She leaned toward me as though itching for a fight.

"Nothing. Sorry."

"Meet the truck at the dock in five minutes."

AS HAD BECOME my custom, I brought a stack of documents from the homes of deported Jews, which Abrielle placed in her bag. We spent an hour discussing the finishing touches on the apart-ment; then Abrielle grabbed her bag, for she would continue to La Maison Benoît after she had walked me out. Abrielle was reaching for the door handle when Herr Pflüger came in.

"*Bärchen!* You're home early." Abrielle's voice was breathier than ever, and she wore a wide-eyed, falsely honest look, like a kid caught with her hand in the cookie jar. "What a nice surprise."

"Where are you going?" he asked, looking at her bulging bag.

"I thought I'd just pop out for a few minutes to . . . get a few things."

Herr Pflüger looked suspicious. "Didn't Zelia do the shopping?"

"I . . . forgot to ask her to get something. Silly me. I'll be right back."

"What's in the bag?"

"Nothing of any importance!"

"Show me." When Abrielle hesitated, he ripped the bag from her hands and went to sit on his new sofa.

Abrielle and I exchanged a glance, neither of us breathing, hoping he would not realize what he had.

"What's all this, then?" he asked, rummaging through the contents. "Where did you get these papers?"

"It's nothing!" Abrielle insisted. "You needn't look in there!"

"These are . . . what? Letters and photographs?" He held up one letter and read a few lines. "These names sound Jewish. Where did these come from?"

"Where did what come from, *Bärchen?*"

He crumpled the papers in his hand and raised his fist. "What is all *this?*"

"J-just some old scraps I found in the street. I thought perhaps we could use them to start a fire."

"A fire? When it's twenty-eight degrees outside? This apartment is already sweltering."

"Mein Herr . . . ," Abrielle began, her voice shaking and her eyes filling with tears. *"Bärchen*, please . . ."

Herr Pflüger said nothing. His gaze was cold when he glanced at me, but much worse when he looked at Abrielle.

"Otto, I beg of you," cried Abrielle, kneeling beside him. "This is all a mistake! I swear I did not know what was going on. She tricked me! Tell him, Capu!"

"She's telling the truth," I said, my voice flat. "I gave them to her. Abrielle didn't know what I was doing."

He stood, gazing at Abrielle with disgust tinged with fear.

"You will be deported," he hissed. *"Französisches schwein."*

Fear, shock, and then anger flitted across Abrielle's face. *"Pig?* You're calling me a pig, you disgusting *Boche?"*

Abrielle surged to her feet and lunged, grabbing for Pflüger's pistol, and he let out a loud exclamation in German. They struggled briefly but he easily subdued her, backhanding her across the face, and she fell to the carpet.

In one smooth move, Pflüger pulled his pistol, aimed, and fired.

A hole appeared in the middle of Abrielle's forehead, black around the edges. She collapsed, her big green-gold eyes open wide, her bright red blood pooling on the plush wool Aubusson carpet.

I froze in shock and disbelief, ears ringing from the gunshot, unable to register what was happening.

Pflüger seemed stunned by his own actions. Stumbling forward, he knelt beside Abrielle on the carpet.

"Maus?" he whispered. He set the gun down and wrapped his arms around her, cradling her dead body. "Abrielle!"

Zelia rushed in from the kitchen. She looked as horrified as I felt, but unlike me, she did not hesitate. She snatched up the gun and pointed it at Pflüger.

He gently set Abrielle's body back on the carpet, then slowly rose to his feet to face his maid.

"What do you think you are doing, madame?" he demanded in French, holding out his hand. "Give me the gun."

Her hand shook, but Zelia's eyes narrowed.

"Give me that weapon *now*," Pflüger repeated. "Or you will regret it."

"*Non*, monsieur. It is you who will regret it. You will regret everything." She steadied the gun by holding it with both hands, and kept it trained on his chest. "The deportations, the shooting in the streets. The loss of so many lives, so many homes. And for *what*?"

Pflüger drew his shoulders back and lifted his head. "Do not be naïve, madame. In war there are only winners and losers. The Third Reich will be victorious and France shall remain defeated."

"I think not. Either way, you won't be alive to see it."

"You wouldn't dare."

"You Nazis have always underestimated us *Französisches schweine.*"

He started toward her.

Zelia pulled the trigger. Pflüger's eyes widened. He clutched at the left side of his chest, stumbled, and collapsed next to Abrielle. He groaned, whispered something, then gasped and fell silent.

Their blood mingled on the expensive Aubusson carpet.

"You'll have to run for it," Zelia said to me. "Quickly. I have friends. They will help you."

"You're in the Résistance?"

"I have friends," she repeated.

"I—I can't run," I stammered. "If I don't return to Lévitan, they'll deport my whole pod."

"If you stay here, they'll shoot you on sight when they learn what has happened."

I thought of Isedore, of Léonie, of Hélène and Victorine. All of them. "I can't be the cause of my friends' being deported."

"Listen to me, Capucine," Zelia said, grabbing my shoulders and giving me a little shake. "The Nazis are losing this war. The Soviets are marching on Berlin from the east, and now the Allies have landed in western France and are fighting their way to Paris. It is only a matter of weeks, even days, before they get here. The Germans know it. The Allies know it. Everybody but Hitler knows it. Even if your friends are taken to Drancy or beyond, the Allies will free them soon enough. You just have to stay alive a few more weeks, a month or two at most. Got it?"

I nodded.

"Good. Now, we must move quickly. Help me pick up those papers."

I crouched to gather the scattered papers, moving slowly and trying not to look at the bodies and the blood.

"Capucine?" Zelia barked. "Now's not the time to fall apart. You must help me. Grab his leg and bring it over here. Don't step in the blood."

Zelia worked with remarkable efficiency, seemingly unfazed by her two dead employers lying on the floor. She wiped the handle of the pistol with her apron and pressed it into Pflüger's meaty hand, closing his fingers around it. Then, with my help, we positioned the bodies to appear as if the slaughter was a murder-suicide, the result of a lovers' quarrel.

"It may not fool the authorities, but it will slow them down while they investigate." Zelia stuffed the papers I had brought into a shopping bag and scribbled something on the back of a torn letter. "Listen to me, Capucine. Go to the butcher at this address and ask for your grandmother's favorite flank steak with flageolets. And then tell him you need the recipe. He will be able to help you."

She pressed the paper into my hand. "Do you understand what I'm saying to you?"

I nodded.

"What do you ask for?"

"Flank steak," I said, sounding like an automaton. "It's my grandmother's favorite, with flageolets. I need the recipe."

"Good. Time to go before the neighbors call the authorities. There are so many backfires and gunshots in the streets these days, we might have a little time, but you never know. There are informants everywhere."

"Wait—the guard," I said. "The one who comes with me—she's waiting for me downstairs."

"We'll take the servants' stairs to the street," Zelia said. "Ready? It's now or never."

"I—"

Pettit appeared in the doorway.

Zelia and I froze.

"*Scheisse*," Pettit swore, her eyes fixed on the macabre vignette on the carpet. "What in the hell?"

I looked at Zelia and said, *"Run."*

"She's right," Pettit said to Zelia. "Go. *Now.*"

Zelia grabbed the paper with the address from my hand, slung the bag with the papers over her arm, and ran to the kitchen. A moment later we heard the door to the servants' stairs close.

Pettit hesitated a moment, then said in a fierce whisper, "You saw *nothing*. Do you understand? When last you saw your friend and Herr Pflüger, they were wrapped in a lovers' embrace." She glanced at her watch. "We left half an hour ago. Got that?"

"But—"

"Do as I say!"

She grabbed me by the arm and hustled me out the door and down to the street, where she ordered Tremblay to ride up front and climbed in the back of the truck with me.

"Listen to me carefully, Capucine," Pettit said when we were underway. She leaned forward on the bench so that her face was close to mine. Her pale eyes were intent, her cheeks flushed with emotion. "The death of a Nazi officer is going to raise holy hell. If the authorities don't buy the murder-suicide story, Zelia will be blamed. But if they learn it happened while we were there, we'll both be arrested and interrogated, and if we don't die from the torture, we'll be shot. You hear what I'm saying to you?"

Her voice sounded very far away. But the fact that Pettit had called me Capucine for the first time scared me. I met her eyes and nodded.

"Yeah, I don't trust you, either," she said. "But if one of us is found out, so is the other. Hell of a thing, isn't it? So let me hear you say it: *We have a deal.*"

"We have a deal. We left half an hour ago, and everyone was fine."

"Good." Pettit handed me a handkerchief and wetted it with water from a canteen. "Clean yourself up before we get back to Lévitan. You have blood on your face."

32

Mathilde

*P*API AUGUSTE BARELY spoke to Mathilde after she refused Victor, and Mami seemed heartbroken.

Mathilde did her best to ignore their unhappiness and continued
to make up excuses to spend as much time as possible at La Maison
Benoît: She was walking in the Jardin du Luxembourg, helping an
old friend with her new baby, sketching the windows at the Cathédrale Notre-Dame. . . .

Everyone in Paris was on edge, assuring one another that the
Allies would be here soon, but rather than slowing down the deportations, the Germans seemed to have stepped up their efforts. More
Jews disappeared, even the very old, the very young, and the ailing,
who could not possibly be of use in a work camp.

One day Mathilde knocked on Antoinette's door and heard
weeping from within.

"Madame?" Mathilde said, trying the doorknob and pushing the door open a crack. "May I come in?"

"Oui, oui, entrez," said Antoinette in a weak voice.

Mathilde found the elderly woman at the table by the window, her head in her hands, a handkerchief beside her. Croissant the cat was on the windowsill and gave Mathilde an imperious look.

"Madame . . . Antoinette . . . what is it? What's wrong?" Fear gripped her. "Is it . . . Did something happen to my mother? Have you heard something?"

Antoinette shook her gray head, wiped her tears, and blew her nose.

"Is it another of your relatives?" Mathilde asked.

"No, child. It's the village of Oradour-sur-Glane. Have you heard of it?"

"No."

"It's in Haute-Vienne. It's been destroyed, the entire village."

"Oh . . . did you have people there?"

She let out a shaky breath and shook her head. "The whole village was massacred. More than six hundred people."

"I don't understand."

"A German Waffen-S.S. company surrounded the town and ordered everyone to assemble in the village square, to have their identity papers examined. They looted the village and desecrated the church, deliberately scattering Communion hosts. Then they forced all the women and children into the church and locked the door. The men of the village, including three parish priests, were led to the barns, where the soldiers shot them in their legs. Once the men were unable to move, they were covered with fuel, and the barns set on fire."

"*No.* That cannot be. That must be an exaggeration . . . ?"

"It's not. A handful of men escaped; they hid in the woods and witnessed everything. Then the S.S. set fire to the church and machine-gunned those who tried to escape through the doors and windows. The only survivor was a woman named Marguerite Rouffanche, who escaped through a rear sacristy window and managed to crawl to some pea bushes and hide."

"I still don't understand," said Mathilde. "I know soldiers can be brutal, but isn't there some sort of code of conduct, even in war? Why would they commit such an atrocity? Who would murder a *child*?"

"The Résistance is growing, becoming more powerful and more effective, and the Germans are scared," said Antoinette. "The leader of the battalion said the Oradour-sur-Glane massacre was in retaliation for partisan activity in nearby Tulle and for the kidnapping of an S.S. commander."

"Does that mean they know they're losing this war?" Mathilde said, wanting the answer to be yes.

Antoinette nodded. "I think so. I think they're panicking. But imagine all the terrible things they can do before they are chased out! My heart aches for those families, for those poor babies. My heart even aches for the monsters who did this—how will they live with themselves? Will they see the faces of those dying children when they try to sleep at night now and for the rest of their lives? Oh, Mathilde, I swear upon all that is holy, I don't know what has become of my country. I don't know how any of us will survive."

Antoinette put her head down and sobbed.

Mathilde brought her chair around the table and sat next to the old woman, holding her and crying her own tears.

WHEN MATHILDE RETURNED to Neuilly-sur-Seine that evening and joined Papi and Mami in the parlor, she told them about the massacre at Oradour-sur-Glane.

Papi snorted. "That's ridiculous. I don't believe a word of it."

"But it's true, Papi—it happened. We can't pretend it didn't. Surely you do not countenance such an atrocity. Please tell me you do not. You are a Christian."

"As are you, young lady, and as such we should know better than to question God's plan."

She gave a humorless laugh. "God's *plan*? Is it God's plan that children be shot or burned alive? Carted off to their deaths?"

"We don't know the details of what happened, and I doubt your account very sincerely. No need to bring histrionics into this discussion."

"It happened," Mathilde insisted. "A lone woman survived the burning of the church and was able to tell the story."

"Perhaps it's not as bad as it sounds, Mathilde," Mami said, looking troubled.

Papi looked discomfited and said, "Atrocities occur in wartime."

"Not like this," Mathilde responded. "And even if they do, that's no defense. What the German soldiers did at Oradour-sur-Glane was barbaric."

"You listen to me, Mathilde. The Germans are a civilized people. They value morality and hard work."

"Now you sound like Father Guillaume, who is either lying or is willfully ignorant about what's happening."

"*Mathilde!*" Mami said, shocked.

"How dare you question the words of a priest!" Papi yelled. "I must say, you think a great deal of yourself lately, young lady. Victor wanted to marry you, but you apparently didn't think he was good enough. It pains me to have to remind you, Mathilde, but the reputation of your mother's family will disqualify you from many good marriages."

"Papi—"

He cut her off. "And what have you been doing lately, eh? Not helping your mami, who has done her best to make you into a lady. Instead of joining the ladies of the church in works of charity, you run around the city on the new bicycle that I bought for you and come home looking a fright. It is long since time to put away childish things, Mathilde. You are a woman now and must start acting like one."

"Yes. Yes, I am a woman." Mathilde allowed her anger to fuel her conviction. She got to her feet. "Thank you for reminding me. And as such, I wish to have control of my inheritance from my father."

"You . . . what?"

"You heard me. It's my money. My father left it to me."

"Mathilde, please. Your dear father—God rest his soul—would not wish you to act in this manner," Mami said.

"That money is for you to start a home with your husband!" Papi shouted. "Not so that you can run off and live like a Gypsy or some other disreputable person."

"You mean, like my mother," Mathilde said flatly.

"And how did that turn out for her, eh?" Papi demanded. "She was arrested along with her communist father. We are well rid of them both."

"Auguste, please," Mami said tearfully. "This is not helping."

"And you refused to help me find her, much less help her,"

Mathilde said, her voice shaking, and she, too, started to cry, which made her angrier. "Why wouldn't you help me, Papi? Do you have any idea how hard it has been for me? Why wouldn't you?"

"You know why."

A wave of calm came over Mathilde, and she realized what she needed to do.

"I cannot collaborate with the Germans anymore. I suggest you think about it as well, for you have thrown your lot in with murderers. I want my money, and then I will go." She looked at her grandmother, who appeared stunned and heartbroken. "I'm sorry, so sorry, Mami. I am truly grateful for everything you have done for me. I love you both. But I just . . . I can't stay here any longer. I just can't."

"Mathilde, *ma petite fille*, where will you go?" asked Mami, crying.

"I'll be at my other inheritance: La Maison Benoît."

33

Capucine

*P*ETTIT AND I had a strange sort of bond after that bloody afternoon. I didn't underestimate her, for I had seen what she was capable of, and I knew she had doubts about me. But for the moment, at least, we each had to trust the other to keep her mouth shut.

The next morning, I was summoned to Herr Direktor Kohn's office.

"Remember what I said," Pettit whispered as she escorted me down to the main floor. "We left the apartment half an hour earlier, and they were fine when you left. If asked, you didn't hear or see anything and know nothing about Zelia. Got it?"

"Got it. But what about Tremblay and the driver? Won't they know what time we left?"

"You leave them to me," she said grimly. "Now, when Herr

Direktor questions you, look scared but honest. Think you can manage that?"

I nodded.

"Of course you can," she said wryly, and knocked on Herr Kohn's office door.

Herr Direktor Kohn stared at me for a long, agonizing moment, then asked, in his high, whispery voice, what I had seen at Herr Pflüger's apartment yesterday.

I looked at him blankly, as if not understanding why he would ask such a question. "Nothing out of the ordinary, Herr Direktor. Mademoiselle Garnier and I discussed the final arrangements for Herr Pflüger's apartment, in particular the choice of a clock for the mantel and a nice work of art for the hallway."

His eyes narrowed. "And did you see Herr Pflüger when you were there?"

"Yes, he arrived just as I was leaving. Mademoiselle seemed surprised to see him in the middle of the day."

"And?"

"And then I left," I said, trying to sound confused. "Herr Pflüger did not address me at all, as I recall."

"Was the maid there?"

"I believe she was in the kitchen, but as I did not see her, I can't be sure."

He rounded the table and stood so close to me that I could smell his aftershave. I forced myself to meet his gaze.

"Did Herr Pflüger seem angry or upset?"

"I cannot say, Herr Direktor. Herr Pflüger did not speak to me."

"Mademoiselle Garnier was once a friend of yours, correct? You spoke with her?"

"Yes, Herr Direktor."

"Did she seem angry or upset?"

"No, Herr Direktor. She did not."

"Were Herr Pflüger and mademoiselle arguing?"

"No, Herr Direktor."

Kohn stared at me for another long moment. My heart pounded and I couldn't seem to stop swallowing.

Finally, he nodded and dismissed me.

"Well done," Pettit murmured as she escorted me back to the office. "You're quite the accomplished liar."

"What do you think will happen now?" I asked.

"I guess we'll see."

For the next few days I was on pins and needles, waiting for another summons or, worse, for me and my pod to be summarily deported. But nothing happened. Perhaps Pettit was right: It behooved Herr Kohn to conclude that I knew nothing about the deaths of Abrielle and Herr Pflüger. If I was involved, then Pettit would be held accountable, and if she was involved, then Herr Direktor Kohn might well be accused of losing control of his staff. A polite fiction satisfied everyone.

I kept thinking of the BBC radio report and what the driver told me, as well as what Zelia had said: that we had to hold on only another month or so. But time dragged like never before. The sound of gunfire in the streets grew more frequent, and our pitiful meals became even more meager due to inconsistent deliveries.

Despite everything, the moving trucks continued pulling up behind the Lévitan, dropping off the stolen contents of Jewish homes.

My fellow prisoners noticed how on edge I was, but I did not confide in a soul. Not even in Ezra. What had happened that day was my burden, not theirs. I tried not to dwell on the harsh blast of Pflüger's pistol, the surprised look on Abrielle's face, the bullet hole in the middle of her forehead. Her bright red blood pooling and mingling with his on the Aubusson carpet.

Most of all, I tried not to think that I had been the cause of Abrielle's death.

When I thought Abrielle had betrayed Bruno and me to the authorities, I had vowed revenge. But I had since realized that it could well have been someone else—my former in-laws, for example, or even a disgruntled customer. It did not take much these days. And even if Abrielle *had* betrayed us, did her helping me smuggle out family papers set right the balance? Had those papers been worth her life? Abrielle did not even fully comprehend the risk she was taking.

I understood the dangers, though. And I had decided for her. Her death weighed on my conscience.

Baron Von Braun came through with a small group of officers for yet another inspection of Lager Ost, during which he again showed off the "little skirts and trousers for German children." The notion was more ludicrous than ever, given the Allied forces were even now fighting their way to Paris. It seemed Pettit and I were not the only ones living out a strange fiction.

Fräulein Sommer kept me busy cataloging the lesser known paintings and the finer pieces of furniture. When we were alone, she would ask about the prisoners and whether they were ready to rise up with the Parisian *levée en masse* if the Allies arrived in Paris. I continued to play dumb, pretending not to understand what she was asking.

"I just want to be of help," she said. "If things go the other way, if Hitler loses control, I would like to be of use."

"In that case, you should get in touch with the Résistance," I said. "I'm sure you are well positioned to be of use. I am afraid I know nothing of these things."

She merely nodded.

Little by little, small groups of prisoners were sent to Drancy "to have their papers clarified," until nearly a third of our number had been taken. The wives of the POWs never returned, and we heard rumors that they had been transported to Bergen-Belsen. The guards were nervous, and our own despair ratcheted up in response.

Every night, Ezra and I slept together, kissed and held each other, but did not make love. I wanted to—I craved his warmth, the scent of him, the feel of him—but I could not stop thinking about Charles.

I told Ezra all about him and even let him read the letter Charles had sent.

"I'm glad for you, Capu. He sounds very special."

"He is. He truly is."

"And you believe he'll come back to Paris?"

"If he can."

"And you'll find him."

"If I can. He . . . Oh, Ezra, you know how I feel about you. But Charles and I have a past. I have amends to make. He asked me . . . He loved me for so long, long after I deserved it."

Ezra gave me his slow, sad smile. "Sounds like a marvelously stubborn man."

"Charles is one marvelously stubborn, glorious man." I cupped Ezra's cheek in my hand, loving the rasp of his whiskers on my palm. "As are you."

And hope was that thing with feathers.

34

Mathilde

MATHILDE WAS TERRIFIED.

In the heart of Paris the night was full of sounds—of voices, some whispering, others shouting; of cars or trucks rumbling past; of boots marching along the sidewalk; of gunshots. Mathilde lay awake, heart pounding, as she tried to convince herself that she was fine, that everything was all right. She would pull her mother's brightly colored quilt over her head until she finally fell back asleep.

All her life, Papi and Mami had been there to protect her and to care for her; all she had had to do was obey. Now she got to make her own decisions—she *had* to make her own decisions. Fortunately, Antoinette was nearby and taught her how to shop for food, which neighbors to watch out for, how to cook a few simple meals.

And it was a vast relief that she no longer had to hide her comings and goings from her grandparents and no longer had to entertain Victor or worry about his feelings.

In the evenings she often joined Antoinette in her apartment, where, despite the warmth of summer, they closed the windows and shutters and listened to the BBC radio news reports of the advancing Allied troops.

One day, Mathilde was making a fan, and she was having a particularly hard time getting some lace to lie just so, when the shop bell rang and Simone greeted her. Mathilde invited her to sit at the small table in the apartment behind the shop and she put on water for tea.

"I can't believe you did it—you divorced your grandparents!" Simone said.

"That's a bit strong," Mathilde replied. "But it wasn't easy, that's for sure. I'm still trying to figure everything out."

"You'll be fine. Get a chance to live a little this way, maybe even have some fun. You deserve it."

"And you?" Mathilde asked as she put a cup of weak tea in front of her old friend. "What are you up to these days?"

Simone sighed and looked glum. "He's married."

"Who's married?"

"Manfred, of course. Who do you think?"

"Your boyfriend is *married*?"

Mathilde could not disguise her surprise. She had been opening her mind to all sorts of new and, to her, radical ideas, but dating a married man was not one of them. She had been raised by her grandparents, after all.

"I know, I know," said Simone. "I don't know what to do, Mathilde."

"I think you do know what to do. You just don't want to do it."

"That's pretty blunt," Simone said, looking surprised. Her eyes narrowed slightly as she studied Mathilde's face. "You've changed."

"War will do that to a person."

"But, Mathilde, it's not that simple. Wolffie's unhappy in his marriage, has been for years now. She's quite the drab country bumpkin. But Herr Hitler frowns on divorce."

"Simone, your Wolffie is not only married—he's a Nazi. How can you be with someone like that?"

She shrugged. "Since when do you care about politics?"

"This isn't just about politics anymore. It's about our very humanity. Simone, open your eyes. Surely you don't countenance what has been happening?"

"What are you talking about?" Simone asked, and Mathilde told her what had happened at Oradour-sur-Glane.

"Well, that's horrific, of course, but that must have been a rogue outfit," Simone said. "I don't see what that has to do with my Wolffie. The German soldiers I've met are very polite, very respectful. They value discipline above all."

"No, they value their 'pure' blood above all, Simone. The rest of us don't matter. Haven't you been paying attention to what's going on?"

Simone shifted uncomfortably. "But Wolffie's not like that."

"Are you sure? Because I have to tell you, Simone, he seems like that to me."

"Why, because he's German?"

"No, because he's a Nazi. A high-ranking officer."

"You don't really know him. Not like I do. He's been so good to me. We have a flat together on the Boulevard de Clichy, not far from the Moulin Rouge."

"But, Simone, look at the bigger picture. He values things you don't, is capable of doing things you would never do. A man like that could never be worthy of you."

"I don't mean to be harsh, Mathilde, but you don't know what you're talking about," Simone said. "And besides, you've always had plenty, much more than I've had. Your own grandfather helps run the Renault factory, after all."

"You think I don't know that? Why do you think I moved out? I love my grandparents, but I can't stand by and watch them support what the Nazis are doing. No one should be able to do such a thing. How can you justify the arrests, Simone? Or the abject cruelty? Your Wolffie is part of that."

"He's really not like that in private. He's so sweet to me when we're alone. And . . . I'm tired of all this wartime scarcity. Aren't you? I mean, I'm young. I should be able to enjoy myself."

Mathilde studied her old friend's face. *Friends forever.*

"Maybe I'm wrong about him," said Mathilde, choosing her words carefully. "I sincerely hope I am. But I'm not wrong about this war or about this Occupation. And I'm worried about you, Simone, because when the Nazis are defeated, then you and everyone else who collaborated with them, including my grandfather, will have to face the injustices you supported."

IN LATE JULY Mathilde rode her bike to Neuilly-sur-Seine in the middle of the day, when Papi would be at work. Mami had come to the shop a few days after Mathilde left, and after many tears and much conversation, they had made up. Papi Auguste was a much harder case. Mathilde loved him, but at least for now, she had no idea how to remain true to herself, and to her new perspective on life, while in his presence—at least, not without making him apoplectic.

As she drew near the clinic run by the nuns on rue Edouard Nortier, Mathilde noticed a crowd milling about. She got off her bike and approached.

"What's going on?" she asked a woman standing at the edge of the crowd, even as her eyes came to rest on the truck pulled up to the curb and guarded by two soldiers, their rifles at the ready. "What are they doing?"

The woman looked at Mathilde with anguished eyes but remained mute.

"They're taking the children," Mathilde whispered. Then louder, she asked the many faces in the throng, "Are they taking the children? Surely they're not taking the children!"

As she said it, the front door opened, and an S.S. officer emerged. Behind him, in a line, shuffled more than a dozen children, the oldest among them carrying mewling toddlers. Each clutched a small bag of belongings.

The elderly nun who answered the door for Mathilde the first time ran behind them, pleading with the soldiers. *"No!* You mustn't! For the love of God—"

One of the soldiers struck her in the back with the butt of his rifle. She cried out and collapsed to the sidewalk. The crowd murmured and surged forward but stopped when the soldier by the truck shouted and raised his rifle.

A pair of younger nuns ran down the steps, reaching down to help their elderly sister. Two soldiers came up on either side of the trio, kicked at them, grabbed them by their upper arms, and shoved them into the truck with the children.

"Anyone else?" demanded the officer, sneering at the murmuring crowd. "We've room for a few more, if anyone else would care to join them."

The soldiers pointed their rifles at the semicircle of bystanders, as well as the clutch of nuns whimpering by the door.

Mathilde stopped breathing. Should she speak up? She would be tossed into the back of the truck with them, and then what? Where would she be taken? Would she find her mother and grandfather there?

"I . . . ," Mathilde began, looking around at the others, wondering if anyone would speak up for her.

The officer fixed her with his malevolent gaze.

"W-where are you taking them?" Mathilde finally managed.

"Would you like to join them and find out?"

Her heart pounded so hard, she thought she might faint, and her courage flagged.

"No?" the officer asked, giving her a contemptuous smile. "I thought not."

He shouted a command in German and climbed into the cab of the truck, and the soldiers piled into the back with the crying children and nuns.

The vehicle rumbled slowly down the cobblestone street.

The nuns shut the door of the building, bolted it from within, and closed the shutters.

One by one, the bystanders dispersed, eyes downcast.

35

Capucine

I WAS SITTING WITH Fräulein Sommer at her makeshift desk in the store's main showroom, making some adjustments to the design sketches for that day's appointments, when I heard a great commotion in the stairwell.

A tall, blond officer had one hand entangled in Isedore's hair and was dragging her down the stairs. A small group of prisoners, led by Ezra, followed them, protesting.

I jumped up and ran over. "What are you doing?" I demanded. "What's going on?"

"Stay out of it," Pettit barked. "Leave this to Herr Wolff. And the rest of you—back upstairs!"

"She's a saboteur," Herr Wolff said, his face red with rage.

I sent a pleading look to Fräulein Sommer. She kept saying she wanted to help. Now was her chance.

"B-but I don't understand," Fräulein Sommer stammered. "Herr Wolff, how could she be a saboteur? She is a prisoner!"

"The clocks she repaired for my dear wife and me stopped working," Wolff replied. "*All* of them. She sabotaged them."

"Well, that is certainly wrong, but surely . . . ," Fräulein Sommer started to say.

"Madame, this is none of your concern," he said coolly. "This is a military affair. She'll help us meet our transport quotas."

Wolff marched Isedore out to the loading dock. I chased after them.

"Wait! It was my fault!" I cried. "I'm the one who told her to do it."

"Shut up, 123. You can't save her," Pettit hissed, then smiled. "But apparently she listened to you. Good job."

I appealed again to Fräulein Sommer, who had trailed us out to the loading dock. "Please, help us! You can speak to Baron Von Braun—he respects you. He'll listen to you."

For a moment everyone, even Wolff, paused at the sound of Oberführer Von Braun's name.

Fräulein Sommer hesitated, then let out a breathy chuckle, shook her head, and said, "I don't think Baron Von Braun should be bothered with something like this. Do you? The man is quite busy."

Two guards picked up the struggling Isedore and threw her in the back of a waiting truck.

Ezra ran past me, toward Isedore. I don't know what he intended, and I never got the chance to find out.

Tremblay lifted his rifle, cried, *"Halt!"*

He fired.

Everyone froze. The gunshot rang in the air, reverberated off the buildings.

Ezra staggered and collapsed on the ground.

"Ezra!" I cried, and ran to him.

Tremblay looked shocked at what he had done. Still, he stepped into my path as if to block me.

Pettit snorted and said, "Let her pass. He won't survive a gut-shot like that."

I kneeled, cradling Ezra's head in my lap, smoothing his dark hair, and murmuring to him, begging him not to die. Barely conscious, he looked up at me, his hands clasped over his wound, which glistened dark red with his lifeblood.

He gave me that little smile. "You see? Sparkles all around you, Fan Girl. I can see them."

"Capu!" Isedore screamed.

I looked up to see Isedore's ashen, bloodied face peering out the rear of the truck as it lumbered down the alley. The canvas flap went down, and the truck went around the corner, out of sight.

I turned back to Ezra. He breathed for a few more moments, started shaking, jerked slightly. Let out one final, extended sigh.

And then the light went out of his beautiful eyes.

36

Mathilde

ANTOINETTE LISTENED AS Mathilde told her what
had happened with the children and the brave nuns.

"I failed them," Mathilde said, crying bitter tears. "I was afraid
and lost my courage."

"There's a difference between courage and stupidity, Mathilde.
What do you think would have happened had you challenged that
officer?"

"I would have been arrested."

"And what purpose would that have served?"

"I know, but . . . I should have done something."

"We must choose our battles carefully, my dear. You *will* do
something—of that, I have no doubt. But it will be something that
will matter, will help make a difference. You will do more good as
a free woman than as yet another prisoner."

"I have to do more, then. Much more. I have to be part of winning our country back, Antoinette."

MATHILDE WAS IN the shop working on a fixed fan, which was easier to make than one that opened and closed. She lifted her hair and fanned the back of her neck, the moving air drying her sweat and making her feel marginally cooler.

The little bell over the door rang and she looked up, hoping to see Mademoiselle Garnier. The woman had not come to the shop in a very long time, and Mathilde yearned for word of her mother.

But it was not Abrielle Garnier or Antoinette or even Simone.

It was Bridgette.

Mathilde dropped the fan, and the two old friends ran into each other's embrace, laughing and crying.

"You're safe!" exclaimed Mathilde. "You're here and you're safe! I can't believe it! I was so worried, so unbelievably worried."

"You're safe, too!" said Bridgette, laughing. "I worried about you as well when I heard you were doing so many deliveries *and* putting posters up around the city! That's so risky!"

"It wasn't much," said Mathilde, blushing. "I feel like I should do more, should have been doing more all along."

"We all feel that way. But you've done a *lot*." Bridgette hesitated, then added, "Are you willing to do more?"

"*Yes.*"

Mathilde had slipped a note to the butcher, informing him that she was no longer in Neuilly, hoping he could get a message to his contacts. She had a nightmare that someone from the Résistance would start pitching pebbles at her grandparents' window when she wasn't there.

And even though she wanted to do more for the Résistance, she was relieved to no longer be putting up posters throughout the city. Scurrying around dark city streets, worrying about encountering soldiers around every corner or running into a man in an overcoat . . . maybe even Simone's Wolffie.

It made her shiver just to think about it.

"Could we sit and have a cup of tea or whatever you have that passes for tea?" asked Bridgette. "I'm not picky."

It was only then that Mathilde noted how tired Bridgette looked. Her boots were caked with mud, and her clothes looked as if she had slept in them. Her dyed-brown hair had faded to a dirty blond, with a center stripe of gold where the hair had grown.

"Of course! What am I thinking? Let's go in the other room, and I'll put on the kettle," said Mathilde as she led the way to the family quarters behind the store. "But how did you know I was here?"

"My parents told me," Bridgette said. "They said you brought them money and food. I can't tell you how grateful I am, Mathilde, for helping them and for keeping my secret. But how did you end up here, at your grandfather's old shop?"

"I just could not live with my grandparents anymore, and it finally dawned on me that I had that money from my father. It's not a lot, but it's enough for now. Until . . . until this horrible war is over. I hope."

"I'm glad to hear it. We all have the right to make our own choices. Speaking of which, I take it you ended things with Victor?" Bridgette asked. "I imagine that was not easy."

"Actually, that was surprisingly easy," Mathilde said.

"I knew you had it in you," Bridgette said. "Poor Victor."

"The only problem is . . ." Mathilde hesitated, loath to confide her true, relatively petty fears to her friend.

"Tell me," urged Bridgette. "Go on, I want all the gory details."

Mathilde shrugged and looked away as tears threatened. Finally, she blurted out, "It's silly, but what if Victor was my last chance? What if Papi is right and no one else will ever want me? I don't want to be an old maid!"

Bridgette looked surprised, then shook her head and began to laugh, that familiar, deep sound that always brought a smile to Mathilde's face.

"Do you even hear yourself?" Bridgette asked, reaching across the table to put her hand over Mathilde's and squeeze. "This isn't last century, my friend. The world has changed. *We* have changed. Here's one thing to come out of this godforsaken mess: We women have fought alongside men in the Résistance, and we've shown our mettle on the home front. We have more options than we used to."

"You think that will continue after the war is over?"

Bridgette shrugged. "I don't know, but I intend to fight for it. I hope you will, too."

The kettle whistled and Mathilde rose to pour the steaming water over a sieve filled with herbs. She brought the teapot to the table, along with two delicate teacups and two slices of toast.

Bridgette inhaled the herbal-scented steam and took a huge bite of the bread. *"Mmm,"* she said, sitting back and closing her eyes for a brief moment. "You know, it's true what they say: The simple things in life really are the best."

"One day soon, I hope, we'll have bread made from real flour. This loaf is made from potato flour. Now, tell me everything you've done since I last saw you, riding away on my bicycle."

Bridgette told Mathilde of the farm family she had stayed with near Nogent-le-Roi and of her work with the *maquis* in the region. She described the small triumphs in the countryside, and how they had developed a series of safe houses for downed Allied aviators, smuggling some into Allied-controlled zones and others across the border into neutral Switzerland. Mathilde described her grandfather's reaction to the atrocities at Oradour-sur-Glane, and cried when she explained how the children had been taken from the nuns. But most important, she told Bridgette about making contact with Capucine, about the fans, and about how her mother had smuggled the papers out.

"Such a brave woman, your mother," Bridgette said.

Mathilde remembered being surprised when Antoinette described Capucine as "brave." That seemed so long ago. She knew better now.

"Where are the papers now?" asked Bridgette.

"The concierge here, Madame Laurent, is an old family friend. She's keeping them safe in the hope that after the war, they might bring some comfort to the families."

"Assuming there are survivors," Bridgette said softly, and Mathilde nodded.

"So," said Bridgette, sitting back, "your mother managed to do her part as well. Even as a Nazi prisoner."

"Even as a Nazi prisoner," said Mathilde. "How—"

The bell rang, and Mathilde went to the shop door.

"Antoinette!" said Mathilde. "Perfect timing. Come in. Let me introduce you to a dear friend, Bridgette Caron. Bridgette, this is the woman I was just talking about, Madame Antoinette Laurent."

"Madame Laurent, it is a pleasure to meet you," Bridgette said.

"Oh, please call me Antoinette," she said as she took a seat at the table. "I am much too old for formalities."

Mathilde poured Antoinette a cup of tea and said, "Bridgette has been telling me about her work with the Résistance and what's next."

"*Vive la Résistance*," said Antoinette with a nod.

"*Vive la Résistance*," echoed the young women.

"What can you tell us?" Antoinette asked.

"The various Résistance efforts have come together as the French Forces of the Interior, or FFI," said Bridgette. "All across France, people are hearing the truth of the war from the BBC and *Radiodiffusion Nationale*: The Allies won a great victory at the battle of Normandy and are advancing toward Paris."

"If the Germans lose control of Paris, they have effectively lost control of France," said Antoinette. "But I worry about what might happen before the Allies get here."

"There's good reason to worry," said Bridgette with a grimace. "The Nazis have increased the pace of deportations, and there are reports of German soldiers placing explosives at strategic points around the city."

"Explosives?" Mathilde asked. "Why?"

"They say the commander of the German garrison, General Dietrich von Choltitz, has been ordered to destroy Paris upon his retreat," said Bridgette.

Antoinette gasped. "*Destroy* Paris?"

Bridgette nodded. "Our intelligence says Choltitz's orders are to blow up the city's landmarks upon departure: the Louvre, the Arc de Triomphe, the Eiffel Tower, the bridges over the Seine—and to burn the city to the ground."

"Why would they do such a thing?" Mathilde asked.

"So that there will be nothing left for the Allies—or for the Parisians, of course."

"I thought the Nazis loved Paris," said Mathilde. "*Jeder einmal in Paris*. Isn't that what they always say? I thought that was why we've been living with them in our streets and cafés and theaters for the past four years."

"If they can't have it for themselves, the Nazis don't want anyone else to enjoy it."

"That's just . . . wretched," said Mathilde.

"And perfectly in keeping with them wanting beauty only for themselves," said Antoinette, reaching out to pat Mathilde's hand. "It is petty, and it is heartbreaking. But it also suggests the Germans know they are losing the war."

"Control is slipping away from them," Bridgette said with a nod. "It won't be easy, but we are going to win."

"What can we do to help?" asked Antoinette. "An old woman like me can be useful. No one pays any attention to me. I might as well be invisible!"

"I said that about myself not too long ago," said Mathilde with a smile.

"*I* think you're both quite remarkable," said Bridgette, then downed the rest of her tea. "And I've always been an excellent judge of character, if I do say so myself."

THEY BEGAN BY speaking with the people in their apartment building, at least those who had not fled, and with the neighbors on their block, save Monsieur Accambray, the fruit monger across the street, whom Antoinette insisted was not to be trusted.

Then Bridgette led them to a shuttered hotel in the fourth arrondissement, whose abandoned-seeming façade disguised a beehive of activity. Dozens of people were making posters and signs, painting the tricolor flag of France on pieces of wood, paper, cardboard, anything at all. In a lot behind the hotel, men in undershirts and berets, cigarettes dangling from their mouths, were camouflaging stolen cars and trucks and blacking out the license plates. A group of women in floral summer dresses were sewing white armbands with "FFI" written in bold black letters.

"Our fighters have no uniforms," Bridgette explained. "We wear street clothes to pass undetected, but during the battle, we will need to be able to identify one another."

On the counter of the old hotel's registration desk sat a huge map of France. Intelligence reports indicated that the Allied forces were expected to enter Paris from the south, and the FFI leadership marked on the map where to position barricades to help funnel the retreating *Wehrmacht* troops and vehicles into the waiting arms of the liberators.

"We need help building the barricades, if you're up for that," said a harried-looking thirtyish woman named Rolande. "We're making them out of anything and everything: crates, furniture, doors— anything, really, that we can find. We're even chopping down some of the beautiful trees along the street to impede the Nazi retreat. Whatever it takes." She looked at Antoinette. "Madame, we need help to sew armbands and to carry messages to other Résistance groups—if you're willing to carry notes in your shoes from one neighborhood to another, I doubt you'd be stopped."

"I would be honored," said Antoinette. "These feet have a few more miles in them."

"My parents have been sewing armbands in their shop as well," said Bridgette. "I'll bring them tomorrow."

"I'll work on the barricades," said Mathilde.

"Are you sure?" Bridgette asked in a low voice. "No one will think less of you if you're not up to it, Mathilde. You've risked your life plenty already."

"That's where you're going, isn't it?" Mathilde asked.

Bridgette nodded.

"Then we'll be there together."

"Bon," said Rolande. "It's settled, then, yes? And there shouldn't be too much risk, at least not until the battle starts. We've posted lookouts around the city to watch for German patrols, so hopefully you won't be surprised." Rolande pointed to the map. "Here's where they need helpers."

For the next several days, they worked frantically to prepare for the coming confrontation, a battle they knew they had to win. The stakes were high: If an uprising of the people, the *levée en masse*, was not well coordinated, the mostly untrained civilians would be slaughtered by the well-armed and increasingly desperate invaders.

On August 14, it began. The employees of the Paris Métro and the police force went on strike. Then the postal workers joined in, and soon so many Parisians had walked off their jobs that city services shut down entirely. Two days later, thirty-five young members of the FFI were betrayed by a double agent of the Gestapo and gunned down in the Bois de Boulogne in the west of Paris. In Pantin, a suburb to the northeast, two thousand men and women were rounded up by the S.S. and deported to Buchenwald and Ravensbrück. Finally, the local gendarmerie refused to continue working for the Vichy and threw their hats in with the Paris uprising.

Cries of *"Vive la Résistance!"* were heard in the streets at all hours of the day and night, often followed by a blast of gunfire.

Mathilde and Bridgette joined other Parisians in constructing the barricades, pushing old cars into place to block the bridges across the Seine, handing out pickaxes to those who were pulling up cobblestones from the streets to make driving more difficult, filling wooden carts with anything they could use to reinforce the barricades. Even young children did their part by shoveling sand into burlap bags and forming long chains to pass the cobblestones, one at a time, to those constructing the barriers.

For the first time in years, Parisians were energized, buoyed by hope.

And each night Bridgette, Mathilde, and Antoinette returned to La Maison Benoît, weary and hungry and waiting for the call to arms.

37

Capucine

*E*ZRA'S DEATH AND Isedore's deportation broke me.

I continued to work because I had no choice, but I felt like one of the eighteenth-century mechanical inventions Bruno had always admired at the *Musée des Arts et Métiers*. Like Vaucanson's duck, which quacked and drank and floated, but never came to life.

Fräulein Sommer did not return to the Lévitan after that terrible day. I still wondered if she had truly turned against the Third Reich, or if she was playing some sort of strange game, trying to get me to incriminate myself and others. Or perhaps she was simply testing the waters to see if she could, if she *should*, switch sides. All I knew was that at the critical moment, when we needed her help, she had not come through.

I told myself I shouldn't judge her—after all, many of us were cowed by the *Boches*. But I did. I judged her.

I unpacked and sorted through crates alongside my pod mates, no longer able to care about the rumors of Allied victories. Those of us who remained in the attic prison heard the gunfire in the streets, occasional calls of *"Vive la Résistance,"* and whispers of Allied forces closing in on Paris.

What it meant for us at the Lévitan was that our jailers became surlier than ever, food was so scarce that we were on the point of near starvation, and the wealthy inmates received no more packages. More of our compatriots were taken away, ten at a time, increasing the workload for those who remained and leaving us with unanswerable questions. Where had they gone? When would our own names be called?

When I wasn't working, I lay on my cot and stared at the little wind chime made of clock parts, thinking of Isedore, and Abrielle . . . but mostly of Ezra. The look in his beautiful dark eyes. The last moment I felt his warmth in my lap, just before his soul left this earth, escaped this prison forever. How I had kicked and clawed at the guards when they dragged me away from his body.

Mordecai had recited the Mourner's Kaddish for him, but without a body, it was impossible to perform the other traditional Jewish rites for the dead. I was not the only one who mourned him; Ezra was a man with many friends.

These days we were allowed to open a few windows, and the occasional summer breeze made the wind chime sway. I watched it for hours and kept thinking of the Hemingway quote about the world breaking everyone, and how "those that will not break it kills."

Ezra never broke.

One Thursday we were not called down to work. Nervous at this unprecedented event but glad for the rest, prisoners napped and chatted, and rumors swirled about what was going to happen next.

Hélène came to sit on Isedore's empty cot.

"Capu, your friends are worried about you. They say you've stopped eating."

I stared at her, unable even to summon a polite denial.

"Have you heard of the Jewish poet and philosopher Yehuda Ha-Levi?" she asked.

I shook my head.

"He was from Andalusia, Spain, and lived— Oh, it must be nearly a thousand years ago. He wrote a poem I think of often:

> 'Tis a fearful thing
> to love what death can touch.
> A fearful thing
> to love, to hope, to dream, to be—
> to be,
> And oh, to lose.
> A thing for fools, this
> And a holy thing.

On the last line, her voice faltered, and tears welled up in her eyes.

"There's more, but I forget the rest. Do you know they took my children? My everything?"

I nodded.

"There's no way to make sense of it," Hélène continued. "I believe—"

"Everyone! Listen up," yelled Pettit. "Let's go. *Now.* Wear your smocks but leave the rest of your things."

"Where are we going?" asked Mordecai.

"To Drancy. To have your papers clarified."

"Everyone?"

"Everyone."

THE SUMMER DAY was warm, and we could hear explosions and the occasional staccato blast of gunfire. The afternoon sun cast a harsh light on the packing crates as we gathered on the loading dock.

We weren't supposed to bring anything with us but our papers, but I hid the little wind chime in my underpants and, at the last minute, grabbed Isedore's beloved clock, shoving it down the front of my dress, where it nestled, absurdly, between my breasts, the erratic ticking seeming to echo my heartbeat. Perhaps I would be able to find Isedore at Drancy and give it to her.

There weren't enough vehicles to transport us all comfortably, so we were packed in like sardines, the guards using their fists, boots, and rifle butts to hurry us along. I was ordered onto a requisitioned city bus, which was driven by a miserable-looking city bus driver, and shoved down the aisle until I was near the rear door.

The bus was filled with whimpers and cries, the prisoners fearing Drancy was only our first stop before our being sent to the horrors of the concentration camp we had been threatened with for so long: Auschwitz.

I could not summon the strength to worry. Perhaps I would be reunited with Isedore, at least. And if we were sent on to Auschwitz, might there be a way for me to find Bruno?

The bus started up with a lurch and the passengers fell into one another, holding one another up as the bus rumbled down the alleyway, away from the Lévitan department store. Was it for the last time? Those who weren't too caught up in their own distress gazed out the windows, seeing the city streets for the first time in months or even a year.

As we lumbered past an empty plaza, I remembered Bruno teaching me how to navigate the bus system when I was just a girl, and how I had always begged to be allowed to reach up and pull the wire to sound the bell for our stop. Out of nostalgia more than anything else, I did so now.

The bell rang. The bus stopped. The doors opened.

For a moment we stood frozen in disbelief. Then we poured out of the bus and into the street.

It took a moment for the guards to grasp what was happening. They started shouting and running after us, but the busload of prisoners scattered in all directions. I heard shots being fired but did not look back. The clock I'd hidden in my dress threatened to fall, so I pulled it out and held it against me.

I ran.

Footsteps rang out behind me, and a hand grabbed me by the arm and swung me around.

Tremblay. Without thinking, I bashed him over the head with Isedore's clock. He cried out and fell to his knees, blood pouring from a nasty gash on his forehead. Enraged, I struck him once more with the heavy metal clock, then threw it at him and for good measure kicked him hard in the stomach.

"That's for Ezra," I spat at him.

I whirled around, intending to flee, but froze.

Pettit. Her pistol was aimed at my head.

My fingers twitched, but I fought the impulse to raise my hands in surrender. Instead, I held her gaze, raised my chin, and braced myself.

If it is to end like this, then so be it. I refused to go back.

A long moment passed.

Pettit let the barrel of the gun drop. Yanking her head in the direction of the alley, she whispered: *"Run, 123."*

For the last time, I obeyed her. I ran.

I did not look back until I turned into the shelter of the narrow alleyway. Pettit was helping Tremblay to his feet, scolding him for letting "a girl" get the best of him. Guards had managed to capture a number of escapees; one was beating a man, and a woman—was it Léonie?—lay facedown in the street. I spied Mordecai among a small group being forced back onto the bus at gunpoint. But at least half a dozen others were running down the street, and I thought I recognized Jérôme fleeing in the opposite direction.

There were more shots fired and another nearby explosion.

I hadn't eaten or slept well in days, but I ran. I ran for my life.

I turned another corner and found the road blocked by a barricade, behind which were men and women dressed in street clothes, resting their rifles on sandbags and cobblestones, pointing them in my direction. They wore white armbands emblazoned with "FFI."

I skidded to a stop, raised my hands high, and cried out: *"Vive la Résistance!"*

"Vive la Résistance!" they echoed, and pulled me to their side of the barricade, just as an armed group of *Wehrmacht* came around the corner.

A bugle sounded. The shooting started.

38

Mathilde

*W*HEN THE BUGLERS, perched high atop buildings throughout the city, blew their horns, the battle for Paris began in earnest.

Coordinated skirmishes broke out all across the city. The FFI fanned out across Paris, ferreting out small units of soldiers, killing many, capturing others. Résistance fighters tossed grenades from third- and fourth-story windows onto German tanks and trucks as they rumbled past in the streets below. German snipers shot at passersby from their stations at the top of the Cathédrale Notre-Dame and the Hôtel de Ville as the *Boches* fought to hold their fortified positions. The FFI held fast to the barricades and fired on the retreating soldiers. Parisians of all types turned out to carry ammunition, ferry provisions, and strip felled soldiers of their weapons.

The famously picturesque cobblestone streets of Paris filled with smoke and blood and broken bodies. Mobile Red Cross units assisted the wounded from both sides, braving bullets and bombs to carry their stretchers to safety.

The Résistance forces commandeered the Grand Palais on the Champs-Élysées for their headquarters, aided by the gendarmerie. German fuel trucks were attacked and captured. The FFI managed to capture the police garrison and seized its cache of weapons, including small cannons and missile launchers, giving them a fighting chance against the armored tanks of the Third Reich.

As many as a thousand Résistance fighters were killed and many more wounded in the battles across Paris, but the Résistance gained the upper hand when reinforcements arrived from the French 2nd Armored Division and the U.S. 4th Infantry Division. Parisians cheered as the convoys of *Wehrmacht* cars, trucks, and tanks fled the city, retreating to the east.

In the end, General Dietrich von Choltitz ignored the command of his Führer to ignite the explosives that would have left Paris "a field of ruins." Instead, on August 25, 1944, he formally surrendered the capitol city, a city that had bowed but had never broken, to the Free French.

Paris was liberated.

ACROSS THE CITY Parisians rejoiced, hanging out their windows, banging on pots and pans, dancing in the streets, and singing *"La Marseillaise."*

"I have to go to the Lévitan," Mathilde said to Bridgette, once the reality of the city's liberation had sunk in. "I have to see if I can find my mother."

"Of course you do," Bridgette said. "I'll go with you."

The young women chose their route with care to avoid possible snipers and the occasional firefights that still erupted between the Résistance and the retreating Germans. Near the Place de la Concorde, they came across the scene of a recent street battle. The air smelled of gunpowder and blood, and a few Résistance fighters milled about, staring at the bodies of several German soldiers.

"Is everyone all right?" Bridgette asked. "Can we help?"

"*Non*, mademoiselle," a young woman with an FFI armband replied proudly. "We took care of these *Boches*."

"Bridgette, look," Mathilde whispered, pointing at the body of a man in an officer's uniform, his unseeing blue eyes staring blankly at the sky. "Isn't that Manfred Wolff, Simone's boyfriend?"

"I think you're right."

"What will happen to Simone?"

Bridgette paused, then said grimly, "I don't imagine it will be good."

"We need to find her," said Mathilde.

"We will," Bridgette said. "But first things first: Let's find your mother."

The windows of the apartment buildings across the street from the Lévitan, which had for years been closed and shuttered, were flung wide open and filled with people waving flags, shouting and cheering. Confetti rained down. A middle-aged woman was playing a flute, and a teenage boy joined in with a guitar. The neighbors sang along in pure celebration.

Mathilde and Bridgette went behind the Lévitan and down the alley to the loading dock, where Mathilde had met the prisoner named Ezra and dropped her fan. But there was nothing there now except stacks of crates and piles of furniture, the store's bay doors standing wide open.

"Looks like they left in a hurry," Bridgette said. "Maybe someone's inside?"

Mathilde and Bridgette entered the warehouse area, then mounted a flight of stairs and peeked through the door leading to the main showroom. There was no sign of anyone. No prisoners, no guards, no one at all.

"Hello?" Mathilde called out, her voice echoing in the vast space. "Is anyone here?"

There was no reply.

They mounted two more flights of stairs to the attic. Light sifted in through tall arched windows, illuminating hundreds of cots and mattresses. Threadbare clothing and black smocks hung from pegs, wooden crates were set up like tables, and stacks of books were piled high. The air was stale and rank with the scent of unwashed bodies, but there was no one anywhere.

Mathilde gazed at the cots, wondering which one had been her mother's. She approached a handwritten calendar on the wall and ran her hand over it. Special dates had been picked out and labeled: *Purim . . . Passover . . .* and finally *Liberation?* with a question mark.

"Were they freed?" Mathilde asked.

"They were probably moved when the Germans realized they were losing control of the city," said Bridgette in a gentle voice. "If they were taken to Drancy, or even somewhere farther away, I'm sure they'll be freed soon by Allied troops."

"I suppose you're right," Mathilde agreed. "Let's get out of here."

Back out in the street, Mathilde spied the young woman she had encountered on the sidewalk once before.

"The prisoners were taken away," said the woman.

"Do you know where they were going?"

She shook her head. "A neighbor told me they were taken, but that's all. I'm searching for my husband, Henri Coën."

"I'm looking for my mother, Capucine Benoît . . . Duplantier," Mathilde said, unsure which name her mother was using.

"I wish you luck, mademoiselle," Madame Coën said.

"And you as well, madame," Mathilde replied. *"Vive la Résistance."*

"Vive la Résistance," responded Madame Coën.

"We'll find her, Mathilde," Bridgette promised, putting her arm around Mathilde as they began the long walk back to La Maison Benoît. "We *will.*"

When they reached the fan shop, they joined Antoinette and watched the celebrating for a while.

"We won," Mathilde said, subdued at the thought of her mother being carted away to an unknown fate. "I can't believe we actually *won.*"

"We certainly did," Antoinette said with a laugh.

"Vive la Résistance!" shouted Bridgette at the top of her lungs.

"Vive la Résistance!" came the reply, echoing down the street as the trio joined in the dancing.

Later that afternoon, General Charles de Gaulle, leader of the Free French Forces, led a joyous victory parade down the Champs-Élysées.

AFTER THE EUPHORIA of liberation came the challenge of getting back to real life. What happened now? How would they rebuild? Where did they even start?

The populace of Paris was hungrier than ever. Dozens of bridges and train tracks had been blown up, and the flour mills in Pantin had been destroyed by German bombs, so days passed without food, even as the people began the grim work of clearing the streets, burying the dead, and trying to locate family and friends who had been injured or deported. Mathilde and Bridgette searched for their third musketeer, but Simone was not at the luxury apartment she had shared with Manfred Wolff, and her brokenhearted parents had no idea where she had gone.

Paris was free, but much of France remained under German Occupation. The Allied forces were gradually pushing the *Wehrmacht* back to Germany, but the brutal fighting continued, as did Mathilde's anxiety over the whereabouts of her mother and her grandfather Bruno. She often found herself worried to the point of tears.

"Be patient, my dear," Antoinette counseled Mathilde one evening as they listened to reports of the progress of the Allies on the radio. "I know it's hard, but if your mother can get to you, she will."

"What if she can't? What if she's already—" Mathilde cut herself off, unable to finish the thought.

Antoinette reached out and squeezed her hand. "If the worst has happened, then you will make an altar for her, and comfort yourself in the knowledge that she knew you loved her and that she loved you. That is all any of us can ask in the end."

After two weeks of famine, the Americans and the British began air-dropping food relief, and the roads were cleared so that trucks could bring flour from the countryside to the city. For the first time in years, Parisian boulangeries filled the streets with the delicious aroma of freshly baked bread. *Real* bread. The familiar, longed-for scent lifted the spirits of the citizenry, almost as much as liberation itself.

Bridgette's parents received word that her older brother was on his way back from Germany, along with other young men and women who had been forced to labor for the Third Reich.

One afternoon Mathilde was returning home with a precious baguette under her arm when she saw half a dozen women being marched through the street, their hair shorn. In a pathetic spectacle, bystanders spat at the women, yelling ugly names and accusing them of "horizontal collaboration" for sleeping with the enemy.

Mathilde was stunned to see Simone among the reviled group, and she scarcely recognized her old friend without her dark flowing hair. Simone appeared diminished and shrunken, and though Mathilde tried to get her attention, Simone never lifted her eyes.

Back at La Maison Benoît, Mathilde did the best she could to keep her spirits up, tending to the shop and distracting herself by sketching and playing with fans and feathers. She couldn't keep the questions from swirling in her mind. Now that Paris was liberated, was there a way she could keep the fan shop open? But even if she could make fans as well as her mother and grandfather—which she couldn't, not by a long shot—who would buy them? They had thrown out the Germans, but it would take a long while for the economy to come back. How long would her money last, and did it make sense to try to convert the store to something else?

The bell rang out over the door, and a beggar walked in.

"One moment," Mathilde said as she ducked into the kitchen to get a heel of bread. "I'm sorry. It's not much but it's all I have just now." She handed the bread to the gaunt woman and returned to her place behind the counter. "If you come back tomorrow, I'll see if I can get a piece of fruit or something to make a sandwich."

The starving woman in the headscarf stood stock-still, the bread cupped in her hands. "Mathilde?" the woman croaked, her voice weak.

Capucine.

Mathilde opened her mouth but could not think of what to say. Instead, she reached for the fan her mother had made for her twenty-first birthday. She had kept it on the counter beside her while she worked, always.

She flicked it open, then closed.

> *Touching tip with finger . . . I wish to speak with you.*
> *Drawing across the eyes . . . I am sorry.*
> *Touch to heart . . . You have my love.*

"Always," Capucine said, grinning even as she started to sob. She touched her hand to her own heart. "You have my love always, *ma chère fille."*

39

Capucine

AFTER MY ESCAPE, I was afraid to go to La Maison Benoît, in case it was being watched. Instead, I took refuge with the Résistance fighters, who politely declined my offer to help with the barricades and insisted that I rest. The most I could manage was to paint a few French flags on scraps of wood and cardboard before collapsing from hunger and exhaustion.

When the battle for Paris was won, two middle-aged sisters who had been cooking for the Résistance fighters took me home with them and nursed me until I was strong enough to walk again. I made them promise to visit me at La Maison Benoît so I could give them fans in gratitude for their kindness.

My reunion with Mathilde was more than I could ever have hoped for. She had grown into such a confident, brave young woman. For that, I would be forever grateful to her grandparents, to her mami Yvette and papi Auguste. Mathilde had read that Louis

Renault was to be arrested and charged with industrial collaboration, and his company was expected to be nationalized. Several of the top executives at Renault were to be brought up on charges and the company was ordered to forfeit its war profits to the government. When Mathilde visited her grandparents, Mami cried the entire time, and Papi seemed a broken man, his future uncertain.

My daughter also told me about seeing her friend Simone, her hair shorn, being abused by a crowd in a spiteful and pitiful spectacle unworthy of Parisians.

War makes some into heroes and turns others ugly. Most of us just muddle through.

We stayed up most of the night, talking and laughing and crying. And then we slept, and in the morning, we awoke to share real bread and coffee with Antoinette. And then we talked some more.

"WHY IS THE fruit monger acting so strange?" I asked Antoinette a few days later as we were locking up La Maison Benoît on our way to meet Mathilde and Bridgette. Ever since I had returned home, I had noticed Monsieur Accambray ducking into his shop or scurrying away whenever he saw me.

"Monsieur Accambray has always been a little odd," said Antoinette.

"But he's acting like he's scared of me." I was so gaunt that my old clothes hung off me like a scarecrow's. "Who would be scared of *me*?"

"He's probably embarrassed," said Antoinette. "And ashamed, assuming he's capable of such a thing."

"Why?" I asked.

She hesitated for a moment, and then said: "It's just gossip, so it may not be true, but according to Madame Trepot, who heard it from Monsieur LaCroix—who heard from his cousin, and *he* really ought to know, since he was a clerk at the municipal office— Monsieur Accambray is the one who turned you and your father in to the S.S."

"*He* is? The fruit monger? Why would he do that?"

"Oh, he and Bruno had that silly feud since you were a child. I imagine he thought it was his chance to get rid of Bruno once and for all."

"That was the only reason?"

"Spiteful people do cruel things, Capu. Like I said, it may not be true, but . . . it does make a certain amount of sense. Monsieur Accambray also wanted your shop space. He's complained about his building for years, and ours is in much better repair. But don't worry. I had a long talk with our landlord. He'll never rent to Monsieur Accambray as long as I'm alive." She shrugged. "When people find out what he did, he'll have a hard time finding friends anywhere in Paris. I intend to make sure of it. I've got plenty of time and nothing else to do."

I smiled and started laughing and then couldn't stop. It was all so absurd. I had suspected Abrielle of betraying us out of petty jealousy, then thought perhaps it had been my in-laws, who wanted to make sure I had no more claim upon my daughter. And all along it was the grumpy fruit monger across the way?

I was still laughing when I spied a slight figure walking down the street toward us. *Isedore.*

I ran to her. After a very long hug, I stood back, studying her.

"*Ça va?* Are you okay?"

413

She shrugged and smiled, but the sadness in her eyes gave her away. "I was scheduled to be deported to Auschwitz, but then Drancy was liberated by the Résistance. The British brought us back to Paris."

"I'm so glad you are here. This is my dear friend Madame Antoinette Laurent. We were just heading out to meet my daughter and a friend. Won't you come? I've wanted you to meet Mathilde for so long!"

We talked as we walked. Isedore cried when I told her about Ezra but cheered up when I described sacrificing her clock to bash Tremblay over the head during my escape. After being liberated from Drancy, Isedore had gone to her family's former apartment in the city. She was heartbroken, but not surprised, to find it stripped of the family's possessions. An elderly neighbor took her in and gave her a letter from distant relatives in New York offering any surviving family members a place to live and a chance to start a new life.

"Will you go?" I asked.

"I think so. It turns out, the Germans kept excellent records of what they did. One of the guards at Drancy confirmed that the rest of my family was taken to Auschwitz. He said it was unlikely"—she caught her breath—"unlikely they survived. Very unlikely. I've made official inquiries but haven't heard anything yet."

"I haven't heard anything about my father, either," I said. "I'm so sorry, Isedore."

"I wonder if we will ever know what happened to them, what they went through."

"Maybe one day when the war is officially over."

"There must be a reckoning, Capu," Isedore said. "Someone must pay for what they did."

I nodded, unsure what to say, for I did not think it would be possible to settle this particular debt to humanity.

We met up with Bridgette and Mathilde at a café, and sat on the terrace, sipping our demitasses of precious coffee and talking nonstop. Other than the fact that our conversation was interrupted by frequent tears, it felt very much like the old days. The before days.

"Capu, have you heard from the American you told me about, the piano player?" asked Isedore, ever the romantic.

"I've written to him," I said, trying to sound casual, as if I did not spend every day hoping for news of Charles. "I don't have a military address, but I asked his family to forward my letter to him. I also sent a letter to him in care of the army's general delivery, just in case. But I haven't heard back."

"It's hard to know whether any of the mail is getting through these days," said Antoinette, patting my hand. "Much less the military mail. We must be patient, as difficult as that is."

"That letter he wrote you was so romantic," said Isedore with a little sigh.

"You should have read the others," teased Mathilde, fanning herself with her hand. "My, my, *my* . . ."

I blushed. I still could not quite wrap my mind around the fact that my daughter had read the love letters Charles had written to me, and I was very glad she had not had access to my side of the correspondence—I feared my missives were much less poetic, and much more explicit, than his.

"There must be some way to track him down." Isedore leaned forward over the tiny café table, rattling our cups. "You have to find him, Capu!"

"You know what? Isedore's right," said Mathilde. "You cannot let him go again. Not if he is the man you think he is, the man that wrote those letters. Instead of waiting to see if your letters reach him, why not try searching for him?"

"How am I supposed to do that?" I asked, though I knew these young women were right. I could not let Charles go again, not now. Not after everything. He might well have moved on, but if there was still a chance for us . . . it was a chance worth taking. "The war's not over. How would I track down an American G.I. on the battlefield?"

"There's a temporary headquarters of the Allied operations right here in Paris," said Bridgette. "It's a place to start, at least."

"I'll go with you!" said Mathilde. "We'll find him. You'll see."

"You seem very confident," I said with a smile.

"And why wouldn't she be?" Antoinette said. "She's her mother's daughter, and her mother is a very brave woman."

"You can say that again," Isedore said, patting me on the shoulder.

We returned to La Maison Benoît to show Isedore the shop. I was able to give Isedore the little clock-part wind chime I had saved from the Lévitan attic, and Mathilde suggested we give her a glorious fan made of eagle feathers—originally from America, after all—for courage on her journey. We hugged one another tightly, and I made Isedore promise to visit again before she left Paris for good, and to write to us from New York.

Then I took a photograph of Isedore and Mathilde, standing side by side in front of the shop's bright yellow Art Nouveau façade.

Two beautiful young survivors, each speaking with her fan.

THERE IS A certain kind of chaos toward the end of a war, the awkward teetering of a world attempting to right itself. I was too young to have truly understood the aftermath of the First

World War, but this time I was brutally aware of the hunger, the broken families, the damaged buildings. The overwhelming sense of loss.

As horror stories began to pour in of atrocities similar to what had happened in Oradour-sur-Glane, and of Nazi extermination camps freed by the Soviet army on the eastern front, we began to fathom the enormity and perversity of the war crimes perpetrated in the name of the Führer. It was so much worse than what the prisoners at Lévitan had been through. So ferociously, callously, *inhumanly* worse.

The day after deciding to track down Charles, Mathilde and I marched to the temporary headquarters of the Allied operations in Paris, where I filled out a long form and we were told to wait. We sat on a hard wooden bench in a busy corridor for what seemed like hours, watching as American and British soldiers and bureaucrats hurried back and forth. I had never realized how much paperwork was involved in waging a war.

At long last we were called in by a small, officious man with spectacles so thick, they magnified his icy blue eyes. He spoke French with a strong British accent, but since my English was limited, I was relieved.

"A Mr. Charles Anthony Moore, from North Carolina," he mused, reading the forms I had filled out. "Who is this man to you?"

"He . . ." I faltered, but only for the briefest moment. I drew myself up and continued. "Charles Moore is my fiancé. He is the man I am going to marry." To my shock I felt the sting of tears in my eyes. "We would already have been married, but for my stubbornness."

The man's stance relaxed, and a slight smile softened the harsh line of his mouth. His voice dropped and he leaned toward me conspiratorially. "A wartime romance, eh?"

I returned his smile. "Actually, no. It was before the war, but it continues."

"And he asked you to marry him?"

"He did. More than once. Stupidly, I refused him."

He tilted his head. "What made you change your mind?"

"The war. After what I have been through, I have learned to appreciate what really matters."

He inspected me for a moment, no doubt noting my baggy clothes, sunken cheeks, and dull hair, the markers of malnutrition and stress.

"You want to move to America. Is that it?"

"No, actually. He wants to move here to Paris."

Mathilde and I exchanged a glance while the clerk sorted through a stack of papers in a file, then made a phone call. He shook his head and said: "He could be anywhere—Normandy, Italy, North Africa, or somewhere in the Pacific Theater. . . ."

I nodded. "I understand. He speaks French and knows Paris well, having lived here for several years, so I thought perhaps he was sent here."

"He speaks French? How well?"

"Very well. And he knows the streets of Paris like the back of his hand."

"A moment, please," he said as he stood and went into another office. Much later, he returned. "You're right. He's here."

"Here?" I asked.

He glanced down at a paper on a clipboard. "Private First Class Charles Anthony Moore was assigned to the Red Ball Express—it's a supply line for the invasion forces up north—but is currently serving as an interim translator attached to a Colonel Barker. They're expected to arrive in Paris in the next week or two."

Excitement surged through me. "Could I get a message to him?"

"Here's his military address," he said, handing me a scrap of paper. "But I must warn you: Given the slow pace of the mail, he's likely to arrive in Paris before your letter gets to him. You'll be able to hand it to him yourself."

FOR THE NEXT several days, time passed at a snail's pace. I immediately wrote to Charles at his military address, but keeping in mind what the clerk had told me, I stopped by the Allied headquarters every few days, hoping to find him in person. I searched the uniformed personnel for his tall, broad-shouldered silhouette, for that smile I remembered so well, for the man I still carried deep in my soul.

Antoinette had kept the documents Abrielle and I had managed to smuggle out of Lévitan, storing them in two big bags. Unsure what to do with the material, I lugged the bags over to the university. I had been wanting to meet Ezra's wife, Michelle, anyway, and I thought she might know of an organization that could sort through the papers and photographs and find the remaining members of the families who might cherish them.

Michelle Goldman was a serious woman of few words.

"Ezra told me about you," she said. "He wrote that you saved him."

"He said—?" I shook my head and fought back tears. "I didn't. I couldn't."

"Let me show you something," she said, opening the top drawer of her desk. She pulled out an envelope and handed it to me. "He bribed a guard to mail it for him."

I studied the neat, slightly slanted lettering, imagining Ezra putting pen to paper in our strange attic prison. Imagining his lithe, graceful hands.

He wrote of how our connection had helped to restore his faith in humanity, in the ability of people to come together.

For if two wounded souls in the midst of horror may yet reach out and find even the smallest semblance of joy, Ezra had written, *then all things are possible.*

His words overwhelmed me. They were just so . . . *Ezra.*

"Please, keep it," Michelle said when I tried to hand the letter back to her. "I'm sure he would have wanted you to have it. Ezra was a profoundly decent person, a fundamentally good, brave man in a world too full of craven cowards. I was honored to know him. Thank you for bringing him joy. Oh, and here." She handed me a framed photograph that had been taken at their wedding. Ezra's face was relaxed, and he looked at the camera with those warm, heavy-lidded eyes and the sad, steady smile I knew so well. "Keep this, too. I have a copy."

"I don't know how to thank you," I said, barely managing to choke out the words.

"No need. As to the papers you smuggled out," Michelle said, riffling through a few of them, "you're right. These could be a real boon to surviving family. It will take a while to sort everything out, as I'm sure you know, but if you'll leave them with me, I'll make sure they find their way to the appropriate organization and, hopefully, into the hands of relatives. The Nazis weren't able to deport all the Jews in France, not by a long shot. Those who survived will be glad to have these."

I wished them luck. Given everything that had passed through Lévitan, it would be a very long process, assuming it was even possible, to reunite people with their stolen property. Mathilde had read that the last train full of plunder from Operation Furniture had been loaded at Aubervilliers station and sent to Germany in early August but had been held on the sidings by French railway workers and had still been sitting there upon liberation.

"One last thing," I said. "I want to be sure that Mademoiselle Abrielle Garnier is given credit for her bravery in smuggling out the papers. I wrote her name down in the notes explaining where everything came from."

She nodded. "Of course. Was this woman working with the Résistance?"

"Not really, no. But she gave her life for it, in the end."

I RETURNED TO the Allied headquarters for the fourth time in a week. Unfortunately, I could not find the clerk who had helped me originally; the last several times I had visited, I was waylaid by an unfriendly woman with a steel gray helmet of hair and dark red lipstick. A brass nameplate on her desk read simply, MRS. SIMPSON.

"You've come here every day for more than a week," she said before I even had a chance to ask after Charles.

"Every other day," I corrected her.

"I don't think you understand. These men have important jobs to do. I gave him the last three notes you've left, so—"

"You *gave* them to him? He's here?"

Mrs. Simpson pressed her lips together.

I felt a spurt of anger tempered with self-doubt. If Charles was here in Paris, why hadn't he been in touch? Or . . . did he not want me anymore?

I blew out a breath and rallied. Whether he still loved me or not, I wanted to see him. I *had* to see him. I needed to apologize and to thank him. I had spent too many nights in the Lévitan thinking about Charles not to see him, at least one last time.

"May I take that chair there?" I asked the surly clerk. "I'll just wait awhile and see if he passes through."

"I'm afraid that's not possible," Mrs. Simpson said. "He's not—"

"Don't tell me they let Fan Girls into this place."

Charles. Wearing an American army uniform, he sauntered down the hall toward me, as tall and strong as I remembered, with that glorious grin. A few wrinkles, a few gray hairs, and more handsome than ever. Beautiful.

I threw myself at him. His arms wrapped around me and squeezed and I inhaled deeply. We kissed and laughed and kissed again. An American soldier passed us in the hall and let out a low whistle. Mrs. Simpson just glowered at us.

I pulled back a little. "I guess we're making a spectacle of ourselves."

Charles gazed down at me with a mock frown. "Since when does *la femme à l'éventail* back down from putting on a show?"

"I'm . . . I fear I'm not that person anymore. Your *femme à l'éventail* doesn't sparkle much these days."

"Pshaw," he scoffed, and gave me a slow, delicious smile. "I could see you sparkling from all the way down the hall. C'mon in here so we can talk in private," he said, and escorted me into a vacant office.

"Why didn't you contact me?" I asked, touching his face gently. "I've been going nuts trying to find you."

He grinned. "Uncle Sam has first dibs on my attention, I'm

afraid. Seems there were some Nazis to deal with. Very bad guys. Real gangster types."

"Is that so?"

He nodded.

"Still," I said, "you could have come by the shop or at least called."

He leaned back on the desk, serious now. "I wasn't sure you wanted me to. You told me to stop writing. And when I wrote anyway, you stopped replying."

I let out a long breath. "Things were getting so bad here, and I thought you would be happier with someone else. Someone shiny and new and unscarred, not a war-torn scarecrow like me."

"You're my one and only. You should know that; I've told you often enough." He pulled me back into his arms and whispered, *"Mon amour, mon Capu."*

Turning my face into his broad chest, I started to cry, and then I couldn't stop. I sobbed and wailed, making noises like a wounded animal. Charles stroked my back and murmured into my hair, and when I finally looked at him, I saw that he, too, had tears in his eyes.

"We have a lot to catch up on, you and I," he said softly.

I nodded, unable to speak.

"Mrs. Simpson tells me you've been making quite a pest of yourself."

"I don't think she likes me."

"She doesn't like that you and I are together. In fact, she doesn't like my being here at all, marring these hallowed halls."

"How do you mean?"

"The American army is still segregated, you know."

"I'm so sorry." I searched his face. What did it mean to risk your life for a country that treated you with disdain? "How— Why are you here, then?"

"I was working as a mechanic on a transport unit when Colonel Barker's translator was killed by a sniper. The colonel heard me speaking French with some of the locals and ordered me to fill in."

"All those French lessons paid off in the end, huh?"

He grinned. "It didn't hurt that I know my way around Paris. Anyway, it turns out that Colonel Barker's a good guy. Mrs. Simpson, on the other hand . . ."

"Well, what's the American expression? 'There's no accounting for taste'?"

"At least she passed on your messages. I'm glad you were so relentless," Charles said with a smile. "It makes me feel wanted."

I laughed. "You are. I promise I will never again give you reason to doubt it. In fact, when can you come to the shop? I want to do something I should have done many years ago: introduce you to my daughter."

Charles nodded, understanding the significance of my offer. "And then you'll marry me?"

"Marriage is an awfully bourgeois institution," I teased, and then added in a serious tone, "But it would be my greatest honor to marry you, Private First Class Charles Anthony Moore."

"'Bout time," he said gruffly.

MATHILDE AND CHARLES got along famously, though it vexed me when they spoke in English, for I struggled to follow along—my daughter's linguistic prowess far exceeded my own. We spoke for hours, for days, filling each other in on everything that had happened in the years we had been separated, first by my foolishness and then by a world war.

Paris had been liberated, and so had I. At long last, I began to open the metaphorical fan box inside my chest and release all the secrets and fears and sorrows I had stuffed away for so many years.

And unlike in the case of unfortunate Pandora, the result was redemptive.

Charles and I were married in a quiet civil ceremony, with Antoinette, Mathilde, Isedore, Bridgette and her parents, and Charles's commanding officer in attendance. We had only a brief honeymoon, as Charles was granted just two days' leave before the army needed him in Belgium, where the Germans were threatening a major counteroffensive in the Ardennes. Charles came to Paris as often as he could, but though he assured me his work as a translator kept him safely behind the front line, I worried. I waited impatiently for a decisive Allied victory, for the moment the war would be well and truly over, for the day Charles was discharged from the army and would come to live with us full-time at La Maison Benoît.

I said a tearful good-bye to Isedore when she left for New York, and over the next few months, I reunited with some of my fellow prisoners. While searching for Bruno, I bumped into Henri Coën, who was also looking for family members. He introduced me to his wife and child, and I rejoiced to learn that Mordecai Krivine was back home with his wife and children and grandchildren, and that Hélène was safe with her sister in Tours. Jérôme had gone to join relatives in London, where he hoped to resume his rabbinical studies. Léonie came into the shop one day and told me that she had found her aunt and uncle, after all: They had still been in Drancy when Paris was liberated.

We former prisoners did not speak about what had happened at the Paris satellite camps of Lévitan, Bassano, and Austerlitz. As the truth emerged about Auschwitz and Treblinka, Dachau and Sobibor, and all the other Nazi labor and death camps, the world was confronted with the sheer enormity of the crimes perpetrated against Jews, homosexuals, Gypsies, communists, and so many others labeled "antisocial" or "degenerate." In comparison with those horrors, being imprisoned as slave laborers in Lévitan had been fortunate.

From time to time, I thought of Pettit. I wondered if she had survived the war and, if so, what had happened to her. I wondered how she had come to be a Nazi prison guard in the first place. But most of all, I wondered why she had intervened to save me on more than one occasion and, in the end, let me escape. I had witnessed the terrible things she was capable of, but also the unexpected acts of mercy. Did Hitler's fascist ideology draw upon the worst impulses of people, or did it turn otherwise decent people evil? Would those who had committed wartime atrocities be able to return to their families and their homes and resume their lives, or had the evil they had done forever left its mark?

Would there be a reckoning, as Isedore had insisted there must be?

All I knew for sure was that there was no easy answer.

I waited for days, weeks, months, but Bruno never returned. But the Germans did, indeed, keep good records, and when the documents were finally released, I found my father's name on a list of the confirmed dead: Bruno Philippe Benoît had died in the gas chamber shortly after his arrival at Auschwitz.

As painful as it was, at least I knew. For a long while I tortured myself. How had I not known, not felt it somehow, when his soul had left this earth? Guilt heightened my grief. Why had I survived when Bruno and countless others had not?

I thought of something Ezra had told me: Jews do not say *Rest in peace*, but *May their memory be a blessing*. Antoinette encouraged me to set some flowers and a candle by Bruno's photograph, and I added a few of his favorite rare feathers. Charles then placed a photograph of his father on the shrine, along with a crumpled pack of cigarettes given to him by a childhood friend and beloved comrade in arms who had been killed in a mortar attack during the advance on Paris. Mathilde asked to include a photo of her grandparents, who, though still alive, had had their lives altered forever, and so our shrine grew to embrace all those killed and injured by the war.

I also added a fluffy pink-and-white fan in remembrance of Abrielle Garnier, my old acquaintance who had once so annoyed me but who had been murdered because she had helped me to do a good deed. Hers was yet another senseless death at the hands of the Nazis.

And then I added two more items: the photo of Ezra from his wedding, and his letter smuggled out of the Lévitan.

I had told Charles all about Ezra, and what he meant to me, and invited him to read the letter.

"I'm glad," Charles said, his eyes revealing torture at the thought of what I had been through. "Glad you found some comfort amid the horror and suffering. I'm only sorry I couldn't have been there for you."

"I'm so thankful you weren't," I said, and kissed him. "I was so happy to think of you safe and sound in America. But I'm so very, very thankful you came back."

Finally, I added one last item to the shrine: the fan that had belonged to my mother, Suzette. It had sat on the rush seat of the chair next to the shop door long enough, a testament to betrayal and abandonment, hope and yearning, love and loss. It was time for a change, and besides, now that Charles and Mathilde and I were sharing the little apartment behind La Maison Benoît, we needed the extra chair.

And then we set about rebuilding our lives and our city.

Epilogue

$\mathscr{A}$RTISTS, MUSICIANS, WRITERS, and freethinkers
began to return to Paris. One of Charles's musician friends, the
trumpeter Arthur Briggs, had been arrested and sent to a camp at
Saint-Denis, where he led the brass section of an orchestra made up
of inmates. Josephine Baker, who worked as a spy for the Résistance,
was awarded France's highest military honors, the Croix de Guerre
and the Legion of Honor medal. She went on to buy herself a castle,
the Château des Milandes, and filled it with a dozen orphans she
adopted from around the world.

As they had in the War of 1914, black American soldiers distin-
guished themselves in the war against fascism through their bravery on the battlefield, fighting to free the democracies of Europe
despite the rampant discrimination they faced at home and in the
military. And just as had happened after the Great War, many
Americans stayed on or moved to Paris after the war, enticed by the

relative openness of the culture. Leroy "Roughhouse" Haynes opened a restaurant in Montmartre called Gabby and Haynes, serving corn bread and collards, yams and fried chicken. Charles and I became regulars, sometimes eating alongside the likes of authors Richard Wright and James Baldwin.

Jazz clubs and bars started reopening on Montmartre, in the Quartier Latin and elsewhere. At Aux Trois Mailletz, Le Tabou, and Le Caveau de la Huchette, the beloved *"entartete Müsik"*—degenerate music—was gleefully played into the wee hours. Occasional skirmishes broke out over whether New Orleans–style jazz was truer than bebop or vice versa, but that was the way of artists.

There was no demand for expensive handmade fans in postwar Paris, but with the assistance of a generous landlord and the help of my daughter, I kept La Maison Benoît open and began to reach out to the old couture houses for work with designers who were starting to rebuild their businesses.

Hitler killed himself and the German forces surrendered in May of 1945, but the war in the Pacific raged on for another few months until Japan accepted defeat, which meant it took a full year after I escaped that wretched bus for World War II to come to an official end.

When peace was at long last declared, we went out to celebrate. I spritzed myself with the last of my Habanita de Molinard perfume and pulled on an outdated—but very sparkly—dress, and Charles accepted the offer to play a few songs onstage with the band. Ringing our table in the audience were my dear friend Antoinette, Henri Coën and his wife, and my lovely daughter, Mathilde, and her wise and kind friend, Bridgette. The two young women had become inseparable, and I wondered whether their closeness might develop into something more than friendship. But that was up to them. Freethinking was no longer a crime in Paris.

Surrounded by music and my loved ones, I took a moment, breathless from the dancing and the joy and my astonishing good fortune.

We had been broken as a people and as a city, but as we had before, we were rising from the ashes. Perhaps this time we were not as blithely optimistic as we had been following the First World War, for we had learned only too well what could happen if we failed to heed the warning signs of intolerance and hatred.

I thought often of what Ezra had said: that when we are *dépouillés*, stripped down to our essence, we must confront, and accept, who we are. I found a copy of the poem Hélène had recited to me after Ezra's death, and I read it often.

Because I now understood that to love what death can touch may be foolish, but it is also holy.

And it is oh so human.

Author's Note

The Paris Showroom was inspired by true events.

During World War II, 795 prisoners of the Third Reich were forced to work in the three Parisian satellite camps, Lévitan, Bassano, and Austerlitz, from July 1943 until August 1944. During that time hundreds were deported to Drancy, and from there to Auschwitz or Bergen-Belsen. Tens of thousands of Jewish homes and businesses in France were emptied not only of valuable art and furniture—which were usually claimed by the Nazi elite—but also of saucepans, children's toys, and even lightbulbs, which were sorted, cleaned, and repaired by prisoners before being packed to be sent on to Germany.

Certain scenes—such as the Nazis' use of prisoners to test the gas masks in case they had been sabotaged, and Capucine's improbable escape from the bus while being transferred from Lévitan to

Drancy—are based very loosely on actual historical events. The story, however, is entirely a work of fiction.

I read dozens of articles and books while researching *The Paris Showroom*. Among the most helpful were:

Dreyfus, Jean-Marc, and Sarah Gensburger. *Nazi Labour Camps in Paris: Austerlitz, Lévitan, Bassano, July 1943–August 1944.* New York: Berghahn Books, 2011.

Gensburger, Sarah. *Witnessing the Robbing of the Jews: A Photographic Album, Paris 1940–1944.* Bloomington: Indiana University Press, 2015.

Shack, William A. *Harlem in Montmartre: A Paris Jazz Story Between the Great Wars.* Berkeley and Los Angeles: University of California Press, 2001.

Sharpley-Whiting, T. Denean. *Bricktop's Paris: African American Women in Paris Between the Two World Wars.* Albany: State University of New York Press, 2015.

Smith, Meredith. "The Civilian Experience in German Occupied France, 1940–1944." History Honors Paper, Connecticut College, 2010.

Acknowledgments

I am always grateful to my wonderful editor at Berkley, Kerry Donovan, for helping transform my messy first drafts into coherent books. And to the ever-wonderful literary agent Jim McCarthy, who always has my back and works to foster careers, not just book sales.

This is my first purely historical novel, and I am enormously grateful to my historian sister, Dr. Carolyn Lawes, for her invaluable contributions to the story—through academic research, continuous brainstorming, and the actual process of writing. I would like to offer special thanks to Dr. Sarah Gensburger for opening my eyes to a phenomenon I had never heard of: Nazi prison camps in Paris. Her thorough and fascinating research was crucial to the novel.

I am beholden to fabulous author Faye Snowden for her sage feedback and commentary, and for encouraging me to write about the Harlem Hellfighters, as well as the interwar era in Paris. Many thanks to my dear friend Linda Harrel for her generosity in reading my work, and for sharing (and correcting!) details of Jewish faith and traditions. And *merci beaucoup* to Francophile Jacquie Wiesner: Your linguistic and editing abilities are unmatched! Thank you for making me look good.

As always, many thanks to my writing community, especially Sophie Littlefield, Dr. Nicole Peeler, Rachael Herron, and Adrienne Bell. I am always grateful to voice artist Xe Sands, who has become the voices in my head as I read through my own books! And to my website maven, Maddee James, thank you for your support and friendship.

And special thanks to Hanna Toda, for letting me be Mama; to Cole and Luc Stauffenegger, Sophia, Amelia, and Isla; and to Susan Lawes, for the sisterhood.

And just so everyone knows: Nugget is still the best dog in the world.

And, finally, to Eric Stauffenegger: For the wine, the song, the travel, the love. *Merci.*

THE PARIS SHOWROOM

Juliet Blackwell

Questions for Discussion

1. Do you think a work of fiction, such as this novel, is able to illuminate aspects of a historical event that a textbook or a documentary film cannot? If so, in what way?

2. Capucine seems rather passive in the beginning of *The Paris Showroom*, willing to accept her lot in life. Why do you think that was? Did she have other options?

3. Why was Capucine arrested? In what ways did her experience as a political prisoner differ from that of a typical Jewish prisoner?

4. What did the Lévitan department store, the big square house in Neuilly, and La Maison Benoît symbolize in the story? Would it be too much to characterize them as "characters" in the novel?

5. Some people find jazz music exhilarating, while others find it annoying or simply boring. What do you think of 1920s jazz? What role does music play in the story?

6. In many big cities, including Paris, the interwar period was a time of social openness that often pushed society's mores. Why do you think that was? How might it have contributed to the general failure to recognize the threat of fascism?

7. *The Paris Showroom* alternates between two stories. Capucine's unfolds mostly within the department store prison, while Mathilde's is set in a Parisian suburb and on the streets of Paris. Did you

prefer or feel closer to one character's voice? Why do you think Blackwell chose to tell the story from two perspectives?

8. Many of us become our best selves only after undergoing difficult experiences. How do you think Mathilde's life might have unfolded had she not experienced the trauma of the war?

9. In what ways does religion shape how the various characters experience and interpret World War II and the Nazi Occupation?

10. For most of the novel, we know Charles only through Capucine's memories and his letters. What did he represent for Capucine? In the end, do you think he lived up to her image of him? How do you imagine their relationship might fare over the years?

11. During the Occupation, some Parisians actively collaborated with the Nazis, while many others pretended not to see, or chose not to react to, what was going on around them. What factors do you think influenced individual responses to the Occupation? Had you lived at that time and place, do you think you would have risked your freedom and your life, or those of your children and family, in order to resist?

12. Would you say Bruno and Isedore were morally purer than Capucine?

13. Why did Capucine leave Mathilde with Auguste and Yvette Duplantier and then choose not to be involved in her daughter's upbringing? In your view, was that an understandable choice, given the situation? Was it a forgivable choice?

14. How did Mathilde's friendships with Simone and Bridgette affect her understanding of what was happening in Paris during the

Occupation? How did the choices these two friends made shape Mathilde's transition from girlhood to womanhood?

15. How did Mathilde's experiences during the war affect her view of her mother?

16. What role did Madame Antoinette Laurent play in the story?

17. Given Grandpère Auguste's responsibilities to his family and his workers, was it understandable that he collaborated with the Nazis? What do you think happened to Mathilde's grandparents at the end of the novel? Do you think their fate was deserved?

18. Many people are aware of how the Nazis plundered valuable works of art during the war, but fewer have heard of *Möbel Aktion*, or Operation Furniture. What was the significance of the Nazis seizing everything belonging to a family—not just valuable items but also everyday items—as described in *The Paris Showroom*?

19. In your view, which was truer: Capucine's love for Charles or her love for Ezra?

20. Why was ritual so important to the prisoners at the Lévitan department store? Why did those in charge permit the prisoners to celebrate some religious holidays?

21. How would you characterize Abrielle Garnier? Well-intentioned but clueless? Self-centered but not vicious? Something else?

22. What do you think Pettit's backstory is? How would you characterize her relationship with Capucine? Why do you think she did what she did at the end?

23. Do you think Capucine and Mathilde will be able to resurrect La Maison Benoît as a fan-making house? Should they even try?

24. What do you think is the key to Capucine's survival and escape? Pure blind luck? Her unique personality and skills? Being at the right place at the right time?

25. Rare feathers were mentioned only briefly in the book, but it was an article on this topic that gave Blackwell the idea of writing a story involving a fan-making shop. Have you ever given any thought to fans and feathers, and the role they have played in the past? Had you ever heard of the "language of fans"?

26. It's always challenging for an author to use real historical events as a backdrop for a novel—and exciting as well. Given what you know about WWII history, did *The Paris Showroom* ring true for you? What artistic liberties do you think Blackwell took to bring this novel to life?

27. The novel quotes a poem about love that was written centuries ago and includes the following lines:

> *A fearful thing*
> *to love, to hope, to dream, to be—*
> *to be,*
> *And oh, to lose.*
> *A thing for fools, this*
> *And a holy thing.*

What does this poem mean to you?

28. What is the theme of *The Paris Showroom*? Would you say there is a moral to the story?

Don't miss Juliet Blackwell's

OFF THE WILD COAST
OF BRITTANY

Available now

Natalie

And we're off, to continue our adventure on the Île de Feme,

renovating a historic guesthouse and opening a gourmet restaurant!

Because when you grab life with both hands and hold on tight,

you never know where it might lead:

perhaps even to a rocky island off the Wild Coast of Brittany.

Stay tuned. . . . This tale is not over.

—last line of the international bestseller *Pourquoi Pas?*
A Memoir of Life, Love, and Food by Natalie Morgen

*T*HINGS ARE NOT *going according to plan.*

Natalie Morgen sat at a little metal café table on the stone terrace outside her guesthouse, watching the latest herd of tourists surge off the ferry.

An aroma of anise rose from her glass, melding with the smoke from her cigarette and the scent of the sea: a mélange of dead things and salt, of the abundant seaweed and muck that marred the shallows during low tide. Island sounds wafted over on the ocean breezes: the histrionic seagulls squabbling over a bucket of scraps Loïc had tossed out the back door of Pouce Café, the rhythmic lapping of the waves in the snug harbor, the murmurs of visitors enjoying lunch at outdoor tables, the occasional clacking of a *pétanque* ball hitting its mark.

Natalie imagined the newly arrived tourists mistook her for a native sipping her glass of pastis—though most of the actual natives preferred beer or hard cider—and enjoying a sunny day on the beautiful island.

And sitting here like this, Natalie could almost convince *herself* that life was good. That everything was going according to her carefully thought-out plan. Lounging on the terrace of her ancient guesthouse, its rusted iron gates still secured with a heavy steel chain because the Bag-Noz was not yet open to guests even though accommodations were well-nigh impossible to come by on the Île de Feme during tourist season.

Bobox strutted by, clucking in contentment. The fluffy white hen had come with the house and had made herself a little nest in the shed. Ridiculously long snowy white feathers on the top of her head quivered and swayed with every confident step, reminding Natalie of stylish Parisian ladies in photographs of yore, parading along the Champs-Élysées in their feathered chapeaux.

Paris. What had Audrey Hepburn said? "Paris is always a good idea"? *Maybe for Audrey—she was rich and beautiful.* Absentmindedly scratching at a mosquito bite, Natalie realized she was clenching her jaw, willed herself to relax, took another sip of pastis, and turned her attention back to the ferry passengers.

Trying to get their bearings, the newcomers weren't talking much as they staggered along the walkway that hugged the thick stone seawall. Some carried inflatables and beach toys; others clutched scraps of paper with instructions directing them to their rented guesthouses or to the Ar-Men, the only hotel on the island. It must have been a rough crossing: Most of the children and more than a few of the adults were decidedly green around the gills. A storm had thrashed the region yesterday, and though to the unpracticed eye the sea today appeared calm, Natalie had lived on the island long enough to have learned a few things from the locals, such as how to read the water.

Or, at the very least, when to ask a local to read the water for her.

Even after a storm appeared to have passed, waves lingered and surged. The swells rippled out and down, the awesome energy of the sea needing time to settle, to balance, to find its footing once again, lulling sailors and landlubbers alike into a false sense of security only to slam them with choppy water if they dared venture too soon onto open sea.

Sounds like a metaphor for life. Natalie made a mental note to post this, or some poetic version of it, on her social media accounts. She should post some photos as well. It had been a while. Too long. She had a lot of followers to keep happy.

Her readers loved the snapshots of Natalie's life on an island off Brittany's Côte Sauvage, or "Wild Coast," where she was renovating an ancient guesthouse with the proceeds from her bestselling memoir. In fact, some of the new arrivals lurching off the ferry might well be women of a certain age who had read Natalie's inspirational tome about finding love and self-fulfillment through the art of French cooking, and had decided to come to the Île de Feme in search of love and self-fulfillment themselves.

But as Natalie had learned, in a most painful way, the Île de

Feme was still an *île*—an island—which meant that if you didn't bring it with you, you weren't likely to find it here.

How could she explain that her Prince Charming—*le prince charmant*—the man she had fallen head over heels for, the reason she had come to Brittany in the first place, had turned out to be a lying, cheating, spendthrift schmuck who left her high and dry in the middle of their guesthouse renovation?

Even his name was annoying. *François-Xavier.* Being French, he insisted she say his entire name, every time: *Fran-swah Ex-ah-vee-ay.* A full six syllables. *Six.* She once made the mistake of addressing him simply as François and he accused her of calling him by another man's name. *A classic case of psychological transference*, she thought with grim humor, knowing what she now knew.

François-Xavier claimed it was an American thing to give people nicknames. He was forever blaming her quirks on Natalie's being American, but in this case it might have been true. In college Natalie's roommate had introduced herself as Anastasia—a mere four syllables—and everyone on their hall immediately shortened it to Ana. Natalie had fought her entire childhood against being called Nat because it sounded like the bug, which her sister Alex insisted she was: Nat-the-Gnat, small and annoying, bouncing around ineffectually, her head in the clouds, endlessly searching for some unspecified thing. Natalie had tried to retaliate by calling Alex "Al," but in that irksome way of smug elder sisters, Alex had embraced the name, stomping around the family compound, singing at the top of her lungs, loudly and proudly, the old Paul Simon song "You Can Call Me Al."

Which wasn't fair. Nobody wrote songs about gnats.

Natalie never managed to outmaneuver her four older sisters, and Alex, the closest to her in age, had been by far the most difficult.

Anyway. François-Xavier. She supposed two names suited a man with two faces. Still . . . that gorgeous face flashed in her mind: the sloping, intensely blue eyes; the sensual, full lips; the hint of dark golden whiskers glistening along his strong jaw. The way he looked at her as if she were not merely desirable but that he had waited a lifetime to meet her, that he was ready to share his life with her, wanted to create a family with her right here on his native island, where they would play *pétanque* in the sunshine, drink *apéro* curled up in front of the hearth, and cook together, transforming classic ingredients into sumptuous dinners through the dedicated application of traditional French techniques. And then they would linger for hours over elaborate meals with friends and extended family and guesthouse visitors.

That was the plan.

At the moment her cupboard contained half a box of crackers, an open bag of dry-roasted peanuts, and a single fragrant cantaloupe well on its way to rotten. Natalie had forgotten to put an order in with the mainland store that shipped to the island, so today's ferry brought no bundle of supplies with her name on it. She supposed she could buy something from the island's small but well-stocked "general store" that primarily served the tourists, but if she did, then the shop's owner, Severine Menou, would know Natalie's business, which meant soon *everyone* on the island would know Natalie's business.

Better to do what she usually did these days: eat the ample *menu du jour* at Milo's café, blaming it on her torn-up kitchen, and stick to peanuts and stale crackers—and plenty of pastis—the rest of the time.

François-Xavier would be appalled.

What was she going to *do*?

Keep your head down and the pretense up. At least until she figured out her next steps. She had told everyone that François-Xavier was on a business trip to Paris, scouting for kitchen help for the gourmet restaurant they were supposed to be opening in the large dining room of the Bag-Noz Guesthouse. No one was surprised; he traveled to Paris frequently, after all.

This time, though, François-Xavier had no intention of coming back. How long would it be until people started asking questions? Also, the construction workers hadn't shown up this week and Natalie was afraid to ask why. It might be because today was *le quinze août*, a national holiday. Or just because it was August, and a lot of French people took the entire month off for vacation.

Or maybe the workers hadn't shown up because Natalie hadn't paid her latest round of bills. When he left, François-Xavier siphoned off the majority of their shared bank account, leaving her to get by on a few hundred euros and maxed-out credit cards until she received a check from her publisher for the book under contract, a follow-up to *Pourquoi Pas?*

Her jaw tightened again. Her current work in progress was meant to be all about her perfect life with her perfect French chef fiancé, and to be accompanied by a liberal smattering of recipes and mouthwatering photos of the meals she and François-Xavier prepared—what her agent referred to as "French food porn."

Natalie took a deep quaff of her pastis, let out a long sigh, and watched as Bobox scratched the ground in her incessant search for something appetizing in the sandy soil of the weed-strewn court-yard.

François-Xavier was supposed to run the kitchen, and Natalie was supposed to run the guesthouse, and it was all supposed to be beautiful.

But things had not gone according to plan.

JULIET BLACKWELL is the pseudonym for the *New York Times* bestselling author of *Off the Wild Coast of Brittany*, *The Vineyards of Champagne*, *The Lost Carousel of Provence*, *Letters from Paris*, and *The Paris Key*. In addition to writing the beloved Witchcraft Mystery series and the Haunted Home Renovation series, she also co-authored the Agatha Award–nominated Art Lover's Mystery series with her sister.

CONNECT ONLINE

JulietBlackwell.net

JulietBlackwellAuthor

JulietBlackwell